180°
MAGNETIC

JIM SCHOENDALLER
JEANNE C. STEIN

TEITELBAUM PUBLISHING

180 Degrees Magnetic

ISBN - 978-1-7337980-5-1

Teitelbaum Publishing

Cover design and illustrations by Leslie Waara

ACKNOWLEDGMENTS

Whereas this book has taken an unexpected amount of time and effort, there are several individuals that I wish to recognize.

My wife Amy and daughter Natalie - Thanks for your patience, understanding and encouragement.

Jeanne C. Stein - Thanks for investing your time and writing prowess to turn a mediocre work into a real novel. Your expert rewriting breathed literary life into the characters and made the scenes vivid.

Deanne Conte, mom #2 - Thanks for your feedback and support and for introducing me to Robert Teitelbaum, your publisher friend.

Robert Teitelbaum, Teitelbaum Publishings - Thank you (and your staff and associates) for giving an unknown, first-time author a chance.

I wish to thank my subject matter experts for their valuable assistance - Jim Cook, founder of the Victoria Sailing School who did a review of the sailing; Chuck Korus, chance meeting on a plane who happened to be a pilot and who reviewed the plane crash scene for aeronautical accuracy; Dr. Valerie Wassill, doctor and ballroom dancer who reviewed the first assault scene for medical accuracy.

I also wish to thank my beta-readers for reading part or all of the various drafts and providing their honest feedback - Shirley Yook, friend and lead singer for the dance band Perfect Harmony who restlessly waited for the next installment to review; Steve Bohn, sailing and ballroom dancing friend who provided detailed feedback; Steve Mufford, chance meeting on a plane who provided detailed feedback and suggested the book include boat diagrams and a glossary; Janet Johnson, aunt and retired federal judge, who reviewed a very early draft.

Jim Schoendaller

I'd like to add a quick thanks to Jim for sharing his work with me, and to his wonderful wife, Amy, and daughter, Natalie (my unofficial goddaughter and tennis partner.) They are more than friends to me—they are family.

Jim mentioned all his contacts who added to the accuracy of the book—to that I want to add my thanks as well. And to my own husband, Phil, and daughter, Jeanette: you have always encouraged me to spread my writing wings. I couldn't do it without you.

Jeanne C. Stein

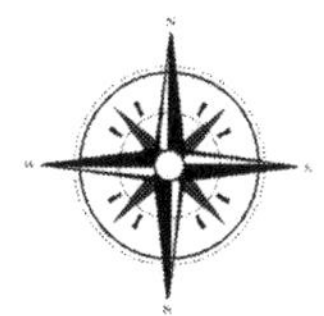

What in the universe was I thinking? This friendly poker game was seriously out of hand. If I lost, which I probably would, I'd have to partake in an orgy. Worse, I was dragging my best friend Tracy into this madness with me.

What was supposed to be a relaxing Casino Night at our hotel had morphed into a prequel for God knows what.

"So if I bet my room key and lose, you and your friend get me and my friend for two days until we leave?" I asked, glancing back at my friend Tracy.

"That's right," Charles said.

"And remind me again what your key fits?"

"My key fits *The Lady Anne*, a two-year-old Clarriage Sixty-Eight worth three million dollars."

I had read about the Clarriage in sailing magazines but

had never seen one. Clarriages were way out of our price range.

He continued, "One of my lawyers will do the paperwork and you, Ms. Pat Taylor, will own a luxury sailing yacht, free and clear. There will be no taxes, no tricks, no lies, and no bullshit."

Tracy spoke up. "Who's your friend?"

Charles looked around the room. "He was here earlier. I don't see him now."

"And what would you expect of my friend and me?" I asked, my breathing suddenly quick and shallow.

"Sex. Anything we want."

"No rough stuff," I said, hardly believing I was buying into this.

"There would be limits."

From behind me, I heard Tracy chug her drink.

I considered the odds. I was one hundred percent certain that he wasn't bluffing.

The steel-drum band was on break and it was strangely quiet. There was no way he could be serious, I told myself, but judging by the way he looked at me and dangled that key on the end of a gold keychain like a lure, he was.

So I did the sensible thing. I took a break by leaving my hole cards facedown on the table and said, "I need a minute."

Tracy grabbed my hand and pulled me away from the table.

"He's kidding, right?"

"Has to be," I said, but even in my own head, I didn't

sound convinced. Tracy and I had been unsuccessfully sailboat shopping in Tortola. After two days of arrogant salesmen who thought we couldn't afford anything we'd looked at and dirty bilges that would take a ton of money and work to be seaworthy, we had nothing to show for our efforts. It was worse than buying a used car.

"Maybe flying over here from the Strictly Sail Show in Miami was a waste of time," I said with a sigh. "Hell, maybe our idea of buying a sailboat and starting a charter service is a pipe dream."

"We covered a four-day show in one day," Tracy said. "That booth offering used charter sailboats for sale looked promising enough for us to change our plans and fly over here."

"And we've still got all day tomorrow to see what else is available," I replied.

"If you don't win a Clarriage Sixty-Eight tonight," Tracy said with a laugh. She pointed to the sign in the lobby for the big Valentine's Day party that brought us here. "For twenty dollars, we got free drinks, free buffet, and free casino funny money … and just maybe …"

"So you think I should go for it?"

"Can you win?"

"Possibly. The odds are against us."

Tracy laughed again. "We're no innocent eighteen-year-olds just out of high school. I don't know what Mr. Williams's friend looks like, but he's not half bad for an older man. A weekend of fucking for a Sixty-Eight Clarriage? They'd have to use protection, of course, but I know I've done guys for a lot less. I think we should go for it. Winning a Clarriage would be like winning the lottery."

"Except when your lottery ticket doesn't come in, you don't have to spread your legs."

Her eyes twinkled. "Are we in?"

I looked hard at my best friend to see if she had any reservations. She looked right back at me. She didn't. We'd both dressed up in our new gift-shop island outfits and followed the music to the party. After eating, Tracy played roulette and I played poker. We agreed to pool our winnings and redeem them for hats, T-shirts, and perhaps even a bottle of rum.

Why not a sailboat?

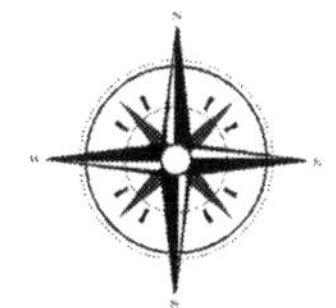

CHAPTER 2

Four players remained at the poker table. Me, Charles T. Williams, and a father and son from Chicago. Charles was on my left and the other two had seats on my right. Charles and I had the most chips.

A local woman was dealing and distracting both the father and son by wearing a very low-cut top that clearly showed an elaborate tattoo of a bird on her chest. It looked like it had been painful.

Like all experienced players, I had quickly sized up my opponents. The father and son were playing very timidly, folding or calling but seldom raising. I categorize those types of players as donators. The other donators at the table had already left, disgusted at getting beaten by a woman, and a blonde one at that, even for funny money.

Charles was my main concern. He was soft-spoken and

played correctly. I hadn't noticed any tells and he hadn't bluffed yet. He was winning because he played smart and got good flops. My only advantage might be that he was drinking more than I was since I had earlier told the bartender to make my Rum and Ting mostly Ting.

Even though until now we had been playing for prizes and the money wasn't real, I always give card games, be it poker, hearts, spades, or bridge, my full concentration and play to win. I especially enjoy poker because I believe it is easier to win money from other players than it is to win money from the casino.

As the evening wore on, there had been small talk during shuffles. Charles knew Tracy and I were shopping for a sailboat. I knew that Charles was a very recent widower. He also said he owned a Clarriage and came over from St. Thomas to Tortola to sell her in non-US waters. I surmised he was very wealthy but very depressed. His wife's death probably explained why he was on his fifth or sixth single malt scotch. While he didn't pay the dealer's tattooed cleavage any attention, his eyes did follow Tracy whenever she'd stop by, especially when she leaned over, revealing her own cleavage. I figured he couldn't help himself. She was cute and he was a man.

The current hand was dealt. Since Charles had the dealer button, I was first to act. I got a jack and a king, suited. The big blind was thirty dollars, but instead of calling, I raised it to one hundred dollars. I calculated that calling that amount would put the Chicago son nearly all in as he was running low on chips. As I expected, Charles and the big blind dad called, but the small blind son folded. One down, two to go.

The flop was two queens and the nine of diamonds. Both queens were red. Dad checked, which probably meant the flop hadn't helped him and he had only called because it was relatively cheap for him to do so.

Now it was my turn to bet. Since my cards were both diamonds, I had nothing made but a fantastic hand to hit. I bet another two hundred dollars to see if I could steal the pot.

That wasn't happening. Without hesitating, Charles went all in. Dad immediately folded. Two down but the stakes had just gone up.

Based on the speed of his all in, I put Charles on a full house or worse, four queens. His previous pattern of play indicated he wouldn't have acted that quickly with just two pair or three of a kind.

I had a straight draw, a flush draw, and even a straight-flush draw. I needed a straight flush to beat a full house or four of a kind. If I called and lost, the game would be over and all of my hard-earned chips would be history. To say nothing of the side bet.

But I was used to playing poker with construction workers. I kept my best poker face and hesitated to see if he'd react. When he didn't, I calmly called. I was still tired from sailboat shopping, had been sitting long enough, didn't need any T-shirts or hats, and the rum was cheap enough to buy if I wanted a bottle or two to take home.

It is customary in Texas Hold'em for players in this situation to turn their hole cards face up and let the hand play out. However, Charles politely instructed the dealer to wait. His action totally surprised me. I was curious why he could possibly be stalling when he had so quickly gone all in.

He quit fiddling with the ignition key and placed it in the center of the table. He looked at me. I reached into my handbag and placed our room key next to his.

CHAPTER 3

Random, disjointed thoughts flitted through my brain. The name of the sailboat was *The Lady Anne*. My middle name was Anne, Patricia Anne Taylor. Tracy's middle name was the same, Tracy Anne Palmer. Same name as the sailboat.

My hand was diamonds and, coincidently, the old movie we had watched on cable last night was *Gentlemen Prefer Blondes*, starring Marilyn Monroe. Marilyn was blonde, same as me, same as Tracy. Also, Marilyn sang "Diamonds are a Girl's Best Friend." There was no way all of this was coincidence; it had to be fate.

Charles turned over his two queens, then casually sipped his drink. This man was calm. He had the poker face from hell. The crowd gasped slightly. They gasped again when I turned over my cards, the jack and king of diamonds. At that moment, Charles, Tracy, and I looked at the dealer.

She said the bet was crazy and she'd have to find her boss.

Charles politely instructed her to continue dealing, since this was a simple side bet between the young ladies and himself.

The dealer looked at me, but I couldn't think of anything to say so I just nodded. My heart was pounding and I felt weak, so I relaxed by leaning back in my chair and exhaled softly. The dealer took a deep breath, looked nervously at the crowd, and slowly burned the next card.

Fourth street was the two of diamonds.

That made my flush, but we were still behind his nearly unstoppable four queens. Charles took another sip. I took a sip. Tracy slammed down the rest of my drink and shifted her weight back and forth, then took my hand, gripping it tightly.

The dealer burned another card. There was total silence. I think I could hear my heart beating. All eyes were on the dealer and the deck she was holding. The river card was worth either an expensive sailing yacht or an orgy. The whole room knew that I needed the ten of diamonds. If any other card came up, Tracy and I were screwed—literally.

Tracy squeezed my hand and told the dealer to get on with it. A sizable crowd had gathered around the table, watching.

The dealer gingerly placed the river card next to the deuce. I saw the dealer smile. Tracy's grip intensified. I focused. It was a ten. I squinted, focusing harder. It was red. I leaned forward to be absolutely certain. It was a diamond.

I had hit an inside straight flush.
I had beaten four queens.
My hand was the winner. Unbelievable.
I shouted, "Holy fuck!"
Tracy let go of my hand and hugged me.
I hugged her back.

CHAPTER 4

The crowd began applauding. We let go of each other and looked at Charles.

He was staring at the cards. He reached out and touched the queens. Then he touched the ten. It was the only card in the deck that could have beaten him. He shook his head.

He then looked up toward the ceiling and closed his eyes. He remained that way for several seconds, taking deep breaths. Finally he opened his eyes and looked at me.

Charles reached into the pot of chips and deftly removed our room key. He looked at it for a second and then handed it back to me. He slowly picked up his ignition key and handed it to me too.

"You played well, young lady," he said.

I could not believe how calm he was. I was waiting for him to start making excuses, but he just finished his drink and then bowed his head slightly in our direction. The crowd was still applauding me for my spectacular win.

Tracy looked at me, eyes wide. "Did this really just happen?"

As if in answer, Charles reached into his jacket pocket and removed a thick passport. He handed it to her, instructing her to hold it for him. "This is to show that I'm serious. Meet me for breakfast tomorrow morning at ten," he said. "I am a man of my word and will begin the process of transferring ownership this evening."

He shook my hand, then Tracy's. "I have a feeling you will take wonderful care of *The Lady Anne*."

Then he bid us "Fair winds and following seas" and nonchalantly made his way around the table, behind the dealer. Charles whispered in her ear and put something into her hand. The dealer smiled, quickly pocketed whatever it was that he gave her, and whispered something back. With that, Charles T. Williams walked away. He didn't look back.

"Can you believe I hit an inside straight flush, almost a royal?"

"If I hadn't seen it, I wouldn't have believed it," Tracy said. "You were amazing. As far as I'm concerned, you just won the lottery."

"Now I have to pee really badly," I said. "So gather up our winnings and go trade them for T-shirts, hats, rum, and whatever else you want."

When Tracy met me by the restroom a few minutes later, she held up two bags. "I used all of it. Got a bunch of hats and

T-shirts, some rum, and both of the band's CDs. I had each member of the band autograph them too. They congratulated me on our big win. None of them could believe what had just happened."

We headed back to our room, each carrying a bag of loot, giggling all the way. The two guys who passed us probably thought we were drunk.

Actually, I was only semidrunk. What we were were luxury sailing yacht owners.

CHAPTER 5

Tracy confessed she had way too many sweet rum drinks and crawled on to my bed, sideways. I covered her, took a shower, and then crawled into her bed. I slept poorly. I kept thinking that I'd never see Charles T. Williams again, but I was confused because his passport was on the dresser. We were both awakened by the eight thirty a.m. alarm.

Tracy was moving slower than usual, but she hadn't gotten sick so that was good. She looked better after her shower. We took our time getting ready. I didn't have much work to do with my short hair and Tracy had learned that hairdos in the Caribbean quickly turn into "hair don'ts" because of the humidity. She twisted her shoulder-length hair into a ponytail and we went looking for Charles just before ten o'clock a.m.

Charles waved at us from his table. He asked how we had

slept and was very much the gentleman, even standing before we were seated.

His politeness worried me. I wondered how anyone who had just lost a super luxury sailing yacht worth three million dollars could be that polite.

"Are you staying at the hotel too?" I asked.

He chuckled. "No," he replied. "I'm staying aboard *The Lady Anne*. Probably for the last time." But there was no acrimony in his tone.

He motioned to the waiter. "I've taken the liberty of ordering for us."

A breakfast platter of lox and toasted sesame bagels, fresh fruit, assorted cheeses, wonderful coffee, and freshly squeezed carambola juice appeared. As we ate, he detailed his plan for our day.

"We'll gather your luggage from the hotel, and you'll accompany me in my skiff back to St. Thomas and *The Lady Anne*."

Tracy held up a hand. "St. Thomas is quite a ways. No offense, but we don't know you."

She glanced at me and I nodded agreement. "We don't feel comfortable going all that way alone with you. We are also uncomfortable checking out of our hotel without first seeing *The Lady Anne*."

"I understand." He thought for a moment. "There is another option. We can take the ferry to St. Thomas and then a cab over to the harbor. It's nearby. After you have finished your inspection, I will run you back to Tortola or you can retrace your route on the ferry." He smiled. "However, you may find that you want to sleep aboard. If not, you'll still have your rooms."

Tracy whispered in my ear that she was okay with the arrangements. I nodded our acceptance.

Charles made a telephone call then and told whoever was on the other end that we'd all be taking the ferry back and to meet him aboard.

Tracy raised an eyebrow. "Was that the friend you referred to in the poker bet?" she asked when he'd disconnected.

"*The Lady Anne*'s captain," he replied. "And yes, it was." Nothing in Charles's voice, his mannerisms, or his demeanor betrayed any sort of creepiness. He insisted on paying for breakfast, but kept looking at his watch. At precisely eleven fifteen, Charles picked up his cell phone. It rang less than thirty seconds later. He handed the phone to me.

The caller introduced himself as David Goldbloom, one of Charles T. Williams' many attorneys. He started speaking quickly about legal documents when I interrupted by saying I was giving him to my accountant. I handed the phone to Tracy.

Tracy took the phone, and after repeating several times that she understood, she gave the attorney our names, addresses, email information, and cell numbers. A few minutes later, Tracy handed the phone back to Charles, who concluded the call.

Tracy turned to me. "An LLC owns *The Lady Anne*," she explained. "Not Mr. Williams, per se. We are going to be the

new managing partners. Since we had both been liable for"—
she paused—"well, let's just call it carnal participation if he
had won, Charles wanted us to be seventy-thirty partners,
with the larger share going to you, since you had been the one
actually playing. Understand?"

"Perfectly."

"The papers will be scanned over later this afternoon."

Now that the formalities were over, Tracy and I excused
ourselves to go to our room. We gathered together our passports, along with Charles's, and a change of clothes. Just in
case. If *The Lady Anne* was all Charles described, we might
decide to stay aboard tonight after all.

The three of us took a cab to the ferry dock. Tracy and I
were both excited and nervous at the same time. Charles made
mostly small talk, but he did ask about our sailing experience.

I told him that Tracy and I had purchased an introductory
sailing class on Groupon and had enjoyed it so much, we took
more classes.

"We've completed the basic keelboat class, the coastal
cruising class, and the bareboat chartering class," I added.

Charles looked amused but didn't comment. I could tell I
was not impressing him.

Tracy saw it too. "Well, the final class entailed sailing from
California to Catalina and back," she said. "We went out on a
forty-foot monohull and returned on a forty-two-foot catamaran. We passed all of the exams and have those three certifications."

"Are those the biggest boats you've sailed?" he asked.

When we nodded, he asked, "Was it just the two of you sailing to Catalina and back?"

I shook my head. "There was a total of eight students and two instructors, but we did have two boats."

Charles grinned a devilish grin and looked away.

The ferry ride was enlightening. Tracy took some scenery pictures while Charles told me about his philosophy. He had been raised distrustful of the government, so his holdings were in real estate and hard assets, not cash. He had properties all over the world. He and his late wife used to love to travel; they had homes in Europe, the Middle East, even in Africa, but their home base was in New York, and from there they sailed *The Lady Anne* to many foreign ports. His tone was wistful as he told me these things, and I could tell he was going to miss those sailing adventures.

"Why in the world did you make that bet?" I asked him when he finished.

He shrugged. "Call it an old man's folly," he said. "I'd watched you and your friend in the hotel. You're both so young and full of life. I wanted to taste that again. I don't even know if I'd have gone through with it had I won."

But there was a sparkle in his eye. And I knew. He would have.

There were mostly locals aboard the ferry this morning, not many tourists. The Sir Francis Drake channel was turquoise and tranquil. The scattered islands looked peaceful from the water. The hues of blues and greens were calming. We passed several sailboats reaching in the breeze. Many of them were charter boats. I could picture myself at the helm of any of the smaller ones. *The Lady Anne?* She might be a challenge.

The marina was a short cab ride from the ferry terminal. The cab dropped us near a gated pier. I relaxed a little when the guard knew Mr. Williams by name and let us all pass without questions. Tracy took some more pictures.

We took a short walk down a gangplank to the docks, where we followed Charles, being careful not to get smacked in the head by the protruding bowsprits. There were several large sailboats and a few big powerboats, all secured neatly in their slips. There weren't any people milling about. If it had been busier, it would have helped calm my nerves.

Finally, Charles stopped in front of a massive sailboat. "Lady Anne" was printed neatly on the bow. That was her, floating proudly in her berth, a Clarriage Sixty-Eight.

I stopped so fast that Tracy bumped into me from behind. I was completely shocked at how big a Clarriage Sixty-Eight actually was. I scolded myself for not googling images beforehand and felt completely unprepared. *The Lady Anne* made the forty-foot monohull we had sailed to Catalina look like a child's bathtub toy.

"This thing is really big," Tracy whispered as she turned and took a selfie.

I just nodded, speechless and in awe.

Charles had not lied about *The Lady Anne* being a superb vessel. We followed him alongside. There was not one mast, but two. There were rigging and lines everywhere. Her white fiberglass, uncluttered deck positively glistened in the noon sun. On the stern was a US flag. It barely waved in the light breeze. *The Lady Anne* looked fast, seaworthy, complicated, new, and expensive. She also looked long and tall and wide and really big.

Charles climbed a small stairstep, unhooked the lifeline gate, stepped aboard, and then suddenly stopped and turned toward us. He didn't speak; he just stood there, waiting.

Remembering my first sailing lesson, I drew a breath. "Request permission to come aboard?" I asked.

CHAPTER 6

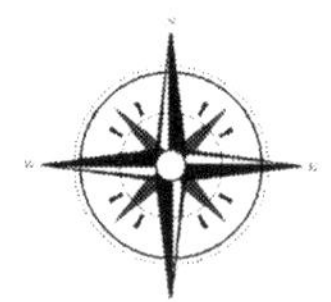

For a man who was mostly emotionless during our previous encounters, being aboard *The Lady Anne* seemed to have energized him. After giving us permission to come aboard, Charles hustled aft and proceeded to ring the large brass bell that was fastened to the mast behind the cockpit. He rang it twice, grinning at us the whole time. It had a beautiful tone and was surprisingly loud.

"Aren't those used to signal the time?" I asked. "Is that what you're doing?"

He replied, "Historically they are, but I'm welcoming the new owners aboard, one ring for each special guest." He looked up at it. "Nowadays the bell is required safety equipment for vessels over twenty meters in length. It can also be used to ring in the new year, to welcome dignitaries aboard, or to mourn the passing of a sailor."

As Tracy and I proceeded through the cockpit toward Charles and the bell, another man emerged behind us through the hatch from below.

He was of medium build, clean-cut, smartly dressed in nautical white, sporting a captain's hat, and probably in his forties. Charles introduced him as Daniel Pincus, captain of *The Lady Anne.*

"Welcome aboard," he said, extending his hand first to me, then to Tracy.

Daniel had a firm handshake and appeared very professional. Still, there was something about that first impression that made me nervous. Call it woman's intuition, but I just had a bad feeling.

I glanced at Tracy. Our eyes met for a tenth of a second. Judging from her silent look, I sensed she felt the same.

Captain Pincus shook his head. "I was at the hotel last night."

I felt color creep into my face. His tone said he knew all about the wager.

He turned to Charles. "We'd be having a different morning if another card had turned up, wouldn't we, sir?"

Charles waved a hand. "The poker game is water under the bridge. Your remark is inappropriate. I don't want it referred to again." His tone was sharp.

Captain Pincus stiffened, apologized, and excused himself below.

But my gut feeling persisted. Captain Pincus was not a man to be trifled with. There was something dark and dangerous in his demeanor, and I would be glad to see the last of him.

Since we were aft, Charles began the tour there. He pointed out all the yacht's many attributes in considerable detail. Charles was obviously proud and acted as if he was the designer, builder, owner, and salesman.

Tracy whispered in my ear, "Hope Captain Pink-Ass doesn't come with *The Lady Anne*."

I desperately fought bursting into laughter at Tracy's mispronunciation of Pincus.

We followed Charles all the way around, trying to keep up with his descriptions. He opened a lazarette. It contained life jackets and some tools. It was so neatly organized that it looked like a display from a boat dealer. So different from the sailboats we'd been looking at. But then, we hadn't been looking at three-million-dollar Clarriage Sixty-Eights, either.

We made our way over to the primary helm station. He had me insert my key, which to my delight fit, and he had me start the engine. There was a brief alarm tone and then the engine roared to life. He pointed out some of the electronics, how to operate the adjustable keel, and how to open the hatch's combination padlock.

When I switched the key off, the motor kept running, so Charles grinned and demonstrated how to stop the motor by pulling on a knob. He explained how that knob starved the fuel and thus stopped the engine. Now that he had mentioned it, I remembered that from sailing to Catalina. Satisfied we understood, he motioned us to follow him below. I was careful not to stumble going through the hatch, but fortunately, there was a handhold. We descended the steep steps into the main salon.

Captain Pincus was waiting below with four crystal flutes of champagne. When he leaned close to hand me one, his breath smelled like he had started without us.

Charles made a toast. "To *The Lady Anne*'s new owners," he said. "We wish you fair winds and following seas."

We all clinked glasses, but Pincus's lack of expression betrayed him. I was certain he was pissed.

Pincus excused himself to his cabin and Charles continued with the tour.

Besides the main salon with its large table, we marveled at the modern galley, saw the two forward guest cabins, an apartment-sized washer and dryer, a rigging station with spools of line, and bags of extra sails. There were storage compartments everywhere.

The heads were spotless and odorless. Charles explained that three of toilets were the low-water use, vacuum-flush type like cruise ships used. He mentioned that regular toilet paper was okay but to use it sparingly and not to flush Kleenex, Wet Wipes, paper towels, feminine hygiene products, or anything that hadn't been "eaten first." A polite way of putting it. He added there was access to remove clogs, but it was a big job.

We headed back through the salon. Charles pointed out the sophisticated electronic, navigation, and communication systems.

Next was the engine room, and it was remarkably clean.

Again, nothing like the cramped, filthy engine compartments we had been poking around in two days before.

We passed through another watertight door and continued aft, stopping at the crew's quarters' open door.

Pincus invited us in to look around. The cabin was small but adequate. It had two stacked berths and a semi-private small head. Despite the open hatch, this head smelled like the heads on other boats and not like the ones we had just seen elsewhere on *The Lady Anne*.

My nose told me why. "This toilet flushes with sea water, right?" I asked.

Charles confirmed that it did. "The odor comes from the bacteria and algae in seawater," he said. "Let me show you how it works."

Charles opened the valve, pumped the bowl wet. "You do your business without toilet paper. Pump the bowl dry. Remember to close the valve before you leave."

There was a small, stainless-steel, hands-free-opening lidded trash can next to the stool and I smiled slightly, knowing what it contained. I made a mental note to myself to make sure Tracy emptied that one. Tracy's eyebrows were raised, and I'd be willing to bet she was thinking the same thing—only that *I* would be the one emptying it!

There were two large duffel bags on the upper berth and Pincus was packing a third. I noticed an empty champagne bottle in a nearby wastebasket. I don't believe Tracy or Charles saw it. The certainly explained his breath. I expect he knew

Tracy and I weren't likely to keep him, though nothing had been said. We left him to his packing.

The workroom room was next, and it was neatly organized and well supplied with tools and lots of spare parts. It was followed by the owner's suite.

The main focal point of the spectacular owner's suite was the raised king-size bed, setting atop a drawer storage base. It was made of dark-colored wood and it was simply beautiful. There was a small peninsula desk with one chair on each side, a large, flat-screen television, and a spacious closet.

The head was clean and odorless and larger than I expected. It contained double sinks, a combination tub and shower, and shelves for additional storage.

"Your place or mine?" Tracy asked a little breathlessly.

I didn't blame her; I was pretty dazzled myself.

"I guess we'll have to flip a coin," I replied, only half kidding.

Charles smiled. "There's plenty of room for both of you, I think," he said.

Overall, the yacht's interior was well lit and cheery, spotless and truly in pristine condition. There was a lot of polished, rich-looking woodwork, and the open hatches let in a welcome breeze. I wanted to see more, but Charles motioned for us to follow him. He whispered that he had something important to discuss and put his finger across his lips.

He led us through the salon to the first cabin and quietly closed the door. Keeping his voice down, Charles started in, "Daniel has been my employee for the last two years. He is a very competent captain, licensed and completely familiar with the operation and maintenance of *The Lady Anne*. Sam, his brother who is currently off island, serves as my chef. He is a competent sailor as well, and is a valued employee. They are the two individuals responsible for keeping *The Lady Anne* shipshape and helped my late wife and I sail the boat."

Charles paused. "I can see he hasn't made a good first impression on you. That's my fault, since the matter of the terms of the bet were entirely my doing. I had had too much to drink. But as I told him, that's water under the bridge. I am offering to keep both Daniel and Sam on my payroll for as long as you require. They will take you anywhere you want to go."

I had a fleeting thought that it was easy to see where Pincus wanted to take us: probably from behind. But I kept a pleasant smile and didn't say anything. We all returned to the salon and Charles then called for Pincus to join him topside so Tracy and I could discuss his offer in private.

"What do you think?" I asked Tracy quietly when they had gone.

"No way can we keep Pincus on board. That guy gives me the creeps. We'll be lucky if he doesn't come back looking for a three-way since he missed the orgy."

"I've got the same vibes," I said. "But realistically, *The Lady Anne* is too big for just us to manage."

Tracy waved her arms around. "Yes, but I seriously love this boat so let's just find us another captain."

"Okay," I murmured, sinking into a surprisingly comfortable recliner. "We've got at least four options. One: Try to find a captain and crew here and sail with them to wherever we decide. Two: Go back to work and arrange for a crew to deliver *The Lady Anne* to us. Three: Move our timeline up and just leave her here until we can quit our day jobs and return for her. Four: Admit that she's too much boat for us and list her for sale, then buy or trade for something we can manage."

One by one we quickly discussed the options. We could conceivably find a crew to deliver *The Lady Anne* to Tracy's brother in Florida, but that would mean finding a place to berth her and slips for a boat this size would be pricey. Neither Tracy nor I were ready to change professions yet, either financially or emotionally, since we are both in our mid-thirties and peaking in our careers.

Tracy said it best when she declared she seriously loved this boat. I'd only been on board a couple of hours, and I did too. Although *The Lady Anne* initially seemed colossal and a bit overwhelming, she was so well designed that after Charles's brief tour, I felt really comfortable aboard. Selling her and settling for something else—something less—seemed unthinkable.

That left only one option.

I looked at Tracy. "We've got to find a captain and crew and sail *The Lady Anne* to Florida. We can keep her near your brother's place. We'll go there on vacations and familiarize ourselves with her until we're ready for the next stage—until we feel comfortable enough to start our charter service." I held out my hand. "Agreed?"

Tracy grabbed my hand and shook it enthusiastically. "Agreed, partner!"

We rejoined the men topside. For the first time, I felt a twinge of nervousness. How would Pincus react when we told him we didn't wish to continue his services?

Tracy took the lead. "We want to thank you, Charles, for your very generous offer, but we are going to pass. We plan to hire our own crew to sail *The Lady Anne* home."

I watched Pincus for his reaction. There wasn't one. He had been leaning against the cockpit table, and except for a tightening of his shoulders, he didn't move. His face was turned toward the marina so I couldn't see his expression. Somehow that disturbed me more than if he had thrown a tantrum.

Charles sighed and said that he understood. He turned to Pincus. "You and Sam will be paid for the rest of your contracts," he said. "Your lodging and travel arrangements will be taken care of. You may fly with me back to New York on the Gulfstream if you like."

He held out his hand. "Thank you for your two years of excellent service. I'll miss you."

Charles's obvious feelings for the man made me wonder if Tracy and I had made a mistake in dismissing him so quickly. Pincus shook Charles's hand and was outwardly very gracious, but his face had colored, and when both men passed us to go below, the look he threw me made the hair stand up on the back of my neck.

"That could have gone much worse," Tracy said, lowering her voice.

"He's not stupid or drunk enough to make a scene in front of his boss," I replied.

"Do you think we're done with him?"

I suppressed a shudder. "I hope so."

In a few minutes, Pincus and Charles re-emerged from below, carrying the duffel bags we had seen in the crew's quarters. I started to relax. It looked like Pincus was going to leave without any trouble.

Pincus left his gear on the dock alongside *The Lady Anne* and walked away. He returned a few moments later with a dock cart, loaded his bags onto the cart, waved at Charles, and started off.

I breathed a sigh of relief.

But he had only gone a few feet when he stopped.

"You really are stupid bitches," he said, turning to look up at us at the lifeline. "You'll never make it out of the slip, much less the marina. Charles, it's not too late to call this fucking fiasco off. Reclaim *The Lady Anne*. Who are they going to complain to? The bet wasn't legal, I'm sure."

Charles looked shocked at Pincus's outburst. "You're out of line, Daniel," he said. "If you don't go on your way, I'll call security. We certainly planned to collect if I'd won, didn't we? It's only fair I keep my part of the bargain."

Pincus stared at me. "You'll regret this," he growled. "Mark my words."

Maybe he *was* stupid or drunk or both. When he turned his back on us to stalk down the pier, I felt my shoulders loosen, relieved. I was hoping that was the end of Captain Daniel Pincus.

Charles sensed my unease. "No need to worry," he assured me. "Daniel will settle down. It's not easy for a man like him to lose his position. In addition to a generous six-figure salary, *The Lady Anne* has been his home for the last two years. But I'll see that he and his brother are well taken care of."

"Now." He clapped his hands together. "I've a few more surprises for you two."

Tracy and I exchanged glances as he took our arms and led us below.

"Not like Pink-Ass, I hope," she mouthed to me behind his back.

I stifled a laugh.

CHAPTER 7

Charles closed the main hatch, the overhead hatches in the salon, and then closed the curtains, darkening the salon considerably. He then excused himself for a moment.

Tracy and I exchanged questioning glances. We watched as he made his way aft down the passageway, going into the workshop. I'm not sure Tracy noticed, but I moved toward the main hatch, our closest exit. I suddenly felt very apprehensive.

He returned with an Allen wrench and a small screwdriver. Without a word, he proceeded to one of the ubiquitous stainless-steel grab rails located throughout the interior. He glanced around again.

Whatever he was going to do was obviously a secret.

He then loosened the setscrews at each end of the rail. He motioned to Tracy to support the rail while he removed it from its brackets. Tracy didn't drop it, but her expression indicated it was heavier than she expected.

Using the screwdriver, Charles deftly loosened the plug in one end of the rail. He removed an old rag and tipped the rail downward. Paper coin rolls began sliding out. He caught the first one and opened one end.

I couldn't see very well from my vantage point, but I heard Tracy's breath catch. "Is that what I think it is?"

Charles didn't reply but simply nodded. Tracy took something in her hand, looked at it carefully, and then brought it over to me.

It was a gold coin, a Canadian Maple Leaf.

Charles motioned around. "Each of these rails hold rolls of gold coins," he quietly explained.

Tracy and I made brief eye contact with each other but didn't say anything. I wasn't sure what to say.

Charles continued. "I think I made my position clear earlier," he said. "I don't trust the government. I don't trust paper money. I only carry gold, twenty-four karat gold coins which are 99.99 percent pure. They are easily exchanged in any country, for any local currency. They have no serial numbers and are impossible to trace."

"You're not nervous about carrying gold coins around?" Tracy asked.

"I've never had a problem," he replied. "Although I don't flaunt them either." He held the coin up. "Gold is odorless, so undetectable by customs dogs. The supply is in plain sight, which I've always felt is the best way to hide anything."

He pointed to the rail. "This one isn't quite full, but the rest are."

Tracy took a few reflexive steps backwards. I could feel my heart pounding, but Tracy was close to hyperventilating. I knew what she was thinking. Considering the number and length of the grab rails that I'd seen on *The Lady Anne*, and at the recent price of gold, *The Lady Anne* was carrying hundreds of thousands of dollars' worth.

"Why are you showing us this?" I asked.

"Because I'm leaving the gold aboard."

His calm reply caught me completely off guard. "You can't be serious," I said. "You've already lost *The Lady Anne*. You don't know Tracy and me. You must have a family who'll object to you giving away their legacy—"

Charles stopped me with an upturned hand. "My family is well provided for. You and Tracy have a chance to start a new life. Didn't you come here to purchase a sailboat to do just that?"

"When we were ready, of course," I said. "But what you're offering is too much. How can we accept?"

Charles's expression grew wistful. "Life is too short and opportunities to start anew few and far between. Look on me as that rich uncle we all fantasize about having who dies suddenly and leaves you his fortune. I only ask that you follow your hearts and don't waste a single moment making your dream a reality. Start today. This minute. I'll be following you two on your journey."

He turned away then and put the coin back in the roll and

reunited it with its companions. He reinserted the rag in the rail so the coins wouldn't slide back and forth or vibrate.

Tracy and I helped him replace the rail, and when it was done, Charles invited us to be seated while he opened the curtains and the hatch.

Still in shock over what had just transpired, I sank into the closest recliner. Tracy looked at me, eyes wide, and all I could do was shrug. I kept thinking I would awaken any moment and find this all a strange and wonderful dream.

Charles poured us all some single malt scotch and I accepted the glass thankfully.

He raised his glass and we all three touched rims, the clear, bell-like ring of good crystal the only sound in the hushed cabin.

No, this was not a dream. This was really happening.

While Tracy and I sipped, Charles left us to retrieve a small duffel bag from the owner's suite.

"Is that all you're taking?" Tracy asked.

He nodded. "Keep anything you like aboard and donate the rest," he said.

He checked his phone and announced the paperwork from his lawyer had arrived.

"Can we print it here?" Tracy asked.

Charles pulled up the forms on *The Lady Anne*'s computer, turned on the printer, and soon Tracy was methodically reviewing a hard copy. "As agreed, the law firm has retained a .01 percent interest in case they need to act as our agent sometime in the future." She looked over at me. "That can easily be amended out if we later if we choose. Otherwise, Goldbloom has done a nice job."

Charles picked up a pen from the desk. "Ladies?"

Tracy and I signed where indicated, Charles did too, then he took a picture of the signature page and sent it back to the lawyer.

Tracy and I looked at each other. I released a breath. In less than twenty minutes time, we had acquired complete owner-ship and control of *The Lady Anne.*

"What will we need to clear ports?" Tracy asked.

"Everything is here." Charles added the scanned signature page to a stack of papers stored in the navigation station. He also pointed out where some spare keys, relevant account pass-words, and the lock's combination were kept.

Charles took our glasses, then washed, dried, and put them away.

Tracy was looking at him, a strange expression on her face. Finally, she said, "Charles, is there any personal service we could perform for you?"

"What?"

Charles and I both expressed our surprise in that one word uttered simultaneously.

Tracy shrugged. "Look, if the bet had gone the other way, we would have fulfilled our obligation." She waved a hand around. "After all we've gotten from you, I'd be happy to—"

There was a moment of awkward silence. Charles looked down and away.

I understood what Tracy was doing, and I half expected he'd accept, but was I ready to go through with it?

Color crept up Charles's neck. "I thank you for the offer," he said. "But I'll pass." He grinned. "However, if our paths should cross again—"

That was the perfect exit line. Charles hefted his bag and we left the salon for the marina office.

At the office, Charles introduced us to the manager as *The Lady Anne*'s new owners. "They're hiring their own crew," he added, "so the Pincus brothers should no longer have access. If you happen to spot either of them, please call the authorities. The slip will continue to be paid by me for as long as they need."

The manager made the necessary notes, welcomed us, and we left the office.

We stood together for a moment, Charles looking out over the marina. "I hope you find happiness with *The Lady Anne*," he said. "I certainly did."

He turned to go, but I stopped him with a hand on his arm. "Almost forgot," I said, digging into my bag. "Your passport."

He took it and dropped it into his duffel.

"How do we get in touch with you?" Tracy asked.

I swear she had tears in her eyes.

Charles put a finger to his lips and leaned close. "I refuse to be monitored by the government, so I won't use telephone or email for communication except just this way. Ever heard of 'foldering'?"

"Old spy trick," she said, grinning. When she saw my look of astonishment, she added, "I read a lot of thrillers."

Charles nodded. "Old spy trick. Here's how it works. Should the occasion arise that you need to contact me, use *The Lady Anne's* computer and the email account you find there. Write a message with the subject line "Four Queens" and save it to the draft folder. Just to the draft folder. Don't send. I will access the email account and respond the same way." He paused. "And of course, you can always call my lawyer. You have the number. He always knows how to reach me."

"The other way is more fun." Tracy grabbed him in a hug. "Thank you for everything," she said.

Charles T. Williams grinned, backed away, and saluted. Then he picked up his bag and strolled away without a backwards glance.

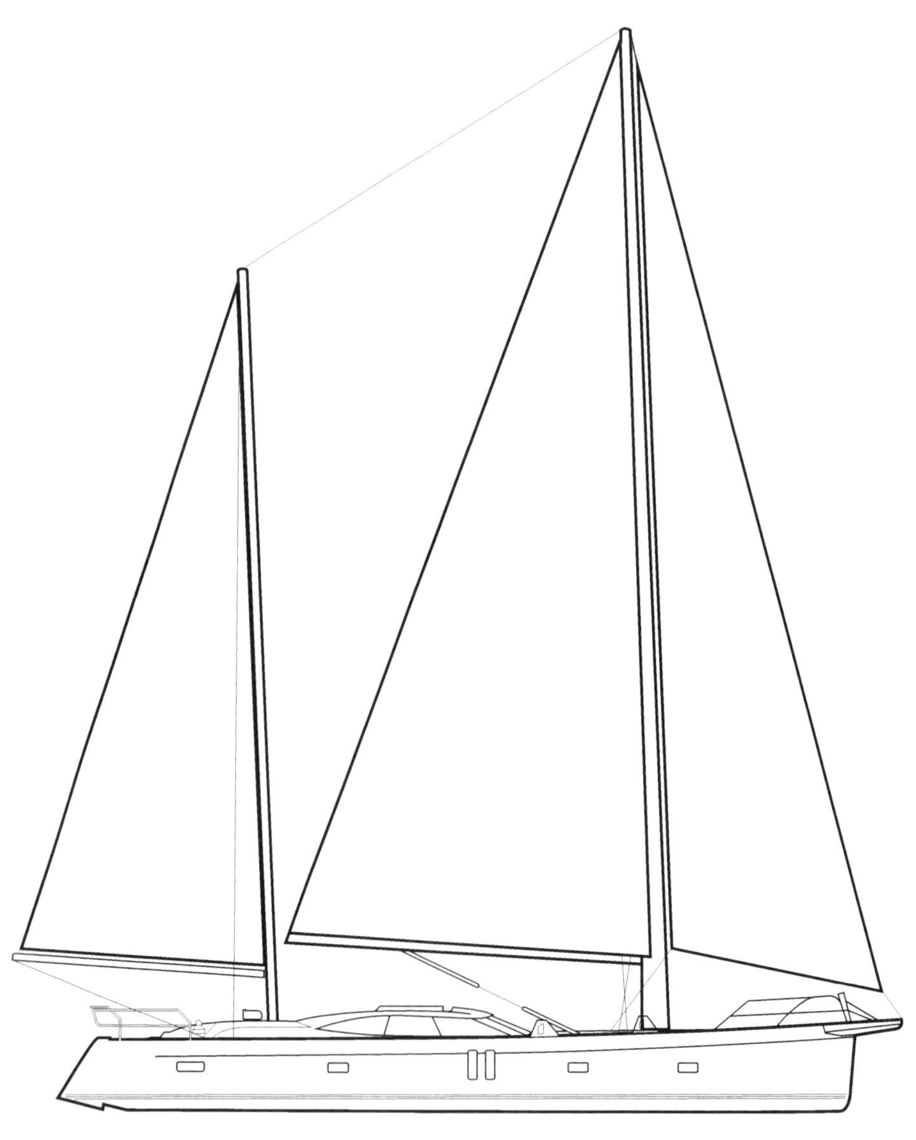

THE LADY ANNE
VESSEL OVERVIEW
NOT TO SCALE

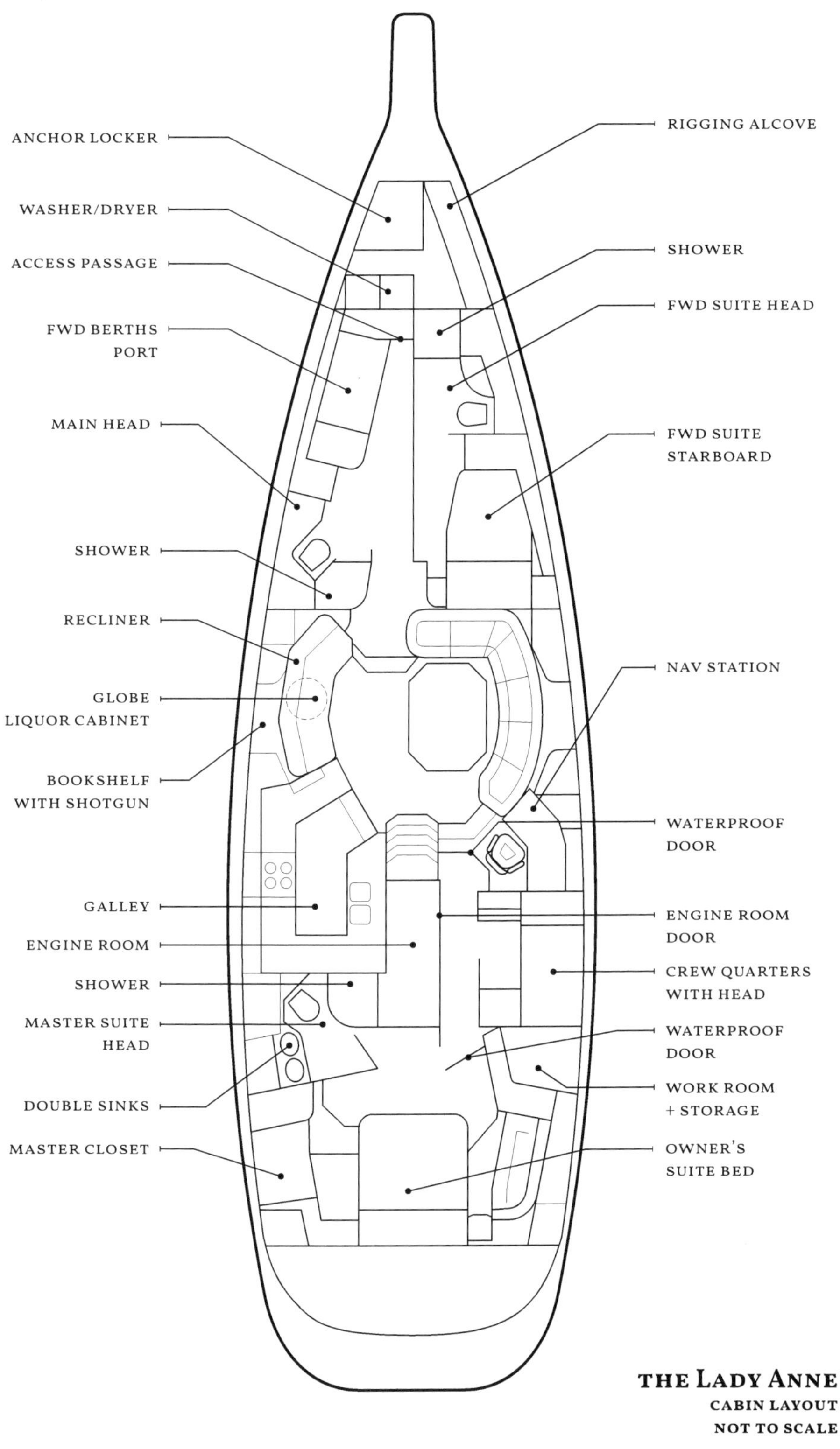

ANCHOR LOCKER
WASHER/DRYER
ACCESS PASSAGE
FWD BERTHS PORT
MAIN HEAD
SHOWER
RECLINER
GLOBE LIQUOR CABINET
BOOKSHELF WITH SHOTGUN
GALLEY
ENGINE ROOM
SHOWER
MASTER SUITE HEAD
DOUBLE SINKS
MASTER CLOSET
RIGGING ALCOVE
SHOWER
FWD SUITE HEAD
FWD SUITE STARBOARD
NAV STATION
WATERPROOF DOOR
ENGINE ROOM DOOR
CREW QUARTERS WITH HEAD
WATERPROOF DOOR
WORK ROOM + STORAGE
OWNER'S SUITE BED
THE LADY ANNE
CABIN LAYOUT
NOT TO SCALE

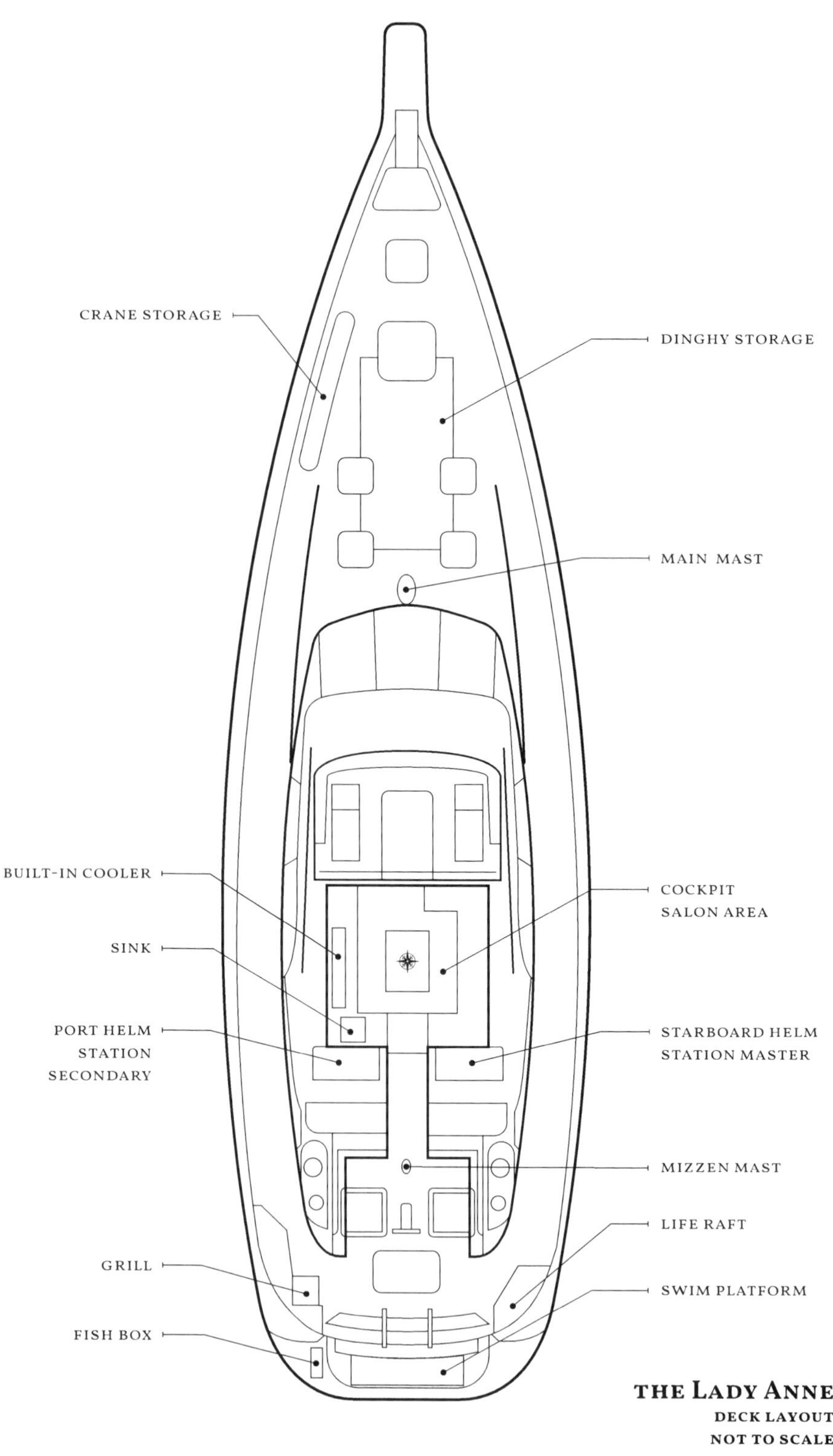

CRANE STORAGE
DINGHY STORAGE
MAIN MAST
BUILT-IN COOLER
COCKPIT SALON AREA
SINK
PORT HELM STATION SECONDARY
STARBOARD HELM STATION MASTER
MIZZEN MAST
LIFE RAFT
GRILL
SWIM PLATFORM
FISH BOX
THE LADY ANNE
DECK LAYOUT
NOT TO SCALE

CHAPTER 8

We watched Charles walk down to the pier and into a taxi.

"Well," Tracy said.

I gave her a nudge with my elbow. "Personal service?"

"It seemed the least we could do. And I liked him, didn't you?"

"Enough to screw? Not sure."

"Let's go back to our hotel," Tracy said. "I feel like sleeping aboard tonight."

We'd brought a change of clothes for just this reason, but why keep the hotel room? Five minutes later we had locked *The Lady Anne* and headed for the ferry.

We quickly packed and checked out, but by now it was getting late. The sun sat low in the sky.

"We should have listened to Charles and checked out this morning," I said.

Tracy shrugged. "Would you have felt comfortable riding in the skiff with Pink-Ass?" she asked.

"Be careful who you use that name around," I warned. "You never know who might hear."

It was almost dark when we finally arrived back at the marina. The guard at the marina gate was different from earlier, but he let us pass after checking our IDs. As we toted our suitcases below, *The Lady Anne* seemed cavernous and eerily quiet.

"We are definitely going to need help," I said, switching on some lights. "There's no way we can manage *The Lady Anne* by ourselves."

"Let's get a list of available captains from the marina office," Tracy said. "They're sure to know someone local."

We were stashing our clothes in closets and drawers, pulling Charles's things out to take ashore later. I said, "We can conduct interviews and eliminate the creepers, or maybe get an all-female crew."

"Even with great references, we'll still be alone at sea with strangers."

We kept working silently until Tracy suddenly stopped and snapped her fingers. "I know exactly who we can get," she said.

I raised an eyebrow. "Who?"

"You know him too, and he's qualified to captain a Clarriage Sixty-Eight."

"Who?"

"He can teach us how to crew for him, and the three of us can sail the boat back to Florida."

I picked up a nearby pillow and threw it at her. "Who do we possibly know like that?"

Tracy grinned. "Reid Adams!"

"Reid Adams, our old sailing instructor from Colorado?"

"Jackpot," Tracy exclaimed, looking quite pleased.

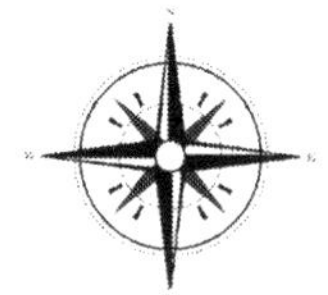

CHAPTER 9

The sun shining through the open hatch woke me from the most restful sleep I had experienced in months. I found Tracy in the galley, already dressed and looking through the cabinets.

"What's the plan?" I asked.

"Breakfast."

"Okay, then what?"

Tracy said, "You familiarize yourself with *The Lady Anne* while I try to get in touch with Reid."

She had pulled a box of cereal from one of the cabinets and set the galley table with bowls, a carton of milk, and a couple of bananas. We took our places and began to eat.

"We'll also need to go shopping at some point," she said, munching.

I agreed. I've never been a cereal person myself.

After breakfast and dishes, I busied myself looking through the lockers, cabinets, drawers, and closets. I started a couple of lists: to-do and shopping. Most of the clothing would need to be disposed of. Some of the basics, especially toiletries, would need replenishing.

Tracy spent her time on *The Lady Anne*'s notebook computer, connected to the marina's free Wi-Fi, looking for Reid. She left a message with the sailing school for Reid to call her, but they hadn't yet responded.

Just before noon, Tracy shouted, "Got it! I think I tracked Reid's cell number. It's amazing what's online. Scary, too," she added under her breath. Then, "There's no answer on the cell, but I've left a message and sent a text."

We left *The Lady Ann* to eat salads at a local place near the marina.

"We had a productive morning," I said, brandishing my lists. "But there's still lots to do."

"But most importantly, we found Reid." Tracy said. "Now let's hope he calls us back. What should we offer him?"

"See if you can get him for two hundred dollars per day plus expenses."

"What if he wants more?" Tracy asked.

"Pay him whatever he wants. *The Lady Anne* has us covered."

Tracy raised her glass. "Here's to Charles, a really generous man. A little eccentric, but really generous."

We giggled and touched the rims of our iced tea glasses together.

We spent the afternoon exploring our new home, Tracy's phone always within reach. At seven that evening, it rang. Tracy grabbed it, said hello, then gave me the thumbs-up.

Reid.

I listened as Tracy spoke with him. They had quite a lengthy conversation and by the time she rung off, I was wild with anticipation.

"We're good," Tracy said, smiling profusely. "He's got a valid passport and if we don't mind paying for expensive airfare, he can be on our dock two nights from tonight. He will fly to St. Thomas, connecting through San Juan via Miami. I gave him directions to the marina."

"Did he accept the two hundred dollars?"

"Yes, two hundred dollars per day, plus expenses. We'll need some cash to reimburse him when he gets here, so put that on the list. He said he'd take a check for the airfare since he'll just charge that to his credit card. He sounds really excited but told me it was too early for an April fool's joke, so we'd better be serious about this."

We gave each other high fives. We'd never been more serious.

CHAPTER 10

For the next two days, Tracy and I were busy. We explored and cleaned *The Lady Anne* from bow to stern, topside and belowdecks. About the only thing we couldn't do was scrub the hull below the waterline, but we donned masks we found aboard and since there were signs prohibiting swimming, we quietly made our way into the water. Like everything on *The Lady Anne*, the hull looked clean and well maintained. The prop was ding-free and looked new. There was a single strand of seaweed caught on the keel, but Tracy swam under the boat and removed it. Charles and the Pincus brothers were nothing if not meticulous about service.

Back on board, we played music as we worked, breaking only to eat or to run errands. We found a coin shop in town and cashed in a few of the Maple Leafs for a little over five thousand dollars, the most cash Tracy or I had ever had. We stowed it with the ownership documents in the navigation station.

Finally, we were finished. "She's as clean as the day she was delivered," I said proudly.

Tossing another empty water bottle into the trash box, Tracy wiped the sweat from her forehead and agreed. Again, more high fives.

As we cleaned, we found clothing we weren't going to keep and stashed it in the crew's quarters. We also found another printer, a long skinny one that was used to print charts on demand. Someone had written detailed instructions on how to print charts and for practice, we set it up on the salon table and printed a color chart of the waters surrounding the US and the British Virgin Islands.

We also discovered something else.

Concealed on the bookshelf was a false front set of books that pulled out to reveal a big orange tube. There were also two boxes of shotgun shells, one unopened, one of them partially full, and a cleaning kit in the space. Tracy pulled everything out and arranged them on the table.

She picked up the tube. "Think there's a gun in here?" she asked.

Considering what we'd found with it, I nodded. "Seems likely. Can you get the tube open?"

After a little effort and a few choice words, Tracy finally got the watertight end loosened. "There's a gun in here, all right," she said, peering inside.

"Well, let's see what we've got."

Carefully, she tipped the tube downward and a shotgun began sliding out.

"Assume that it's loaded and be very careful," I told her, moving closer.

When it was fully exposed, she laid it carefully on the table. There was no name on the barrel, but underneath it was stamped, "Mossberg, Made in U.S.A., North Haven, Conn, 500 12 GA."

"What do you think Charles did with this?" Tracy asked.

"A better question," I said, "is why was it hidden?"

She shrugged. "Well, now that we found it, what should we do with it?"

Neither Tracy nor I were crazy about guns. I'd done some shooting with my father, but it had been a long time. Still, we would be out on the open ocean and if nothing else, it might be a comfort to know we had protection.

Tracy was eyeing me, wanting me to make a decision. "Let's google the gun," I suggested. "At least find out how to load and unload it."

We found some YouTube videos not only on how to load and unload it, but also how to hold it, aim it, and fire it. It was loaded, so we unloaded it while we examined it. We also watched a video on how to clean it. The cleaning kit in the video was different than the one we had but we got the idea.

We reloaded it and put it back in its storage tube.

"What happens if a customs agent asks us if we have any weapons?" Tracy asked, placing everything back in its hiding place.

"We'll say no," I replied without hesitation. "Don't you always say it's better to beg forgiveness than to ask permission? Besides, it was only luck that we found it. What are the chances anyone else would?"

We finished putting all our cleaning supplies away and set about fixing dinner. We had chicken salad, accompanied by a bottle of wine from Charles's liquor supply. We were having vanilla ice cream for dessert when there was a noise topside.

"That must be Reid," Tracy said as she scurried topside. "He texted earlier that he had landed in St. Thomas."

I busied myself putting our dinner things away. I could hear voices but couldn't quite tell what was being said. I headed topside.

I was barely to the steps when Tracy came down headfirst through the opening, nearly hitting me. She crashed into the deck with a loud thud.

I knelt beside her. "Oh my God, Tracy. Are you okay?"

She didn't answer, didn't even move. I checked her breathing and looked for any blood. Out of the corner of my eye, I saw someone coming below toward me.

"Reid, what happened?" I asked, jumping to my feet.

But it wasn't Reid; it was Daniel Pincus.

Before I could react, he kicked me in the head on his way below. I fell over next to Tracy. I started to get up, but he grabbed me by the back of my neck and slammed my face into the deck. Then, something hard hit me in the back of my head.

CHAPTER 11

I awoke to the rumble of the engine. I could feel the boat surging through the water. My face hurt and my nose was throbbing. When I tried to raise my hands, I discovered that they were tied. I was bound hand and foot at the salon table.

Tracy was seated next to me, slumped forward. Her hands were also tied. She wasn't moving.

I didn't see any blood, but her stillness made my heart race. "Tracy. Can you hear me?"

She didn't respond. I kept repeating the question, louder, more urgently. Still no response. Now I was close to panic.

Pincus came below. He had traded his nautical whites for all black, including black gloves and a black stocking hat.

"Thought I heard you," he said.

"If you hurt Tracy, I'll kill you."

He looked at me as if I'd just said the dumbest thing he'd

ever heard. Given the circumstances, he was probably right. He lifted her head by her chin, then let it fall back again. "Nah, she'll be okay. She was awake earlier. She must have passed out again."

"Where are you taking us?"

"We're headed to St. Croix. We'll pick up my brother there, refuel, reprovision, and then the four of us are going to have some fun. All the way to South America." He smiled at me, the smile of a predator. "Of course, not all of us are going to make it."

My head started spinning. "You need to let us go right now, before you do something that you'll regret. You can't just make us disappear. We have families, friends who will miss us —come looking."

Pincus laughed. "You'll not simply disappear. Accidents happen at sea all the time. Especially with inexperienced sailors on their first voyage. It will all be very sad."

"You really think you'll get away with murdering us?"

"Murder? There can't be a murder without a body. And between here and the 500 miles to South America, the water is very deep, the course is very lonely, and the sharks are very hungry."

He seemed to have thought this through. "Why are you doing this?" I asked quietly.

"Because you two sluts fucked up my life," he snapped. "I had a plan and when you caught that ten, you ruined it."

I looked away from him, toward the bookcase. Pincus saw where I was looking and then said, "Well, you're smarter than you look. Congratulations. You found the gun. Go for it. Oh wait, you can't. You're tied up. Too bad."

Tracy moaned and moved her head a little. Pincus paused and felt her neck.

"Her pulse is normal; she'll recover."

"She needs medical attention."

"When I get done with you two, the only medical attention you're going to need is an autopsy." He chuckled at his own wit before continuing. "When Charles gambled this boat away, he screwed me and my brother. Now I'm going to screw you. I'm going to use you and your cute friend until you're both used up. As soon as Sam is aboard, the party is going to begin."

"Why South America?" I asked, clutching at anything to change the subject from this maniac and his plan.

"A market for all the gold we're carrying."

"You know about that?"

"Yeah, I know about the gold. I've spent a year devising a way to steal it. I've got a foolproof plan. It will be the perfect crime. Long tacks across oceans give you plenty of time to think, and to make plans."

"So, what's the plan?"

At first, the way Pincus peered at me, I thought he would refuse to say more. After a moment, though, he said, "For being a smart man, Charles wasn't that smart. He should learn to put tools back in their proper place. There aren't that many Allen screws on board and when you're on autopilot in steady conditions, you have nothing to do but look around.

Yeah, I found the gold, and then I devised the perfect way to steal it."

"How?" I asked.

"Sam and I would have delivered *The Lady Anne* to some distant port after Charles and his wife completed their vacation. But this time, *The Lady Anne* was going sink in deep water with all crew lost and nothing but a *Mayday*, an emergency EPIRB signal, and floating debris for clues. Of course, we would have transferred the gold to another vessel and then just quietly slipped away. Charles kept enough gold on board to set us up for life. It was foolproof until his wife died and he wanted to sail back with us. Then you caught that fucking ten and I was no longer captain."

He checked Tracy's pulse again and then continued. "So now I've got a new plan. Fuck the girls to death, take the gold, ditch the boat and the bodies, leave no witnesses, and live happily ever after in Venezuela, which is a nonextradition country. You know that pirates did this exact same thing in these very waters a couple hundred years ago and now they make movies about it."

Tracy moaned again. She lifted her head, looked at me, and asked, "Pat, what's going on?"

Her words were slurred and her eyes clouded.

"Pincus," I said, putting as much venom as I could in those two syllables. "He's a psycho who thinks he and his brother are going to use us for sport until we get to South America."

All the time I was speaking, I held Pincus's eyes with my

own. "Then he thinks he's going to kill us and dump our bodies. But he's going to find we're not that easy to kill. In fact, Mr. Pink-Ass, you'd better be fucking sure—"

Pincus's face colored and he took a step toward me. "What did you just call me?"

He made a fist but stopped when suddenly *The Lady Anne*'s engine throttled back, and she began to slow.

Pincus started for the ladder. "I'm going to check that," he said, heading topside. "And then we'll see who's got a pink ass."

As soon as he was out of sight, I began tugging furiously at the lines that were biting into my wrists.

"Tracy," I said. "We've got to get out of here before Pincus comes back. He's going to kill us. Can you help untie me?"

Tracy had slumped forward again and wasn't answering.

"Tracy," I repeated more urgently. "We're dead unless we can get out of here now!"

From the corner of my eye, I spotted a shape moving in from behind me. I braced myself for whatever was going to happen next and opened my mouth to scream.

A hand pressed against my mouth. I was ready to chomp down on the fingers, bite them completely off, when my head was forcibly turned to the side.

It wasn't Pincus.

"Shh," Reid said. "Be quiet."

I'd never been so happy to see someone in my life. "Where did you come from?" I whispered.

As he untied my hands, he said, "From the marina. I saw Tracy get pushed through the hatch. Figured something was up. So I swam over and stowed away on the swim platform alongside the dinghy."

"Figured something was up, huh?" I quickly loosened the lines binding my feet and began trying to rub feeling back into my wrists. "Quick, untie Tracy. There's a gun over there on the bookshelf. I'll go get it."

Reid began untying Tracy's hands while I stumbled over to the bookcase. My feet felt like lead weights, they'd been tied so tightly. Something else to thank Pincus for later.

I made it over to the bookcase and pulled the books toward me, thinking how smart it had been to reload the shotgun before we put it back in its hiding place.

But something was wrong. The tube was gone. I stared at the empty space for a few seconds, knowing Tracy and I had put it back.

"No, no. It has to be here." Frantically I began looking around the salon. I knew that our lives depended on finding that tube and getting the gun out quickly.

"Looking for this?" Pincus said.

Neither Reid nor I heard Pincus come back down. Now he was standing five or six feet from Reid, pointing the shotgun at him.

"Move and you're dead." He moved closer toward Reid, but his eyes were on me. "Do you think I'm a fucking moron?

Do you think I'd leave a loaded shotgun unattended, especially since there'd be a good chance you and your nosy girlfriend might find it?" He smirked. "Or maybe old Charles himself showed you where it was. He'd want to be sure you girls would have protection."

He poked the gun into Reid's chest. "Who the hell are you?"

Just then Tracy raised her head and looked around. Her eyes widened when she took in the scene. "Reid? Is that you?"

The fact that she recognized Reid relieved me. At least if she had a concussion, it was a mild one.

Pincus glanced at her, then back to Reid. "And who is Reid?"

Tracy answered him, although her words were slow and her speech slurred. "Reid Adams, our sailing instructor from Colorado."

Pincus moved toward Reid. "How did you get on board?"

Reid backed away until he was up against the bookcase. "I saw you push Tracy down the ladder. I waited until you cleared the slip, then swam over and climbed on the swim platform. When I saw my chance, I snuck down here."

Pincus pointed the shotgun at Reid's face. "Let me see your phone. Now."

Reid reached into his back pocket.

Pincus stopped him with the shotgun. "Slowly," he said.

Reid gingerly pulled out his phone and held it up.

"Drop it and move away, slow, real fucking slow."

Reid did as ordered, moving so that he was between me and Pincus.

Pincus examined the phone. "This thing is all wet. Did you call anyone before you took your swim?"

Reid shook his head. "Didn't have time."

"Then it doesn't work, does it?"

"Probably not," Reid said.

Pincus lowered the barrel of the shotgun slightly and reached into his back pocket. He produced one of the hand-held VHF radios Tracy and I had seen earlier by the navigation station. He looked at it for a minute.

"Well, Mr. Sailing Instructor," he said. "There is a radar blip headed this way, but if your phone doesn't work and since I didn't hear a distress call go out over the radio, I'm guessing you didn't have time to call for help. It's probably a local out on a night run."

Pincus put the radio back in his pocket and tossed Reid's phone toward the galley. He raised the gun so that it was pointed at Reid's chest. "Now what to do with you?"

Reid looked over at me. "Who is this guy?" he asked.

His tone was far from flattering, and I was afraid for a minute Pincus would react by hitting him—or worse. Instead, though, Pincus answered himself.

"A few days ago, I was the captain of this boat," he said. "Until the fucking owner got drunk and lost her in a poker game to these two cunts." He motioned with the shotgun toward Tracy and me. "Tie them up and don't try anything funny. If they get loose, I'll kill you all, right here, right now."

Reid tied us back up, tying Tracy first, softly apologizing as he tied us. When he was finished, Pincus motioned him away and inspected the knots. My bindings weren't as tight as before but still tight enough that I couldn't get loose. Before leaving Tracy, he pulled her top and bra up, exposing her breasts.

I couldn't believe I was back where I started.

Pincus approached Reid, pointing the barrel at his head.

"If you blow my head off with that shotgun," Reid said, "you'll blow a hole in the hull. You do realize that, right?" Reid's voice sounded like he was asking a question of a not-so-bright student.

Pincus touched the gun to Reid's forehead. "Put your hands in your pockets."

Reid did as he was told. Pincus stepped close and kneed Reid with such force, Reid expelled a hiss of pain and surprise. His hands jerked to grab himself and he fell forward to his knees. Pincus kneed him again, this time under his chin.

Reid toppled over backwards, curled into a fetal position, still holding himself.

Raising the gun high out of the way, Pincus began kicking him.

"Stop it," I screamed. "You'll kill him!"

Pincus paused, glancing over at me. "You may be right. Sam and I may have use for him later." He picked up a length of line and used it to tie Reid's hands behind his back.

I breathed a sigh of relief thinking his attack on Reid was over, but I was wrong. When he was done, he kicked Reid again in the ribs three or four times.

By now, Reid offered no resistance.

He dragged Reid a short distance and propped him up into a sitting position against the bulkhead. Then he reached down and slapped him until Reid moaned and opened his eyes.

"Do you fuck your students?" he asked.

Reid shook his head as if to clear it. "What?"

"Do you fuck your students?" Pincus asked again.

Reid struggled to sit up. "No," he said.

Pincus motioned to Tracy and me. "Not even two good-looking pieces of ass like that?"

"No, I don't fuck my students."

Pincus straightened up. "Too bad. I was hoping you could give me some pointers about what they like. You know. Do they like it straight? Or maybe they're into something kinky? Any women who would wager an orgy against a yacht must be into more than the missionary position."

Reid narrowed his eyes. "What are you talking about?"

Pincus laughed. "Oh, they didn't tell you how they won *The Lady Anne*?"

"A poker game," Reid answered. "They won it in a poker game."

"And you never wondered what they had to bet that was worth a three-million-dollar yacht?"

I groaned inwardly. I'm sure Tracy didn't tell Reid what we had put up—our bodies.

Reid was staring at me. "No. They never mentioned what they had bet."

Pincus walked past me, laid the shotgun down on the salon table, and then turned my chair around so that I was facing Reid. He reached down and grabbed my crotch.

"They bet this. A weekend of sex with my boss and me. Anything we wanted. Isn't that right, bitch?"

Reid snorted. "Well. I'd say they got the better bargain, wouldn't you? Pat's a smart card player. I'm sure she saw a sucker bet from a mile away."

It was not the reaction I was expecting. Pincus, either, gathering from the way his face colored. But he recovered quickly.

"Well, if you can't give me any pointers, I suppose I'll have to find out for myself how she likes it. And I guess you'll just have to watch. If you're a good boy, maybe you can have a piece of what's left when Sam and I are finished."

"Sam?" Reid asked.

"My brother," Pincus replied. "We're on our way to pick him up. I was going to wait for him but what the hell, let's get this party started."

Pincus grabbed my hair and pulled me up. He dragged me over to the salon table and shoved me facedown onto the surface with such force I was sure if my nose hadn't been broken before, it was now. Pain knifed through me, and I tasted the blood as it spilled onto the table.

"Leave her alone," Reid said.

Pincus glared at him. "Or what? What are you going to do?" He walked over to him. "One more word and I'll gag you. If I were you, I'd shut the fuck up and enjoy the show."

My heart was beating a crazy tattoo in my chest. I felt Pincus behind me. He grabbed my neck with one hand, forcing my face into the table while he yanked my shorts and panties down with the other.

I felt cool air on my exposed rear. I began kicking, but he pinned my legs.

"Now, who were you calling a Pink-Ass?"

I tensed up. I felt his hand on my ass. He rubbed it before delivering a hard slap. I jumped and tried to squirm away, but I couldn't move. He laughed and slapped me again. Then I heard a zipper. I couldn't believe what was about to happen.

I was staring right at the shotgun next to me, but I couldn't reach it with my hands tied and my legs pinned.

I looked over at Tracy. She was slumped backward in her chair, topless. Her hands were again tied, but this time in front, resting in her lap. She had passed out again. I was secretly glad. She wouldn't see what was coming.

Pincus was rubbing his cock against me. I squeezed my butt cheeks together. I remembered what I had been told in a self-defense class. Do whatever you have to in order to survive.

"Please don't do this," I pleaded.

He leaned down, his breath hot against my cheek. "Do what? If any card other than that fucking ten had come up, wouldn't we be doing just this?"

He was forcing my legs apart now, his fingers probing, poking.

I heard Reid suck in a breath. I felt tears burning, so I clenched my teeth and closed my eyes.

Pincus was right, of course. I'd made the bet. Stupid. Maybe I had this coming…

"This is the United States Coast Guard. Heave to and prepare to be boarded," a booming, amplified voice commanded from outside.

Pincus stopped but kept me pinned. I opened my eyes.

"How did you call them?" he yelled at Reid.

"I didn't call anybody," Reid answered. "My phone doesn't work. You saw for yourself."

"This is the United States Coast Guard," the voice repeated louder and with more urgency. "Heave to and prepare to be boarded."

That's when I started to scream.

CHAPTER 13

Pincus tried to put his hand over my mouth but I continued to scream.

"Give yourself up," Reid said. "You haven't raped her yet and you haven't committed murder. This is the time to give yourself up."

"Fuck you!" Pincus replied. He crawled off me and pulled up his pants. He looked at the shotgun but didn't pick it up. The radio fell out of his pocket but he didn't pick that up either.

He started for the ladder. Before he reached it, two armed, uniformed sailors came below. They stopped at the sight of Tracy, topless and slumped over in her chair, a bound Reid, and me, half-naked with a bloody face.

It probably wasn't something they saw every day.

Pincus, for all his bravado, put his hands up and gave up without a fight.

While they hustled him up the ladder, a Coast Guard medic started for me, but I waved him to Tracy. He draped his jacket over her and did a quick exam. I straightened and pulled my shorts back up, feeling both mortified and angry thinking about what Pincus had come close to doing.

In the meantime, two more guardsman had come below. I answered their questions, telling them about the poker game (leaving out the orgy wager part) and how Daniel Pincus, the man they had in custody, had gotten fired after we took over and came back for revenge. I didn't mention the gold, something I was pretty sure he wouldn't bring up either, but I did mention his brother, Sam, waiting in St. Croix.

Reid filled in who he was and how he had gotten aboard. He was approaching *The Lady Anne* on the dock when he saw Tracy get shoved below. He didn't have time to do anything but drop his bags and silently enter the water—phone, passport, wallet, clothes, and all. He swam over and crawled onto the swim platform, hiding there until Pincus went below.

He overheard Pincus's plan to get rid of Tracy and me, so he slowed the engine and snuck below through an unfastened forward hatch. Like me, he omitted the part of the plot where Pincus was to steal the gold and sink *The Lady Anne*. I would have to ask him why when we had a chance to be alone.

When Reid finished, I asked the guardsman taking notes, "I don't want to sound ungrateful, but who called you guys?"

"The guard at the marina," he replied. "He thought he had

given Reid the wrong slip number and went looking for him. He found Reid's bags on the dock and saw Daniel Pincus backing *The Lady Anne* out of her slip. He remembered the notice from the day shift that the Pincus brothers were no longer to have access. Seeing him at the helm of *The Lady Anne* was suspicious. He made the call."

"What are you going to do with Pincus?" I asked. "You have him locked up, right?"

The two guardsmen looked at one another.

I got a cold chill. "You don't have him?"

"He came topside with us," one said. "But struggled free and dove overboard. We're searching the immediate waters but haven't found him yet."

I closed my eyes. The dangerous lunatic was still out there.

Across the salon, I heard Tracy giving her statement. She collaborated my story as best she could, having been unconscious most of the time.

Then it was my turn to be examined. The medic discretely asked if I had been raped. I answered no. He looked at my nose, my bruised wrists and ankles, then catalogued our injuries.

"You were very fortunate no one was hurt worse. Ms. Palmer has a head injury, most likely a concussion, and should have an MRI or CT scan as soon as possible. You have a broken nose that needs a medical or surgical assessment, again as soon as possible. Your cheekbones do not appear to be broken. Your bruises will heal, but they'll get worse before they get better. You'll have two very black eyes for a while too.

"Mr. Adams has two broken ribs, but his breathing sounds good and his lungs don't appear to have been punctured. He should seek medical attention if he has any trouble breathing.

"You both need to keep an eye on Ms. Palmer. Get her immediate medical attention if you notice any worsening headaches, unequal pupils, or vision changes."

As he finished his instructions, he said softly, "You three are extremely lucky we came along when we did."

The captain came down then. He consulted with the medics, excused them, and turned to me. "The medics tell me you should return to St. Thomas for further treatment right away. Ms. Palmer needs a CT scan. We've been unable to locate your assailant, but we will notify the St. Thomas and the St. Croix police about the incident. They'll be on the lookout for him."

Reid and I followed the guardsman topside, leaving Tracy resting below. We thanked them and watched them move off. Saying thank you seemed so inadequate. I knew we owed them our lives.

Reid saluted the captain and said, "*Semper Paratus.*"

Smiling, the captain returned the salute. "*Semper Paratus.*"

I held up a hand to say goodbye.

After they left, I asked Reid what *Semper Paratus* meant.

"It's the motto of the Coast Guard meaning 'always ready,'" he responded.

I nodded. "It's a good motto."

Reid and I got Tracy into bed and then, taking a flashlight and the shotgun, quietly went topside and made our way all around the boat, shining the light along the hull and out into the water as far as the beam would go. We checked in and around the dinghy and the swim platform, concerned that Pincus might be treading water nearby, watching and listening to us, preparing to come back on board the same way Reid had.

I wrapped my arms around my waist. "Let's raise sail and get out of here," I said.

"Back to St. Thomas?" Reid asked.

I didn't answer but left Reid to go below. I retrieved the paper chart Tracy and I had printed earlier and returned topside with it.

"We can't go back to the marina," I said, laying the chart on the table. "Not without knowing what happened to Pincus."

Reid shrugged. "My bags are there," he said. "And the medic said Tracy needed a CT scan."

I studied the chart.

"Puerto Rico," I whispered. "Plot a course for Puerto Rico. By ferry, it's only a few hours away. We should be able to make it on *The Lady Anne*."

"What about my luggage?"

"Can cash cover what was in your bags?" I asked.

He paused and then nodded.

"Then we're not going back. It's not safe. Plot the course please, and I'll replace everything there."

Tracy appeared from below, holding a bag of ice cubes against her forehead. "Where are we going?" she asked.

"Here," I said, pointing again to Puerto Rico. "We're going here."

She raised an eyebrow. "I heard you whispering. You're afraid Pincus is out there somewhere, listening?"

"If he is," I said grimly, hoisting the shotgun, "we'll be ready this time. But you go back to bed. Reid and I can manage."

Tracy looked again at the chart. "I don't want to lie down, I want to help."

While Tracy got our current position from the GPS, Reid plotted our course and I raised the sails. Given all of *The Lady Anne*'s electric winches, it was easy. Reid took the helm and we started sailing toward Puerto Rico in the dark, with a blanket of stars above. But after a while, Tracy went back down below, her headache worse. Her pupils looked okay, but I knew we'd have to get her to a hospital as soon as we landed in San Juan.

I took the wheel while Reid took the gun and patrolled the decks, patrolled below, then patrolled topside again. Then he repeated the process. Satisfied Pincus could not possibly be on board, he sat down next to me.

"So," he said, "what was this about gold?"

I explained Charles's fantastic gift.

"Who exactly is Charles?"

I told him what I knew, which wasn't a whole lot.

"And you really bet a weekend with two men you never met before for a chance at a yacht?"

"Not just a yacht. A Clarriage Sixty-Eight."

He gave me a raised eyebrow.

"Yes, yes. It was stupid and dangerous. Charles seemed like a very nice man. Who knew he would have a psychopath for a friend."

Reid sighed. "So the plan is to take *The Lady Anne* to Florida until you and Tracy can get a charter service started."

"That *was* the plan."

"*Was* the plan?"

"I can't help thinking about what almost happened. If you hadn't have shown up when you did, or if the guard hadn't gone looking for you and seen Pincus take the boat out, Tracy and I would be sailing toward a horrible death. We would have been killed and disposed of in deep water. *The Lady Anne*, a Clarriage Sixty-Eight luxury sailing yacht, my beautiful Clarriage that I won fair and square, would be gone. My family would be told I was lost at sea."

My breath ran out and I felt tears sting my eyes. "Who knows how many other Pincus's are out there. What happens if Tracy and I get another psycho charter? How do we protect ourselves against that?"

Reid took my hand. "I can think of one way," he said.

"What's that?"

"Hire the right crew. And the right captain."

"I plan to be captain," I said with a smile.

"Then hire the right second officer."

"That's Tracy."

He shook his head. "Okay. Any room for a sailor who brings his crew flowers?"

"You bought us flowers?"

"Of course I bought you flowers. I had flowers for both of you. Purple for you and yellow for Tracy. They're on the dock with my bags."

"So you'd be willing to crew with us? Become business partners?"

He spread his arms out wide. "Who wouldn't want that life? We would need a cook, maybe a couple of deckhands when we actually started to accept charters, but we could make this work. I have some money saved to contribute. I can't think of a better way to see the world."

"Don't you have a girlfriend? I seem to remember a curvy redhead who met you at the dock after lessons."

Reid shook his head. "That's been over for a while. Nope. No attachments. Free as you and Tracy."

I liked the idea of partnering with Reid. A lot. He was an experienced sailor and nice to look at—a plus on long days at sea. I tilted my head and sized him up. Tall, lean, ruggedly handsome, but with a kind face. And unattached.

"I have to run this by Tracy," I said after a moment.

"Understood," he said.

I grinned. "Okay. Make a list of what was in your bags and be sure to include the flowers. Tomorrow we go shopping."

"Aye-aye, Captain."

Up until now, an adrenaline rush had kept me going. Now, for the first time since the Coast Guard left, I let myself relax. Immediately, my nose began to throb. I covered my face with my hands.

"You okay?" Reid asked

"I need an ice pack," I said, starting to get up.

Reid stopped me with a hand on my arm. "You stay. I'll get it."

He left for the galley and I rested my head on my hands.

I could only imagine what I looked like—two black eyes, swollen lips, busted nose. When Reid came back with a small bag of ice cubes, I pressed it against my face. "When we take Tracy for the CT scan, what do I say when they see my bruises?" I asked. "Tell them I ran into a door?"

"If you're embarrassed by the truth, tell them you were in a car wreck," Reid replied. "Both of you. I'm sure they'll accept it. You should be checked out too, you know."

The day was beginning to take its toll on me. I yawned and Reid stood, pulling me up with him. "I'll take the watch," he said. "Go below with Tracy and get some sleep."

I started to object but he held up a hand. "I'll come get you if I need to. You need rest or you'll be no good tomorrow. Go on. Get some sleep."

Sleep sounded like a wonderful idea. I left him in the cockpit and headed below.

CHAPTER 14

The rising sun shining in my eyes woke me. I was in the owner's cabin. Tracy was sleeping beside me in the king-size bed. Neither of us had taken our clothes off, but just fell across the big bed, exhausted. We were covered by a blanket, though, so I figured Reid must have come down and covered us up.

I felt a slight side-to-side motion from *The Lady Anne*. I passed Reid in the galley, said good morning, and went directly up on deck to find she was hove to and saw land in the distance.

Reid emerged from below with a cup of steaming coffee.

"Puerto Rico?" I asked, pointing.

"San Juan. I single-handed the boat over here through the night. I didn't trim for speed, so she didn't heel. I kept the ride smooth so as not to wake you. Then I heaved to and I've been waiting for you two to wake up." He handed me the coffee. "She's a beauty to sail."

He picked up the shotgun. "I don't think it's necessary, but I'll take another look around. I left a cruising guide on the salon table. Look it over and decide where you want to dock for the day."

He left and I went into the salon. I remembered from our exploring that Charles had an impressive library of cruising guides and charts, no doubt accumulated during his cruise time with his wife. Reid had found a cruising guide for Puerto Rico. I sipped my coffee and flipped through it. There was also a large paper chart of the entire island.

By the time Reid returned, I'd made up my mind. "The San Juan Bay Marina," I told him. "Here. The cruising guide says it's the best for mega yachts and there are medical facilities nearby. There's also a Costco where we can provision."

"I'll put the gun away and radio ahead for a slip."

Reid left the cabin and I relaxed back in my chair, enjoying the coffee. I familiarized myself with the facilities at the marina, specifically the fact that it was only a few minutes to a hospital, restaurants, and shopping areas. Just what we needed. An added plus was that there was a twenty-four-hour security patrol.

Reid appeared. "All set. Fee is per foot per hour or per foot per day. I asked for the day. Gives us plenty of time to get Tracy and you checked out in a hospital and the shopping done."

"I'm fine," I said.

"Let's just make sure," he said back.

Noon found us in a nice big slip, nearby to some very impressive motor yachts. It was with a sense of pride that I noticed the looks *The Lady Anne* got as we docked. She held her own with every one of those boats—even the ones much bigger and fancier. But it was the fear of frightening small children with my bruises and broken nose that had me pulling a hat down low on my head and putting on my sunglasses.

Reid replaced the Virgin Islands' flag with a Puerto Rico flag. He reminded us to fly the flag of the host country from the starboard spreader. I vaguely remembered reading that in my sailing textbook.

I waited until we were ready to go on shore to wake Tracy. She managed to get a little coffee down as she changed clothes, but getting her to a hospital was first priority.

I gave Reid cash from our stash to pay our fees. I took the rest of the cash with me. I could have used a credit card, but a credit card can be traced. I didn't want to leave a bigger paper trail then we needed to.

Reid found us a local driver with a minivan who would stay with us for the day. He spoke English and didn't question our car wreck story, which was a relief. He drove us to a hospital only five minutes from the marina and said he'd wait for us in the waiting room in case we needed a translator.

The emergency room was empty when we went in. Luckily, the nurse on duty spoke English and, like our driver, accepted the car wreck story. When we had finished the paperwork, she asked who would like to be seen first.

"Tracy," I answered quickly. "She hit the windshield pretty hard."

Tracy grabbed my arm. "Come with me."

The nurse nodded that it would be alright, so I went with her, leaving Reid and the driver to wait.

The doctor on duty was a young, handsome Hispanic whose broken English added to his charm. His examination was thorough and when he was finished, he turned to me.

"Your friend has no sign of neurologic compromise. She appears alert, oriented, and her pupils are equal. She will need bed rest," he said. "She should take it very easy for at least a week. If her eyesight changes, her headaches worsen, or she should begin to vomit, take her to hospital immediately. If her speech becomes slurred or she loses consciousness, she must go to hospital. Traumatic brain injury is not something to take lightly, do you understand?"

"Does she need a CT scan?"

He nodded. "I'm ordering one for her and one for you as well. I'll know more after your exam."

"Will you know the results today?" I asked.

"The radiologist is here today so I will probably have your results in a few hours, but no later than tomorrow."

"If we choose not to wait, can you call, email, or text me if there are any problems?"

"Certainly," he replied with a smile.

I didn't bother to tell him that we wouldn't be here for more than a day, but since our trip to Florida shouldn't take us too far from land, I figured we could always get ashore if we needed to.

He was talking to Tracy now. "Bed rest means just that. No reading, watching television, writing. Nothing that might bring on a headache."

She shot me a pleading look. "What can I do?"

"What you can do is listen to the doctor," I said firmly.

He turned toward me. "Now. Let's check you out."

My turn.

He turned my face this way and that, poked at my nose (which made me yelp), and shone a light in my eyes.

"No serious damage," he said. "Your cheekbones are undamaged and there doesn't appear to be any broken bones or nasal obstructions."

I was relieved.

He continued, "Your nose is slightly out of alignment but doesn't require surgery. I can realign it manually or you can let it heal by itself and it shouldn't be overly noticeable."

I didn't really want surgery in a foreign country unless it was absolutely necessary.

As if reading my thoughts, he said reassuringly, "Your perfect nose will be less so now. But a small bump will add character."

I rolled my eyes and he and Tracy laughed.

We followed him and got our CT scans. Tracy went first. When it was my turn, I tried hard to remain still and ignore the buzzing noises as the machine operated. The entire procedure was painless.

"There's one more person I'd like you to look at," I said as we followed the doctor back to the waiting room.

But Reid and the driver had conveniently disappeared.

The nurse behind the desk saw me looking around. "The men said they'd wait for you at the van," she said.

I took care of the charges with cash and thanked both the doctor and the nurse for their help.

"Let this be a lesson to you," he told us. "Always wear your seatbelt."

Tracy began grumbling the moment we got back to the van.

"He can't be serious," she said. "Bed rest for a week? No way."

"Is that what the doctor said?" Reid asked.

We were on the road to the shopping area. "It is," I said. "And why didn't you stay in the waiting room? You should have been checked out too. Pincus worked you over pretty hard."

He shot me a look and I gulped. There goes the car wreck story. The driver didn't seem to be paying attention, though, so I shook my head and lowered my voice. "Well?"

"I'm fine and my breathing is fine. No discomfort, no laboring, and not much pain," he said. "The worst is the sore ribs. And there's nothing that can be done about that."

We were approaching our first stop—a marine supply store.

Next door was a café.

I pushed some bills at the driver. "Take Tracy to the café and wait for us there."

"What?" It was a cry of indignation.

"You can get breakfast. We'll join you when we're done. Listen, it's either that or we take you back to *The Lady Anne* right now. Your choice."

Tracy climbed out of the van. She followed the driver into the café, only stopping once to give us the finger.

"She seems fine to me," Reid commented dryly.

We walked up and down the aisles, finding the items Reid had brought with him and now had to replace: a handheld GPS with two sets of extra lithium batteries; a handheld VHF radio with extra battery and charger; PFD (personal flotation device) with an integrated safety harness and two extra CO2 inflation cartridges; a six-foot tether; a survival whistle; a hand bearing compass; parallel rules; divider; fingerless sailing gloves; duct tape; dive mask; waterproof flashlight with extra batteries; thru-hull plugs; multi-tool; rigging knife with marlin spike; one hundred feet of orange paracord; light sticks; motion sickness pills; biodegradable soap; two pair of polarized sunglasses, each with a retainer strap; and some nice binoculars.

I poked at one of the items in the basket. "Seasick pills? Is there something you need to tell me?"

"You ever make a two-hundred-mile offshore passage?" he asked.

I let it go.

He also got some clothes, offshore rain gear, a fleece jacket, a swimsuit, two hats, and sailing shoes. I liked his shoes so much that I bought a pair for Tracy and me too. I also bought sailing gloves and rain gear for us. He picked two nice duffel bags and when we had paid, carefully packed his purchases in them at the checkout counter. I settled for a large plastic bag.

Reid stowed the bags in the van while I went to get Tracy and the driver. While she was trying on her new shoes, I asked if there was a Walmart or a similar store nearby and he said there was. This time though, when we got there, Tracy refused to stay in the van.

Reid's purchases were personal this time: underwear, socks, T-shirts, shorts, a sweatshirt, a belt, a calculator, spiral notebooks, pens, pencils, some snacks, some ginger ale, sunscreen, and some toiletries. Near the toiletries, he paused at the display of condoms. He looked at Tracy and started to blush.

"Did you have those in your lost bags?" Tracy asked.

"Yes," said Reid, looking very uncomfortable.

"Well, you better replace them," said Tracy matter-of-factly. "You never know."

I winked at Tracy.

We took everything out to the minivan. We still had plenty of room, so I figured the next stop was Costco.

"We need to make another stop first," he told our driver. "A music store. Is there one nearby?"

"What for?" Tracy asked before the driver could reply.

"We need to replace my trumpet."

"You brought a trumpet?" Tracy blinked at him. "Can you play?"

"Of course I can play," he answered. "I used to play for the president."

Tracy and I exchanged glances.

"I'll tell you about it later," Reid said.

At the music store, Reid picked out two instruments and tested them. He really could play. Everyone in the store gathered around to listen and clapped for him when he stopped.

After a few minutes, he made his decision which trumpet to take, and I paid.

"You are a man of surprises," Tracy said back at the van.

"You ain't seen nothing yet," he said.

At Costco, I could see Tracy was tired. "You are staying here," I told her. "No arguments. It's either that or I take you back to the hospital and tell them to admit you."

"The doctor was cute," Tracy said. "But I'll be good. I'll go inside to the concession stand and get a cold drink." She hooked her arm with the driver's. "Come with?"

He grinned and once I'd used my card to get us in, the two of them headed for the concession area.

I wasn't happy using my card, another trail to follow if someone was diligent, but it was the only way to take advantage of what I figured would be an expensive trip.

And it was. Four stuffed carts later we were back at the van trying to fit everything in.

"Were you able to replace everything?" I asked Reid on the way back to *The Lady Anne*.

"Everything except my sailing and scuba certifications and logbook," he replied. "When I got your call, I figured I'd take us around the British Virgin Islands for a few days after my arrival. We could practice sailing and anchoring *The Lady Anne* at the local tourist spots. And I would have liked to dive the wreck of the Rhone. Pincus changed those plans. When we get to Florida, I can replace the certifications, no problem."

"But until then," Tracy said with a twinkle in her eye. "You can't really prove you're qualified to sail a Clarriage, can you?"

There was a brief moment of silence before we all started to laugh.

CHAPTER 15

I ordered Tracy to wait in the van and hold our new flowers. For once she didn't argue with me. The driver, Reid, and I unloaded all of our purchases, stacking them neatly in an adjoining parking space. I paid the driver, adding a big tip. He said to call him if we needed another ride and to feel better after our accident.

That story was getting a lot of mileage.

I sent Tracy ahead to *The Lady Anne* with an easy job to do: send Charles an email. We thought he should know about Pincus. She would ask him to call us as soon as he saw the message.

It took three dock carts and several trips to unload all our purchases. Tracy stayed topside, watching the mountain of supplies grow alongside *The Lady Anne*, waiting for her phone to ring. She had placed our flowers—roses for her, sunflowers for me—in a bucket of water on the cockpit table. It had to be the ugliest vase I had ever seen, but seeing the flowers made me smile. It made *The Lady Anne* feel like home and, at least for the moment, safe.

Reid and I fashioned a two-person assembly line, moving the Costco boxes aboard, then carrying them to the hatch, sending them below, and finally stacking them in the salon. It was hard work for two people in the heat. When the last box was below, Reid finally commented on my provisioning.

"There are ports between here and Florida, you know," he said. "We have enough provisions here for a circumnavigation."

"I don't want to run aground on a lee shore and starve to death while waiting for help," I said.

"Fair enough, but are we expecting company? There's enough food here to feed half the marina."

I poked his arm. "You'll thank me later when you get the munchies."

Tracy joined us below and just shook her head. "This looks like a warehouse now. Where'd the boat go?" She cleared a space to sit and with her phone and began taking pictures of the once clean and neat salon.

Reid ripped open the nearest case and handed each of us a bottle of water. Even warm, it tasted good. I drained one and helped myself to another.

When Tracy aimed her phone at Reid and me, I made an excuse to go to my cabin. I didn't want a reminder of what Pincus had done to me in the salon. Besides, it was the perfect time to try an aloe skin care cream I had purchased today at a special display inside Costco. The saleswoman boasted that using her product three to four times a day would get rid of my "car wreck" bruises very quickly. I was skeptical, and it was expensive, but I'm also vain enough to hope the product was as good as advertised. I hated the way everyone in port kept staring at my face.

Finally, Tracy admitted she was tired. I got her tucked into bed for a nap and rejoined Reid in the galley. He had his hands full of canned goods that he was lining up in one of the cabinets.

"Sleeping arrangements," I said without preamble.

He turned and raised an eyebrow.

"Tracy and I want to offer you the owner's cabin," I said. "It seems fair—"

"No." Reid held up his hand. "You and Tracy are the owners. I'm hired help. Besides, I will be perfectly comfortable in the forward cabin. It's plenty big enough. There are two of you and only one of me."

He didn't seem likely to change his mind, so I gave in. Besides, truth be told, I was excited about claiming that owner's suite for our own. I might have to convince Tracy, but she had been as awestruck as I when we first saw it. And the "guest" cabin Reid picked was pretty nice in itself.

We made some headway with the groceries, so we took a break from the boxes. While Reid put his things away, I finished packing Charles's old clothes in two black trash bags along with the few things Pincus and his brother had left. I stowed them in one of the other cabins along with cases of water, pop, Gatorade, and canned, bagged, and boxed food. I put the bulky items like toilet paper, Kleenex, and paper towels in the top berth of the forward, port side cabin.

Looking over the sea of supplies scattered about, I wondered out loud if I hadn't gone a little crazy in Costco.

"A little crazy?"

Reid's voice at my elbow made me jump. I hadn't realized he had come in and was standing behind me.

"How many flatbeds did we have? Four? Five? I should have hired a truck, not a minivan. It's a good thing *The Lady Anne* is sixty-eight feet long. She's packed."

We finally had everything stowed when there was a knock on the hull.

A chill raced down my spine as Reid and I looked at each other. That feeling of safety I'd experienced a few minutes before vanished with the thought that Pincus had tracked us down again.

"Who is it?" Reid called.

"It's Charles T. Williams. Request permission to come aboard?"

I let out a sigh of relief and scrambled topside. Tracy must have heard him too, because she bounded to his side, wrapping her arms around him in a hug of welcome.

"Permission granted," she said, "How did you get here so fast? I just wrote the email."

Charles held Tracy at arm's length, peering at her, then did the same to me. "Did Daniel do all that?" he asked, his voice shaking with anger. When I nodded, he lowered his voice and said, "That bastard should get the same treatment."

Then he hugged me so hard, it made my breath catch.

"I'm so sorry," he said. "I had no idea he was capable of violence."

"You still have no idea," Tracy said dryly. She turned to Reid, who had followed me topside. "I want you to meet a friend of ours. He's going to help us crew *The Lady Anne* to Florida."

He shook Reid's hand. "I'm glad you're here for the girls," he said. Then he put a finger to his lips. "I've something important to tell you. Let's go below."

It was deja vu as we followed Charles into the salon. As before, he closed the hatch and the curtains. He motioned for us to be seated at the table.

"First of all, I'm glad you are all okay," he began. "If something worse had happened because of Captain Pincus, I would never have forgiven myself. I feel directly responsible for the pain and suffering caused by my employee, someone I considered my friend. To say I'm shocked at his behavior is a massive understatement. After ocean crossings together, you'd think you'd know someone, but I guess you really never do."

"We don't blame you, Charles," I said.

"Nevertheless, after what's happened, I decided I needed to let you in on another of *The Lady Anne*'s secrets."

"You mean the shotgun," Tracy interrupted.

"No. Not the shotgun. I expected you to find that. But there's something else. She leaves a footprint."

"A footprint?" Reid asked.

Charles nodded. "I had a tracking device installed before I took delivery. It's similar to what parents install in a teen's car. It tracks location, speed, day, and time, and I had it installed mainly to see if *The Lady Anne* was ever used for smuggling when I wasn't aboard."

"So you were able to track us?" I asked.

"Yes. Anytime the power is on, engine, generator, battery or shore power, the tracker starts recording GPS coordinates, speed, and the date and time. The file is then uploaded to the cloud via the first available connection, be it Internet, cell phone, or satellite phone. The data can then be accessed with a password."

As the three of us exchanged glances, Charles continued. "After I left you in St. Thomas, I periodically checked on *The Lady Anne*'s whereabouts. I wasn't spying, I was just concerned that you might not be able to get her back to the mainland. When I saw her head for St. Croix and then stop partway, I began watching full time. When she didn't return to her slip but headed for San Juan, I began making inquiries. I knew something was wrong. The dock manager in St. Thomas confirmed it. When you docked in San Juan, I flew over on my Gulfstream and waited at the airport until I had your exact position. I missed you this morning, so I came back this afternoon."

"How much did the dock manager tell you?" I asked.

Charles frowned. "He gave me a copy of the Coast Guard

report. I have a feeling coming back to exact revenge over a lost job isn't the whole story, is it?"

I shook my head. "It was the gold he was after," I said. "He knew about it. His plan was to pick up his brother and head for South America. Tracy and I were to be sex toys until they got to Venezuela. Then they'd get rid of us, scuttle *The Lady Anne*, and disappear."

"He almost got away with it too," Tracy said. "Reid managed to sneak on board, but Pincus discovered him with us before we could get free. He took a beating too."

"I saw the report," Charles said. "I can't apologize enough for what you three have been through. The police were waiting at the slip. They still need to interview you. They don't know you diverted here."

"It was the dock guard who called the Coast Guard," Tracy said. "He saw Pincus at the wheel of *The Lady Anne*."

"We owe that man our life," I said.

"And I will see he gets a reward," Charles said. "It's the least I can do." He waved a hand. "But there's another reason I'm telling you about the tracker." He paused, then said, "If I can track you, so might Captain Pincus."

Alarm traced an icy finger across the back of my neck. "You think he knows we're here?" I asked.

"He might. I didn't think he knew about the gold and I was wrong. I don't believe he knows how to access the tracker, but I don't want to bet your lives on it. I look at the three of you and I'm determined not to underestimate Daniel Pincus again."

"Can't we just turn it off?" Tracy asked.

"I'm afraid it was installed by the builder and is not user accessible. But I had the access password changed and my tech people assure me it can't be hacked from the outside. Pincus may know you're here, but he won't be able to track you once you leave."

"Then we need to get going," Tracy said, standing up and looking anxious.

"I have three armed associates who are keeping *The Lady Anne* under constant surveillance until you clear the harbor. You won't see them, but they are very close. I can personally guarantee your safety."

"Are they coming with us?" I asked.

"If that's what you want, I'll make it happen," Charles replied.

Reid took a deep breath, looked straight at Charles, and said, "Pincus evaded capture by going overboard. We were miles offshore when the man jumped. The Coast Guard couldn't find him, so either he's a good swimmer or he drowned and we can all relax."

But Charles looked grim. "It would be a mistake to assume that Daniel drowned. Both he and Sam were athletes, three-time top fifty Ironman finishers to be exact. Four or five miles in open water would not be a problem for either of them."

More bad news. An uncomfortable silence stretched between us until I broke it with sigh. "Well, there's nothing we can do tonight. Charles, would you join us for dinner? I think we may have enough food on board for all of us."

Tracy snorted and Reid laughed.

"Yes, Charles," Reid said. "I do believe we can scrape together dinner for the four of us."

Charles accepted, not knowing what Tracy and Reid found so amusing: that we could have fed fifty people and still had provisions left over.

CHAPTER 16

We dined topside to enjoy the evening air. I might have been apprehensive about it if Charles hadn't pointed to one of the men he had hired to watch us. The man was as wide as he was tall, built like a wrestler. He had a fishing line dangling over the dock railing, but his eyes were on us. Charles assured me the other two were just as impressive.

Reid took over cooking duties, duties Tracy and I were only too happy to relinquish. He grilled rib eye steaks and asparagus while Tracy prepared a salad. Charles chose a bottle of Rioja Gran Reserva from the impressive collection he had left for us. He opened it and poured it into a carafe to breathe while we put the finishing touches on dinner.

We talked during dinner, Charles asking each of us to tell

him our stories. We were relaxed and at ease, and I motioned to Reid. "You start," I said.

"I'm retired military and before being shanghaied by these two, I taught sailing and skiing in Colorado." He smiled at me. "I gave Pat and Tracy sailing lessons last year. They were good students and very eager to learn."

"You can support yourself with sailing lessons?" Charles asked. "In a landlocked state like Colorado?"

"And skiing, don't forget," Reid said. "But I have other sources of income. My folks left me a small strip mall. I live in the basement apartment below the Subway Sandwich Shop." He laughed. "I eat a lot of free subs. I also get free haircuts and free laundry from other tenants. It's the good old barter system. Between my military pension, part-time work, and rental income, I can pretty much do what I want."

Charles nodded. "Sounds ideal. What branch of the military were you in?"

"The Marines . . . but I wasn't what you'd call a typical jarhead. I started piano lessons when I was four but switched to trumpet when I was ten. I graduated college with a degree in music. When I enlisted, I auditioned for, and was eventually accepted by, 'The President's Own' United States Marine Band. It was a great gig for twenty years. I got to travel and play for official White House and Marine Corps functions."

"Anyway," Reid concluded, "that's my story. When Tracy called and offered me a job to help sail *The Lady Anne* back to Florida, the timing was perfect. Sailing lessons won't begin until ice-out in April, and I can pick and choose when I want to teach skiing. So here I am."

"How did you get into sailing?" Charles asked then.

"I used to sail with friends, and I liked it so much, I took some classes and got into racing. I've crewed the Newport-Ensenada race on a Catalina 470 and the Baja Ha-Ha on a Jeanneau 45. I've also crewed some San Francisco regattas on a J/44. I heard about an open sailing instructor position from a friend, applied, and got hired with one interview."

Charles tipped his glass toward Reid. "Then I can rest easy that *The Lady Anne* is in good hands."

Tracy started to pour herself a second glass of wine.

I stopped her. "Maybe not a good idea," I said, "until we know you're out of the woods. Concussions are not something to fool around with."

Charles agreed with me, reaching across the table to push a tall bottle of water toward her. She shrugged, but filled her glass with water and sat back.

"So," Charles said, turning to me, "I take it you're the voice of reason in this duo."

Tracy snickered. "You wouldn't say that if you saw her grocery shop," she said.

But she reached out and squeezed my hand. "Pat is the best friend anyone could ask for. "We met at the health club where I worked. I taught an early morning fitness class two mornings per week and we hit it off right away. It was a bad time in my life—I'd just gotten a divorce. I needed a diversion and Pat suggested I might like to go with her for a sailing lesson. I did. And the rest is history."

She smiled at me. "My nine-to-five job was with an accounting firm. When Pat's remodeling business needed an accountant, I volunteered. Now it's my full-time gig. I handle all her accounting, taxes, job costing, purchasing, budgeting, and payroll."

Charles turned to me. "You have a remodeling business?"

I nodded. "My dad was a handyman. I started working with him when I was twelve. I have a degree in engineering. Built my business from the ground up, adding finished living space over freestanding garages. I caught my former accountant stealing and when I learned that Tracy was an accountant, I hired her full time."

"Not married? No boyfriends?"

I shook my head. "Never had the time to date."

"But don't think men don't notice her," Tracy said. "With those long legs and that blond hair, she stops traffic."

Charles laughed. "I believe it. You're both good-looking women. But when did you get the idea you'd like to run charters?"

"I was tired of fighting for my place in the man's world of engineering, so I may have casually mentioned my idea of sailing the world to Tracy once or twice," I said.

"And I was tired of accounting. The bad memories of my husband's infidelities weighed heavily, too, so I may have casually replied that I'd like nothing better," Tracy answered.

I winked at Charles. "And did I mention that I like to play cards? Especially poker?"

That got a chuckle.

We finished eating. I cleared the table with Charles's help and he and I did the dishes. Reid cleaned up the grill while Tracy made coffee and opened a package of Costco cookies for dessert.

When we were back on deck with a pot of coffee and cookies, Charles complimented Reid on the meal.

Rick looked pleased. "Can't go wrong with Costco steaks. A little olive oil, salt, and freshly ground pepper and the grill does the rest. The asparagus I cooked on foil with Italian dressing, dried basil since I didn't have fresh, and grated Parmesan cheese."

"Where did you learn to cook?" Tracy asked.

"Someone told me cooking classes were a great way to meet women," Reid answered with a chuckle.

"I guess it didn't work," I said. "Since you're still single."

"You guess right. I'm still single, but now I can out-cook my dates."

We sipped our coffee and nibbled cookies, enjoying the warm evening air, the gentle motion of *The Lady Anne*, and a comfortable camaraderie that surprised me when I thought about it. Tracy and I, on the deck of a beautiful sailboat, *our* sailboat, with two men we'd only just met. Yes, we knew Reid a little better, maybe, because of our sailing lessons, but there had never been any personal interaction between us. Charles came into our lives in a bizarre set of circumstances that I probably wouldn't have believed if I'd read about it in a book! Yet here we were, together, because of the luck of the draw—literally.

"What are you thinking about, Pat?" Charles asked. "You have the strangest look on your face."

I smiled back. "Nothing important," I said. "But I think it's your turn now. You told Tracy and me a little about your philosophy of life, but Reid might enjoy hearing it."

"I would." Reid poured a second cup of coffee and offered the coffee pot around. When we'd settled back into our chairs, Charles started in.

"I am guided by four simple tenets. One: own property, people will always need somewhere to live. Two: own precious metals, don't trust the government's fiat money. Three: pick rich over famous, every time. And four: protect your anonymity."

"That's a tall order in today's world," Reid said.

"You're right," Charles agreed. "I know that only too well. So rather than try and keep my name out of search engines, I've taken a different tack—hide in plain sight. I've had my tech people create over five hundred fictitious personas with every variation of my name: Charles T. Williams, Charlie Williams, Chuck Williams, et cetera, et cetera, designed to mislead anyone looking for information about me. I suppose a determined reporter will find me one day, but up until now, *Forbes, Fortune, Barron's* and *Money* magazine don't know I exist. That kind of anonymity is precious and rare nowadays."

"You recently lost your wife?" I asked softly.

"Yes. Anne."

"How long were you married?"

"We were married for forty-four years." Charles let his gaze sweep the harbor. "She died while we were in Europe. An accident. I suppose I should say she was lucky to go quickly and not suffer. But the truth is, I hate that she's gone. I hate that with all our money, there was nothing I could do to prevent her dying. I hate that there were still things we wanted to do and places we wanted to go."

His voice broke. We all remained silent until he composed himself. "She was cremated in Spain and her ashes scattered over the Atlantic, as she wanted."

I searched my mind for something to say to ease Charles's pain. Obviously he was heartbroken. I could see how it hurt to speak about her. In a heartbeat, the mood on *The Lady Anne* had changed from light to somber. He continued to fight tears when he told us how much they loved being on *The Lady Anne*, that of all of their toys, this was their favorite. This was their escape, their passport to adventure.

It became very quiet.

"Charles," I said. "Are you sure you want to part with her?"

He nodded. "Since Anne's passing, I've used the time aboard *The Lady Anne* to grieve. Sailing her now wouldn't be the same. It was the reason I stopped in the Virgin Islands. I'd decided to list her for sale. It was sheer coincidence that I was in your hotel in Tortola the night of our"—he chuckled —"our infamous poker game. No," he said after a moment's reflection. "I take that back. It wasn't coincidence, it was fate."

He stood. "*The Lady Anne* is meant for adventure. She's meant for new horizons. I can't think of a better tribute to Anne than to leave her in your hands. I'll take my leave now. I want to thank you for dinner and for letting me get to know you all a little better. We have only one matter left to discuss: are the three of you comfortable attempting to sail to Florida on your own or do you want my men to accompany you?"

CHAPTER 17

I'd been so caught up in Charles's story that I'd forgotten about his offer to send the three hired guns with us. He excused himself and went below, closing the hatch behind him to give us a chance to talk in private.

"I don't want Pincus to come back, ever," Tracy said.

"I agree," I said. "He may know we're here now, but if Charles had the codes changed, Pincus won't know where we're going once we're under way."

"And I'm not so worried about him finding us in open water," Reid added. "We can see him coming and we still have the gun."

"It's being in port that's the problem," I said, looking around. "It's way too easy to sneak around the fences and gates if you don't mind getting wet."

"So what if Charles had his men meet us at the ports

between here and Florida?" Tracy asked. "How many stops are there?"

Reid thought for a moment. "I plotted the course this morning. If I remember correctly, it's about three hundred nautical miles to Puerto Plata in the Dominican Republic. It's another one hundred miles or so to Provo in the Turks and Caicos. Then it's another two hundred to Eleuthera in the Bahamas and another two hundred to Miami. Those distances are quick and dirty, but they're close."

"So," he continued, "if Charles's men could meet us at marinas in Puerto Plata, Provo, and Eleuthera, that would help ease our minds. I don't think we have to worry about Pincus once we get to Florida."

Tracy and I agreed, and I called Charles topside and told him what we'd been discussing. He made a note of our ports of call and said his men would be waiting at each one.

Slipping his notebook back into his pocket, he asked, "Where are you headed in Florida? Are you going to Miami?"

Tracy shook her head. "We'll most likely end up further North. My brother lives in Orlando and said he'd find us a marina on the Atlantic side, probably close to Daytona Beach."

"If he can't," said Charles, "let me know. I have lots of contacts." Charles let a moment go by before saying, "There is another alternative if you're up for an adventure. Take her south through the canal and then sail on to Hawaii."

"Hawaii?" I repeated. "Why Hawaii?"

"Anne and I had a little compound near Kailua on the

island of Oahu. There's a marina nearby. The three of you could sail *The Lady Anne* there. It would be a wonderful inaugural trip. When you arrive, you can stay for as long as you want."

I looked at Tracy, then at Reid. "It would mean being gone a lot longer than we planned."

But Reid was shaking his head. "That's a fabulous offer and I'd love to consider it. But that's a serious passage that will take weeks. If my memory serves, it's about one thousand miles to the Panama Canal from here and then another four thousand to Hawaii. It would require a lot of planning and weather timing and more experience than the three of us have." He looked at me. "Why don't we start with getting *The Lady Anne* to Florida and then we can take the time to seriously consider the most generous offer I have ever heard."

"That's a well-thought-out response, young man," Charles said. "I feel very confident having you onboard *The Lady Anne.*"

I sighed. I knew Reid was right. We'd have to have a lot more sailing experience under our belts before we could attempt a passage like that. But someday…

Charles was speaking again.

"Now what's this about Reid playing the trumpet in the President's band?" He turned to him. "I'd like to hear you play. Did you bring your trumpet?"

Tracy grinned. "Bought one today. Reid, go get it."

Reid went below, returning in a few moments with his trumpet. He played scales to warm up, then launched into the

"Girl from Ipanema." He followed it up with "A Taste of Honey" and an oldie, "Cherry Pink and Apple Blossom White."

There was a high note on the end of that one and when he hit it, I got goose bumps. "I've never heard that song before," I said.

Charles smiled. "Well before your time, young lady," he said. "I'm surprised you know it, Reid."

"It's a trumpet player's classic," he said.

"Well, I, for one, never heard anything like it," Tracy said. "You are incredibly talented. I can understand why you had that twenty-year career."

Reid started to put his trumpet away, but Tracy begged for one more. "Even a short one," she said.

Reid grinned. "How's this?"

He played "My Funny Valentine" and the melancholy music floated out over the harbor like a gentle breeze. People on boats near us had been listening as Reid played and now, as the last notes faded, they broke into spontaneous applause.

Charles was smiling. "What a wonderful way to end the evening." He stood. "I'm going to leave the three of you alone and say goodnight."

"Where are you staying?" I asked, walking him toward the exit gate.

"I've made arrangements nearby, but I'd like to return in the morning and go through the boat's systems."

"Systems?" Tracy asked, joining us by the exit gate.

He nodded. "Where to access extra gasoline and propane,

how to fill a scuba tank, how to stow the skiff for a long passage, and how to work the water maker. You have a complete set of manuals and could figure everything out by yourselves, but I'm happy to show you, if you don't mind."

"That would be great," Tracy said.

"I'll come by around seven thirty. That will give us a few hours and then you can be underway by say, ten thirty."

"Perfect," I said. "And thank you so much."

"Sleep well, feel better, and I'll see you in the morning."

We waved goodbye. I looked around, but the man I had seen before fishing from the dock was no longer in sight. I wasn't worried though. Charles was nothing if not thorough. I knew his men would be very close by. We went below for the night, Reid securing the hatch behind us.

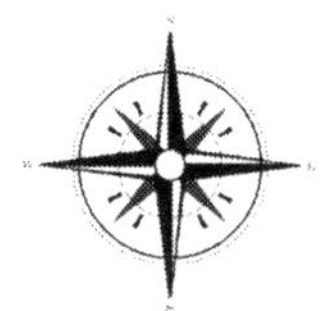

Charles was punctual and we were ready. Reid and I had notebooks and Tracy, her phone to shoot video of anything complicated. I sensed we were all excited; I knew I was.

He began by quoting from the sale's brochure, "She is self-contained and designed to cross oceans and then live aboard for an extended period in complete comfort." Then Charles started at the bow and worked his way aft, pointing out the anchor station, the spinnaker pole's concealed storage, and the carbon fiber crane that retracted and tilted down into its own storage compartment on the port side. It was used to stow the skiff on the foredeck during long passages.

He showed us where the freshwater rinse was and advised us to rinse the salt off the skiff while she was hanging over the side. It would save having to hose off the deck later.

He pointed out the integrated solar panels in the cabin top, opened the propane locker with dual tanks, and demonstrated the electric and manual operation of the winches.

"I didn't know they made plastic propane tanks," Reid said.

"They're fiberglass, not plastic," Charles answered. "And they're great because they're not as heavy when empty. Plus they're not opaque so you can easily see how full they are."

We moved to the cockpit. Charles traced an inlaid compass rose in the center of the cockpit's large teak table. He looked sad for a moment and I guessed he was thinking of his late wife, as the design was something she might have chosen.

He demonstrated how to deploy the Bimini top and the cockpit curtains. He pointed out a large compartment underneath a cushion with a drain. It held a Pelican cooler that would keep ice for over a week. You could drain the cooler without having to lift it out.

Tracy said, "That's a big cooler. Why do we need so much ice?"

Charles answered, "There's some nice fishing gear below. You'll need ice for the fish box. If Reid can cook fish half as well as he can cook steaks, you're in for some good eating."

We had already sailed and docked her from the helm stations and knew where the pushbuttons were to raise and lower the keel, but he did give us a quick radar lesson. He also showed us how to interface the autopilot with the GPS and do an electronic chart overlay. Tracy videoed that part since he covered it very quickly and it was a little confusing.

As we worked our way aft, Charles said the skiff could easily be hauled up on the swim platform and towed fairly efficiently for short distances of say two hundred miles or less. Beyond that, or in heavy weather or a following sea, he recommended she be secured to her base on the foredeck.

The dinghy, or skiff as Charles called it, was a fourteen-and-one-half foot Rigid Inflatable Boat, or RIB. Its center console and sixty-horsepower Honda outboard motor gave it a top speed of over thirty miles per hour. Charles pointed out her built-in fifteen-gallon fuel tank, brackets for holding two scuba tanks, and her water-repellant travel cover.

There were four vented lockers near the stern, above the swim platform. One held extra gas cans for refueling the skiff. The second held a diesel generator. He explained it had ample power but cautioned us not to turn on everything all at once. The third contained a compressor and fittings for filling scuba tanks.

The last locker held spare propane tanks over the fish box and a big orange duffel bag. You could see the propane level, but only three of the tanks were full. Charles didn't like that, or the fact that all of the gas cans weren't full. He suggested we top them all off before leaving.

Reid pointed to the duffel. "What size is that and where's the EPIRB emergency locator beacon?"

"That's an eight-person life raft and there are two EPIRBs, one in the cockpit and one in the owner's closet."

I looked at Tracy, who was looking at me. Having to

abandon ship and activate a rescue beacon was something we hadn't given a thought to. I suddenly realized that in an emergency, all the things we were learning could mean the difference between life and death. It was discomforting and concerning, and I was glad there were three of us taking these lessons. I was also glad to see Reid taking notes.

Charles continued the tour. He showed us how to operate the freshwater shower and the saltwater rinse. On deck, we saw the fishing rod holders, the stainless-steel propane grill, which Reid had used the night before, a US flag flying from the stern, two throwable horseshoes on the stern rail, and the boarding ladder.

"How many people does it take to sail her?" Tracy asked. "Will three be able to manage it?"

"Once you're away from the dock, if all of her systems are working, she can be sailed by two," Charles replied. "One helmsman and one handling all the sheets. If you're racing, flying the spinnaker, or anchoring, you need more crew. If you add night watches into the equation, additional crewmen will make it easier."

"But didn't Pincus leave the dock by himself?" asked Tracy.

Charles nodded. "If there's no wind or current, one person could untie the dock lines, climb aboard, and motor away. For safe docking, you really need three—one at the helm and one to handle each dock line."

I was thinking that yesterday Reid sailed her from the

Virgin Islands to Puerto Rico by himself, and at night. I looked up to find Reid looking at me and suspected he was thinking the same thing. We smiled at each other.

"So we are good with only the three of us?" Tracy asked.

"Three is perfect. Three can get her in and out of the slip, handle the sails, anchor, and manage the night watches. Once you start on longer voyages, though, or start that charter business, I would suggest at least two more. Now let's go below. I've still got a lot to show you and the clock is ticking."

We followed Charles to the engine room. He showed us the two hundred-horsepower marine diesel. He stated that with shore power, or under engine or generator power, the galley fridge and freezer would cool automatically. He also said the water maker would have power, the hot-water tank would begin heating and the batteries would be charged.

"Charles, what's her tankage?" Reid asked.

"She holds eight hundred gallons of diesel, four hundred gallons of fresh water, one hundred gallons of wastewater, and twenty gallons of hot water."

"Is that enough hot water for showers?" Tracy asked.

"Best to use the solar showers that are kept in the fish box," Charles replied. "That twenty gallons supplies all fixtures, including the washing machine and the dishwasher."

Reid nodded. "I often used solar showers as a way to conserve water, especially when there were kids aboard. It's easy and quick. Fill the bladder with fresh water and place it in the sun for a few hours. It holds enough water for two or possibly three showers if you don't dawdle."

"What does she draw?" I asked, thinking of the charts we had below. Each was marked with depth as well as the configuration of the shoreline and seafloor.

"*The Lady Anne*'s keel is retractable, but even with the keel up, she'll hit anything within seven feet of the surface. With her bulb keel down, she needs sixteen feet, assuming there are no rocks or tide issues. Best you always stay in deeper water than you draw."

I could see Reid nodding. None of this was news to him. Gave me a sense of security and I appreciated him even more.

"What about batteries?" Reid asked as we continued our walk-through.

"There are three house batteries and two starter batteries, one for the diesel and one for the generator. The selector switches are under the navigation station." Charles snapped his fingers. "I almost forgot to mention that the cabin top is properly angled to catch rainwater and can funnel it into the freshwater tank. Just be sure to rinse any salt off the collectors or you'll have to drain and flush the entire system." Charles laughed and added, "That mistake will only happen once."

As we moved on, Tracy took video of which valves to open and close to macerate and discharge the wastewater. She also videoed his instructions for making fresh water. All of the systems were clearly labeled in French, English, Spanish, and German. There were a lot of valves, but everything was logically laid out.

Charles pointed out the compass and knot meter in the crew's quarters and the owner's suite and said they were handy to confirm course and speed without having to go topside. He also showed us where he kept an expensive-looking Sony high-definition camcorder. He said we were welcome to it and should use it to document our voyage. He gave Tracy a five-minute lesson in how to use it. He said it took much better video that any smart phone. I thought that it should, considering its size.

Besides the shotgun, the bookcase held sailing books, DVDs, and CDs. There were numerous cruising guides and chart books. A small metal case held cards and poker chips. I wanted to say something clever about irony but thought better of it. The bottom shelf held large black binders which contained instruction manuals and maintenance records.

Tracy and I had already found his liquor cabinet, concealed in the old-world style globe in the salon. Moving to the galley, he showed us where the shut-off valve was for the propane stove.

The navigation station had rows of electronics, radios, and a satellite phone. There was a wireless weather station that contained a dedicated weather-fax machine. There was another collection of cruising guides here as well. Beneath the over-sized chart table were numerous rolled paper charts. He told us we could print our own, which Tracy and I already knew how to do.

We went into the forward cabin on the starboard side, Reid's cabin. It had a queen-sized bed and its own head. From his cabin, we proceeded forward through a narrow passageway and accessed a stacked washer/dryer and the fishing gear.

We continued to the rigging station with its inventory of various spools of lines and a toolbox of rigging tools. There were several bags of extra sails. Reid noticed some racing sails that seemed to please him.

Then he pointed at a yellow storage bag. "The drogue? What size is it?"

"Twenty-four-foot diameter, rated for a ninety-foot boat," Charles replied.

I remembered from our sailing lessons what a drogue was and how it's used. I hoped never to have to deploy what amounts to a funnel-shaped sea anchor to ride out a storm.

The anchor locker was our last stop. The topside anchor was rigged with a substantial amount of chain.

As if reading my mind, Charles said, "She has two hundred fifty feet of one-half-inch high test chain spliced to three hundred feet of nylon anchor line. She can anchor in water between seventy and one hundred twenty-five feet deep. The bitter end is tied off and secured here."

There were three extra anchors and extra nylon rope. He pointed out the freshwater rinse to reduce odors. There was also a spare electric anchor windlass for easily raising the anchor, still in its original carton. He told us there was extra chain in the workroom.

As we returned to the salon, Charles showed us the water-tight doors that would divide *The Lady Anne* into separate compartments in the event of an emergency. He showed where to access the bilge and the keel's hydraulics. He demonstrated a small lantern with a red lens that would preserve our night vision. He cautioned about using that above deck so as not to present a confusing lighting pattern to other vessels at night.

Reid grinned and asked, "So why does a pirate captain always wear an eyepatch?"

"That's a Hollywood effect and not real," Tracy said.

"From having a hook and an itch?" I joked.

"It might be because the captain was blind in one eye from taking noon sun shots for navigation," Charles stated, sounding confident.

"Actually the pirate captain wasn't blind at all," Reid said. "He wore a patch to preserve his night vision. Belowdecks, he would switch the patch to the other eye and then back again when returning to daylight. In that way, he could see quickly in dark or light. That could be the difference between life and death when fighting belowdecks with a cutlass."

Having expected a joke, we were all impressed.

Tracy looked tired. Charles was ready to leave, so she said goodbye and went to our cabin to rest. Reid and I took Charles topside.

"You really should reconsider transiting the canal and setting sail for Hawaii," Charles said as we walked with him down the dock. "You understand all of *The Lady Anne*'s systems and you seem to be provisioned for an extended passage."

"We don't have that kind of experience," Reid replied. "Not yet. But someday."

Charles shook his hand and turned to me. "I've not a

single regret leaving *The Lady Anne* in your care," he said. "Fair winds and following seas, Pat."

We hugged and he left us.

Our adventure was about to begin.

CHAPTER 19

By late afternoon we had refueled everything that needed refueling and were ready to head to Florida via Puerto Plata in the Dominican Republic, Provo in the Turks and Caicos Islands, and Eleuthera in the Bahamas. It was about three hundred miles to Puerto Plata, and we were all topside. I looked to see if I could spot Charles's men, but the big man I saw yesterday was nowhere in sight.

While Reid and I handled the dock lines, Tracy took the helm. She looked nervous, but followed Reid's instructions. It was just like a sailing lesson, except the boat was bigger and the marina more crowded.

Reid adjusted the radar controls to his preferences. We gathered around the display, watching how the blips corresponded to the other boats we passed.

We worked our way twelve miles offshore and then angled

toward Puerto Plata. Reid retrieved the Puerto Rico flag, leaving *The Lady Anne* flagless except for the ever-present US flag flying from her stern.

Tracy watched the knot meter as I helped Reid trim the sails. After a few small adjustments, the boat heeled a bit and Tracy announced our speed had increased nearly two knots. He went below to dump the wastewater. When he returned topside, he was carrying the shotgun and an empty Costco box.

"This seems like a good place to practice a man-overboard drill," Reid said as he threw the box over the side and yelled, "Man overboard!"

Tracy immediately changed course to a beam reach, sailed out about six boat lengths, tacked, sailed back. and then headed up into the wind and heaved to, stopping the boat within five feet of the still-floating box.

"That was perfect," Reid said as he adjusted the mizzen sheet and walked to the lifeline. "You were paying attention in class!" He hefted the shotgun. "Now let's see if this thing shoots."

Holding the shotgun's pistol grip with one hand and holding the ribbed slide below the barrel with his other hand, he pointed the barrel clear of the boat, switched off the safety, and fired.

I clapped my hands to my ears. "Wow! That thing is loud."

Tracy was leaning over the lifeline. "You hit it," she said. "Blew a hole clean through."

He handed Tracy the shotgun. "Your turn."

He showed Tracy how to pump in a new shell and operate the safety. She listened, glancing once at me to raise her eyebrows. We'd both watched the videos and practiced loading and unloading, but she didn't give it away.

Finally she fired, hitting the box almost dead center.

Reid laughed. "Annie Oakley," he said.

"It jumps quite a bit," she warned, handing it to me. "Hold tight."

My first shot was high and missed the box completely. I hit it with the second one though. The recoil didn't bother me as much as the noise.

Reid took the gun. "Good job," he said. "Now that I know you know how to use this, we'll reload it and put it away."

"What about the box?" I asked. "It's coming apart, but we can't leave it in the water, can we?"

Reid tried to retrieve the box with a boat hook, but it had gotten so soggy, it fell apart. I felt bad for littering but not bad enough to jump in after it.

Reid put the boat hook away and motioned for Tracy and me to join him around the cockpit table. "This is the first time you two will be sailing at night," he said. "Let's go over what you'll be doing."

I fished my pen and notebook from the pocket of my jacket.

"Fire away."

"First, we'll set a watch schedule. Two, the most important way to avoid collisions is by keeping a vigilant lookout, so keep sharp. Three, wear your PFD and stay tethered or clipped in. Four, have a jacket, snacks, and drinks close by. Five, wake me immediately if you begin to suspect something, *anything*, might be wrong."

"So what's the watch schedule?" Tracy asked.

"We'll do two hours on, four hours off during the day and three hours on, six hours off at night. I'll take the first night watch, followed by Tracy and then Pat."

"How do we avoid collisions?" I asked. "Especially at night."

"By keeping an eye on the radar and remembering the night navigation rules. If you see a white light, you're probably overtaking another vessel, so be alert. If you see both red and green lights behind us, something is probably overtaking us, so again, be alert."

"What do we tether to?" Tracy asked.

"We'll rig a jackline right down the center from the bow pulpit to the stern rail. That's what you'll clip to," Reid answered. "Before it gets dark, we'll also adjust the sails so they won't need a lot of attention. Trimming at night is much harder than trimming during the day, trust me."

He went on, "We'll run the generator to top off the batteries and then we'll switch on the proper lights for night sailing and switch off everything else. We don't want to present conflicting light patterns to other vessels. Conserving battery power is always paramount so we don't find dead batteries in the morning."

"What about bathroom breaks?" Tracy asked.

"Pee before your watch or have a bucket in the cockpit."

"What about eating?" I asked.

"We can celebrate with a grand meal when we get to Puerto Plata," Reid said. "In fact, I'd like to cook something special to commemorate your first night passage. Between now and then, I recommend you stay hydrated but eat sparingly and nothing greasy or creamy. And we'll bring some ginger ale up. That helps if you're feeling queasy."

"Have you ever been seasick?" I asked.

"I've been seasick twice, but both times it wasn't the sailing, it was the diesel fumes from a powerboat. Believe me, it's no fun."

"But we're sailing, not motoring. So no fumes, right?" Tracy sounded slightly nervous.

"We're sailing as long as the wind holds," Reid said. "We'll also start a log, make hourly entries, and plot our position on the chart."

He retrieved one of his spiral notebooks and made some columns for date, time, position, heading, speed, and notes. He had Tracy complete the first entry while I marked our GPS coordinates on the chart. It was right on the course line Reid had drawn earlier. Her note said, "Puerto Plata, here we come."

The late afternoon sun hovered just above the horizon. Tracy still looked nervous.

"Are you up for this?" he asked her. "I can sail her through the night if need be."

Tracy and I exchanged glances. I knew I was ready. Tracy

hesitated only a second before she said, "No. I can do this. Let's rig that line."

We rigged the jackline and trimmed the sails, then brought up ginger ale, bottled water, extra jackets, and a bucket. Reid went below then to take a nap, telling us to wake him in an hour for the first watch.

"Are you sure you're ready for this?" I asked Tracy when Reid had gone below.

"I'm right on the edge between scared and excited."

"Me too." I gave her a quick hug. "You go below and try and get some rest before your shift."

"I can't believe we're about to sail out of sight of land at night," she said.

I laughed. "Me neither. This is going to be great." I put my hands over my ears. "By the way, are your ears still ringing too?"

CHAPTER 20

Late morning of the third day of our passage found us having a light lunch of fruit and granola bars together in the cockpit. We had stood uneventful watches for two nights and were only a few hours from making port.

I didn't have any life experience to compare to our long sail. It seemed to be somewhere on the line between peaceful and boring. The chart plots showed Reid made more miles during his shift. His tacks were more efficient. He certainly had more experience, being a racer at heart, but Tracy and I were getting faster.

On the second day, Tracy had fished for hours without a single strike. Dolphins swam in our bow wake and that was really cool. I tried to get some video, but they didn't stay with us long enough.

The Lady Anne was handling perfectly. I understood why

Charles enjoyed crossing the ocean, but I was ready to sleep tied up to a dock, not constantly moving.

The autopilot was engaged and Reid was nearest the helm. There was a radar contact, so he took his new binoculars and began glassing. After about thirty minutes, he suddenly scrambled belowdecks. I didn't have any binoculars, but I could see there was definitely something straight ahead. I hoped he hadn't gone below to get the gun.

In a moment, Reid returned without the gun. Instead, he had his trumpet. Now I was really curious.

He handed Tracy the binoculars.

She shrugged at me and lifted them to her eyes. "We've got company," she said, grinning.

It took an hour for three tall ships to reach us, sailing in a staggered formation. Reid had me steer closer and told Tracy to get the good video camera. We passed within two hundred yards. Their crews were on deck, waving at us, and we waived back. The crew members were all dressed in blue-striped white shirts, and all looked to be young.

"Who are they?" I asked.

"Could be a class," Reid replied. "Or they're heading for a race. There are Tall Ship regattas and races all over the world."

Reid grabbed his trumpet and began to play.

As we passed the tall ships, Reid played the theme from *Pirates of the Caribbean.* Their crews began whooping and hollering. The second ship ran up a pirate flag and the crew all donned triangular pirate hats. At that moment, I wished *The*

Lady Anne had a pirate flag too, but if she did, we hadn't found it.

Tracy got the whole thing on video and I shot some with my phone. I could see them videoing us as well. The third ship ran up four signal flags and Reid stopped playing and grinned.

"What do those flags mean?" I asked. The last one was red, white, and blue but not a US flag, and not the French flag either.

Reid laughed and said, "It reads *S-U-Y-T*." He kept laughing.

"What's *S-U-Y-T*?" Tracy asked.

Reid was now laughing so hard he could barely talk. Finally he managed to say, "It means show us your tits."

Before I could react, Tracy put down the camera, pulled off her top, unhooked her bra, and faced the tall ships. She raised her arms and started waving.

We heard them whistling and then a moment later, they fired a cannon.

Tracy turned to me. "Come on, Pat, don't be a prude."

I glanced at Reid, but he had picked up the video camera and continued filming. So, not wanting to be a prude, I followed Tracy's example. I stripped off my shirt and bra and faced the ships. But while Tracy seemed completely at ease, I felt color flood my face. I could imagine the other ships were videoing us the same way we were them, but I figured they were far enough away that no one could recognize me.

At least, I hoped so.

I looked at Reid. "Come on, Reid," I said. "Take your shirt off too."

Reid grinned, put the camera down, peeled off his tee, and danced a jig. That brought on another round of cheering and a boom from the cannon.

In a few minutes, they had passed on their way. After putting my bra and top back on, I said, "Well, that was unexpected."

Tracy looked at me, eyes twinkling. "When I get this uploaded to YouTube, it will go viral. Reid, you got it all, right?"

I looked at him, horrified. "Reid, you didn't—?"

Reid held up a hand. "Don't worry, Pat. Your modesty is intact. At least from this point of view. Can't promise what the boys in those ships got." He circled his eyes with his fingers. "Zoom lenses, you know."

"Have you seen the tall ships at sail before?" I asked, still thinking about the possibility I might appear topless on somebody's YouTube account.

Reid pulled his T-shirt back on. "I've only seen them in port, never at sea."

"You've never seen these in port either," Tracy said slyly. She cradled her breasts and winked.

"Touché," Reid said, looking away.

Tracy laughed and put herself back together. "Our first adventure at sea," she said.

We gave each other high fives. I noted *"S-U-Y-T"* in the log and on the chart.

Tracy put the camera below and returned with a cruising guide for the Dominican Republic/Haiti. We perused the marinas in Puerto Plata and decided to try the Ocean World Marina. Reid hailed them on the radio and made arrangements.

The channel depth was twelve feet, so before we got to the outer buoys, we started the engine, furled the sails, and raised the keel. The book mentioned dinghy theft, but we hoped it would be okay secured in its cradle on the deck. Besides, if Charles was true to his word, we'd have three guardian angels waiting for us in port.

After we docked, we ran into trouble with the customs officer. I figured we might have to dispose of our fresh fruits and vegetables, and possibly the meat in the freezer, but all he demanded was that we surrender our flowers. His inspection was so quick, we could have been carrying a ton of drugs and he would have missed them. He did ask about my bruises and again, the car wreck story worked. Tracy told me the bruises were improving, but they looked the same to me. The "miracle" cream I paid a fortune for didn't do much but moisturize.

Besides the permit fee, the customs officer wanted another four hundred dollars cash for an unofficial "special" fee that he couldn't really explain. After pointless arguing, I finally caved. Then he asked for an additional one hundred dollars cash crew fee if Tracy or I were going to leave the boat.

"Why just us?" Tracy asked. "Why not Reid?"

The customs officer smiled. "The captain doesn't pay," he answered smugly.

I was tempted to set him straight on just who the captain of this boat was, but for all I knew, the fee for a woman captain might be twice as much, so I paid that also. Tracy told him we wanted a receipt, which he provided, albeit reluctantly and scribbled illegibly on a scrap of paper.

He didn't ask about firearms, cigarettes, or liquor but did want to know if we had any pets. I can't even imagine how much the family dog would have cost. Finally he stamped our passports and we were cleared into the Dominican Republic. I was ready to explain why there was no exit stamp for the Virgin Islands, but he either didn't notice or didn't care.

There was an advertisement posted about a casino on the premises.

Reid wriggled his eyebrows. "Feeling lucky? They probably have a poker table or two."

I grinned. "Do we need another boat?" I asked.

Just out of curiosity, Tracy went online to see if other boat owners had run up against the same kind of exorbitant fees that we did.

"Listen to these comments," she said. "'The whole country runs on tips. Bring lots of cash.' And this one: 'All the officials are crooked. My advice: avoid the island.' There are more like that too."

I sighed. "Well, we've already paid. Luckily, we're only staying one night."

Tracy laughed. "I'll bet he took the flowers for his wife."

"You're probably right," I said.

Reid called one of Charles's men to see if they knew we

had arrived. As I expected, they had watched us sail in and had booked a room in the hotel overlooking our slip. He assured Reid everything would be safely looked after.

While the customs officials were shady, the resort itself looked nice and safe. Tracy and I decided to look around. I left my phone with Reid in case there was trouble. He'd be able to reach us on Tracy's.

CHAPTER 21

Tracy and I wandered around the marina for an hour, more to stretch our legs than anything else. The casino was bright and busy, bustling with tourists. We heard people speaking in languages from all around the world. This might be an expensive place to slip, but it was a popular one.

When we returned from exploring the resort, it was obvious Reid had been very busy. The cockpit table held a bowl of fresh guacamole, neatly surrounded by Costco chips.

"Wonderful," Tracy said after gobbling down a half dozen loaded chips. "What's in it? There's a taste I don't recognize."

"Maybe the green bean pepper?" Reid said. "The rest is pretty basic guac: avocados, onion, garlic, dried cilantro, and fresh lime juice."

"What's a green bean pepper?" I asked, smacking my lips in appreciation. "And where'd you get the avocados?"

"After you two left, I was hosing the salt off the decks when a local fisherman came by selling live lobsters from his small boat. They looked fine, but after hearing what Tracy said about the island, I was leery."

"You bought lobsters?" Tracy asked eagerly. She dropped a bit of guacamole on her top and scooped it up with a finger that she promptly popped into her mouth. When she saw me watching, she said, "What? This is too good to waste."

I grinned and Reid continued. "No, not right away. But a guy on a Canadian-flagged boat two slips away saw the lobster man and came to make a purchase. He vouched for him, so I bought three."

"So he also had the avocados?" I asked, taking another bite.

"No, but while dealing with lobster man, another small boat came over. This guy had fruit and produce. The Canadian guy vouched for him as well, so I bought some grapefruit, limes, papaya, mangos, avocados, bananas, and a pineapple."

"And the green bean peppers."

"He also had hot peppers, but scotch bonnet and habanero are too hot, so I took his advice and bought some bell peppers and some 'gringo-hot' peppers that actually do look like green beans."

Reid ducked below for a moment and returned carrying a plate of fruit kabobs. Each kabob contained pieces of mango, papaya, and banana and were lightly glazed with a sugary lime-juice glaze. I ate two by myself and they were delicious.

Reid went below again and we heard the blender running. Shortly, he passed three glasses topside.

Tracy took a big sip. "Wow, is this amazing. What is it?"

"It's a Reid Adams' Hurricane."

"Potent," I said. "What's in here?"

"Blended passion fruit juice, light rum, dark rum, orange juice, lime juice, a little sugar, and some ice cubes."

Reid went to the grill, platters of pineapple wedges and lobster in hand. Tracy and I kept him company while he grilled the pineapple and the lobster tails. When everything was cooked to his satisfaction, we passed everything below and dined at the salon table.

Reid refilled our drinks while Tracy played a CD she had gotten the night of the infamous poker game.

We ate until we were stuffed—no leftovers from this meal. And when he apologized for not having made dessert, I groaned. "I couldn't eat another bite."

Reid made another blender of hurricanes and refilled our glasses.

Tracy and I toasted his culinary skills.

He toasted back with an Irish proverb: "There are good ships and there are wood ships, the ships that sail the seas. But the best ships are friendships, and may they always be."

We clinked glasses and drank. Then Reid excused himself topside to give *The Lady Anne* a quick inspection. When he returned below, he refilled his glass and took a seat next to Tracy.

"All secure for the night," he said.

I was sipping my drink when Tracy scooted close to him. "Why haven't you made a pass at either of us?"

I almost choked but put my drink down to see what Reid would say.

He was quiet for a moment. "The day the owner hired me to teach sailing, he told me three things. One: don't let the students drown. Two: don't hit anything with the boat. Three: don't sleep with the students."

"We aren't students anymore," Tracy reminded him.

"Is this you talking or the booze?" he asked.

"I'm not drunk," Tracy said.

I could feel my heart beating faster. Did I want this? My experience with sex up to this point had been with men I'd had long relationships with. Strictly one on one. And I kept flashing back to Pincus. The memory was still raw.

I watched Tracy's face as she bantered with Reid. I envied how easy this seemed for her.

"You know I'm old enough to be your father," Reid was saying.

"Pardon me," Tracy said. "But I don't believe I asked you your birthdate.

Tracy's CD had long since ended and there was total silence.

Then they were both looking at me.

I stood up. "You two kids have fun," I said.

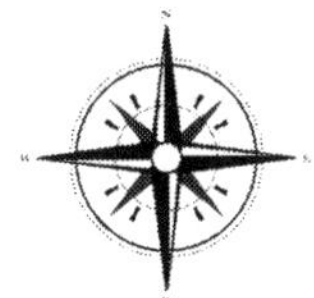

CHAPTER 22

The next morning, I awoke to a gentle rap on the stateroom door.

I sat up. "Come in."

Reid, dressed and showered, came in bearing a breakfast tray.

"Are you all right with last night?" he asked. He put the tray on the bedside nightstand. "Coffee, grapefruit, cottage cheese."

"You and Tracy are two adults," I said smiling, reaching for the coffee. "And I can tell Tracy likes you."

"And you?"

I laughed. "I like you too. It's just not as easy for me." I winked. "Give me time."

Light from the window flooded the room. "What time is it?" I asked.

"Almost ten thirty a.m." His face reddened. "Tracy's still asleep."

I took a spoonful of cottage cheese. "Everything all right topside? Do we still have our dinghy?"

"Everything looks fine."

Tracy appeared at the door, a lopsided smile on her face. She stood on tiptoe and planted a kiss on Reid's cheek. "Thanks for last night," she said. She sank down on the bed and took a drink from my coffee cup. "You missed a good time."

Reid blushed again. "I'll go make another pot of coffee. You two think about what you want to do today."

When he left, Tracy poked my arm. "You okay with what happened?"

"You're the second person to ask me that. I'll tell you the same thing I told him. Of course I am. You and Reid are adults."

"So, what about today?"

"I'm sure there are plenty of things to do and see on the island," I said. "But frankly, after our welcome by the customs official, I'd just as soon get out of here."

Tracy nodded. "And the longer we stay, the more money we'll owe, I bet."

Reid returned then with coffee for him and Tracy.

"How soon can we get under way?" I asked.

"Two hours, give or take," he answered. "We'll have to check out, but if you two take care of that, I'll get *The Lady Anne* ready to sail."

Tracy took her coffee and put on some clean clothes, Reid went topside, and I climbed out of bed. I was glad there was no awkwardness between the three of us. I pulled on shorts and a halter and ran a brush through my hair.

And before this trip has ended, I thought, *who knows what might happen.*

Two hours later, we set sail, leaving Puerto Plata in our wake … and a good chunk of change for slip fees, electricity, dumping our trash, resort fees (though none of us had used any of the resort's amenities), the water Reid used to hose off the deck, and a fee to leave the Dominican Republic. If Tracy hadn't produced yesterday's receipts, we might have had to pay those fees again too.

"Those customs guys are making money hand over fist," Tracy grumbled, filing the new receipts away.

Reid chuckled. "And that is an old nautical term," he said. "Crews used to climb the old-time rigging hand over hand or hand over fist. Successfully climbing hand over fist meant you had reached the top."

"Remind me to get some more cash at Provo," I said. "Another port like this and we'll have nothing left."

"I'll go with you and we can check out the shopping," said Tracy, rubbing her hands together.

"We should have plenty of time for that," Reid said. "And while you two run your errands, I'll do a little shopping myself. See what I can come up with for another special meal."

Tracy sidled up to him. "What about dessert? Can you handle another dessert like last night?"

Reid's face reddened. "I believe I can handle it."

We were under full sail, on course to Provo in the Turks and Caicos Islands ninety miles away. Reid was at the helm and Tracy was trying her hand at fishing.

She chose a heavy neon-pink lure from the assortment Charles left, about ten inches long, in the shape of a fish, but with a white mouth which made it look like it was smiling. I thought it was cute, but Reid was positive that no self-respecting fish would ever hit it. Despite his continuous jokes about her lure selection, he helped her rig it and showed us both how to work the reel.

I was examining the course Reid had plotted to Provo and Tracy was aft, watching her rod, when she suddenly yelled, "Fish on! Fish on!"

Reid and I could hear the reel screaming before we even looked back. The pole was bent way over and the line was going out extremely fast. Tracy grabbed the rod but couldn't get it out of the rod holder.

"Go help Tracy," Reid said. "I'm heaving to."

While Reid got *The Lady Anne* stopped, Tracy and I manhandled the rod out of the holder. About one half of the line was gone and whatever was hooked was still speeding away.

There was no way Tracy could hold the rod by herself. I yelled to Reid for help, but he didn't answer. I glanced toward the cockpit but couldn't see him.

The Lady Anne was oscillating slowly, first one direction

and then back again. Line was still being peeled off but not as quickly.

Reid joined us then, carrying the fighting belt and the gaff. He wedged the gaff in the stern rail and then strapped the belt around Tracy's waist. He guided the gimbaled rod butt into the receptacle on the fighting belt. After it seated into place, Tracy was able to hold the rod without any help.

She began cranking, bringing the line in slowly. The rod was still bent way over, but Reid assured us it wouldn't break. Tracy just kept reeling. She had to be tiring but she didn't complain.

I got my phone and shot some video. We had no idea what she had caught. At one point, Tracy looked at Reid and managed to say in a breathless voice, "No more lure jokes."

Finally, she got the fish close, only to have it run out again, taking line with it. Tracy began cussing but kept reeling. Reid showed her how to "pump" the rod up and then reel down and wind in the slack.

The fish ran three times, but each run was shorter. It was obvious the fish was tiring. We were all anxious to get a look at it. Sweat was pouring down Tracy's face but she wouldn't quit.

Then suddenly, the line went slack. Tracy nearly toppled over backwards; only Reid standing close behind her kept her from hitting the deck.

The fish had escaped.

"Shit." Tracy, exhausted, kept reeling.

I leaned over. "What's that on the surface?"

Reid made his way to the edge of the swim platform. "Stop reeling," he told Tracy. He reached into the water.

"Well," he said. "You did catch something." He turned and held up the pink lure with a hooked Dorado head. No fish, no tail, just the blue-green and yellow, slightly squared head.

"What happened?" Tracy asked.

Reid pointed to the sheared edge where a bigger fish had chomped on it, leaving the front part of the Dorado's blue dorsal fin. Judging from the size of the head, Tracy had hooked a really nice fish.

"Probably close to three feet long," Reid said.

"Yikes," I said. "How big was the shark that did that?"

I got the head unhooked and threw it back.

Tracy looked wiped out. She sank down in a heap on the deck. "Do you think you could put the rod away?" she asked me. "I'm done for the day."

I did, while Reid brought her a bottle of water.

She downed it in one gulp. "That sucked," she said.

"How big do you suppose the shark was that got it?" I asked again.

And again, nobody answered. I don't think any of us wanted to think about how big the shark had to be to take that kind of bite.

Reid readjusted the sails and we were shortly back on course. After the second bottle of water, Tracy looked better.

"No more lure jokes."

"Yeah, I heard you," Reid said, grinning. "No more lure jokes." His grin got wider. "How about a shark joke?

Tracy groaned.

"Why do sharks prefer salt water?" he asked.

Tracy and I shrugged.

"Because pepper water makes them sneeze."

This time we both groaned.

"Pat, you'll like this one. What kind of shark likes to gamble?"

I didn't know. Neither did Tracy. Reid smiled and said softly, "A card shark."

I shook my head.

"Okay, try this. Why don't sharks attack lawyers?"

I knew this one. "They don't eat their own kind."

He shook his head, waited a second for Tracy to answer, and when she didn't, he answered, "Professional courtesy."

"Are you done yet?" Tracy asked.

Reid shrugged and turned to the logbook. His entry said, "Partial Dorado, big shark."

I drew a crude picture of a shark next to our position on the chart and a frowning stick figure holding an empty pole. Tracy didn't think it was funny either.

CHAPTER 23

Later that afternoon, I had the helm while Reid and Tracy were below, resting in preparation for night sailing. We hadn't timed our departure very well, and now it looked like we wouldn't make port in Provo until sometime after dark.

My sail-trimming skills had improved and we were making nine knots without much heeling. I could have gone faster, but I tried to keep the ride smooth while they were napping.

The ocean was endless, and we hadn't seen another boat in quite a while. Besides *The Lady Anne* and the clouds, there was nothing out here but wave after wave. But the autopilot was working perfectly and we were right on course.

The hatch was open and suddenly, I heard Reid playing. The song sounded familiar, but I couldn't place it. They were supposed to be resting, but apparently not.

Then he hit a bad note. "Okay, no big deal," I told myself.

After the second bad note, I was amused.

After the third, I suspected something wasn't right. I glanced around and, satisfied there was nothing but open seas ahead, I went below.

Tracy and Reid were in his cabin. The trumpet was on the cabin sole, as were their clothes. I didn't want to see anymore. I scrambled topside.

But apparently I wasn't as quiet as I thought. In a minute, Reid and Tracy were back on deck with me.

"Who's driving?" Reid asked, pulling his T-shirt over his head.

Tracy was wrapped in a beach towel. "Are you upset?" she asked.

I answered Reid first. "I have everything under control. We're in open seas on autopilot. I only planned to kid you a little about the clinkers you were hitting. Now I know why."

I turned to Tracy. "No. I'm not upset exactly. I just wasn't prepared to see you two humping like rabbits when you were supposed to be resting for tonight's watch."

Tracy shrugged. "It wasn't planned. It just happened."

Reid motioned Tracy and me to sit at the helm with him. "I think we need to talk."

"Last night was unexpected for me," he began. "Maybe I should have ignored Tracy's question. Chalked it up to the booze. But it wasn't the booze, was it? And you said yourself, Pat, Tracy and I are consenting adults. Unattached. We've done nothing wrong."

Tracy nodded. "When my ex cheated on me, I was livid. But there was no cheating going on last night. Or this morning. I won't apologize for enjoying sex. I want more. But you can't be upset, Pat."

I listened as she continued.

"And as I recall, you called Charles's orgy bet. What would you have done if you'd lost? Renege? That doesn't seem like you at all."

I didn't have an answer for that. In fact, I felt ashamed I'd even started this conversation.

Reid took up where Tracy left off. "We find ourselves in an unconventional situation. But if you look at everything that has happened since your poker game, this whole damn trip is pretty unconventional."

I took a deep breath.

Tracy said, "People on a cruise eat way too much and gain ten pounds. But they justify it by saying they're on vacation so it doesn't count."

I looked at her, not quite connecting the dots.

She continued. "So I'm on vacation and I'm not going to gain ten pounds. Instead I'm going to lose ten pounds because I plan to have lots of sex." She nudged me. "You could, too, you know?"

Reid put his arm around Tracy. "She's right. We could make this work."

"Let's do whatever we want," Tracy said. "Who knows when we'll get this chance again? What happens on the boat, stays on the boat, like Vegas."

Reid said, "I admit, I want you both. You and Tracy are kryptonite. Either one of you would bring Superman to his knees. Gorgeous and smart, bruises or not, you're both incredibly sexy. I want you together. I want you separately. I want you right now and I'll want you again in an hour. But I want both of you."

Tracy was smiling. "See? No competition. No jealousy."

I let a moment go by, collecting my thoughts, evaluating my feelings. I've always been conservative, always worried about how people saw me, what image I was projecting. I had the chance now to break out of that mold. Could I do it?

Tracy and Reid were both watching me. "Can I have some time to think about this?" I asked. "But I promise, no interference. You and Reid can pursue your sexual exploits with no fear of disapproval from me." I grinned. "And I promise not to break in on you unannounced again."

Reid grinned too. "Okay. Now I better get my ass below and get some rest."

Tracy and I watched him go.

"He does have a nice ass." I said.

"So you and I are cool?" Tracy asked.

I nodded. "We're cool." I sighed. "Have you ever been compared to kryptonite before?"

CHAPTER 24

The Lady Anne arrived at the Blue Haven Marina on Providenciales in the Turks and Caicos Islands later that evening. We had intended to land at the Harbor Club Marina near Sapodilla Bay, which was closer, but it was full. We passed a lot of impressive motor yachts on our way in, but few sailing ships. And none as big as *The Lady Anne.*

The customs man was waiting for us at our slip. One of his first questions was if we had any firearms. We had all agreed to lie if asked and then deny knowledge if they happened to find the gun, but he seemed satisfied with the "no."

I was sure all of our fruits and vegetables would be a problem, but they weren't. It took longer to fill out the forms than his inspection took, and soon we were cleared. He said we had a beautiful vessel, the nicest sailboat he had seen. It was a relief to only have to buy an inexpensive permit and not be charged an additional dozen "special" fees. I already liked it better here. Plus, he accepted my car wreck story, didn't ask a lot of questions, even adding he was glad it wasn't worse.

He departed with a smile and we soon had *The Lady Anne* secured for the night, the blue Turks and Caicos flag fluttering in the breeze.

We had a quick snack and then Tracy and I went to our cabin and Reid went to his.

I brushed my teeth, undressed, and slipped into bed, but sleep was far from my mind. I couldn't stop thinking about our earlier conversation. So what exactly did I think was wrong with having an open sexual relationship with Reid? Tracy certainly was, and she seemed to be enjoying every moment. No one else had to know.

Then the pragmatist in me reared its ugly head. What if Reid and I fell in love? What if the three of us fell in love? When we got back to Florida, to the real world, how would we resolve whatever romantic entanglement we'd formed? How would I feel if he chose Tracy? How would she feel if he chose me?

My head spun these thoughts around until I was dizzy.

And then I quietly climbed out of bed, being careful not to wake Tracy.

Florida was a long way off. For once in my life, I was going to live in the moment.

I wrapped a towel around me and quietly, made my way to Reid's cabin. His light was still on; I could see the soft glow under his door. I knocked.

Reid answered the door, a book in one hand. He had stripped to shorts and his face reflected his surprise at seeing me.

"Expecting Tracy?"

He smiled and shook his head. "No. I think fishing did her in."

"Just the fishing?"

He raised his eyebrows. "Have you come to any conclusions about what we discussed this afternoon?"

I dropped the towel. "What do you think?"

CHAPTER 25

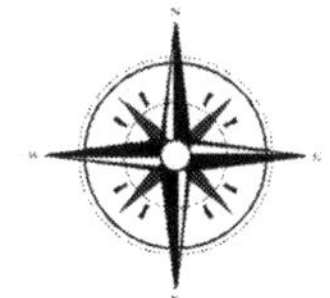

Tracy knocked on Reid's door and announced breakfast was ready. She didn't say anything when I followed Reid out, dressed only in one of his T-shirts.

And she didn't appear upset or surprised.

Instead, when Reid proceeded us to the galley, she grabbed my arm, grinned, and gave me a high five.

"I'll be right with you," I said, continuing to my cabin. "I want to change."

But I had more than clothes on my mind. I wanted a few minutes to myself to process how I felt. Tracy was right, Reid was a wonderful lover. I was hesitant at first, wondering if I'd made a mistake in going to his cabin. But he didn't rush me. He let me set the pace. We kissed for a long time, then he began a slow exploration with fingers and lips until I was ready —more than ready.

I closed my eyes, remembering the sensations. I pulled Reid's T-shirt over my head and held it to my face. His scent—the musk of sex—was still on it. It awakened a long dormant need in me. It had been some time since I'd been in a sexual relationship with anyone, and now I realized how much I'd missed it.

I sighed. Well, this was either going to be the best or the worst thing that had ever happened to me. Two women and one man.

I almost felt sorry for Reid.

Tracy was waiting for me when I walked into the galley. She had made turkey bacon to go with the last of the grapefruit, and Reid was busy with the coffee pot. She pulled me aside and whispered, "Can't wait to get you alone. I want all the details."

Since the plan called for us to split up, we finished breakfast and got ready to go. Reid needed groceries and would take care of that. I gave him the cash I had on hand and Tracy and I took a few more coins from our stash. She and I would find a place to exchange them and do our own shopping after.

It was the first time Reid saw how we accessed the gold. He whistled when he realized the fortune we still had left.

"Thank you, Charles T. Williams," he said.

Tracy and I echoed the sentiment.

We all left together, agreeing to check back at lunch. Once again, I gave him my phone. I offered to replace his, but he said it could wait. I was glad I had added an international calling plan.

It took Tracy and me awhile to find a place willing to trade our gold for currency. The US dollar is the official currency of Turks and Caicos and we were offered the going exchange rate, less a small fee. Even at that, we walked out with almost five thousand dollars.

As we went from place to place, she peppered me with questions about my night with Reid. Yes, I told her, Reid is a wonderful lover, and yes, I want to do it again. But no, I won't discuss positions or oral sex or how many orgasms I had and no, I'm not ready for a threesome yet.

She jumped and clapped her hands. "Yet. You said not ready *yet*. That's not *no* or *never*."

I rolled my eyes. We were in a little boutique and Tracy had spotted a red bikini that left little to the imagination.

"Go try that on," I said, hoping to distract her from what was becoming an embarrassing conversation. I was learning that my friend Tracy was more of a wild child than I'd ever imagined.

At noon, Reid called. Tracy told him to meet us at a quaint little restaurant the shop clerk had recommended. It wasn't far from the marina and when he joined us, we had a delightful meal consisting of conch chowder, salads with jerk chicken, and rum cheesecake for dessert.

Tracy leaned over to me and whispered, "I wonder how much sex we have to have to work off that cheesecake."

I'm sure Reid heard her, but except for a slight uptick at the corners of his mouth, he didn't react.

"Behave yourself," I hissed, feeling heat flood my face.

Back at the boat, we took turns sharing our purchases. Reid wouldn't tell us what he'd gotten for that "special" dinner tonight, but he did present us with flowers. I took them to the galley to find a vase. I could hear Tracy through the open hatch.

"Look," she was saying. "Our own pirate flag. And a set of signal flags so the next time we get a request to show our tits, we can respond with 'drop your drawers.'"

Reid was still laughing at that when I rejoined them. She was holding up the bikini. "You like?"

"Is that street legal?" Reid wondered.

"Gotta keep you interested," she replied. She pulled another bag from her tote. "The guy at the sports shop said some of the best deep-sea fishing in the world is off these islands. He showed me some lures to try. I bought the lot."

Reid cleared his throat. "Okay, your turn Pat. You get a bikini too?"

Hardly. What I pulled from my tote was a new fleece for the night watch and a pocket-sized rigging knife/marlin spike.

Reid chuckled. "I can see who the practical one is."

"One of us has to be," I said.

"You should have gotten a bikini too," Tracy said to me. "Or at least a sexy nightie."

"Why?"

"To keep our man interested."

I bristled a little at that but before I could respond, Reid did.

"Are you kidding? Either of you could wear yellow rain gear and I'd be turned on."

I moved away and muttered under my breath, "Tracy, when you wear that bikini, you'll turn on every man on the island."

But Reid and Tracy were staring at each other and didn't hear me.

CHAPTER 26

Reid shooed us topside so he could cook in private. He made us promise not to peek. He was very secretive.

Tracy and I took her flags topside. We wanted to see what it took to hoist them. The pirate flag was easy using the port side signal flag halyard on the main mast spreader. The *S, U, Y* and *T* flags took a little more effort. Tracy went below to get some line from the rigging station.

I remembered how she and Reid had been eyeing each other a few minutes ago. "Come right back," I said.

She grinned and promised not to get distracted.

"Whatever Reid is cooking smells delicious," she said, returning. "And see? No distraction."

"He wouldn't let you stay."

"He wouldn't let me stay." She sighed. "Not even when I offered to model my new bikini."

I shook my head. "The flags?" I reminded her. At least she remembered the line.

Before long we were finished and could raise the letters from the mizzen mast spreader. Since we were in port, surrounded by families, we quickly lowered and stowed those flags in a cockpit locker along with the rest of the signal flags.

Reid called to us from the galley. "Hey, you two. I need some beer for the dinner. Want to run to the marina store?"

Tracy grinned at me. "Why don't you go? I'll see if I can help—"

I grabbed her hand and pulled her with me. "Oh, no. Why do you think he asked us BOTH to go? Only a few days and he knows you so well."

But we were laughing as we made our way off the boat. On the way to the marina, we walked past a couple of young, blond teens who looked like the models for every Southern California surfer poster I'd ever seen. They were standing on the foredeck on a sleek Albemarle fishing boat that looked brand-new.

One of them called out to us. "Hey! Saw your flags. We'll show you ours if you show us yours!"

I looked at Tracy. "Maybe we should have waited until we were out at sea to hoist those flags," I said.

But Tracy had already flashed them. It happened so fast, I hardly had time to process it before the boys started whooping and whistling. I rolled my eyes. "You are incorrigible," I said, pulling her away.

Luckily, as the boys' parents turned to see what the

commotion was all about, Tracy and I were disappearing into the shop. I held my breath until I was sure no one was storming after us for corrupting minors. Instead, by the time we had made our purchase, their fishing boat was out of the marina.

When we returned to *The Lady Anne,* there was a family on the dock looking at her. Did they see what happened and were here to complain? I sent Tracy on board with the beer.

"Can I help you?" I asked.

The man shook my hand and introduced himself and his wife as Scott and Cathy from Kansas. They were on vacation and decided to show their kids the marina. *The Lady Anne* caught their eye.

I invited them aboard, letting the two kids, maybe ten and eleven, explore topside. They were well-behaved and asked some surprisingly good questions, especially the older one, who asked if the sail was like a plane's wing, only vertical. "It is," I said. "And that was a very good question."

Tracy joined us and immediately took a liking to the kids. She had them help her hoist the pirate flag while their mother took pictures.

After exploring for a few minutes, Scott asked if we'd consider taking them out sailing.

About that time, Reid came up from the galley. "You'd have to ask the captain," he said, shaking Scott's hand and motioning in my direction.

"Well," I said. "We haven't had passengers aboard before. We've only had the boat for a week. We're taking her to

Florida, and we're eventually going to start a charter business."

"How about an hour's sail?" Scott said. "We'd happily buy you dinner in return."

Cathy and the kids had gathered around. It was clear from the expression on all three faces that they were eagerly awaiting my answer. I looked at Reid. "You've already started our dinner. Can it hold for a little while?"

Reid nodded. "I'll take care of that right now."

He disappeared below deck and we prepared to sail.

My phone rang just as Tracy was piloting *The Lady Anne* out of the slip. It was one of Charles's men. He asked why we were leaving so soon and if everything was alright. I assured him that it was and told him we'd be back in a little over an hour. I felt relieved, knowing he was watching.

With the boys lending a hand, we unfurled all the sails, stopped the engine, and headed offshore. After a few tacks, Tracy let the kids take the helm and try it themselves. They called out commands and were exuberant. Cathy took lots of pictures and video.

Tracy showed the kids how to quickly stop the boat by heaving to. First she had them "sheet-in" or tighten the genoa, mainsail, and mizzen sail. Then she had them announce we were "heaving to" so the crew wouldn't think we were tacking. She had them tack like before but without releasing the genoa. It began to back fill but wasn't released to change sides. They eased the mainsheet and turned the wheel so the rudder was parallel to the genoa. She then had them ease the mainsail itself and the mizzen sail until *The Lady Anne* was slowly oscillating back and forth. She locked the wheel and proudly announced, "Great job, helmsman."

I don't think I've ever seen two kids happier. I turned to Scott. "I think you need to get a boat," I said.

He shook his head. "Only real large lake is Kaw Reservoir and we don't live close enough to it to justify buying a boat. But"—he smiled—"I hear you three are going into the charter business. I'll leave you a card. We may be your first customers."

He checked his watch. "I guess that's enough sailing for today." The kids looked crestfallen, but Tracy took them below deck to fill out the log entry, saying they were our first guests. Reid took over the sailing and once back at the marina, he executed docking maneuvers while Tracy, Scott, and I handled the lines.

Once docked, Scott got a passerby to take some group photos of all of us on *The Lady Anne*'s bow. Again, Scott insisted that Pat, Tracy, and I meet them for dinner at a restaurant of our choosing.

"We do already have dinner plans," I explained. "But thanks for the offer. And it was our pleasure to have you on board."

Cathy shook my hand. "I can't believe you're sailing all the way to Florida through the Bermuda Triangle. Aren't you the least bit nervous?"

Ah. I hadn't thought of that before now. Before I could

respond, Scott handed me a business card. "Remember what I said. First customers."

We hugged the kids, exchanged email addresses, and promised to share photos. Then they were on their way back toward the resort.

It dawned on me as I watched them go that my bruises must be a lot better. I hadn't had to tell my car wreck story. And I hadn't frightened the children.

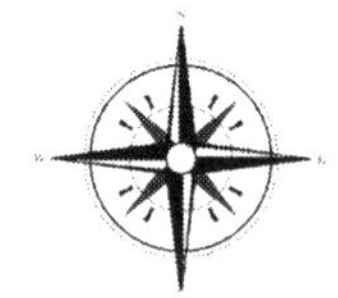

CHAPTER 27

As soon as they left, Reid headed back to the galley and said he'd call us for dinner in about an hour. Tracy and I hosed off the decks and then showered below and cleaned up. I half expected Tracy to reappear in her new bikini, but thankfully, she didn't.

While we were setting the table, Tracy paused. "I heard what Cathy said to you just before they left," she said. "Are we really sailing through the Bermuda Triangle?"

Reid answered from his place at the stove. "Depending on which charts you look at, we've been in it since leaving San Juan."

"Do you believe in it?" I asked.

"I don't know," he replied. "Maybe. Strange things happen at sea. We've got Internet here. Tracy, Google it."

Tracy took a seat and opened up the laptop. She began

paraphrasing: "The generally accepted boundary of the Bermuda Triangle, or Devil's Triangle, is the area between Miami, San Juan, and Bermuda, but that is subject to interpretation. Planes and ships have disappeared, but the exact numbers vary. The insurance companies say there are no more accidents in that area than anywhere else."

She continued, "If you accept the Bermuda Triangle is real, there are paranormal explanations such as lost Atlantis technology and alien abductions. There are also natural explanations such as the Gulf Stream, bad weather, compass variation, the Sargasso Sea, methane gas, electronic fog, freak waves, et cetera."

"How can there be *compass variations*?" I asked.

"It says, there's an area where true north and magnetic north are the same and that gets you into accidents because you travel in the wrong direction."

"True north? Magnetic north? I didn't know there was a difference," Tracy said.

Reid nodded. "Let's see if I can explain it. The earth rotates on its axis once a day. The ends of the axes are the north and south poles—true north and south. But the earth is one big magnet, and a compass needle aligns itself where the northern lines of attraction enter the earth, a point currently in northern Canada I believe. The horizontal angular difference between true north and magnetic north can vary by a few degrees or many degrees, and it changes every year, making the need for charts of declination or local calibration essential."

My head was spinning. "A few degrees difference. That

could mean a difference of a few *hundred* or even a few thousand kilometers? I had no idea it was so much. No wonder a ship could get lost. A captain would naturally think he was looking at magnetic north and could make a huge error."

Reid nodded. "Exactly."

I took a breath. "I've never heard of the Sargasso Sea either," I said to Tracy. "What does it say about that?"

Tracy consulted her screen. "It says it's an area bordered by currents where there are huge mats of heavy Sargassum seaweed and no wind. Boats and small ships get stuck, the propellers get jammed, and sailboats get becalmed. Without a rescue, the crews eventually starve to death, or the boat is found with no crew aboard."

Reid turned. "The Sargasso Sea encircles Bermuda, much farther north and east of where we're going." He followed up with, "What about the Gulf Stream?"

"The heavy current will carry you away from your reported position. Rescuers end up searching in the wrong area for lost boats."

"Does it give any documented incidents?" I asked.

"Yeah, a whole listing, even some military stuff. Most of the accidents are explained away, but for some, a cause was never determined."

Tracy's expression was suddenly anxious. "I wish Cathy had never mentioned the Bermuda Triangle."

Reid excused himself for a minute. Then from the open door of his cabin, we heard the theme from *The Twilight Zone*, softly at first, then building to a crescendo. I joined in with scary woo-woo noises.

Tracy snapped the laptop closed and stowed it. She was not amused.

Reid came back to the galley, dodging the dish towel Tracy flung at him. "Take your seats, ladies," he said. "Dinner is served."

And what a dinner it was, beginning with baked crab dip and toasted French bread slices.

While Tracy and I feasted on the appetizers, Reid went topside with a covered plate from the fridge. He returned about twenty minutes later with the same covered plate and a big smile. He changed the music from the soft rock we'd been listening to, to Jimmy Buffet's "Cheeseburger in Paradise." As the song ended, Reid served cheeseburgers, exactly as the song said. Lettuce, tomato, kosher pickle, French fries, everything. He had even chilled the glasses so the beer was really cold.

"Why are these cheeseburgers so good?" I asked.

"Yeah," Tracy echoed. "Really good. What's your secret?"

Reid grinned and said he used a secret ingredient: ice water.

"Ice water?" I echoed.

"Yes. Put some ice water in the hamburger mix and then the burgers slightly steam from the inside as they cook. It keeps them moist."

I had never heard of that but made a mental note to remember.

For dessert, he served homemade key lime pie, complete

with a chocolate graham-cracker crust, whipped cream, and a curly lime garnish. It was a fantastic finish to a great meal. Neither of us could believe Reid could make a key lime pie that good in our little galley. If he hadn't put half of it away for another meal, I believe the three of us would have devoured the whole thing right then and there.

As if that wasn't enough, Reid announced it would be movie time in one hour. He insisted on cleaning up the grill and doing the dishes. He banished us from the galley. Tracy and I went to the salon where she wrote a Four Queens email updating Charles, and I looked through the cruising guide for the Turks and Caicos.

"What is there to do here?" Tracy asked when she was done.

"Well, we've already done our shopping. Everything else is diving, fishing, or beach related. There are also lots of tours to the nearby islands."

"That's it?"

"No. We could also tour a conch farm, go parasailing, go to a casino, go birdwatching, go whale watching, go horseback riding, or go see where shipwrecked sailors carved their names into stones a long time ago."

Reid joined us in salon, went to one of the cabinets where Charles's collection of movies was housed, and opened the doors. While he perused the titles, he asked, "Does any of that sound good?"

Tracy took the book from me and began flipping pages.

"I'm game for whatever you two want to do," I said.

Then Tracy stood up and said loudly, "Wait! I found what we can do. It says it right here."

She grinned and began reading, "We can go sailing aboard a fabulous yacht with a handsome sailor who is a gourmet chef and a virtuoso trumpet player and who will gladly fuck your lights out for dessert."

I raised my hand and said, "Let's do that."

"Yeah," Reid said. "Let's do that."

The smell of microwave popcorn filled the air. "I can't believe I'm saying this," I said, sniffing. "But even after that meal, the popcorn smells wonderful."

Reid motioned toward the cabinet. "Pick a movie."

Tracy and I narrowed it done to two choices: *Unforgiven* or *Monsters, Inc.* Tracy said she wasn't really in the mood for a children's movie, so the western won out.

The popping stopped so Reid disappeared into the galley and returned carrying a large bowl of popcorn.

"Cue it up," he said, settling himself between us at the table.

But somewhere between the opening credits and the first ten minutes of the movie, I fell asleep. When I awoke, Tracy and Reid had disappeared. The movie had been put away, the television turned off, and the popcorn bowl left half full on the table. I could hear whispers from his cabin.

Smiling, I took the bowl to the galley, saved the popcorn, washed the bowl and put it away, and went quietly to my cabin. Tracy and Reid were obviously enjoying another dessert.

CHAPTER 28

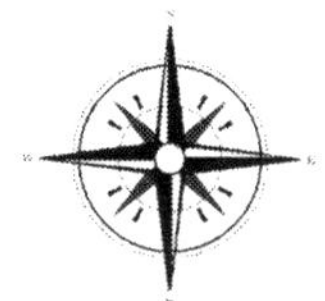

I awoke before either Tracy or Reid, so I went to the galley to start breakfast. While the coffee was perking, I checked the email draft folder.

We had a reply from Charles.

He said that his associates had failed to locate Pincus. Using the coordinates from the night of the attempted kidnapping, they had plotted an area of shoreline where Pincus would have likely come ashore, assuming he hadn't drowned.

They found no sign of him. There was, however, a report of a stolen motorcycle in the area at about the right time. If Pincus had stolen a motorcycle, he could be anywhere on St. Thomas, possibly still waiting for his brother. Charles said they would keep looking, and in the meantime, we could rest assured his security guards would continue to watch out for us.

When Tracy and Reid appeared for breakfast, I read them Charles's email. It enforced our decision to forego the tourist attractions and sail on. So we cleared through customs and joined the queue at the fuel dock.

"We've got plenty of fuel," Tracy said, eyeing the line. "I don't like the idea that Pincus is still somewhere out there. Let's get underway."

"We've got two hundred miles until our next port at Eleuthera," I said. "Even if we get a little behind schedule, I feel better topping off the tanks."

Reid agreed with me. "It makes us all uneasy that Pincus is still at large. But that's all the more reason we want full tanks."

Once we had refueled and were clearing the channel, Reid could see Tracy was still feeling anxious. He put his arm around her shoulders and asked, "How do buoys make a living?"

Tracy and I looked at each other. "Is this another of your lame jokes?" I asked, narrowing my eyes.

He looked askance. "Lame joke? Me?"

"Okay," I said. "I'll bite. How do buoys make a living?"

"They get tipped by the waves."

Then he started to laugh. Tracy looked down and shook her head.

I walked away and retrieved the Turks and Caicos flag.

Reid didn't even seem to notice that he was the only one laughing.

Soon, though, we were making good time. The wind and sea conditions were favorable, and it looked like another great day for sailing. Before long, we passed a dozen fishing boats, all trolling in the same area. Tracy let out a line with one of her new lures, but didn't have any luck. She didn't seem to mind. Instead she looked relaxed for the first time since we'd left port, watching the bright-green, rubber-tentacled lure skip, gurgle, and bubble in our wake.

Our depth finder had been mostly useless since we left Puerto Plata. It only had a 1,000-foot maximum scale and the water was much deeper than that everywhere except near the islands. When I looked at our course for Eleuthera, I noted that we would be sailing over water that was over two miles deep in places. I remembered something Reid had told nervous students in class when sailing deep water. "Sailing in thirty feet of water is no different than sailing in 10,000 feet of water. The boat doesn't care."

As we passed Mayaguana, we spied a lot of sea birds feeding on the surface. We altered course to move closer, thinking it might be a great fishing area, but again, nothing hit.

Tracy switched back to the pink lure. She was sure she could catch something in the deep waters surrounding Samana Cay, Rum Cay, San Salvador Island, Cat Island, or Eleuthera. Our plotted course would take us over some ridges and areas that were still deep, but shallow enough for the depth finder to see them. We decided to try and troll over those "humps" if we could stay close to our planned course. Maybe fishing would be better at those depths.

Tracy said she was going to give the pink lure about an

hour and then try a different one. Between her new lures and the tackle box below, I was sure she'd eventually find one the fish liked.

Reid told her to fish until dusk, hoping she'd catch a good eating fish for dinner. In the meantime, we passed Samana Cay, rumored to be where Columbus first landed. I don't know what we were expecting, but except for the fact it was uninhabited, it looked like every other island we passed.

Fishing was a bust once again, so Reid worked his magic with what we had on hand. He made us ham rollers—thin ham slices spread with cream cheese, rolled around a kosher pickle spear, and cut into bite-sized pieces. He made two plates full and we ate them all. The last of the key lime pie was dessert.

The sun was setting, so we prepared to sail through the night. Before retreating to his cabin, Reid decided to shower. Using the solar shower on the stern, he stripped down in front of us. We whooped and clapped, and he entertained us with a bump and grind. I laughed, but Tracy was licking her lips and fidgeting.

I could tell she wanted to join him.

"Go for it," I whispered. "I'll take the helm and won't watch."

But she frowned. "After you fell asleep during the movie last night, I screwed him. It's your turn."

"There are no *turns*," I said, annoyed. "We're not keeping track. If you want to fuck Reid, go for it."

Tracy's face reddened. "I don't know if it's the boat or

sailing or Reid. But I'm thinking about sex more than usual. When we get home, I know I'll have to go back to bean-counter Tracy, but right now—"

"You don't owe me an explanation." I stood up. "Reid is right over there, wet, naked, and available. Flash your smile and go for it."

Tracy grabbed my hand. "When your watch is over, he'll come topside to relieve you. I think you should relieve each other. Have some fun. It's okay to be naughty. I won't tell."

With that, she started to undress.

I glanced over at Reid. He was watching Tracy. He caught my eye and smiled. I don't think he heard what Tracy and I had been talking about. It probably wouldn't have mattered if he had.

But I did think Tracy was wrong about one thing. When we got home, she wouldn't be able to go back to her old life anymore than I would be able to go back to mine.

CHAPTER 29

There was still another hour left on my shift when Reid joined me topside.

"You're early," I said, secretly happy for the company. It had been an uneventful stint and I'd had a hard time staying awake.

Reid said, "Go forward a little on the starboard side and look up."

"What?"

"I've been watching something through the overhead hatch in my cabin. Go over by the mainsail and tell me what you see."

His tone was serious, and I unclipped my PFD and did as he instructed.

The sky was overloaded with stars. They seemed extra bright and so close that I could almost touch them. There were solitary points of light along with clusters. The Milky Way stretched across the blackness, twinkling with its thousands of stars. The sky shone even more spectacularly than usual, wrapping around *The Lady Anne*'s sails like a blanket and extending to the horizon.

"Do you see it?"

I jumped. I hadn't heard Reid come behind me and his voice at my shoulders startled me.

"See what?" I asked. "I see the stars. I see flashes of bright colors from the bioluminescence in our bow wake. I see dark water with frothy patches of white abeam. Is that what you mean?"

Reid shook his head and pointed. "Look there. That bright light above us and to the right."

"Bright light?" I asked. "Like from another vessel?"

Reid took my elbow and pointed. Still, I only saw lots of bright stars. I shrugged.

"Keep watching," Reid said. "You'll see it."

"What am I looking for, an airplane?"

"I don't think so." Reid was still pointing. "It's yellow. It's moving and it's yellow."

Then I saw it. A pale-yellow light that had just dropped straight down. "The yellow one? Got it," I said. It would have been difficult to see from the port side helm station with the mainsail blocking my view, but it was clearly visible from this vantage point.

"Keep watching."

The light climbed for a minute or so, then it dropped straight down again.

"Comets don't do that, do they?" I asked, a little shiver of fear chasing down my back.

"No. It's not a comet and it's not a shooting star because there's no tail or aura. A satellite would hold a steady course. And planes don't suddenly drop like that unless they're in trouble."

"Could it be a helicopter?"

"No. A helicopter might hover, but not that high and not in that pattern. And I might not have heard it below, but we'd hear it topside. Besides, this is the third time that it's worked its way down. Two other times it worked its way up. It's like the light is going up and down a staircase."

"Are you sure there's only one light?"

"No. I'm not sure. I have very limited visibility from my cabin and a restricted view from the salon. I lose it when it goes too low and I lose it when it gets too high. Either there's just one light going up and down or there are at least five *somethings* that I've seen."

As I watched, the light was definitely getting lower and now making its way behind us.

"Go get the video camera," Reid said then. "And wake Tracy. Tell her there's a UFO behind us."

I stared at him. "A UFO?"

"Unidentified flying object, right? I'm not saying it's from outer space. But it's certainly unusual and I think we should make a record of it." He paused. "Oh. And Tracy's in my cabin."

When isn't she in his cabin? I thought. But he sounded so unconcerned about the light that it alleviated some of the fear I'd been feeling earlier. After all, it was a great distance from us. And all the literature I'd ever read about UFOs offered some perfectly natural explanation for strange lights in the sky.

I went below, got the video camera, and woke Tracy. I only told her that Reid wanted us topside. I decided to let him tell her why.

CHAPTER 30

Tracy rubbed the sleep out of her eyes. "Did I oversleep?" she asked, sitting up. She was naked from the waist up.

I tossed her a T-shirt. "No. Reid just wants us both topside."

She threw me a puzzled look, but when I didn't offer any more explanation, she swung her legs out of bed and slipped into the T-shirt and her shorts.

Reid was waiting for us. He took Tracy aside and pointed to the yellow light, now on the rise.

"What is it?" she asked.

Reid had fetched the binoculars while I was below, and he handed them to her. "What do you think it is?"

Tracy peered through the lenses. "I have no idea. Some kind of military experiment?"

Reid handed me the binoculars next. They didn't help much. And now our mysterious object was directly astern and much closer, still glowing pale yellow.

Tracy took the video camera and moved to a good spot, clear of the rigging, and began shooting.

"I think the light's changing," I said.

"I see it too," Reid said.

What had been a steady, pale-yellow light was now different. Other colors alternated like strobe lights on a dance floor.

Tracy kept videoing, saying, "Isn't this cool?"

I marveled at how calm she was. My heart was beating a tattoo in my chest so loudly, I thought for sure they could hear.

I jotted down our GPS coordinates in the log, thinking we might be glad to have exact documentation.

"Look! Over there!" Reid suddenly shouted, pointing.

Tracy followed his line of sight and swung the camera around.

About 500 yards to port, the ocean was churning—getting lighter. There wasn't a buoy or a reef in sight, and it wasn't from another ship. The light seemed to be coming from just below the surface. It was intense but diffused by the water, making the sea glow like emeralds.

Reid stared. "Oh, fuck," he said.

"What's wrong?" I asked, glancing back.

"That green light's a submarine and the yellow light isn't a UFO, it's a drone." Reid passed a hand over his face. "I think

Tracy may be right. We've wandered into the middle of a military exercise."

His voice was calm, but there was an unmistakable sense of urgency in his tone.

"Are we in trouble?" I asked.

"I hope not, but they might confiscate the camera. Tracy, you better stop videoing." Then he added, "I just hope it's our military."

The drone that had moved in behind us was now flying low, maybe twice as high as our mast. Besides the yellow light, it displayed oranges and reds. The new colors were faint but more frequent. There was no engine or propeller noise. There were no blips on the radar, even after Reid adjusted the sensitivity. It was puzzling to think that something we could see, the radar couldn't pick up.

I saw the video camera lying on the cockpit table and wedged it under a cushion, just in case.

I looked toward the submarine. Its light was nearer the surface and getting brighter. It was displaying the same subtle yellow, red, and orange variations as the drone, albeit with a greenish tinge.

"I don't think that's a submarine," Reid said finally.

"Why not?" I asked.

"Because if that light was on the conning tower, we'd see the rest of the sub, or at least its shadow."

"Is it another drone?" Tracy asked.

"I'm not aware of underwater drones."

"I'm getting a bad feeling," I said. "What should we do?"

"Let's get some distance," Reid said. He started the engine, shifted into forward, and told me to furl the genoa and the mizzen sail, but to leave the mainsail up for stability.

I had just begun to secure the sails when the light we thought had been a submarine broke the surface.

There was no submarine, no vessel of any kind we could see—just a bright yellow light. It floated on the surface of the water like a giant bubble.

Tracy retrieved the camera and began videoing again. The drone had moved directly above the lower light. Both lights now flashed the same colors.

"Are they communicating with each other?" I asked.

As if in answer, the intensity of the colors increased. Then, on the forward part of the lower light, three large black spots appeared, blocking out a portion of the light. The spots slowly changed color, from black to gray.

"Tracy," I asked breathlessly. "Are you getting this?"

Before she could respond, three beams of gray light shot out, like witches' fingers, reaching across the darkness to grasp *The Lady Anne.*

My body tingled, felt electrified. I glanced at my hand. It glowed a dull silver color. My legs, too. I looked over at Reid and Tracy. Tracy was still videoing, alternating the camera between Reid and me and the strange lights. They, too, had the same luminescence, like a white shirt under a blacklight. I wondered if the phenomenon would show up on video.

I found it curious that the boat wasn't glowing, just the three of us.

Then, as quickly as it began, the gray fingers of light retracted. Reid, Tracy, and I looked at each other. The tingling was gone. Our skin returned to its normal color.

I took a step toward them when a huge flash of light exploded from astern, lighting up the night sky for miles in all directions.

I screamed and instinctively closed my eyes. But the brilliance was as powerful as the sun. Pain exploded behind my eyelids. I heard Reid and Tracy crying out too.

It only lasted a few seconds before winking out like a switch being thrown. Cautiously, I opened my eyes and squinted into the darkness. Both lights were still astern and still glowing yellow, but the flashes had stopped. And they were moving. The lights were getting further away.

I looked around. "Something's ahead, coming right at us," I gasped, pointing.

At the same time, Reid yelled, "Oh shit. Fog ahead."

"Where did that come from?" I couldn't keep the fear out of my voice. Minutes ago, the sea had been clear, the sky star filled.

"It just appeared," Reid answered, his own voice registering alarm. "Whatever that shit is, it wasn't there five minutes ago."

CHAPTER 31

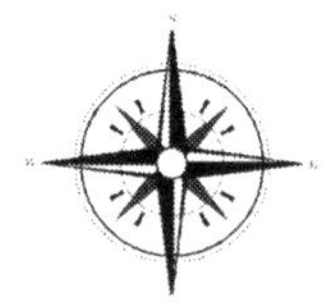

"Hold on," Reid yelled from the cockpit as he swung the boat around, away from the bank of fog that appeared out of nowhere. The mainsail wasn't sheeted in tight and the boom came flying across. Fortunately, I saw it coming and ducked.

As the boat lurched, Tracy nearly fell over. She wrapped her leg around the stern rail for stability and kept working the camera.

"More fog, dead ahead," Reid shouted.

I saw the fog ahead and then glanced behind us. That fog was still there.

Reid increased our speed and changed course.

As the bow came around, fog surrounded us again, moving across the surface of the sea as if it was something alive, determined to block our path.

"We're cut off," I hollered. "This isn't normal."

Tracy lowered the camera. "I'm getting scared," she said.

"Hang on," Reid said. He changed course again. But a moment later, there was more fog in that direction.

He called for Tracy to move away from the stern and join us at the helm. She acknowledged.

Reid made another hard turn. Everything bounced as *The Lady Anne* crossed her own wake. Waves crashed over the bow. I moved closer to Reid. Tracy did too.

"We've got trouble," Reid said, pointing at the compass.

Reid was steering a straight course, but the compass needle was slowly turning. Not spinning as such, but rotating more than it should have been. He tapped on the glass, but the needle kept turning.

I watched the fog as it circled around us, getting closer and closer, moving in from all sides.

"This is crazy," I said. "Fog doesn't move like this, does it?"

Before anyone could answer, we motored right into it.

It was warm and damp, stinging my eyes. As it wafted over the decks, the engine sputtered and the instrument lights flashed. Reid jerked his hands off the wheel as if he'd been shocked. The engine sputtered again, and then it just stopped, taking the power for the instruments and our lights away. Reid turned the key off, then back on, and pushed the starter button but nothing happened—no clicking, no noise, no alarm tone, no nothing. Flipping various switches on and off didn't do anything either.

We had lost power.

With our momentum and the mainsail up, *The Lady Anne* was still making way. We could barely see the bow, much less any farther.

"Pat, manually furl the mainsail," Reid said.

"Should we be stopping?" Tracy asked. "We need to get out of here."

"We're sailing blind," Reid replied. "We need to stop and wait for this confounded fog to lift. We also need to get the power back on. Now, can you find me a flashlight?"

Tracy started opening compartments and lockers in the cockpit while I finished furling the mainsail. I couldn't see very well and the fog burned my eyes, but the mainsail finally felt like it was furled completely in.

Tracy located the cockpit flashlight but when she tried it, it didn't work. She hit it against her palm and shook it. "Now what?" she said. "I know it's not the batteries. We put in fresh two days ago."

"Pat," Reid said. "Please go below. There's another flashlight under the steps. Get that one. Then check the breakers. We need power."

I slowly made my way toward the hatch through a mist growing heavier, denser, and thicker. In less than ten seconds, the visibility had gone from poor to none. I held my hand directly in front of my face and couldn't see it. Nor could I see Reid or Tracy. The air became heavy, making it harder to even breathe.

"Are you guys still there?" I asked.

"We're here," Tracy replied, sounding more and more alarmed. "Do you have the flashlight yet? Does it work?"

"Hang on," I said. I wasn't about to tell her I hadn't started below yet and add to her panic.

I heard Reid trying to calm her, telling her that we had temporarily lost power but that *The Lady Anne* was completely seaworthy. He instructed her to grab something solid and to clip herself in. She said she had forgotten her PFD.

And she was crying.

CHAPTER 32

I had to feel for the outline of the hatchway and, holding firmly to the handholds, gingerly descended below. The air wasn't quite as heavy and breathing was easier, but I still couldn't see anything. I remembered that the yellow, water-proof flashlight was secured underneath the steps, next to the fire extinguisher. After a bit of groping around, I finally located it.

"Got it," I shouted. I switched it on. It had worked in St. Thomas because I had personally tested it, but it wasn't working now.

Shit. "No good, it's dead" I hollered up. "Now what?"

"Did you check the breakers?" Reid asked.

"Negative, I can't see anything down here."

"Go to my cabin and get the light sticks," Reid hollered back. "They're either in the closet, in one of the duffel bags, or they're in a drawer. I can't remember if I unpacked them or not."

"Pat, please hurry," Tracy added.

She was still crying.

I closed my eyes, took a labored breath, and forced myself to relax. I knew where Reid's cabin was from here and I knew where the closet was. Finding a duffel bag should be fairly simple. Finding a package of light sticks in the dark that had been buried in a drawer might be more challenging.

Regardless, I told myself, *go get the damn light sticks.*

I kept my eyes open, even though I couldn't see anything, and started forward, taking small, hesitant steps. I kept one hand in front of my face and reached with the other, feeling the heavy air for any obstacles.

I felt my way past the table, through the main salon, and was soon at Reid's cabin. The door was open. I visualized entering the room and looking at his closet. Then I got down on my hands and knees and crawled over to it.

There were no light sticks in the first duffel, but I did find them right on top of the second. I was ready to yell my good fortune when I decided it might be prudent to try one before I got everyone excited. What if none of the light sticks worked either? I didn't know how much more disappointment Tracy could take.

The bag opened easily but the stupid foil wrapper was much tougher. Finally I got a tear started and quickly removed the plastic tube. Grasping each end, I gently bent it until I heard the inner tube snap. I shook it vigorously and a soft blue light appeared.

The blue glow was comforting. I released a breath I hadn't known I was holding. I grabbed five light sticks and cautiously made my way topside, stopping briefly at the circuit breakers. None of them had tripped. I tried resetting them but with no success. Then I grabbed Tracy's PFD from the salon table where she'd left it.

While I was at the nav station, I saw my phone. We might not have service out here, but it had a light, a bright one. I knew my phone was charged but when I tried to turn it on, it was as dead as everything else.

Tracy saw my blue light appear topside and applauded as I rejoined them. Reid got two yellow light sticks opened and working, one for each of them. I kept the blue one, even though it was the dimmest of the three. I handed Reid the spare light sticks and told him it wasn't the breakers causing the trouble.

The fog had gotten thicker and felt even heavier. I held my light stick about a foot in front my face and could barely see it.

Reid excused himself to go below, determined to find a flashlight that worked. He returned with a few choice words about not finding a working flashlight, but he did have one of the handheld marine radios. He also said he had closed and dogged all of the watertight doors, just as a precaution.

Like the flashlights, the radio didn't work either. Reid

called an emergency meeting. We all huddled around the helm, our eyes and lungs burning from the fog soup.

"We'd better talk about this fog first," he said. "I'm sure you remember from class that when navigating in fog, the biggest danger is collision. Under normal conditions we'd designate a lookout, hoist a radar reflector, and make sound signals."

"A lookout?" Tracy said. "We can't see two fucking feet in front of our faces."

"I know."

I could tell Reid was making a conscious effort to soothe Tracy. "And a radar reflector would be tricky to rig in the dark. But we could ring a sound signal."

"What if it brings the lights back?" Tracy looked around. "They might still be out there."

"So might another ship," Reid said. "We don't know how far we've drifted."

Reid left the helm and made his way to our bell. He rang the bell rapidly for a few seconds, waited a bit, and then rang it again.

There was no answering signal.

When he returned, he said, "I think we can be pretty sure we haven't wandered into any military exercise." He shone his yellow light stick on the compass. The needle was still spinning.

"We should have never furled the mainsail. Let's raise it and get out of here," Tracy said. "At least try to clear the fog bank. I'd rather take my chances on a collision rather than stay here."

"There's no wind," Reid said. "And we have no power to motor out."

He was right; the air was now very still. "We need another plan," I said.

"Look," Tracy said then. "Pat, you're an engineer and Reid, you sail for a living. Between you two you should be able come up with something. So think. Now!"

Reid and I looked at each other, nearly bumping heads. "What do you do when you're in a sailboat that has no working engine, there's no wind for the sails, and you need to move?" I asked.

"Could we swim and pull her behind us?" Tracy asked.

I knew then how desperate Tracy was to get out of here. She's obviously forgotten about the size of the sharks that we'd be sharing the ocean with, even if such a thing were feasible.

Rather than plant that vision in Tracy's head, I replied, "*The Lady Anne* is too big. We'd never be able to manage pulling her."

"We could find or make a paddle," Reid suggested. "There might be one on board." Reid paused a minute. "Or I could turn the wheel back and forth quickly, in effect sculling with the rudder."

I snapped my fingers. "Or if the dinghy will start, she could tow us," I said.

CHAPTER 33

We contemplated the logistics of using the dinghy. We would have to see if there was power to crank the Honda outboard. If there was, we'd next have to use the crane to get her into position to be lowered over the side. But since the crane's winch was electric, we'd have to rig a line and pulley. And we'd have to do all that working by the limited glow of light sticks.

"Doesn't sound feasible, does it?" I admitted.

"And even if all of those things happen and the dinghy can tow *The Lady Anne*, both vessels will be operating in zero visibility," Reid added.

Suddenly, Tracy gave a little yelp. "The fog's getting thinner," she said.

I looked. The fog was definitely dissipating and breathing became easier. What had been blackness was now light gray.

But with the lifting of the fog, something new came into view—flickers of light getting brighter and closer.

"Are we moving?" Tracy asked.

Without a point of reference, it was difficult to know for certain, but it felt like *The Lady Anne* was moving forward. I thought about throwing my light stick over the side to see if it stayed parallel to us or not but immediately dismissed that idea as wasteful and foolish.

Semicircular patterns of bright light formed ahead. It was like some sort of archway or tunnel was taking shape. I wiped the salt from my eyes. I could hear our bow breaking water. *The Lady Anne* was definitely moving, and picking up speed.

Tracy grabbed the binoculars. "Something's ahead," she said. "I can't tell what it is."

"Another ship?" Reid tried to steer but couldn't change our course. He went to the other helm station and turned that wheel. No effect.

We were on a collision course. Using the whistle attached to his PFD, he blew five short blasts, the danger signal.

There was no response.

Reid signaled again. The bright flashes were closing in fast. Steering was ineffective, and without being able to run the engine in reverse, there was no way to slow down.

Intermittent flashes of the whole color spectrum danced before us. Showers of sparks, like the kind welding produces, rained down. The electrical disturbance, or whatever it was, loomed ominously dead ahead.

The fog was now gone and the entire area, illuminated. At

the speed we were moving, if we couldn't alter course, a collision was imminent. But with what?

Reid hollered that the compass needle was spinning so fast it was just a blur. For the first time I can remember, he sounded scared. He ordered us below.

I went first, followed by Tracy. Light was shining in through the hatch, main windows, and portholes and we could see quite clearly. Neither of us spoke. I don't think we knew what to say.

While Tracy watched, I opened all the circuit breakers. If we were going through an electromagnetic disturbance, I didn't want to "fry" all of our electronics. I wished I had closed the valves on the propane tanks, but I hadn't thought about them until now. I hoped they wouldn't explode.

I climbed halfway up the steps and peeked out.

"What kind of electrical storm is this?" I asked Reid, trying to sound calm.

"I don't know," he answered. "But you two better brace yourselves."

I latched onto the closest grab rail and told Tracy to do the same.

"Do you smell that?" Reid asked.

I sniffed, not sure what I was supposed to be smelling.

Then…

"Ozone." Although I hadn't smelled it since my college labs, I recognized its unique odor immediately. My skin began to tingle.

I looked up. Sparks were being drawn to the metal masts

and to the standing rigging, the metal cables supporting the masts. Little flashes of yellow and white danced along the metal cable lifelines and the metal stanchions that held them. The smell of ozone was getting stronger. My skin crawled with the static electricity that seemed to be everywhere.

I glanced back at Tracy. She clung to her handhold, whimpering.

Then I called to Reid. "Come below," I said. "Before you get electrocuted."

CHAPTER 34

Reid didn't respond, and with all the hissing and crackling from the sparks, I wasn't at all sure he could hear me. He had let go of the metal steering wheel, but electricity continued to arc around him.

I went topside, carefully avoiding anything alive with electricity, determined to help him. At first I thought the low frequency hum I felt more than heard was my imagination—a by-product of the electrical storm.

But it was getting louder.

The scene on deck was surreal. Large bolts of electricity danced all around. Some made contact with any metal, others just flashed close by. There were cascades of sparks falling all around. The hum was getting louder.

My muscles began to twitch. Simple movements became difficult. I began coughing, nearly overwhelmed by the stench of ozone. The skin on my arms and legs felt burned and bruised.

I was facing aft but felt heat behind me. Turning, I saw what was ahead.

In front of our bow rose an archway. The heat came from a brilliant white light at the top. It was like looking into the sun. Before I could turn away, the light began to rotate.

The hum was so loud, I could no longer hear the hissing and popping of sparks. The light moved around so that it shone on the starboard side. I could no longer see waves or ocean. I wondered if *The Lady Anne* was sailing into hell. I wondered if I was going to die.

I looked over at Reid. He was still at the helm, electricity arcing from the wheel to his belt buckle. When he fell to his knees, it galvanized me into action. I screamed at him to come below.

Tracy tapped the back of my leg, making me jump. I hadn't seen nor heard her come topside. "What's going on?" she yelled.

"Reid's in trouble," I said. "We have to get him below."

Reid was still on his knees and hadn't moved. His eyes were closed. I couldn't tell from here if he was breathing or not. Telling Tracy I'd be right back, I crawled through the cockpit to the helm and grabbed his arm. I tugged but he tipped forward, facedown.

I rolled him onto his back and put my ear to his chest. His heartbeat was strong and steady. For a split second, I was elated. He wasn't dead. At least not yet. I cupped his face in my hands and yelled at him to follow me. He opened his eyes and looked at me, but there was no recognition. Electricity arced everywhere and I was getting shocked. I started coughing again and felt pain in my chest. I feared I might pass out from the overpowering smell of ozone. I tried to remember if concentrated ozone was toxic or flammable or inert. I couldn't, though it hardly mattered.

I grabbed the collar of Reid's PFD and started backing up toward the hatch, dragging him behind me. Tracy was waiting at the hatch, reaching for me, offering her hand and yelling for me to hurry. She was coughing as well.

We were almost there when Reid stopped. I pulled hard but he wouldn't move. He was stuck on something. There was a frenzy of raging electrical discharges all around. The hum had become so loud that my ears hurt and my head began throbbing.

Tracy saw my predicament and crawled toward me. "What's holding him?" she yelled.

It took us a few minutes to find the problem. Reid's safety tether was still connected to the jackline, but the tether had caught on something. I got shocked when I touched the metal snap, but I managed to get him unhooked.

With Tracy's help, we dragged him forward, through the hatch and down the steps. I told Tracy to secure the hatch. My skin was alive with shocking sensations. Reid looked distressed, but he was still alive, breathing, and now conscious.

He tried to sit up.

I put my hand on his chest and forced him gently back

down. "Not yet," I said. "We need to stay away from anything metal."

"What's going on out there?" he asked then. "And what's that sound?"

I shook my head. "I have no idea. It started about the same time as the light."

We bunched together in the middle of the salon. Through the portholes and windows we watched the berserk electrical melee raging topside. Streaks and flashes lit up the salon until we didn't know whether it was day or night.

The cabin reeked of ozone but less so than topside. There were fingers of sparks jumping around the metal in the galley and on the grab rails. I noticed that Tracy's hair was standing on end, like it had been moussed by a sadist. The loud crackling and popping sounds topside were much more muted below. The hum sounded like someone had maxed-out the bass volume on cheap speakers.

I cautiously peered through the main windows. I could clearly see the bright light rising up on the port side. It had circled completely around *The Lady Anne.*

Suddenly, the hum's volume increased tenfold, going from discomfort to pain. It sounded like a jet engine was belowdecks with us. Simultaneously, Tracy, Reid, and I slammed our hands over our ears. I winced in pain and screamed.

At the same time, we were bathed in more light. It shone in through the portholes and the windows, illuminating *The Lady Anne* inside and out.

Even with my hands pressed hard against my ears, I couldn't take the insane noise any longer. I knew I had to sit down or I would fall down. I saw Tracy lying on the cabin sole, her hands pressed over her ears, grimacing in pain. Her mouth was open, but I heard no scream. I tried to see how Reid was fairing but my vision began to blur. My eardrums ached as if ready to rupture.

I swallowed and then yelled as loud as I could in a futile attempt to relieve the pressure. But there was no relief. If I could have surrendered, I would have. I closed my eyes as tight as possible and waited for the end.

CHAPTER 35

I must have passed out because the next thing I remember is waking up on the cabin sole on my back. The deafening noise had stopped, there was no ozone smell, and my skin was no longer tingling. My ears were still ringing, and I had a serious headache. *The Lady Anne* was rocking, heaving, and pitching about. I sat up and looked around. Reid and Tracy were lying on the floorboards. I called their names and they moved, but didn't speak.

The light shining in through the side portholes looked like normal daylight, not the supernova light that nearly blinded us before. I wanted to check on Reid and Tracy, but whatever was causing the boat to rock was getting worse. I had to check it out.

The Lady Anne was really bouncing, making it tricky to get the hatch open. The bright daylight hurt my eyes, but I staggered topside. I grabbed the nearest handhold and boosted myself up, trying to see what was happening.

Using one hand to shield my eyes from the bright sun, I looked out over the water.

Whales.

There were whales surrounding us—at least a dozen groups of about a dozen whales each. One group swam past in loose formation. I could hear them chattering with each other in chirps and low trilling sounds. As I watched, several of them rose up out of the water, their heads very close together, less than twenty feet away. When they hit the water with a sound like gunshots, *The Lady Anne* was rocked by the impact waves.

I finally realized the whales were feeding as a group on small, silvery-colored fish scrambling around them. The smell of fish hung in the air, but it was an improvement over the ozone.

Whales fed on all sides. I had no idea what kind they were, but guesstimated their length at eighty to ninety feet. They made our boat look small. There were also huge flocks of big birds dive-bombing the surface around the whales, feasting on the whales' scraps.

Flocks of birds didn't worry me. The proximity of the giant whales did.

I made my way to the helm and sat down. I needed to get us out of here before one of these majestic monsters hit us, accidentally or on purpose. I tried to start the engine but there was still no power. I shouted for Reid or Tracy, but there was no answer.

I rubbed my temples. It looked like it was up to me to find a solution.

There was a light breeze blowing, probably less than five knots. The whales were moving slowly. It suddenly dawned on me to just sail away. Five knots might be fast enough to get clear. I would have to determine if the sails had been damaged by that ferocious electrical storm, but if they were serviceable, I'd be able to get us underway.

I discovered the genoa burned on the wrapped edge. I wouldn't be able to see what condition the mainsail or mizzen sail were in, however, until I unfurled them.

I cautiously hauled out the mainsail. If it was burned, I didn't want to tear it. As it inched its way along the boom, *The Lady Anne* responded, picking up speed.

A pod of whales fed a scant ten feet away, rocking *The Lady Anne*. Another large whale crossed directly ahead. I steered behind him, missing his giant tail by a few feet.

Six more whales were headed right at us, on a collision course from the starboard side. They looked like a formation of locomotive-sized torpedoes. About thirty feet away, they dove at the same time. I gripped the wheel tightly and braced for collision. While I calculated all six of them would clear the hull, I was certain one of them would hit our keel. Fortunately they all passed below, surfacing on the port side as if I hadn't been there.

The immediate area ahead was clear of whales, giving me a

chance to think. I debated raising the mizzen sail and unfurling the genoa, but trying to handle a sixty-eight footer under full canvas with no help and no electric winches seemed overly ambitious and way too risky.

I steered evasively, knowing that I didn't want to ram a whale and damage the hull. Without a lookout to guide me, I just did my best. There appeared to be fewer whales and fewer birds ahead to the right, so I continued in that general direction.

After a few more near misses that had my heart racing, *The Lady Anne* sailed clear of the commotion. With the nearest whale at least 100 yards away, even though I could still hear them, I was finally able to relax.

Self-congratulations were in order. I had single-handedly sailed *The Lady Anne* out of danger. I had no idea where we were and no idea where we were going, but at least the feeding whales were getting further away.

"Hey, are you guys okay down there?" I hollered below.

This time, Reid emerged topside, saying Tracy would be up shortly.

"You don't look so good," I told him. "How do you feel?"

He rubbed his forehead. "I have the mother of all migraines," he said. "And I think I could sleep for a week. But nothing's broken." He held up his arm. "Got some serious bruises though."

He gave me a once-over. "You look like you came through practically unscathed."

"Not exactly," I replied. "I don't think my ears will ever

stop ringing." I motioned to the whales feeding en masse off our port side. "It's a good thing I came to when I did."

Tracy joined us, trying to run her fingers through hair that looked like it might never get untangled. Her bottom lip was swollen and her legs were covered in bruises. She gave up on her hair after a moment and like Reid, began rubbing her temple.

"Headache?" I asked.

"And my ears hurt."

Reid went over to the cockpit fridge and retrieved three bottles of water. They were still cold. I don't think I'd ever had a better drink.

Tracy wiped her hand across her mouth and winced. "Now I feel like I've been in a car wreck." She narrowed her eyes and looked at me. "Aren't you even sore? You look pretty good."

I laughed. "It's the short hair."

"Next port I'm getting my head shaved," she mumbled. She looked out over the water. "Are those whales?" she asked, pointing.

"Let's talk about those whales," I replied.

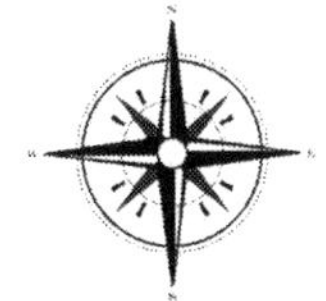

CHAPTER 36

I recapped waking up to a pitching, rolling vessel and the discovery of the feeding whales. I explained my decision to sail us out of danger after several near collisions.

Reid was impressed. "That's quite a feat, sailing under mainsail all by yourself."

"Do you know what kind of whales they are?" Tracy asked.

"The really big kind," I answered.

Tracy wasn't amused.

"My guess is they're humpback whales," Reid said, looking through the binoculars. "They are usually only about fifty feet long, but these look much bigger." He turned to me. "Have you seen any whale-watching boats nearby?"

"No. Why?"

He shrugged. "Seems to me with the whales being that active, there'd be sightseeing boats around."

He was right. I got a queasy feeling in the pit of my stomach. Why hadn't we seen any sightseeing boats? Or boats of any kind for that matter? And we still had no idea where we were.

I kept my thoughts to myself. Tracy didn't need to share my anxiety, but I could tell Reid had the same thing on his mind.

We took a few minutes to finish our drinks and look around, each visually inspecting *The Lady Anne*.

Both masts seemed okay, but the standing rigging was a little blackened after exposure to so much current during the electrical storm. We still had no power to start the engine or run the electronics. The decks were wet and seemed to be coated with some kind of film or residue and were slippery. That smell of ozone was now replaced by the smell of fish—a little less noxious, but unpleasant nonetheless.

Reid took the helm while I went below to reset the circuit breakers. He also asked me to check the bilge. Tracy offered to come with me, but I told her to stay in the cockpit and take it easy.

She waved away my concern. "I'm fine. Or at least I will be after a good night's sleep. I want to help. I'll stand by the hatch and relay your reports to Reid."

I nodded and went below. I checked the bilge first. To my relief, it was dry. Tracy passed the information to Reid.

"Reid says very good on the bilge, now what about the breakers?" she said.

I moved to the panel and closed all the circuit breakers I had opened before the electrical storm.

Nothing. No power. The batteries were dead.

Given the bright sunlight, the charging circuit should have indicated something, but there was no reading. The solar panels should have been trickle-charging the batteries but weren't. I needed to find out why.

"Negative on the power. Stand by, I'm coming up."

I went topside to see if the panels were cracked or broken. They looked intact but were covered by the same thick, dirty film as the decks. I returned below for a bucket of hot, soapy water, but the pump wasn't working either. So I poured a liquid degreaser into the bucket, grabbed some microfiber cloths, and headed back topside to clean the solar panels.

"Tracy, will you check to see if the solar showers are still bungeed to the stern rail? If they are and they're hot, please bring them to me."

Tracy was back in a flash with both solar showers. As I hoped, they were both hot. I soaped and scrubbed while she regulated the water. Whatever the coating was, the hot water and degreaser removed it. Before long, the panels were clean. I returned below. The batteries were being trickle-charged. I physically accessed all of the batteries. They had not been subjected to salt water and looked fine. They were just dead.

I pumped a fist in relief. "Okay, they're charging," I yelled.

I smiled at the sound of their clapping.

I continued my inspection. The engine appeared undamaged and I was sure it would start when the batteries were charged.

At least, I hoped it would.

Surprisingly, there were lots of dead roaches near the engine and the batteries. They were the first bugs I had seen aboard and not a welcome sight.

I changed the battery selector switch so the entire output from the solar panel was directed to the starting battery, not the generator or house batteries. I then opened all the breakers except for the charging circuit. I didn't want anything draining the system. Starting the engine was a priority, as it could then charge everything else.

Tracy joined me below. She wanted a handheld GPS to get our coordinates for Reid. She also grabbed a portable radio, Reid's new compass, and Tylenol for everybody.

"While you're at it, you might brush your hair," I joked.

"Look who's talking," she joked back. It was good to see her smile.

I took two Tylenol and continued my inspection. Working my way through the compartments, I looked for leaks, cracks, and damage. Lots of stuff had fallen over, but other than being messy, belowdecks seemed pretty good. Except for the fact that nothing electrical was working, of course. The compasses in the crew's quarters and the owner's suite were broken.

I came across more dead roaches and even a few dead spiders and centipedes on the deck, which gave me the willies. I knew sailboats had bugs that came in with the local produce or hidden in corrugated cardboard boxes, but when Tracy and I cleaned, we hadn't seen a single bug.

I also found something that worked—the manual head in the crew's quarters. I confirmed that by using it. Then I went topside, told them which head worked, and intended to continue my inspection, but Reid and Tracy stopped me with more bad news.

The handheld GPS and the radio were dead. So was her phone. Surprisingly, Reid's new compass was working but without knowing where we were, he didn't know which course to steer. Tracy asked me how fast I could get an outlet working so she could charge her phone.

I couldn't give her an answer.

I summarized what I had found below, and Reid gave Tracy the helm so he could accompany me while I continued my inspection. I think she was relieved to stay topside since my report of the dead bugs made her cringe. Reid hadn't commented about that. I suspected he was accustomed to bugs aboard.

The decks were covered with the same slippery guck that had been on the solar panels. Other than lots of blackened metal, nothing appeared damaged. The hull was intact, at least above the waterline, but since we weren't listing, and since there was no water in the bilge, we figured it was okay.

We inspected the sails next, hauling out the mizzen sail but not unfurling the genoa. Without power to the winches, we were better off without it.

It was a relief to see that other than being a little blackened along the edges, the sails weren't torn or damaged. *The Lady Anne* did have replacement canvas, but we agreed that replacing the sails wasn't a high priority.

I took Reid below and showed him the meter indicating the batteries were being charged.

"You've done a good job, Pat," he said. "It was smart directing the charge to one battery. Once it's fully charged, we can try to start the engine."

"Just remember, it's charging really slow. This may take a while," I replied.

He just smiled and asked if I had a plane to catch. I smiled back.

There was a flashlight laying on the table but like everything else, it was dead. On a lark, I removed its batteries and then got two new ones from our Costco stash. I held my breath while I replaced them and switched it on. It worked. I was elated.

Reid hollered up to Tracy, "Pat got a flashlight working! What size and how many batteries does that handheld GPS take?"

"Two. Lithium," she called back shortly.

Reid had purchased lithium batteries in San Juan and went to fetch them. When he returned, he gave me a hug, hefting the flashlight.

"That was brilliant," he said.

"That was lucky," I replied.

CHAPTER 37

We joined Tracy topside. In a few minutes, Reid had replaced the batteries in the GPS and switched it on. It beeped a few times and then went into "acquisition mode," searching for satellites. While we were waiting, I got a second GPS unit working. It, too, went into "acquisition mode."

Remembering yet another handheld GPS in the navigation station, I went below to try that one. Same result. It was dead, started up with fresh batteries, but could find no satellite lock. Puzzling.

We gathered topside. Reid handed water around.

"We need to make a plan," Reid said. "We can keep sailing away from the whales, but until we know our position, we should stop. We don't know how long it's going to take to charge the batteries and I don't think we should drop all the sails and just drift. Heaving to would be better."

Tracy and I agreed and set about unfurling the genoa, then immediately heaved to.

The slippery guck on the deck made the job harder than it should have been. Just scrubbing with salt water didn't help, so Tracy and Reid followed my example with the solar panels and used the remaining solar shower hot water and more degreaser to scrub a clean path around the decks.

Leaving them to their cleaning, I tackled the helm compasses. I took them both apart. Their internal needles were broken, the plastic domes cracked, and they each had a big air bubble, signifying fluid loss. Neither were level, probably due to the gimbals breaking under the stress of high-speed spinning.

There was nothing I could do. We didn't have a replacement helm compass or spare parts in the workroom, and the compasses in the crew's quarters and owner's cabin were unrepairable as well. We were now forced to navigate using Reid's hand bearing compass alone. It wasn't nearly as convenient nor as accurate, but it was the only working compass we had. I was suddenly thankful he had bought it.

I reported the situation to Reid and Tracy. I asked why his compass wasn't broken. It turned out the needle mechanism had been tightened for shipping and couldn't spin like the others. When he loosened the needle, it worked.

"In your next email to Charles," I said to Tracy, "mention that we need new helm and cabin compasses. If we don't hear back from him before our next stop, we'll buy them at the next chandlery."

Tracy excused herself below and Reid moved next to me. He looked serious.

"I'm very concerned about none of the GPS units being able to get even one satellite lock," he said quietly. "Do you suppose they're all fried?"

"Fried units wouldn't be searching for satellites, would they?" I replied. "They'd have blank screens."

"So what do you think is wrong?"

I thought for a moment. "Could be the units have internal damage, or something is blocking reception, or…"

He motioned me to keep my voice low. "Or what?"

"Or there was simultaneous failure of all the satellites."

The enormity of such a thing happening caused us both to pause. "No," I said, putting steel in my voice. "That just couldn't happen."

"What about that electrical nightmare we lived through last night?" he said. "Is it possible that could have caused it?"

Tracy called up from below. "Hey, you guys, there are a *lot* of dead bugs down here. What do you suppose killed them all?"

Her question broke the tension building between Reid and me.

"They probably all got electrocuted by the static electricity," I answered, glad to be able to solve at least one problem. "Just sweep them up."

I knew Reid had been whispering so Tracy wouldn't hear.

He didn't want to frighten her with the prospect of navigating without GPS or even a known starting point.

It was scary for me too. I pulled him closer and whispered, "It's not likely that three different units would have the same internal failure preventing a signal. Maybe they can't get a signal because there is no signal to get. Maybe the military has turned off civilian access."

"Why would they do that?"

I shook my head. "They wouldn't, unless something really bad happened."

"Like what?" Concern darkened his face. "You don't suppose we sailed through the aftershock of a nuclear war, do you?"

I held up a hand. "Whoa. A fiberglass boat would not have survived that, and while that might explain the flash of light, I don't recall heavy fog and ozone being by-products of a nuclear explosion."

He was listening intently.

"Whatever is wrong with our GPS units appears to have affected them all. I wouldn't count on any of them working again."

I could tell Reid didn't like the answers I was giving him anymore than I liked giving them.

After a moment, he squeezed my hand.

"Hey, I teach students how to navigate without electronics," he said, standing and pulling me up with him. "So that's just what we'll do."

He smiled. "Put one of the GPS units on the cockpit table and leave it turned on. Just in case."

"Good idea," I said, smiling back. "Just in case."

CHAPTER 38

Tracy joined us topside. She had a dustpan full of assorted dead bugs which she disposed of over the side.

"Makes us look like really bad housekeepers," she said.

"Boats in the tropics have bugs," Reid said. "They thrive in the warm, moist environment. Without regular attention, they are just a given."

"Well, *The Lady Anne* doesn't have any now, at least none that are alive," she said.

Tracy took the dustpan below and returned with three oranges and a bag of chips.

"Got in and out of the fridge fast," she said. "And I'm happy to report it doesn't look like anything spoiled."

I peeled my orange. It was still cold and sweet. "Hits the spot," I said, grabbing a handful of chips. "I'm going below to check the charge."

The gauge indicated a minimal charge. At this rate, I feared it might take two to three days to have enough battery power to start a diesel engine. If we couldn't get the engine started, I worried how Tracy might react.

I tidied up from the aftermath of the electromagnetic disturbance. I was still looking for problems I might have missed earlier, but thankfully, I didn't find anything more than a few dead bugs Tracy had missed. I was thankful there weren't any dead rats. I remembered reading that a rat can climb a dock line and get on board unseen. That was not a pretty picture.

I got two more flashlights working by simply changing batteries, and was glad I had bought in bulk.

All the while, I was thinking about our predicament. I was an engineer. I should have been able to figure out what was wrong with our electronics.

In a few minutes, I had it.

I returned topside, saying, "I have a theory about why all our electronics are dead."

Reid and Tracy moved closer.

"Going through the electrical disturbance seems to have drained any batteries that were connected in a circuit, even if the power switch was turned off. That's why the boat won't start and why flashlights, radios, cellphones, GPS units, et cetera won't work. They all had their batteries installed and connected."

Having their undivided attention, I continued, "Now I'm not sure why it happened, but fortunately for us, batteries that weren't installed or connected don't seem to have been drained."

"So if Reid's lithium batteries aren't dead, why won't the GPS unit work?" Tracy asked.

"The GPS unit is working, it just can't find satellites to give us our coordinates."

"Why not?"

I paused, debating how I was going to answer her question without alarming her. I glanced at Reid, the conversation we'd had earlier foremost on my mind.

Reid caught my gaze and answered for me. "Tracy, we're not sure why we can't connect to any satellites. The electrical disturbance might have damaged the GPS circuitry or perhaps it disrupted the satellites' systems like it did ours."

She raised one hand in a questioning fashion, looking perplexed. "How does a satellite's system get damaged?"

Reid shrugged. "Let's just wait until Pat gets the engine started. That will give us power to the radio and the satellite phone. We'll make some calls, figure out where we are, and be in a port in time for dinner. Now, Pat, please continue with your theory."

Reid's answer seemed to calm Tracy, so I continued. "Anyway, connected batteries were drained, disconnected ones weren't. Had I known or foreseen this, I would have disconnected the boat's batteries before the storm. After, I could have restored power by simply reconnecting them."

"But it won't work on everything," I cautioned. "For instance, Reid, what time is it?"

He looked at his watch. "It's stopped. It's battery powered."

"So are all the clocks below. Even if you replace the batteries and turn on Charles's fancy atomic alarm clock, it won't know the time. Those clocks rely on a signal from a satellite. No signal, and they'll all flash twelve o'clock."

"So what do we do?" Tracy asked.

"The only thing we can do," I answered. "We're going to make a log entry. It won't have the time or our coordinates, but I think it's important we detail what we went through. We're probably good with the date since I don't believe we were unconscious for a whole day. While you and Reid work on that, I'm going below to check the charge."

Tracy said, "I have two things to say. First, didn't Reid buy an extra battery for his replacement VHF radio?"

"You're right," Reid said. "I do have an extra battery and I charged it back in port. That radio should work. It's in my duffel bag. I'll be right back."

"What's the second thing?" I asked as Reid disappeared below.

She grinned. "How do I *turn on* an atomic alarm clock? Wear my red bikini?"

Seeing her smile made me feel better.

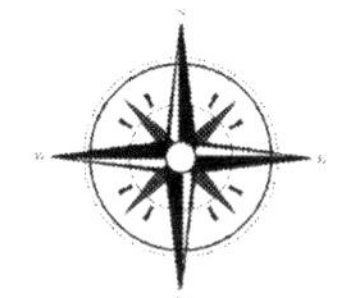

CHAPTER 39

R eid returned topside, radio in hand. He began broadcasting immediately. "*Pan-pan, Pan-pan, Pan-pan.* This is the sailing ketch *The Lady Anne*. Is anybody receiving?"

I stared at his radio, willing someone to answer.

"Why isn't he broadcasting a *Mayday*?" Tracy asked me.

As Reid repeated his call, I quietly answered her. "Remember our radio lessons. *Mayday* is for extreme distress, *Pan-pan* is for urgency."

"I'm feeling pretty fucking distressed," she snapped back.

"Maybe, but we're not sinking or on fire and nobody is dying," I replied. "We're not in immediate danger, we're just powerless and lost."

Reid switched channels and repeated his call, twice.

No response.

He switched back to the original channel, sixteen, the emergency and hailing channel.

"What's the range of that thing?" Tracy asked, looking more and more agitated.

"About five miles," Reid answered. "But once we get the main radio working, it will be closer to twenty."

"Are you sure it's working?" Tracy asked.

"It appears to be transmitting."

"Then why isn't anybody responding? Isn't channel sixteen monitored by the Coast Guard and all commercial vessels? Wasn't that a test question in class?" The volume of her voice rose with her frustration.

"Tracy, try to relax," I said. "Let's get the engine started and you can try the main radio. Okay?"

I directed Reid to move to the helm and Tracy to the cockpit. Then I went below, telling them to cross their fingers.

The meter indicated a slight charge, nowhere near enough to start the engine. Dejected, I returned topside.

Tracy read my expression and asked, "What's wrong?"

"The solar panels are charging the battery but it's going to be a while before it's charged enough to start an engine."

"How much of a while?" Tracy asked.

"Maybe tomorrow, maybe the next day. The system wasn't designed to fast-charge a completely dead battery."

"You're fucking kidding, right?" Tracy's voice had escalated from cautious to shrill.

"It doesn't look like she's kidding," Reid answered before I could.

"Do you expect us to be hove to for a couple of days?" she uttered. I sensed she was on the verge of tears, or worse, panic.

Reid must have sensed it also because he asked calmly, "Pat, are there any other options to charge a dead battery?"

I worked the problem logically. We needed more current to charge the battery. The solar panels were clean and working and supplying all they were capable of. So either I needed more power or a smaller battery that would still be capable of starting a diesel engine.

"Take your time," Reid reassured me. "Reason it out."

"Perhaps I should direct the charge to the generator starting battery," I finally stated. "It will require less power to start and then it could be used to quickly charge the other batteries."

"Very nice," Reid smiled.

"How long will that take?" Tracy grumbled, still upset.

"Probably another day or so," I replied. I didn't want to upset her, but I figured it was better to guesstimate long rather than short.

Reid's expression indicated he wasn't thrilled with that answer either, so he said, "Pat, any other options?"

They were both watching me, waiting. Suddenly I had an idea. "Go get me the generator manual," I said to Reid. "I want to check something."

He went below and returned with the owner's manual. I scanned the index and found the page I wanted. A moment later I exclaimed, "Just like I had hoped, this model has a manual start feature."

They followed me aft, to the generator. I loosened four thumbscrews and removed an access plate. There was a short piece of rope with a plastic handle on one end and a knot in the other. There was also a gear with a notch. The knot fit into the notch and the rope wrapped around the gear.

With both Tracy and Reid peering over my shoulder, I switched the generator to manual and then pulled the handle. It finally started on the twenty-eighth pull. Tracy hugged me so hard she nearly cracked my ribs.

I stowed the rope, replaced the access cover, and then went below. In the workroom, I found a little red portable battery charger. If I remembered correctly, it had a start engine feature.

I connected the negative black clip to the starting battery, disconnected the solar panels, got charger power from a nearby electrical outlet, and then shouted topside, "Get ready to start the engine."

"Ready," Reid responded a few seconds later.

I connected the positive, red clip, flipped a switch on the charger, and hollered, "Hit it!"

I held my breath.

It seemed like an eternity before I heard the shrill alarm tone indicating power. A moment later, the engine cranked—once, twice—then roared to life.

I let out a whoop!

Tracy and Reid started clapping and cheering.

"Keep it running," I hollered up. I kept the "or else" to myself.

I had never liked motor noise in a sailboat. Until now. The throttle increased. The rumble of the diesel was suddenly very comforting.

One by one, I began closing circuit breakers. There was a strangely welcome *beep* as the various electronics powered up. I disconnected the charger and reconnected the solar panels. Then I changed the switches to charge all of the batteries. I tried the satellite phone, but it was looking for service. So was the navigation station GPS. I began charging my phone and another handheld VHF radio. I also switched on the water maker and verified we were making hot water. At some point, I really needed a shower. Satisfied I'd done all I could, I returned topside, anxious to make port, any port.

With the engine running, Tracy's spirit markedly improved. She gave Reid back his radio and began broadcasting on the main radio. Despite its longer range, there was no response to her *Pan-pan* call.

"Let me check something," Reid said, going below. A minute later we heard his hail over the main radio. He and Tracy chatted for a minute, confirming to motor-sail to the nearest port and report what had happened.

"What was that all about?" Tracy asked after Reid signed off.

"He just confirmed both radios are transmitting and receiving," I said. "Pretty clever, huh?"

"Then why hasn't anyone answered?" Tracy asked.

A very good question. Too bad I couldn't come up with a very good answer.

Reid came back topside, and we regrouped in the cockpit. We set to work plotting the precise coordinates I had hastily noted when we encountered the strange lights: Twenty-three degrees, 14.1 minutes north; Seventy-four degrees, 17.5 minutes west. They put us north-northwest of Samana Cay. We agreed there was a margin of error as we had no way to measure how far we had drifted or sailed away from the whales, but it was a reasonable guess.

I got a pencil and a piece of paper and we started listing our options.

We discussed whether to continue to Eleuthera, turn back for Provo, or head due west for Long Island, which was about forty-five miles away. According to the cruising guide, Long Island had several small settlements and an airport.

San Salvador Island was about the same distance and on the way to Eleuthera. It also had an airport, but if we missed it, we could find ourselves in open water.

Samana Cay was only about twenty-eight miles behind us south-southeast. But it was uninhabited.

The north tip of Crooked Island was below us, about twenty-three miles due south. It was sparsely populated, but did have an airport. If we missed it, we should pass Inagua Island on the way to eventually Cuba or Haiti. Inagua Island had a salt factory, a bird sanctuary, and an airport.

The underlying problem was we weren't sure of our current position and sailing a few degrees off course, for any distance, could easily take us past our target without ever seeing it, even using radar.

Now that we'd weighed our options, it was time to come up with a plan.

"Okay," I said, consulting the list. "We can continue to Eleuthera, turn back to Provo, head for Long Island, or sail for San Salvador, Samana Cay, Crooked Island, or Inagua on the way to Cuba or Haiti."

"If we continue on our original course for Eleuthera one hundred and fifty miles away," Reid said. "And missed it to the north or the east, we'd be in the Atlantic. There are islands along the route, but we have no guarantee we'll see them. I'm not thrilled about the prospect of venturing into the vastness of the Atlantic."

"It's the same with San Salvador, isn't it?" I said, consulting the charts we had spread on the table.

"Then that's two down," Tracy said, taking my pencil and drawing lines through Eleuthera and San Salvador. "Next?"

"We could head west for Long Island," I said. "It's pretty big and we should be able to find it. But remember it's very shallow throughout the Bahamian Islands, especially west of Long Island, and *The Lady Anne* is not a shoal-draft vessel. With a working GPS and *The Lady Anne*'s charts, we might have safely navigated around the Great Bahama Bank, but without either, due west toward it seems way too risky."

Tracy crossed another name off the list.

After more discussion, we were pretty sure we could retrace our course to Samana Cay. If we found it and were positive it was indeed Samana Cay, we would have a fix and then reevaluate. We eventually dismissed that choice too.

Sailing to an uninhabited island just didn't seem all that practical.

Another down. That left Crooked Island. It was much closer than Provo and was inhabited.

Upon making port, we would report what had happened to the authorities, replace any non-working equipment, make any necessary repairs, get some rest, tell Charles we were okay, and then regroup and start over for Eleuthera. I was sure Charles could bring us necessary parts and equipment on his plane.

"Speaking of Charles," Tracy said. "Won't his tracking device have stopped working when the power went out?"

"Yes," I said. "Nothing electrical worked."

"Then either he'll report us as missing to the Coast Guard or the tracker will come back on and he'll send a boat or a plane to see if we're okay," she said.

"Good thinking, Tracy," Reid said, smiling. "I had forgotten about that. Well done."

"But we're bound to find the authorities before they find us, right?" I said.

While I had welcomed the Coast Guard once, I had no desire to be the focal point of a massive search now. After all, *The Lady Anne* was fine, and we hadn't been injured.

Reid nodded. "Let's get under way," he said.

The three of us gave each other high fives. We had made our decision—to sail south, course 180 degrees, magnetic.

CHAPTER 40

"I don't understand," Tracy said.

I looked up. I was seated cross-legged on the deck where I had parts from the two helm compasses in front of me. I'd thought maybe I could salvage enough to make one working compass. I thought wrong.

I sighed. "What don't you understand?"

"We've been motor-sailing about two hours, right?"

"Right," I answered. "Although when I set the clocks, I did have to guess the time. But you're right, it's been just over two hours."

"And during that time"—Tracy counted off on her fingers —"we've gotten the dinghy battery charging, all the systems working, the decks cleaned topside, and we all had much needed showers."

"And your point?" Reid asked, joining us.

"We've dodged the wheel to hold course 180 degrees and we've been making nearly nine knots. So we should have traveled about nine times two with is eighteen nautical miles, more or less."

Reid and I looked at each other. Reid nodded.

Tracy continued, "So if we were only about twenty-three miles from Crooked Island two hours ago, why don't we see it, or more importantly, why isn't it showing up on radar?"

"Well obviously we weren't where we thought we were," Reid answered.

"And that doesn't bother you?" Tracy fired back. "Motoring at nine knots for two hours, plus the thirty-six-mile range of the radar on a relatively steady course away from our last known position should have put us within sight of land by now."

Before I could respond, she continued, "And why doesn't anyone reply to our *Pan-pan*? Why can't any of the GPS units get a signal? Why doesn't the satellite phone work? Why won't the weather fax connect? Why is there no phone service? Why haven't we seen any other boats or planes? I guess I'm not really perplexed, I'm scared. I vote to broadcast a *Mayday* and activate the EPIRB!"

"If no one is responding to our *Pan-pan*, they probably won't respond to a *Mayday* either," I said.

"Pat's right," Reid said.

"What about the EPIRB? Don't we have two emergency locator beacons aboard?"

I got up and checked the one in the cockpit. Its battery

was dead. "Dead battery," I said. "And I'd be willing to bet the one in our cabin is dead also."

"Can't you charge them?"

Reid answered for me. "Wouldn't make a difference since they rely on satellite tracking and radio transmissions. So even if Pat could get the EPIRBs working, we most likely won't get any response. Plus, EPIRBs are only to be used in an emergency situation, and I'm not sure our situation qualifies."

Reid was trying to sound matter-of-fact and reassuring. It didn't look to me like Tracy was buying it.

"I wish you two would quit telling me what we *can't* do."

Tracy's face reddened. I was right. Not buying it all.

She stood up, her hands curling into fists. "A *Mayday* isn't appropriate. Activating the EPIRB isn't appropriate. Why have an emergency locator beacon if we won't use it? We're fucking lost. Say it. We're fucking lost. We're burning up our fuel and we don't know where we're going."

Reid stood up too. "It's okay, Tracy," Reid replied. "It's okay."

"No, it's not fucking okay. Do you know where we are? No. Do you know where we're going? No. Do you know how deep it is? No, just that it's over a thousand feet, maybe way over. Hell, we're on a three-million-dollar yacht and we don't even know the fucking time."

She glared at us for a moment, then stomped out of the cockpit.

I looked at Reid. "You know she's right about most of it."

Reid nodded. "I'll bring her back."

Reid caught up to her and led her by the hand back to the cockpit.

"You're right," he said. "We are temporarily lost and we are burning diesel."

Tracy looked at him and wiped away tears.

"This is a sailboat, so we're going to sail. Pat, is everything charged?"

"I'll have to check but except for some handheld stuff and the fancy camera, probably," I replied.

"Good. Pat, within twenty minutes, I want the diesel shut down, the keel down, the sails up, and *The Lady Anne* trimmed for speed. I've got a few things to do while we're under power and then we'll use the wind."

"We're still lost," Tracy barked.

"We're not lost," Reid said. "We are exactly right here. It's those pesky islands that aren't where they're supposed to be."

Tracy shot him a narrow-eyed look, but the corners of her mouth tipped up slightly.

"Here's the plan," Reid said. "We're going to sail our agreed upon course, 180 degrees. Sooner or later, something will show up on radar."

"What if nothing shows up before dark?" Tracy asked, sounding more curious than scared this time.

"We'll heave to and keep watch until daybreak, then we can resume course. If we don't sight land before the next nightfall, we'll change course and head due west, towards the North American continent."

"What about the Great Bahama Bank?" I asked. "Aren't we

in danger of hitting it if we go west? The water there is only six to nine feet deep."

"We should be well south of that by then, but we'll keep an eye on the depth gauge. It registers anything below one thousand feet. No reading means deeper water than that, which isn't a problem. Sound good?"

Tracy and I both nodded.

Reid took Tracy's hand. "Tracy, you can broadcast a *Mayday* all you want if it will make you feel better. We know the radio works. It's only a matter of time before we get an answer. We're also going to fly two flags—November and Charlie—an international distress signal."

"So, while we're busy doing all that?" I asked Reid. "What are you going to be doing?"

"I'm going to be making us something to eat. I'm starved, so I know you two must be hungry too."

CHAPTER 41

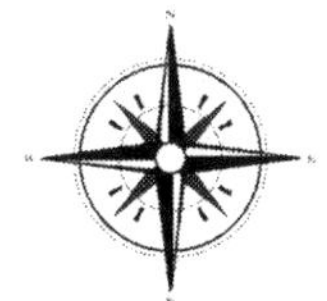

Leaving Tracy at the helm, I followed Reid below.

"I think I can rig something to tell the time," I said. "I did it in a science lab once."

He raised his eyebrows. "Then have at it, professor."

I scrounged around below and found what I needed for my project: a ruler, a pencil, scissors, tape, and a box of cereal. I left him in the galley preparing lunch and returned topside.

I cut an eight-inch square out of a piece of notebook paper from our log. I drew an upside down *T* and then measured out fifteen-degree angles on both sides. Once the angles were penciled in, I numbered them from six through twelve and then back to six. I cut a cardboard gnomon pointer fin from the cereal box flap and taped it so it angled upward from the bottom of the *T*. Then I taped the eight-inch square base to the back of the cereal box for support.

"Is that thing going to work?" Reid asked as he returned topside with three peanut butter and jelly sandwiches and some grapes.

"It should; hang on."

I took the hand bearing compass and asked Tracy to slow *The Lady Anne* down and keep the boat steady. I placed my homemade sundial on the open deck and oriented it with the compass. The shadow registered a little after three o'clock p.m.

"Ta-da!" I proclaimed with a flourish.

Their loud clapping and whistling indicated they were both impressed.

"How accurate is that thing?" Reid asked as he made a log entry.

"Probably within thirty minutes since I can't make any adjustments for latitude and longitude. I also aimed it with a compass which finds magnetic north, and I don't know how much to adjust for true north variation. And I can't adjust for the equation of time since I don't have an accurate watch and it's nowhere near high noon."

While I thought that a good, complete answer, it was greeted with blank stares from Reid and Tracy.

"Ah, thirty minutes is close enough for me," Reid said, passing out sandwiches.

"Me too," Tracy echoed. "Great job."

"We've run the engine enough to complete charging," Reid said. "After we've had a chance to eat, let's get ready to sail."

"Aye, aye," Tracy responded.

I was relieved to see she seemed much more relaxed now.

While the water pump was working, Reid refilled all of the solar showers and I disconnected the battery charger from the dinghy.

"This still might need more charging before it will start," I warned.

"Understood," Reid responded, smiling.

I took one last sundial reading, grabbed a sandwich, and went below to discontinue charging operations and to shut down all noncritical electrical systems. I also reset the clocks to three thirty p.m. I wanted to get Reid's watch working, but I hadn't seen any batteries that small so I didn't bother opening it up.

I stowed the sundial in a safe place. While it might not have earned an "A" grade at university, I was pleased with it.

A few minutes later, I gave Tracy the signal and she shut off the engine.

Immediately, the magical feeling of continued motion under sail enveloped me. I helped Reid trim the sails, and soon *The Lady Anne* was making over eight knots, leaving a bubbly, frothy wake in the azure water. Tracy had the helm, grinning and much happier.

So was I. I tipped my face to the sun and wind and pretended for a moment we were cruising near St. Thomas. It was a lovely fantasy.

"I had planned a nice dinner in Eleuthera," Reid said, bringing me back to the present. "But this will have to suffice for now." He finished his sandwich.

"Tease us," Tracy said. "Tell us what was on the menu."

Reid shook a finger. "Nope. It may still work, so don't look in the fridge."

We finished the grapes, our hunger curbed.

Reid gathered up the napkins and paper plates, then asked, "What do you think? We unluckily sailed into World War III?"

The question stunned Tracy and me into silence.

After a moment, I said, "If we'd been the target of a cruise missile or submarine, we'd be dead. And since when are the Bahamas a strategic military target?" I thought a minute longer. "If nuclear weapons had been fired at major US cities, there would still be emergency broadcasts from cities not under attack, wouldn't there? Or even other countries."

Tracy had been quiet during the discussion but suddenly she shouted, "Hey! The radar found something!"

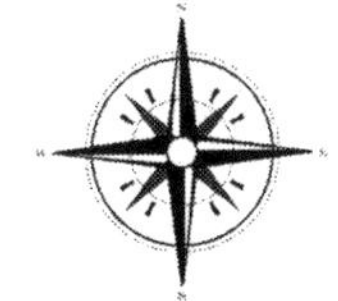

Reid and I scrambled over. The radar had made a contact: a land mass twelve miles distant.

Reid grabbed the binoculars. There was nothing in sight, but the display indicated otherwise.

"Why something just now at twelve miles?" Tracy asked. "Doesn't the radar have a thirty-six-mile range?"

"Under optimum conditions," Reid answered. "But things like the curvature of the earth, the height of our antenna, and the height and quality of the target can hinder a radar's efficiency. Even choppy water can disrupt the signal."

Whatever the contact was, the radar was locked on it, so we decided to change course and take a look. I made a log entry. We were all excited at the prospect of finding land or possibly another vessel, though to show up on radar it had to be a large one.

At eight knots, it didn't take very long before a low-lying island came into view. Reid was the first to give the "Land ho" shout.

When we were one-half mile out, the water changed color. In a few seconds, the depth meter went from no reading to four hundred feet and then to sixty. We furled the genoa and slowed down, watching the depth meter.

Reid stayed at the helm with Tracy while I went forward with the binoculars.

"The shoreline is very rocky," I reported. "There are low, jagged outcroppings and no trees that I can see."

"What about buildings?" Reid asked. "Do you see structures of any kind? Antennas? Signs? Warning buoys?"

I shook my head. "No. Nothing."

"I see flocks of birds," I said. "Most of the higher rocks are white."

"The waves and the tide keep the lower rocks free from guano," Reid responded.

"That's bird shit, right?" Tracy asked.

"Right," Reid answered.

Tracy kept roughly parallel to the shoreline, calling out fifty to sixty feet of water. I continued glassing. Except for the birds, I concluded that this side of the island, at least, was barren and uninhabited.

The radar indicated circular barriers approaching. The water ahead was light green. Judging from the way the waves were breaking, Reid surmised there were rocks or exposed reefs ahead. We decided to start the motor and get a closer look.

By the time Tracy had the engine started and Reid had furled the mizzen sail and partially furled the mainsail, the depth meter read forty-five feet.

I went forward to point out obstructions in our path. Reid went amidships to watch as well. Tracy began calling out the depth. She would turn *The Lady Anne* away quickly when one of us spotted a hazard, but then angle back in as we passed. She called out the depth constantly. Reid raised the keel. *The Lady Anne* now drew seven feet.

There were some large patches of brownish seaweed floating about and we tried our best to avoid them.

"Sargassum seaweed?" Tracy asked.

I could tell by the tone of her voice that she was hoping it was. At least then we'd have a clue where we were.

But Reid shook his head. "My guess, we're too far south."

We followed the light green water into a small bay. It offered minimal protection from the open sea, but it was better than nothing. The sun was getting lower, so this seemed like a logical place to stay for the night.

Reid and I prepared to drop the anchor while Tracy slowly circled, keeping us well away from the surrounding rocks. The bottom was rocky and this was far from an ideal anchorage, but we didn't have many options. Tracy put us in twenty-four feet of water and Reid let out one hundred twenty feet of chain. Tracy powered backwards to set the anchor. It caught on the first try.

We idled in neutral, waiting to see if the anchor would hold. Reid glassed the surrounding shoreline but saw the same things I did—nothing but rocks and birds. Tracy broadcast a *Mayday* and sounded five short horn blasts.

There was no response.

The Lady Anne tugged lazily at the anchor, testing her leash. The water was clear, our chain visible, the anchor held.

"On your next email to Charles," Reid said, "thank him for having the chain marked every ten feet. That's very helpful."

"Is that unusual?" I asked as Tracy nodded that she would.

"It is on the boats I've raced. They only carry about thirty feet of one-quarter-inch chain. Two hundred feet of big chain would be just too much weight in the bow."

With no working GPS, we couldn't use the "anchor alarm function," so we'd have to remain vigilant. Reid took compass bearings off some identifiable rocks to make sure we didn't stray into exposed reefs.

With *The Lady Anne* stable at anchor, we were free to attend to other matters. Tracy made a log entry and then began checking the chart, trying to identify the island. She also got the cruising guide and consulted that as well.

I went below to check our electrical status. I was relieved to see the main batteries were fully charged. All indicators looked good.

Reid took more bearings and then, satisfied the anchor was holding, started the generator and shut down the engine. That gave us power and allowed me to keep charging the rest of the dead electronics. I also put the charger back on the dinghy's battery.

We still had no satellite or cell phone service and no working GPS. Tracy wasn't able to find an island with the depths of this one on the chart and there had been no responses to her *Mayday*.

In spite of all that, it felt strangely reassuring, safe even, to be anchored near land, lessening the gravity of being lost and without communications.

CHAPTER 43

A certain peacefulness floated over me. With it came fatigue.

The Lady Anne rode well at anchor. Her decks were freshly swabbed, and she was nice and clean. A slight breeze was blowing into our anchorage, so Reid unfurled the mizzen sail to keep us pointed into the wind. He also switched on our anchor light.

"I have a suggestion about dinner," I said to Reid, yawning.

"It's going to be a surprise," Reid answered.

"Can we save it for another night?"

Reid's mouth drooped in disappointment. "But I had planned something special."

"I know. And Tracy and I appreciate it. But we're all dead tired. How about we do something easy?"

"I agree," Tracy added. "Let's make something simple tonight and save your special dinner for when we can really enjoy it."

"Well, there's nothing that can't keep another day or two. Let's see what we can throw together."

Since it only took a second for Reid to agree, I suspected he was feeling the impact of the last couple of days too.

We went to the galley and, after a few minutes, decided on wine, cheese, and soup. With everyone helping, it didn't take long to pour wine, cut up cheese, and heat two cans of soup. We carted our bounty topside and ate in the cockpit where we could keep an eye on things. Reid wanted to be absolutely certain the anchor was holding before we all went to sleep.

As was becoming a habit at dinnertime, Reid proposed a toast: "Don't lie, steal, cheat, or drink. But if you must lie, lie in your lover's arms. If you must steal, steal a kiss. If you must cheat, cheat death. And if you must drink, drink with friends."

We clinked glasses and drank. Then Reid held up his glass again. "And here's to Pat. Thanks to her, our batteries are charged, the engine started, and we now know what time it is."

I laughed. "Within thirty minutes or so."

"Within thirty minutes or so," Tracy and Reid echoed as we touched our glasses together.

We then enjoyed our simple meal. For canned soup, it was delicious. The cheese cubes were a nice compliment. After, Tracy opened the Costco box of Snickers bars for dessert. We debated opening a second bottle of wine but decided that in our fatigued state, one was enough.

We were alone in the bay, surrounded by nature's simple splendor: rocks, sea birds, and water. The sun set, bisected by the horizon, casting its last rays in blazing splendor over the sea. Darkness slowly overtook us. Other than the muffled noise from the generator and the occasional bird cry, the anchorage was very peaceful.

After one more unsuccessful *Mayday* attempt, Tracy turned off the radio and the remaining GPS for the night. While she did the few dishes and cleaned up the galley, Reid grabbed a flashlight and he and I walked the deck.

We didn't talk at first, lost in our own thoughts. We were safe tonight. But after?

"Worried about tomorrow?"

I hadn't realized Reid was watching me, or that my anxiety showed so clearly on my face.

"Aren't you?"

He shrugged. "We've done everything we can. What happens next is out of our control."

"Maybe that's what has me so worried."

Reid looked out over the water. "We're pretty good problem solvers, you and I. Whatever happens, we'll cope the best way we can."

I looked away. Figuring out what drained the batteries was one thing. Making a sundial was another. Finding a way back home in uncharted waters, something else entirely.

We were aft. The anchor hadn't budged, and everything

looked good. Reid switched off the generator and I put the ignition key in my pocket.

Now we were plunged into total silence. Except for the anchor light, the enveloping darkness made me shiver. I scurried to the well-lit salon below. Reid followed, closing the hatch behind him.

The salon felt even more cozy and comfortable than usual, perhaps because we were all tired. Tracy suggested watching a movie but since that would mean restarting the generator, we decided against it. Besides, I for one knew I'd be asleep before the opening credits finished running. Whether it was the wine or everything that happened in the last couple of days or the anxiety about tomorrow, exhaustion settled over me like a blanket.

I stood up. "I'm going to bed."

Tracy yawned. "Me too. I'm so tired."

"Me, three," Reid said. He left first, waving goodnight.

Tracy and I were alone in the salon. Suddenly, I didn't feel quite so safe anymore. "Did you notice how dark it is outside?" I said, peering out the window.

Tracy joined me, looking out. "You know what we should do?"

I shot her a look. "What? And don't say have sex with Reid because I'm too damned tired for a three-way."

"Not have sex. But we should sleep with him. We could get the gun and all sleep in his cabin."

I raised an eyebrow. "Not a bad plan," I said. "I'll grab the gun and meet you back here in two minutes. And dress for *sleep*."

Shortly, we were knocking on his door.

"It's unlocked," Reid answered.

Tracy walked in first and I followed, carrying the shotgun.

Reid looked surprised. "Is this a mutiny?"

"We don't want to sleep alone," Tracy said.

"Anchored in the dark by a rocky island that isn't on the charts is kind of creepy," I said.

Reid took the shotgun and propped it beside the nightstand. "Don't expect to get laid," he said. "I'm way too tired."

He crawled into bed and held up the covers. Tracy scooted in. I closed his cabin door, switched off the light, and joined them in bed.

The last thought I had before drifting off was that Tracy was getting her three-way after all.

CHAPTER 44

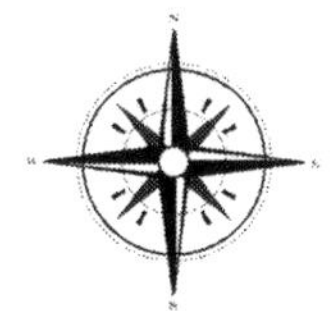

Reid got out of bed, which woke me. The morning sun lit the cabin. Reid grabbed his clothes and went to the head on tiptoes, obviously trying not to wake us. I remained still and quiet and soon he left, closing the door behind him.

Tracy stirred. "Are you awake?"

"Yep." I sat up. "How'd you sleep?"

"Considering it's the first time I've been in bed with a man and didn't fuck him, not bad."

It was my first time, too, but my reaction wasn't quite the same. I was happy for the company. Sex never entered into it.

"Do you think about sex all the time?"

"Pretty much."

And she didn't even blush when she said it.

I swung my legs over the side of the bed. "I must be missing a chromosome," I said.

"You're not missing anything," Tracy said back. "You just need to learn to relax and not take things too seriously. Stick with me, you'll lose your inhibitions in no time."

She climbed out of bed. "Let's go see what Reid's got for breakfast."

The table in the galley was set when we joined Reid. There was coffee in the pot and bagels, cream cheese, and fruit on the plates.

We took our places.

"You girls sleep well?" Reid asked.

I half expected Tracy to answer him the same way she answered me. Instead, she smiled sweetly and said, "Like a rock."

"Pat?"

"The same. Thanks for letting us crash with you last night."

We ate for a few minutes in silence. I was on my second cup of coffee when Tracy said, "So what's the plan for the day?"

"I say we clean up, weigh anchor, and resume course," Reid replied.

"Sounds good," Tracy said.

"I'll start the engine and make some hot water," I added. "I'd like to do laundry."

While Reid and Tracy went to gather clothes to be washed, I retrieved the shotgun from Reid's cabin and put it back in its hiding place. I started a load of community laundry. Tracy and Reid went topside to solar shower on the stern. Tracy winked at me as she followed him up the hatch. I figured she was going to right last night's wrong.

I took my shower alone below. There was enough hot water and I really didn't want to witness whatever Tracy had in mind for Reid. I imagined Tracy was every man's fantasy—willing to have sex anytime, anywhere.

I soaped up. Okay, truth be told, I looked forward to another romp in the sack with Reid. But on my terms—just him and me. I wondered if Tracy would leave him alone long enough for me to fulfill that desire.

I dried off and got dressed. I peeked out the hatch before going topside. Reid and Tracy were dressed, too, so I figured it was safe to come up.

Reid motioned me to join them. "I want you two to raise anchor and get us back into open water. By yourselves."

"Why?" Tracy asked, throwing me a grin. "Are you too tired to help?"

Reid shook his head. "Let's just see if you can do it. Consider it an advanced lesson."

With Tracy at the helm, I went forward to raise the anchor. Since she couldn't hear me very well with the engine running, and since she was also having trouble interpreting my hand signals, I ducked below for one of the handheld radios.

Using the electric windlass and talking to her over the radio worked better than expected. She steered where I needed her to, and she slowed when instructed. Reid was near the dinghy watching, and although he didn't say a word, I could see him smiling.

The anchor hadn't fouled in the rocks and came up effortlessly. When it was securely aboard, Tracy turned *The Lady Anne* toward our exit. With me on the bow radioing directions, she carefully made her way out through the reef. When we were safely back in deep water, she resumed course, 180 degrees magnetic.

"Do we get an *A*?" I asked.

"*A* plus," Reid said. "I'm very impressed with how well you two handled a sixty-eight-footer by yourselves. That was perfectly done."

"The radios helped," Tracy said. "I couldn't hear Pat without them."

"It also helped having an electric windlass," I added. "I'm not sure I'm strong enough to pull in 120 feet of chain by myself."

"You could if you had to," Reid said. "I should have taken a video. I'd show it to all of my future students."

"Thank you," I said.

"We had a great teacher," Tracy said. "Versatile in *so* many ways."

Reid's face reddened while Tracy giggled her little giggle.

CHAPTER 45

Except for the occasional patch of brown seaweed, the water was beautiful shades of blue. There were large, puffy, white clouds overhead and the wind was building. The depth meter read over 1,000 feet, so I felt it safe enough to go below and check on the laundry. It was done. Then rather than run the dryer, I rigged a clothesline in the main salon and hung everything to dry.

When I returned topside, Tracy had turned us into the wind. We raised the sails, lowered the keel, shut off the engine, and resumed our course. Reid popped below and quickly returned, carrying everyone's PFDs. We hadn't worn them much yesterday, but now that things were back to semi-normal, he insisted they be used.

Before long, Reid and I had the sails trimmed nicely. With no GPS, the autopilot didn't work, forcing the helmsman to hand-steer a compass heading, which was difficult enough under normal conditions. With a hand bearing compass in open water and no landmarks to aim for, it was almost impossible. So I took over compass duty, pointing slight course corrections as necessary. *The Lady Anne* was slicing through the waves, heeling a bit, and promising to click off the miles as long as the wind held.

Occasional spray would kiss the foredeck, but the cockpit and helm stayed dry. We had given up on the GPS, satellite phone, and cell phones, but from time to time, did try the radio. The resulting static was discouraging. Still, the radar was working, and we waited patiently for it to display something.

Reid and I were relaxing in the cockpit when there were loud, blowing sounds. We jumped up and looked around, pinpointed the direction of the sounds, and saw plumes of spray.

I stared. More whales. Hundreds of them, directly ahead and on both sides of our bow.

"Should I reverse course?" Tracy called.

"No," Reid answered. "Heave to."

The Lady Anne bobbed on a placid sea as we watched these magnificent creatures swim by. They were a different species than the ones I saw yesterday, still huge but swimming in small groups and headed due east. Several dozen crossed right in front of us. I was sure they were looking directly at us.

We could hear "whale song," low-pitched grunts and groans and higher-pitched chirps. The whales were definitely communicating.

"Do you suppose they are talking about us?" I asked.

"I've never seen this many whales all together before," Reid said, his voice hushed. "In fact, I've never even heard stories about this many whales, at least not in the last few centuries."

After a few minutes, Reid said, "Orcas. They're orcas."

"Killer whales?"

As we watched, another group passed close to *The Lady Anne*.

"Look at that whale in the middle," I said. "What does she have on her back?"

Reid grabbed the binoculars. "It's a baby whale." He was silent for a moment, watching. "I think it's dead."

I snatched the binoculars from his hands. The orca was swimming in the middle of the pod, the lifeless body of her calf flung across her back. After a few minutes, she seemed to tire and slow. I held my breath, awestruck, as a second orca swam beside her and nudged the baby onto its own back.

"Tracy," I called. "You've got to video this."

Tracy got the video camera and began shooting. I couldn't look away.

"I've read about this," Reid said, his own voice hushed. "It was documented in the Pacific Northwest. It's almost a funeral rite."

"Where are they taking the calf?" I asked, wonderstruck by the spectacle unfolding around us.

"I don't know," Reid answered. "It's one of those mysteries of the sea."

Reid went to the helm to check the radar screen. It was clear. Not good.

"Had we encountered this pod at night," he said, "we might have sailed directly into them."

He turned up the sensitivity and blips filled the display.

I don't think I began to breathe normally until the whales were nearly out of sight. And even then, we stayed hove to. We didn't want to hit or be hit by any stragglers.

The whale sighting had been spectacular. Compared to the whales, *The Lady Anne*'s sixty-eight-foot length seemed like a kid's plastic model toy.

Tracy reviewed her footage. "This is fantastic," she said. "I can't wait to get it uploaded."

But Reid looked concerned. "A pod of whales this size should have drawn every tourist boat around," he said. "And at least one local news copter, if not more. Tracy, try another *Mayday*."

Tracy did, but as was becoming the norm, there was no reply but static.

"I want to make the log entry," I said.

Reid nodded and I got the logbook. I recounted what we saw, the behavior of the whales as they carried the lifeless body of a calf, switching turns when one became tired. An almost human expression of grief. I was glad we were here to experience and record it.

After I finished the log entry, we resumed course. This time I took the helm and gave Tracy the compass. She handed it to Reid. She wanted to fish.

She selected a lure with a shiny silver head and long pink and--blue plastic strips concealing a single, large, nasty-looking hook. She said it reminded her of the plastic streamers at the end of the handlebars on her first bicycle.

"I'm glad the whales are gone," I said. "After what we saw, I couldn't bear for you to harm one."

She frowned. "Do you actually think I'd want to hook a whale? A *whale*, for God's sake?"

Reid shook his head and said, "No comment." He took a compass bearing for me.

That lure wasn't out for more than five minutes when the reel started screaming and she hollered, "Fish on, heave to."

My first heave to was unsuccessful. The sails weren't counteracting each other, and I nearly ran over her line.

"This is a monster; don't cut my fucking line," she yelled.

"Get some speed and try again," Reid said, using his calm, reassuring instructor voice.

I exhaled, forcing myself to relax. I replayed the heave to maneuver in my mind. I would give the command to prepare to heave to so the crew would sheet-in all the sails and know not to release the genoa when I tacked. When they acknowledged they were ready, I would tack, bringing the bow through the eye of the wind. When the crew didn't release the genoa, it would backfill, trying to come across to the other side.

I would then gradually ease the mainsail out, further and further, and gradually turn the wheel so the rudder was parallel to the genoa. The mizzen sail would then be eased to match the mainsail. The sails would then counteract each other, forcing *The Lady Anne* to oscillate slowly one way and then back again. We would barely be making way and very inefficiently, the bow swinging over, over, over, slowing, stopping and then back, back, back, slowing, stopping. The process would repeat again and again and again.

As long as the timing of releasing the mainsail and aiming the rudder was proper, the maneuver was fairly simple. Once hove to, the wheel could be locked, thus freeing the helmsman to leave their post. Unless the wind changed significantly, the vessel would stay hove to.

My second attempt was perfect and as we stopped, Tracy yelled for help.

It took all three of us to fight that fish. I was positive the rod would snap, and I begged it to stay in one piece long enough for us to at least see the fish.

"You don't suppose I hooked a whale after all, do you?" Tracy asked, her breath coming in fits and starts.

"I hope not," Reid answered. "Keep reeling."

"If it is, cut the line," Tracy said. She was breathing so hard it was difficult to understand her.

"Just keep reeling."

It seemed like we fought that fish for an eternity, but it finally surfaced right behind the boat and plowed through the waves.

"You caught a marlin, a giant one!" Reid yelled, so excited he jumped up and down. "Pat, get some video of this."

I grabbed my phone and started videoing. The fish broke the water several more times.

I got it all.

Reid's excitement abated when he realized there was no possible way for us to land a fish that big. He looked at Tracy and she nodded. Reluctantly, he used my new rigging knife to cut it loose.

The fish bolted away with a splash and immediately vanished.

Tracy returned the rod to its holder and then collapsed on the deck, eyes closed. She had nothing left, but managed to ask, "Did I lose my lure?"

"Just the hook," Reid replied. "But we can replace it."

"How big was it?" I asked, reviewing my video.

"Probably fifteen feet long and around a thousand pounds I'd guess," Reid answered.

"Will it be okay?"

"The hook will eventually corrode. The fish will be fine."

"Is that the biggest marlin you've ever seen?" Tracy asked from her prone position on the deck. Her eyes were still closed but her breathing was returning to normal.

"Without a doubt. I don't know what Charles and his late wife ever caught, but this has got to be *The Lady Anne*'s record, especially for catch and release."

Reid took over the helm and got us back on course while I got Tracy a bottle of water and helped her sit up.

"That fish was beautiful. I hope we didn't hurt it," she said as she drank.

"As quickly as it swam away, I'm sure it's okay," I said. Then I replayed my video for her.

"Hey, you two, next time catch something that will fit on the grill," Reid said.

Tracy looked up at me. "Bring me the logbook please," she said. "That was the biggest thing I've ever caught! It deserves an entry."

"Was landing it better than sex?" Reid asked, grinning.

I handed Tracy the logbook and she started writing. When she finished her entry, she said, "I don't know about better, but it was definitely a rush."

She handed the logbook back to me.

"You look exhausted. Are you all right?" I asked.

"I could really use a tall glass of cold chocolate milk." She looked a little glassy eyed. "Between the sex earlier and the giant fish just now, I'm feeling the need."

"Wait right here," I said and headed below. We didn't have chocolate milk, but I could put together a good substitute.

I returned topside and handed her a Snickers bar and a coffee cup.

She looked in the cup and asked, "Is this half and half?" She thrust the cup back at me. "Half and half is not milk."

"It most certainly is, more or less. It's made from milk and cream. Add a Snickers bar, and presto, chocolate and milk. Chocolate milk."

"She's got you there," Reid said.

Tracy made a face and took a sip.

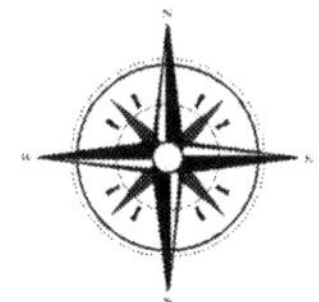

After she finished her "chocolate milk," Tracy made her way to the cockpit table, took a seat, and promptly fell asleep. Sitting up. Ten minutes later, she was snoring.

I joined Reid at the helm, taking periodic compass readings to keep us on course. We were discussing her marlin when the radar displayed a large set of blips at twenty-three miles. After five minutes, the contact was holding steady and appeared to be land. Even though nothing was visible with the binoculars, we made a course change.

I noticed dolphins ahead of us, so I grabbed my phone and carefully made my way forward. I got some video of four of them riding our bow wake.

Swimming in a tight formation, they would surface to breathe, often in unison. One of them seemed to regularly leap out of the water, making a smacking sound upon re-entry. While darting across our bow, they would get so close I was sure we would hit them, but then they would veer away at the last second.

More dolphins appeared. Soon there were about twenty on both sides of the bow. I watched as one pair came in fast from the side, like torpedoes. They didn't hit us but changed direction, accelerated, and swam ahead of the whole group, like they were the new leaders.

Some swam so close together, it looked like they intentionally bumped each other. They were regularly leaning onto their sides, exposing their white underbellies. I sensed they were watching me watching them.

I looked out a little further. What had been about twenty was now one hundred, maybe more. They seemed to rotate in closer, as if in some kind of pattern, swim alongside for a bit, and then move away, only to be quickly replaced by new ones.

These dolphins were very adept at avoiding a collision with our bow. I feared if we did happen to accidentally hit one, we would seriously injure it. It seemed to be a game of chicken, but the dolphins looked happy, playful, and curious, not stressed.

Their intelligence was abundantly clear. The squeaking and clicking noises were obvious communications. The more I watched, the more I was convinced that their orchestrated movements were not random frolicking. These dolphins were "talking" about us and then they were trading places with their friends so they could see. I wondered if they were deciding if we were friend or foe.

I made my way back to the helm so Reid could watch for a while. In my exuberance, I accidentally woke Tracy. She was barely awake, but when she heard there were one hundred dolphins surfing in our bow wake, she insisted on going forward with the video camera.

The view from the bow was spectacular and I debated locking the wheel and rejoining them. But I was at the helm. Safety had to come first. Besides, there were dolphins all around us.

The hundred dolphins grew to several hundred. I had never seen so many dolphins. Everywhere I looked they were surfacing and jumping. So much was happening, I didn't know where to look first. I held my course and enjoyed the once-in-a-lifetime spectacle. I hoped Tracy was getting it all on video. This was likely more award-winning stuff.

Reid and Tracy rejoined me at the helm. They were grinning like crazy.

"Wow, I've never seen anything like this," Tracy exclaimed.

"Me either," I added. "Have you, Reid?"

"Once during a Baja Ha-Ha race, we sailed through three or four hundred, but nothing like this." His smile betrayed his excitement.

"Do you suppose they are swimming with us, or we are just passing through their waters?" I asked.

"There's one way to find out," Reid replied. "We could heave to and see if they stick around."

So I did, executing the stop this time on my first attempt.

As *The Lady Anne* oscillated slowly one way and then back again, the dolphins moved in closer. Many of them stopped right next to us, sticking their heads out of the water and making all kinds of dolphin noises. Tracy got the whole thing on video.

What had been cool before was now incredible. There were probably over a hundred dolphins less that twenty feet away, bobbing out of the water, talking to us.

Reid stripped down to his underwear and said, "Watch this."

With that, he dove off the side and swam toward them.

He moved so fast, I didn't have a chance to argue him out of it. I was leery of him being in the water, but he hadn't asked permission. I told Tracy to keep videoing.

Reid hadn't swum very far when he was surrounded by dolphins. They were close enough to touch and he would grab their dorsal fin and get towed a short distance before letting go and catching another ride.

He hollered that one of us could join him.

I shook my head. "No, thank you. I like the view from here just fine."

Tracy watched for a moment. "Are you sure you don't want to go in?" she asked. "Because I think I do. It looks like fun."

"Go ahead," I said. "But remember dolphins aren't the only fish in the sea. Remember the shark that took your fish the other day."

I probably shouldn't have mentioned it, because the expression on her face told me she did remember—vividly. If she'd been inclined to go swimming, that comment ended it.

Reid swam back closer. "Pat, will you get my mask? As long as I'm in the water, I might as well check the hull."

I went below and found it in his duffel bag.

"Don't drop it," I said, handing it to him from the swim platform.

Accompanied by several dolphins, Reid swam around the boat. I kept a lookout for any non-dolphin dorsal fins. He soon reported the hull was fine and then resumed playing with the dolphins.

After another twenty minutes or so, he said he was getting cold. As he headed back, two dolphins sandwiched him between them and towed him back to the boat. Tracy got that on video too. She was really pleased with what was sure to be great footage.

Reid made his way to the swim platform and climbed aboard.

I handed him a towel. He barely used it before rushing below. He emerged a moment later carrying his trumpet. Hefting it, he said, "I wonder how they'll react to music?"

"I'll keep the camera going. Let's see," Tracy said.

"Do you know any good dolphin music?" I said, chuckling.

"Let's see what happens with a Beatles' song about an octopus."

With that he went down to the swim platform and began playing "Octopus's Garden."

Immediately, fifty dolphins right behind the boat poked their heads out of the water. They faced the boat and quieted, as if listening to the music.

Tracy moved nearer Reid to get clear audio.

I glanced to my right. On the port side, several hundred dolphins were partway out of the water, also looking and listening. It was the same to starboard. I tapped Tracy's shoulder and pointed. She slowly panned all around.

When I looked back toward Reid, what had been fifty a moment ago had increased tenfold. I also noticed that except for the music, it was suddenly quiet. The dolphins had ceased making noise, as if listening politely.

Reid was obviously enjoying the spectacle. He played for ten minutes and as the last note faded away, every one of the dolphins submerged. What had looked like headstones in a cemetery was now bare ocean.

"Tell me you got that," I said to Tracy, my mind reeling at what had just happened.

She smiled and nodded. "Where do you think they all went?"

The words had just left her lips when the dolphins were back, circling the boat. Their level of chattering increased to its loudest level yet. A few were even jumping clear out of the water. Some would protrude their heads and then violently shake them up and down.

"I think they're applauding," I said. "Tracy, keep the camera going. Reid, play another one!"

Reid began playing. Once again, the dolphins surfaced, quietly watching and listening.

Reid didn't play as long this time. When he finished, he faced the nearest dolphin and loudly announced, "That was 'Beyond the Sea' by Bobby Darin."

"Are you talking to the dolphins?" I asked, laughing.

As the dolphins submerged and resumed their circling, he added, "Thank you very much. I'll be here all week."

Several dozen dolphins surfaced in unison and responded with more chattering and violent headshaking.

I was dumbstruck. Did they understand him?

Reid obviously thought so, because he smiled a giant smile and loudly thanked the dolphins again. And again, they chattered back. Our two species may not have been speaking the same language, but we were definitely communicating. It was unbelievable.

Finally, it was time to go. At Reid's command, I "unheaved to" by releasing the genoa to the side it wanted to be on and centered the rudder. *The Lady Anne* immediately accelerated on a beam reach.

Tracy shouted out to the dolphins, "We've got to go but maybe we'll see you later."

There was some more chattering and then as if on cue, the dolphins headed away from us.

Reid, Tracy, and I looked at each other. We may have been

lost, but at that moment, I'd guess not one of us would have traded today's experiences for a working helm compass.

Within a few minutes, all but a handful of the dolphins were out of sight.

The few that remained took up position near our bow. Tracy got a little more video and then joined me at the helm.

CHAPTER 47

Reid showered with a solar shower and quickly dressed, but instead of joining us at the helm, he ducked below and returned with a small, dark, blue-black lure.

"During my time racing in Mexico," he said, attaching the lure to a fishing line, "we'd often troll a deep line when we saw dolphins because tuna often swim below them. Let's see if it holds true here too."

He held the pole out to Tracy, but she shook her head. "I'm going to steer for a while. You two have at it."

Reid tried to let the lure out, but we were going too fast and the lure didn't sink but just bounced along the surface, twisting the line.

I furled the genoa, reducing our speed significantly while Reid attached a large weight in front of the lure. This time, Reid was able to get the lure out.

Judging from the steep angle of the line, it had gone pretty deep. He then handed me the rod. I could feel the lure's steady tug, tug, tug. Rather than place the rod in the holder, I decided to hold it.

In less than five minutes, I felt a serious jerk. The line began playing out. I shouted, "Fish on."

I held the rod tightly, nearly losing my balance when the fish took the line. Reid scrambled over and steadied me.

With the genoa furled, Tracy couldn't heave to, so Reid told her to stow the mizzen sail and partially furl the mainsail. She did as instructed, and *The Lady Anne* slowed way down, barely making way. Tracy locked the wheel and joined us at the helm.

This fish didn't head toward the surface but instead went deeper. And then stopped. I began to reel, pumping the rod up and down as Tracy had done earlier. It was tedious work, but I managed to gain a bit of line each time.

I would get the fish in close enough to glimpse, but not close enough to identify, and then the fish would dive again, taking line back out and forcing me to start pumping and reeling all over again.

The fish sounded a few more times, but each dive was shallower. I was getting tired but refused to quit. Eventually I brought the fish a few feet from the stern.

It was a giant tuna. The upper half was blue and the lower part was silvery white. The tuna had little stubby fins between its dorsal and tail. It was around six feet long, but it was very thick and I guessed it weighed two hundred pounds or more.

There was no way we could eat two hundred pounds of tuna, nor did we have freezer space to store it. We had to let it go, but not before Tracy got the camera and shot a video of me smiling and pointing at my big tuna.

Reid managed to release the fish and save the lure on his first attempt. The tuna bled a little but rested for thirty seconds or so before disappearing out of sight.

As I reeled in the slack line, Reid hollered, "Shark," and pointed. We watched as a fin approached from directly astern. Tracy started the camera.

"The blood drew it in," Reid said, quickly exiting the swim platform, pliers in hand.

"It's pretty fair sized. Any idea what kind it is?" I asked.

Before Reid could answer, five dolphins appeared from out of nowhere. They swam straight for the shark, forcing it to turn.

"Are those dolphins crazy?" Tracy blurted out. "They're going to get eaten."

Two dolphins passed right in front of the shark. I watched in horror as the shark opened its mouth, but the dolphins were too fast and darted away.

Another dolphin dove right under the shark, forcing the shark to stop and turn. One more dolphin sped by on the other side. The shark opened its mouth, turned, and made a big splash but was way too slow.

Then, a single dolphin came up from below and rammed the shark in its belly. The shark rolled slightly. Before it could right itself, another dolphin rammed it full speed, directly into its side. We heard the impact. The shark rolled nearly all the way over.

"Tell me you're getting this?" Reid asked, his usually calm voice betraying his excitement.

"I'm getting it," Tracy replied. "I didn't know dolphins could fight a shark."

"They have quickness and agility in their favor. The shark is bigger but slower," I said.

"But he has all the teeth," Tracy pointed out.

"It's five smart dolphins to one dumb shark," Reid said. "I'll bet on the dolphins."

The shark had righted itself and began swimming away.

We watched as the dolphins pursued it, ramming it from one side and then the other. After about the third hit, the shark submerged. We watched but didn't see it resurface.

"Do you suppose they killed it?" I asked.

"Don't know," Reid said. "But they certainly drove it away."

Just then, the dolphins began leaping out of the water and chattering.

"Are they all there?" Tracy asked.

"I think so," Reid said.

One by one, the dolphins—all five of them—splashed directly astern.

"Are they celebrating?" Tracy asked.

"It certainly looks that way," I said.

"Then let's help them." Reid retrieved his trumpet, went to the swim platform, and began playing.

"Man, can that guy play," I whispered to Tracy. "Recognize the song?"

She smiled and nodded as she videoed. "The theme from *The Lone Ranger*, right?"

I laughed. "Close."

The dolphins circled behind us, listening.

After he finished, Reid announced, "Thank you my dolphin friends. I hope you enjoyed the 'William Tell Overture' by Rossini."

Tracy raised an eyebrow. "I thought that was the theme from *The Lone Ranger*."

"The 'William Tell Overture' was used for *The Lone Ranger* theme."

"Well, in any case, it was really cool."

Reid gave a little bow. "Glad you liked it."

The dolphins weren't behind us any longer. We unfurled all the sails and resumed course toward the radar contact. Tracy and I went forward to see if the dolphins were swimming by the bow, but they were gone.

The conditions were perfect for sailing, and after a little sail trim, the three of us watched the miles tick off as the foamy ocean undulated beneath us.

We sailed close to a large patch of floating brown seaweed. There were hundreds, maybe thousands of birds flying, diving, and squawking like crazy. It looked like a good place to troll but we decided against it. We were too tired for another battle if a big one happened to hit.

"The radar shows what looks like land is still fourteen miles away," Tracy said.

"Yes," Reid said, waiting.

"How far away from land do birds normally fly?"

"Gulls can fly fifty miles easily," Reid said. "Larger birds, farther than that, and really large birds, like the albatross, can cross oceans."

At seven miles away, land was clearly visible without needing the binoculars. Tracy tried the radio but there were no replies to her repeated hails. There was also no phone service. The lack of communication was frustrating, but we held our course.

We continued to see plenty of seaweed and birds. Another large dorsal fin surfaced next to us and swam alongside, as if to check us out. It was a hammerhead. Tracy stayed at the helm while Reid and I moved to the lifeline for a closer look.

"That is one big shark," I said.

Reid stood even to the front edge of its hammer, and I positioned myself with the tip of its tail.

I walked off the distance—six paces, or about eighteen feet.

The shark didn't appear aggressive, only curious. Reid switched places with Tracy so she could video it. Soon the shark submerged. If it was following us, we couldn't tell. I glanced around for dolphins but didn't see any.

"Do you suppose those dolphins could have driven that big guy away?" I asked, returning to the safety of the helm. Seeing a big shark that close made me nervous.

"The way they coordinated their attack earlier, they probably could handle any shark smaller than ten to twelve feet," Reid answered. "This one, or a big tiger or great white, might be pushing it."

"I've never seen a hammerhead in the wild before," Tracy said.

"I sailed through a school of them migrating once," Reid

said. "I was also lucky enough to see one eat a ray when I was diving."

"What happened?" Tracy asked.

"I was diving with a group of sailors near Cabo when a nice hammerhead swam past. It was about a ten footer, but didn't seem interested in us. It had no doubt seen divers in that spot before. We watched it swimming very leisurely, just above the bottom. It suddenly dove down, headfirst. When the dust cleared, it was eating a ray that had been hiding in the sand. The ray probably had a three-foot wingspan, but the shark killed it with no problem. Unfortunately, none of us had an underwater camera and we had to leave when other sharks showed up."

"They look weird if you ask me," Tracy said.

"They are apex predators, evolving over centuries. Their wide-set eyes and large head give them excellent vision and highly refined senses. While most sharks don't bother humans, one that big, especially a hammerhead, is not to be underestimated, ever."

"Can I ask you a favor?" I said then, looking straight at Reid.

"Go ahead."

"Would you please not go swimming anymore? When you dove into the water to swim with the dolphins, I was nervous. Now that we know there are big sharks in the water, I'd appreciate it if you'd stay aboard."

Tracy nodded. "I agree." She winked. "After all, you might

lose an appendage I've grown very fond of. That would bite. Get it? Bite?"

Reid and I both groaned. Once more, Tracy had managed to infuse sex into an entirely different subject. I shook my head and rolled my eyes.

But Reid held up a hand. "Okay, I promise. No more swimming with the fishes."

Tracy was reviewing some of her video, sure that everything she had shot in the last day or two was sure to go viral, when it suddenly got dark.

I looked up, expecting to see clouds blocking the sun. It wasn't clouds. It was a giant flock of birds. There must have been ten thousand, flying right over us.

Reid used the binoculars and reported the birds had a fairly big head and a light or white body. Their wings were brown, with a white stripe. He said they might be pelicans, but he wasn't positive. Tracy shot some more video.

"Let's hope they keep moving," I said. "That's all we need, a real poop deck."

As they flew away, the shadows cleared.

We impatiently waited as *The Lady Anne* made way and closed the distance to land. We were anxious to find a marina and report what we had been through.

Tracy had left the cockpit and was at the lifeline glassing when she shouted, "Something's coming at us, port side."

I took the helm from Reid and he scrambled toward her. I watched as she handed him the binoculars and pointed to port, slightly forward. I couldn't see anything, but Tracy was still pointing. She looked excited. I got ready to change course.

Finally Reid turned toward me and said, "It's just a bunch of low-flying birds, hold your course."

They exchanged the binoculars a few times. I still couldn't see anything.

"Correction," Reid said. "Those aren't birds, they're flying fish."

Tracy came back to the cockpit and got the video camera. She was really smiling and said, "There are flying fish everywhere. Thousands of them."

She went to the port side and began videoing. Reid held her with one hand and supported himself against the shroud with the other. I finally saw what they were watching. They did look like birds making splashes between the waves.

A few minutes later they crossed us. The fish were about a foot long and would launch out of a wave and glide one hundred feet or so before reentering the water. Some of them got two to three feet above the waves. I heard a *thud* as one crashed into our hull. It wasn't heavy enough to do any damage, at least not to us.

The thuds got more frequent. At one point, it sounded like a bag of microwave popcorn. Soon there were flying fish floating behind us.

"Do you suppose they're dead or just stunned?" I asked, pointing.

"The impact is killing them," Reid shouted. "Heave to."

It seemed to take forever to get stopped and I continued to

hear thuds. Eventually the thuds subsided as the massive school passed by.

"We've got company," Reid said and pointed.

Tracy moved to a better position aft and resumed videoing.

Ten sharks had closed in on the dead flying fish that were scattered around us. Their dorsal fins weren't very big, and Reid said they were probably only four to five feet long.

Tracy stopped the camera and said, "Let's go. I don't want to see this. I feel terrible."

I got back underway, leaving the sharks astern. What had started out very cool was now very sad.

CHAPTER 49

I resumed course and we sailed on. The depth changed about one-half mile out, so I changed course and paralleled the shoreline. Tracy tried the radio while Reid used the binoculars and reported.

"The shore is really rocky. The vegetation is low and scattered. There are no palm trees. There are no sandy beaches. There are no visible buildings, roads, towers, structures, or wires."

"Do you see anything all?" I asked.

"Just lots of birds."

"That's it?" Tracy asked. "Lots of birds?"

"Hold your course, but so far, this is the most inhospitable looking island I have ever seen."

Tracy tried the radio again and then took a break. She checked her cell phone but there was no service.

Wave after wave passed under *The Lady Anne*'s bow. We continued sailing in silence. Reid kept glassing but the coastline stayed a rocky jumble of boulders and crashing waves. After nearly an hour, we couldn't find anything even remotely resembling a landing. There were no signs of civilization.

We closed on a large rock ahead rising out of the water, a hundred feet high. It was separated from the shore by a narrow channel. The rock was white above the waterline. It looked like snow in the sun, but with all the birds around, we knew better. There were several small caves along the waterline.

Tracy wanted to drive, so I handed off the helm. She continued to parallel the shoreline, watching the depth. It had shallowed considerably. "Can we anchor in ninety feet?" she asked.

"We can if we have to, but let's keep going," Reid answered. "This is too exposed for a relaxing night's sleep."

Beyond the tall rock was another white rock, followed by another and then another. I furled the genoa and we slowed down.

Reid reported what looked like a large bay just beyond a narrow channel, guarded by stone sentinels. Tracy changed course, following his pointing. He asked me to slow us more, so I furled the sails until we were just making two knots.

The water was blueish and looked plenty deep, and the entrance was certainly wide enough for *The Lady Anne* to pass. The floating birds were mostly stationary, indicating negligible current, if any.

We agreed to motor in and check it out. The engine started right up with no problems. Tracy retracted our keel.

Reid went clear forward and began lookout duties. I stationed myself halfway so I could relay instructions. Tracy turned *The Lady Anne* toward the entrance and increased the throttle slightly.

"Do you see any buoys or channel markers?" she asked.

Neither Reid nor I saw any.

She tried the radio again but there was no response.

"What's our depth?" Reid asked.

I relayed that is was sixty feet. He wanted to know when it hit forty. Tracy proceeded slowly. We easily cleared the channel.

The bay was mushroom shaped and large enough for several vessels our size to anchor. Tracy slowed down and made a gradual circle while Reid continued to glass and report.

The bay appeared deserted and the shoreline was rocky and uninviting. The vegetation was minimal. There was just one low spot that looked like a possible dinghy landing site. The bay seemed safe enough to anchor for the evening.

Tracy picked a shady spot near the cliffs, fifty feet deep, and we dropped anchor. Reid let out all two hundred fifty feet of chain plus an additional one hundred feet of the nylon. While we waited to see if our anchoring was successful, we kept the engine running. Although the solar panels were keeping the batteries charged, I wanted hot water for a real shower.

There were several flying fish that had landed on our deck. I had never seen one close-up before. It was interesting how their fins were high on their sides and shaped liked airplane wings. No wonder they could glide so far. I dropped them over the side.

The natural harbor was partially surrounded by white cliffs, about fifty to one hundred feet high. The sides were fairly steep, and it would have been a tough climb to the top.

The rocky cliffs had sparse vegetation. There were small trees growing from between the rocks. About half of them were dead and the other half were windblown. None of them were straight or lush or more than five feet tall. It was obvious they fought hard for survival. It seemed a bleak place to live, even for a tree. We could hear birds squawking and calling.

The water was the color of turquoise and there were small fish darting about. We didn't see anything big enough to fish for, but the small ones were plentiful. Reid decided we should break out the dinghy and go ashore before dinner. The crane worked perfectly and the three of us soon had the dinghy off-loaded. Reid tied it to the stern.

The anchor was holding, so we packed a few things, shut down the engine, closed the hatch, and launched the dinghy.

Tracy got it started and drove while Reid and I watched *The Lady Anne* bob at anchor. She really was a spectacular vessel, anchored majestically in this less-than-idyllic setting.

We zoomed across the anchorage and quickly arrived at our destination. The landing was rocky but manageable. We got our feet wet but were soon ashore. Reid wrapped the bow line around a big rock and made it fast. The dinghy was secured, and *The Lady Anne* still looked stable. Tracy shot a little video and then we moved inshore.

CHAPTER 50

We carefully made our way over the rocks and through a patch of wet sand. Except it wasn't sand. We were walking on seashells, thousands of shells laying in the sand. They ranged from small ones the size of your thumb to some as large as a cucumber. There were speckled, striped, and patterned shells, along with some shells that had very intricate designs.

Reid was leery of the some of the shells. He had seen them before when diving the reefs and kelp beds in Southern California waters. He explained that cone snails had cone-shaped shells. While brightly colored with intricate patterns made them appealing to pick up, there was a living creature inside.

The small cone snails stung like a bee, but the larger ones could puncture wetsuit gloves and their sting could be fatal.

He helped Tracy pick out three of the benign ones for souvenirs.

"Well, at least a few shells from here won't be missed," Tracy said, pocketing her finds.

We tried to step lightly, but crunching shells was unavoidable. Reid shook his head. "I can't believe craft vendors haven't raided this spot. Some of these would bring a small fortune back home."

Over and around the shells, crabs scuttled. And once we finally made our way out of the band of seashells, we were able to climb up on some rocks and look back. The dinghy was still secured and *The Lady Anne* looked fine, so we pressed on.

Where there had been crabs before, now there were lizards scurrying all about us. They were gray, about a foot long, and had a brownish patch along their backs. Running down the center of the brown patch was a chalky white stripe. All the lizards had the same markings. There were no crabs among the lizards.

About two hundred yards inland, we were stopped by a large crevice, four feet across and thirty to forty feet deep, running in both directions as far as we could see. At some point in time, it had cleanly separated from the other side.

"Must have been a hell of an earthquake," Reid said.

"Glad we missed it," I said.

Tracy eyed the fissure. "It's not that wide. We can jump it and keep exploring."

Reid shook his head. "If any of us missed and fell, we'd

have another set of problems. We'd better start back. We can catch a few of those good-looking crabs on shell beach for a future dinner."

"Tonight?" I asked eagerly. Crab was one of my favorites.

He shook his head. "Not tonight. I've already got that covered."

Tracy made one final video of the area. When we got back to shore, we put the camera in the dinghy and the three of us started in catching crabs. They were about eight inches across, reddish in color, with black at the ends of their claws. They were really easy to catch, and we quickly had fifteen between us—plenty for a meal, maybe two.

Reid unloaded the anchor storage compartment and we used that for temporary crab storage. We returned with our bounty to *The Lady Anne*. While Reid secured the dinghy, Tracy and I carefully transferred the crabs to the fish box.

Reid went below to make dinner while Tracy used a solar shower on the stern. I took my shower below. When I returned topside to straighten up the cockpit, Tracy had already changed clothes and was combing her hair. Reid brought up a pitcher of boat drinks and poured the first round. We sipped while he started the grill.

While Tracy and I were enjoying cocktails, four dolphins circled the boat. We could hear them clicking and chattering. We wondered if they were the same ones that had chased the shark away earlier. Were they on sentinel duty protecting us?

Reid returned carrying a platter of brats and peppers.

"Voila," he said. "I am going to make you my special beer brats and peppers."

We followed him to the grill and watched as he set the brats to grill then halved and seeded the peppers, making little boats. He sprinkled them with Italian dressing, basil and Parmesan cheese and grilled them until they were black on the bottom.

They looked so delicious Tracy grabbed her camera and started videoing.

Before the brats were fully cooked, he took them off the grill, split them lengthwise, added chopped green onion, sprinkled them with crumbled cheese and then returned them to the grill.

It was hard to pull ourselves away, but Tracy and I set the cockpit table. I put out a bag of chips and the mustard.

And waited for Reid to bring us our dinner.

Finally, he did.

"These brats taste heavenly," I said. "I have never had a brat prepared like this."

"And these aren't my best," Reid said. "When we get back, I'll have you two over and I'll make them the way they should be. I'll smoke them first, use jalapeño cheddar, and have better mustard."

I finished my first brat and took a second. "I can't imagine anything better than this."

"Well, I'm in," Tracy said, "Hand me another brat and another pepper."

We finished eating and polished off the blender of drinks.

Reid offered to make a second one, but Tracy and I both declined. We were feeling fine and didn't want to push it. It was the perfect meal to end a great day of sailing.

In between savoring Reid's grill craft and making toasts about the dolphins, Tracy dropped a couple of potato chips. Scooping them up, she threw the chips toward the side, aiming for the water. Unfortunately she didn't throw them far enough and they fluttered down to the deck, landing just below the lifeline.

Immediately, a large gray gull swooped in, and squawking loudly, landed on the deck. It devoured those chips like it hadn't eaten in weeks. Before I knew what was happening, another gull flew right at us, just missing our heads. I didn't even have time to duck. That second bird startled me so much, I knocked over the bag of chips and spilled my drink.

Two or three more gulls immediately dived-bombed the cockpit. I quickly picked up the fallen chips and threw them way over the side, thinking the birds would follow.

No such luck. More gulls swooped in. One gull got caught in Tracy's hair. She screamed, knocked it free, and hustled below.

Flinging chips over the side had only intensified the feeding frenzy. Gulls descended from the rocks all around us. Those big gulls were strafing the boat, squawking nosily, and darting all around us.

Hundreds of them left the rocks and headed for us. I grabbed the food from the table and passed it down to Tracy. Then I joined her below. From the hatch, I saw Reid still trying to finish his meal. Two loud, angry gulls landed directly on the table. He tried to shoo them away, but they pecked at him.

Tracy grabbed the camera. "This is a sight too good to miss!" She went topside, videoing those two gulls pecking at Reid, his plate, and even at each other.

The birds had gone berserk. Puffs of feathers floated around us as gulls crashed into the rigging. One gull got caught on the fishing lure and freed itself with a great loss of feathers. Reid grabbed the rod so the bird wouldn't drag it away.

Another of the gulls landed on the grill, which was still hot, and started screaming. It must have been in too much pain to fly away so Reid grabbed it and threw it astern, slamming the grill lid closed.

A big gull smacked Tracy in the back of her head. That was the end of the videoing. She screeched and rejoined me below. All we could do was watch the spectacle through the hatchway. When a gull got too close to the hatch, I'd hit it with the food platter, driving it away.

We could barely see through the cloud of feathers. Reid was shooing birds away, but for every one he chased off, a dozen would take its place. Our vessel was being swarmed. A gull with a bloody wing hobbled by, being chased by other gulls. It was savage.

"Fuck this," I said, handing Tracy the platter.

She moved out of my way when I headed topside with the shotgun.

Reid saw me coming and met me in the cockpit.

"Be very careful with that." He spoke directly in my ear.

"I'm just going to scare them," I yelled above the gull's racket.

"Get clear of the rigging and point the barrel well over the side. That thing will put a hole in whatever it hits. Don't sink us."

I made my way aft and pointed the gun out and slightly up. Reid stood next to me and held my arm. He told me when I was clear to fire. I took a breath, switched off the safety, and pulled the trigger.

Boom went the shotgun.

Whoosh went the sound of a hundred birds fleeing in panic.

I cycled the next shell and fired a second blast.

Within ten seconds, the birds were gone. Except for the ringing in my ears, it was suddenly quiet. There were still feathers floating everywhere, but the birds were headed for the rocks.

Tracy joined us aft. She said there were still some birds aboard. We looked and there were several gulls that had bloody wings. They would scoot out of our way but couldn't take off.

"They probably got hurt when they flew into the shrouds," Reid said. "Hitting those wire cables likely broke their wings."

"What are we going to do with them?" Tracy asked.

"I know what I'm not going to do with them." Reid

picked up an injured gull who promptly tried to peck him. "I'm not starting a bird hospital."

He brought it to the swim platform and let it go in the water. It squawked loudly and moved away.

Tracy and I helped gather injured birds and place them in the water. Then we surveyed the carnage our winged visitors had inflicted. There were feathers and bird poop everywhere. The beautiful *Lady Anne* was trashed.

"Think you shot any?" Tracy asked.

"I wasn't aiming," I said, laughing. "And I don't see any bodies floating around."

"Too bad," she replied. "What a fucking mess."

Reid joined us with brooms, mops, buckets, and sponges. "We've got to clean this up before the morning sun bakes the poop."

He swept feathers over the side while Tracy and I cleaned and scrubbed poop off of everything. The birds had even trashed the dinghy, so we washed that as well. Then we swabbed the decks.

I discovered that one of the solar showers was leaking. It looked like a bird had pecked a hole in it. I patched it with duct tape. I also reloaded the gun and put it away.

We regrouped below, turning on the anchor light and closing the hatch for the night. While Tracy and I did the dishes, Reid looked through Charles's movie collection.

"No way," he shouted, startling us both. He waved a DVD. "Movie time," he said. "Meet me in your cabin."

He started the generator and disappeared down the passageway.

"Whatever he found, he seems very pleased," I said.

"Do you suppose there will be as much action on the screen as there will be in the bed?" Tracy asked, wiggling her ass.

"Don't tell me cleaning up bird shit made you horny?"

"Breathing makes me horny. This vacation makes me horny."

As we walked into our cabin, Reid began playing an upbeat song. I recognized it immediately. I knew what movie Reid had found in Charles's stash.

Reid was in the middle of the bed, patting each side. Without a moment's hesitation, Tracy took off her clothes and joined him.

I hesitated. Tracy's remark about our "vacation" made me realize the uneasy gut feeling I'd experienced since seeing those UFOs was growing stronger.

"Pat?" Reid asked. "Aren't you going to join us?"

"Not right now," I said. "Besides, I've seen this one."

Reid shrugged and started the movie. The credits hadn't finished rolling on Alfred Hitchcock's *The Birds* before Reid and Tracy were entertaining themselves. Either Tracy had seen it before too, or it was too tame after our recent experience. In any case, she was looking for a different kind of action.

I went into the salon, pulled some charts from the library, and settled in to do some research. I couldn't find anything resembling our island, not even anything close, on any chart I consulted. Thinking of the electrical disturbance we encountered, coupled with the schools of whales and dolphins that in our modern day had no parallel and the complete radio silence that greeted every distress signal we'd sent, brought me to a chilling conclusion.

I believed I knew where we were.

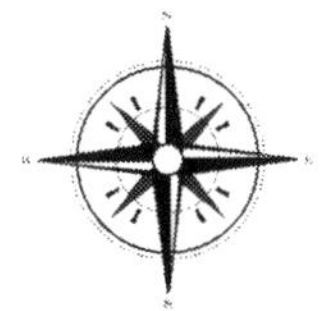

CHAPTER 51

I was awakened the next morning by Reid gently shaking my arm.

"You slept here last night?" he said.

I sat up, looking around. I didn't even remember moving from the table where I was reviewing charts to the recliner in the salon, but evidently I had. I rubbed my eyes and stood. "Doesn't appear you missed me," I said.

Whether it was my tone or guilt that neither he nor Tracy *had* missed me, Reid's face reddened. "We'll stay in my cabin from now on," he said.

"So, it's *we* now. You and Tracy are officially a couple."

"A couple maybe," Tracy said, appearing from the stateroom. "Doesn't mean it's exclusive. Always up for a threesome."

I shook my head. "I'm going topside."

"We'll prepare breakfast," Reid said.

I left them and made my way on deck. The sun was already high in the sky and the water rippled in a gentle offshore breeze. It looked like it was going to be another beautiful day.

While Reid and Tracy made breakfast below, I wondered how I was going to tell them what conclusion I came to last night.

I went to the stern and thought about busying myself with a little casting. But I didn't. I just stood there, admiring the desolate beauty of the cove.

Finally, I heard Reid announce that breakfast was ready. I joined them below.

Tracy had that "just fucked" look and they both looked guilty. Tracy avoided making eye contact with me.

"Really?" I said. "Again?"

I picked up a bagel from the plate on the galley table. "The least you could have done was toast the bagels," I muttered.

We ate for a few minutes in awkward silence. I breathed a sigh and tapped the rim of my coffee cup. "I believe I know what happened to us and where we are."

Reid and Tracy stopped eating and gave me their attention.

"I believe that we went through an electromagnetic doorway into the Bermuda Triangle. And we are now on the other side of that doorway."

Tracy scoffed. "That's not overly helpful."

I ignored her sarcasm. "I can't find this spot on any chart, plus the huge increase in the amount of sea life we have encountered would support a theory I've developed."

Reid leaned toward me. "What theory?"

"First, there are some facts we have to accept—like the lights we encountered that first night were UFOs."

They both nodded.

"If that's the case, an alien being would not want to get discovered. They were operating in an area known for unexplained disappearances precisely because of that. But we took video, in effect documenting their existence."

"That's ridiculous," Tracy snapped. "So why didn't they vaporize us or something?"

But Reid nodded. "Beings advanced enough for space travel may also be more enlightened than we are. Perhaps they avoid killing less-advanced species, like us, unless they can't avoid it."

I continued. "When we took the video, they needed to get rid of us. But since they couldn't or didn't want to kill us, they came up with an alternative, perhaps as they have in the past —send us somewhere where we couldn't show anyone our video."

"Like where?" Tracy asked, her tone still reflecting skepticism. "A parallel universe?"

"Maybe," I answered. "But I was thinking more along the lines of time travel."

"You think the aliens sent us through time to keep us from

showing our video of them?" She stared. "Do you have any idea how crazy that sounds?"

"Yes, I do. It seemed pretty obvious to me at the time of the electrical disturbance that we entered some kind of a portal or tunnel. We exited the tunnel in the same general area, only at a different time, likely an earlier time. Judging from the abundant sea life, a much earlier time."

"That would explain the fact that we've encountered no other people," Reid said. "And why no one has responded to our distress calls. We're virtually alone on the sea."

Tracy rounded on him. "That's ridiculous. You can't be buying this. We're just lost." She turned to me. "Okay, smart lady, if we went through time, prove it."

"The only way to do that is to keep going on our original course. If we find anyone who didn't get here via a similar electrical disturbance, I'll admit my error. We can finish our passage to Florida and put this chapter behind us."

"Why would there be other time travelers like us here?"

"Remember your research? Strange events seem to regularly occur in the area named the Bermuda Triangle. If my theory is correct, time travel would require technology way beyond ours. It would involve areas of science we haven't yet discovered. But some of the forces required to move through time might be electromagnetic. The earth is covered with electromagnetic fields. There is probably something in this area that makes time travel easier than say time travel in the desert or at the poles."

"Like what?" Tracy asked.

"Why do you ski downhill and not uphill?" I countered.

"It's much easier," she said.

"Exactly. The forces of gravity and the laws of physics confirm that it's easier to ski down the mountain than up. The same may hold true here. Whatever the laws of alien science allowing time travel are, it may be easier here in the Bermuda Triangle than elsewhere on the planet."

"So you think all that stuff I found about the unexplained disappearances in the Bermuda Triangle are the result of aliens?"

She sounded less hostile and I breathed a sigh of relief. "Yes, I do."

"And if we find someone else that vanished in the Bermuda Triangle and your theory is correct, they will collaborate having gone through an electromagnetic disturbance," Reid said.

"That's right," I said. "I'd bet on it."

Tracy grinned. "Okay. Let's make a wager. If the next person we find doesn't say they got here through an electromagnetic disturbance, Reid gets to fuck you while I watch."

"Really?" I snapped. "Is everything with you about sex?"

"I guess I watched too much porn with my ex. And I'm getting a little tired of the disapproving looks you give me when you know Reid and I have fucked. So, is it a bet or not?"

"Wait a minute, ladies," Reid said.

"Quiet, you," Tracy barked. Then looking at me, she repeated, "Bet or not? After all, you made a similar bet not too long ago. Won us this yacht."

My temper snapped. "What if I'm right and the next person we find confirms it. What are *you* willing to wager?"

Reid stood. "This has gone far enough." He grabbed Tracy by the hand, pulling her away from the table. "We're going topside."

CHAPTER 52

I finished eating, did the dishes, and straightened the galley, all to delay heading topside. I was not eager to face another hostile Tracy outburst.

When I could put it off no longer, I went up.

Tracy and Reid were standing at the stern rail. Reid saw me approach and said, "Please join us. Tracy has something to say."

Tracy closed her eyes for a minute, then began. "I'm sorry I said what I said. You obviously put a lot of thought into your theory and I didn't mean to laugh at it. I do hope you are wrong and we eventually find a nice Bahamian marina, but if you're not, I commend you for figuring out the reason for the Bermuda Triangle incidents. Will you forgive me?"

"Anything else?" Reid said, looking straight at her.

"We don't have to bet. I'm sorry I threw that out. I'm just

confused and not ready to accept we've been admonished by an alien for taking a video."

"Anything else?"

She looked at him and said, "Reid, I'm sorry I snarled at you earlier. I'm also sorry I drug you into what was obviously a stupid wager."

She looked truly contrite, so I said, "Thank you. I accept your apology. I also hope I'm wrong and if we do get to a marina, I'm buying drinks for the house." I leaned close to her. "And you're right about one thing—I did make a wager just as crazy when I won this yacht."

Reid sent Tracy forward to prepare to get under way. I snagged his arm.

"How did you convince her to apologize?" I asked, raising an eyebrow. "Threaten to withhold sex?"

He smiled. "Well, there was that. But I also threatened to turn her over my knee and smack some sense into her. I'm not sure which threat got through to her."

I laughed. "The sex part, I'm sure. Knowing Tracy, she'd enjoy getting spanked." I shook my head. "But I understand where Tracy is coming from. She's scared. I am, too, because if I'm right, how the hell do we get out of here?"

Tracy was waiting for us forward when Reid and I joined her. "Will we be resuming course 180 degrees?" she asked.

"We'll follow the shoreline that direction," I answered. "Prepare to weigh anchor."

"Belay that," Reid said.

We stopped and looked at him.

"Before we start the engine, I'd like to share something."

"Go ahead," I said. "The deck is yours."

"We may have tough days ahead, but we're on this beautiful boat with people we love. The sea has always held a fascination for me. So much so that I memorized a sailing poem once. It's called "Sea Fever" and it was written by John Masefield. You may have heard it before. Anyway, it goes like this:

> *"I must go down to the seas again, to the lonely*
> *sea and the sky,*
> *And all I ask is a tall ship and a star to steer*
> *her by;*
> *And the wheel's kick and the wind's song and the*
> *white sail's shaking,*
> *And a gray mist on the sea's face, and a gray*
> *dawn breaking.*
>
> *I must go down to the seas again, for the call of*
> *the running tide*
> *Is a wild call and a clear call that may not be*
> *denied;*
> *And all I ask is a windy day with the white*
> *clouds flying,*
> *And the flung spray and the blown spume, and*
> *the sea-gulls crying.*
>
> *I must go down to the seas again, to the vagrant*
> *gypsy life,*

To the gull's way and the whale's way where the
wind's like a whetted knife;
And all I ask is a merry yarn from a laughing
fellow-rover,
And quiet sleep and a sweet dream when the long
trick's over.

When he finished, Tracy said, "I remember hearing the part about a tall ship and a star to steer by. Isn't that from a movie?"

"It was recited by Captain Kirk in a *Star Trek* episode," I answered.

Reid nodded. "So let's get going. We've got a tall ship, a windy day, white clouds, and the sea is calling."

"Can we skip the seagulls part, though?" Tracy asked. "I don't want to live through another *Birds* movie."

So they at least saw some of it, I thought bitterly. Then I caught myself. We needed to stick together. Instead of the sarcastic remark I was about to make, I said, "May we all have sweet dreams together."

"And what was that about blown spume and a long trick?"

Ah, there was the Tracy I knew so well. "Tracy," I said, only half-joking. "That was a beautiful poem. Don't ruin it."

She shrugged. "Sorry."

We got back into open water and followed the shoreline. Rather than stow the dinghy on deck, we towed it behind us in case we needed to make shore.

"So why aren't we headed out to sea instead of following the shoreline of a deserted island?" Tracy asked from the helm.

"Most of the disappearances in the triangle involve boats or ships," I replied. "Maybe we'll find something to indicate someone's passed by this way."

Tracy tried the radio a few times with no success. Reid and I took turns glassing the shoreline. We passed a large cove and then a small one, but both looked deserted. A large point loomed ahead. There appeared to be waves breaking just this side of it.

"Hold your course, Tracy," Reid instructed. "But be prepared to fall off if that's a shoal area where the waves are breaking. And keep an eye on the depth. Pat, keep glassing that area."

We both acknowledged. A few moments later, I called Reid over. "Look over there. What is that?" I asked, barely able to contain the excitement in my voice. I pointed to waves breaking over something. "Does that look like a mast to you?"

He took the binoculars and followed my line of sight. "It sure does."

CHAPTER 53

We reduced sail and Tracy steered us in closer. There was definitely a mast angling up out of the light green water.

"If they ran aground, we don't want to join them," Reid said.

"What's the plan?" Tracy asked.

"We'll find a safe place to anchor and take the dinghy to check it out," Reid replied.

We reversed course and sailed back to the closest cove. It was an exposed anchorage but would be suitable for day use. We quickly anchored and then Reid detailed his plan.

He wanted to dive the wreck by himself, reasoning that Tracy should stay aboard *The Lady Anne* and I should drive him over in the dinghy and wait for him on the surface.

"It's not safe to dive alone," Tracy stated emphatically.

"Are you certified?"

"No. My ex and I were going to learn how but we never went back after the introductory pool lesson."

"How about you, Pat? Are you a certified Scuba diver?"

"No, but I'm a quick study."

Reid shook his head. "Not good enough. Wreck diving is dangerous and not for beginners."

"Why can't we both go with you in the dinghy?" Tracy asked. "Why do I need to stay aboard *The Lady Anne* when the anchor is holding?"

"You need to be here to repel boarders."

I gave him a hard look. "What boarders?"

"If there are any survivors from that wreck, we can't leave *The Lady Anne* unprotected. We're in close enough that someone could easily swim out here from shore."

His answer chilled me, but I knew he was right. Tracy obviously did too. She disappeared for a minute and came back with the shotgun.

"If you teach me how to dive, we can tie the dinghy to the mast and I can join you," I said.

Tracy nodded. "She's right. I'll be fine here, but you shouldn't dive alone."

Reid gave in. "Let's get the gear."

When we assembled all the gear Reid gathered from below, it looked like there was enough scuba equipment spread out on the swim platform for a small expedition.

"We really need all this? *Three* tanks for the two of us?"

Reid answered as Tracy and I helped as directed. "It's a

safety stop. The deeper you dive, the less time you can stay down before requiring decompression. This third tank has two regulators, and we can both breathe off of it on the way up if we need to."

He looked around at the gear. "My chief concern is that we don't have a working dive watch. If we have to decompress, we will have to guess at the time. We'll also have to guess at our bottom time, which again, could become a serious problem."

He helped me put my gear on, explaining equipment functions as he went. The tank was heavy. Then he said, "I have three instructions for you. One, don't exceed your depth limit. Two, don't outrun your bubbles to the surface. Three, never hold your breath."

He had me repeat his instructions, word for word. Twice.

"How deep do you think we'll have to dive?"

"For you, no more than thirty feet." He was checking all the belts and straps on my buoyancy compensator. It fit snugly, but I was able to turn and twist. When he was satisfied, he put his own gear on, adding something he hadn't given me, a large knife that he strapped to his leg.

A few minutes later, we were in the dinghy and Reid headed back to the mast. On the way, he detailed our dive plan.

We would get in the water near the mast and he would show me how to clear my ears, clear any water from my mask, and clear my regulator. He would show me how to "buddy breathe" if one of us ran out of air. Then we would observe the wreck from the surface and if it looked safe, we would descend for a closer look, keeping clear of the rigging and any loose lines.

"Now this is very important, Pat," he said. "We aren't equipped to enter a wreck, so under no condition will we go inside whatever is down there. And there are likely to be sharks. I should have asked you this before we left *The Lady Anne*, but you're not having your period, are you?"

I shook my head.

"Don't worry. Shark attacks on divers are very rare."

He didn't say they never happen, and all I could think of was the huge hammerhead we had seen yesterday.

Then he repeated that without a working watch, we couldn't go below thirty feet, either of us. That was reassuring, knowing he'd be by me the whole time.

He slowly approached the exposed mast. I tied a line to it and looked back toward *The Lady Anne*. She wasn't visible from here. My heart was beating faster.

Reid tested the third tank to be sure it was working and then lowered it over the side, tying it off at about fifteen feet. He confirmed we would stay there for three to five minutes on our return, best guess.

"Are you ready for this? It's not too late to stay aboard the dinghy and wait."

"I'm a lot nervous," I confessed. "And a little scared, but I can do it."

"Being nervous and scared is normal for anyone on their

first dive. But it will be fun and don't forget, I'll be close the whole time."

Then he radioed Tracy that we were going in. She acknowledged.

He showed me how to position myself and rolled into the water. I told myself I could do this and followed him in.

CHAPTER 54

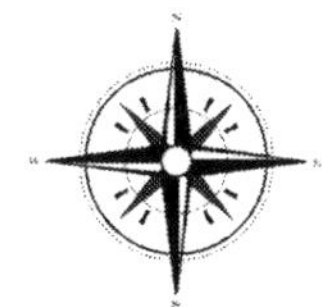

The water was colder than expected and I gasped, my breathing increasing. I poked my head above water. Reid had surfaced with me. I removed my regulator and told him it was cold. He agreed. He told me to wait a minute, to let my body adjust. He was right. After a minute, it didn't feel as frigid, so I submerged and tried it again.

He showed me how to clear the mask. He demonstrated by taking a deep breath, holding the top of his mask firmly against his face, and peeling the bottom edge of the mask back, allowing water to enter. He blew through his nose while tipping his head back. He continued exhaling and then reseated the mask on his face. All of the water was gone.

I did that with no problem, although the salt water burned my eyes. He showed me how to clear my ears. He put one finger on each side of his mask, pinching the soft rubber part of the mask covering his nose. He then exhaled lightly through his nose. I tried that, but as shallow as we were, my ears didn't need clearing. He demonstrated how to clear water from the regulator by pushing the "purge" valve, forcing air through the regulator, blowing out any water. He had already explained how the buoyancy vest operated as an elevator. Push one button to add air, thus going up. Hold the valve over your head and push a different button to release air and submerge. The harder you pushed the button, the more rapid the change.

We submerged three feet and he waited while I relaxed. He made the okay sign with his fingers. I responded I was okay also.

There was nearly unlimited visibility. I tried to slow my breathing and look around. I could see the dinghy's outline above. The safety tank was a little ways below us. I could also see the sunken sailboat. It was on its side, up against a big rock.

We submerged a little deeper. I felt pressure and tried to clear my ears as he had shown. They didn't clear. He must have known that by my expression, so we got a little shallower and they cleared. We went deeper again, all the way to the safety tank. My depth gauge read fourteen feet. My ears were fine.

Again he asked if I was okay. I signaled I was. I adjusted my buoyancy vest like he did until I was suspended. It was a cool feeling. I checked both air supply gauges. I had used more air than he had. He motioned for me to breathe slowly, in, then out. I forced myself to relax.

The boat was about ten feet below us, close to the thirty-foot limit. Reid squeezed my hand and pointed at two sharks in the distance. I tensed up. He again motioned for me to relax. I watched the sharks. They were about six feet long. They didn't seem interested in us. I remembered him saying shark attacks on divers were rare and squeezed his hand back.

I signaled I was okay and we went deeper. I successfully cleared my ears on the way down. We neutralized our buoyancy again, this time about five feet above the boat. My depth gauge read twenty-three feet. I checked on the sharks. They hadn't gotten any closer.

Reid pointed at the rigging. I acknowledged to stay clear of it. We began a slow pass forward, surveying the dead hull below us.

There was minimal barnacle growth on the decks and rigging. It didn't look like the boat had been submerged very long. There were no sails attached. We continued closer. I willed myself to relax. I needed to control my breathing or I would run out of air.

There were some small, brightly colored fish swimming just above the deck. Reid pointed at the sharks. Now there were four instead of two. They were a little closer. Reid signaled we were okay. I said to myself, "I should have let Tracy do this."

The exposed side of the hull was intact. The underside wasn't visible from our angle. Most of the weight of the boat was on its keel. Reid led me over to a shroud and had me hold on. He signaled for me to stay put while he swam deeper.

I watched as he descended by the rock the boat was leaning against. I looked over at the sharks. Now there were six, maybe seven. I repeated to myself, "Sharks rarely attack divers. Sharks rarely attack divers."

Reid tapped me on the shoulder. I jumped. He pantomimed a hole in the underside of the boat. I pointed at the sharks. He signaled okay.

We went a little further forward. The bow was intact, so he had us turn around and swim aft.

When we were over the cockpit, I could see the hatch was open. Reid had me hold the backstay and he swam down to the hatch. I feared he would swim inside, but he just looked in. He accidentally bumped his tank on the boom. I could hear the *clink* of metal on metal quite clearly. I looked to see if the sharks had reacted to the sound. They appeared uninterested. Reid swam back to me. He shook his head and shrugged, as if to say he hadn't seen anything to give us a clue who the crew had been or where they had gone.

There were a few dark-colored starfish attached to the transom, but the boat's name was clearly visible : *Obsession*, Nova Scotia.

The sharks were getting closer. They seemed more curious than aggressive. Their bodies were dark gray and the dorsal fins were a solid color with no colored tips. The end of their tails had a black edge. There were some smaller fish swimming right alongside the sharks, attached to them. Remoras. The name came to me. I remembered reading that they eat parasites on larger fish, protection from being eaten themselves.

Reid acknowledged the sharks and signaled we should resume swimming. We swam a lazy circle around *The Obsession*.

I spotted a gigantic lobster on the bottom. I pointed at it. Reid motioned for me to stay put, descended, followed it for a moment, and then swooped down and grabbed it. The lobster tried to swim backwards, and even pulled Reid along a little, but he held on. Reid kicked slowly back to me, cradling the lobster in his arms. He motioned toward the safety tank and we ascended to it. I made sure not to outrun my bubbles.

We reached the safety stop and I held the line with one hand and Reid with the other. He held on to the lobster. I made a mental note to wait five minutes.

Of course, I watched the sharks. There were at least twenty now. Most of them were deeper, eerily patrolling *The Obsession*. One did come up toward us and I grabbed Reid's arm, but it turned away and rejoined its friends. If Reid was scared, he didn't show it.

I managed to check my air supply. I had just under half a tank. Reid probably had more, so there was no need to switch to the third tank. We just admired our king-sized lobster. It had to be three feet long with no claws, only spiny legs and long antennae.

While we were waiting, a pale blue fish with a neon yellow stripe and matching gills swam by, maybe ten feet away and a little below us. It was followed by another, then another, then another. These fish were about a foot long and spaced fairly close together.

I watched the conga line snake its way past us. I tried to count them but gave up and stopped counting at one hundred twenty. The fish just kept coming, swimming steadily past, apparently unconcerned with us or the sharks.

The lobster had stopped struggling as if also enjoying the parade. I looked behind us and could see the fish procession continuing out of sight. I thought those fish were the perfect size for a shark snack, but the sharks left them alone.

Counting all those fish made me certain we had waited long enough, so we slowly surfaced, again being careful to not outrun our bubbles. It was easier to get into the water than back into the dinghy, but I held the lobster and Reid's fins while he climbed aboard.

We got everything aboard and radioed Tracy we were okay and on our way back. She responded that all was well on *The Lady Anne*. I was glad to be out of the water and motoring back to the boat.

Reid congratulated me on my first dive. I was proud that I hadn't freaked out with all those sharks so close. I held the lobster while Reid drove us back to Tracy. I felt cold again and a little tired.

"Holy shit," Tracy exclaimed when she saw the lobster.

We unloaded the dinghy, Reid directing Tracy to put the lobster in the fish box.

"There are still crabs in it. The lobster won't eat them, will it?" she asked.

"I don't think so," Reid answered.

"Do I need to refill these tanks?" I asked him, hefting one.

"Let's wait till we're motoring. There's no hurry."

Tracy came back from depositing the lobster. "So, are you going to tell me about the wreck? I'm dying to know what you found."

CHAPTER 55

Reid described *The Obsession* and her final resting place.

"She was about a forty footer," he said, looking to me for confirmation.

I nodded.

"I looked in the hatch. Didn't see anything to give us a clue what happened to the crew, but there's a big hole below the waterline on the starboard side."

I looked at Tracy. "There were sharks everywhere but they left us alone."

"So, no bodies?" she asked hesitantly.

"I didn't see any bodies," Reid replied. "And the fact that the sails were removed and not left attached to rot makes me fairly certain the crew had time to abandon ship."

"Tell me more about the hole." I said. "Was it punched in,

indicating collision, punched out, indicating explosion, or sawed neatly, indicating intentional scuttling?"

"It took a wicked collision with something pretty big to smash a four-foot hole through modern-day fiberglass."

"Was the hole more on the side or on the bottom?"

"They didn't run aground if that's what you're asking. They were rammed. The impact was straight from the side."

"How old do you think this wreck is?" Tracy asked.

"Judging from the modest amount of sea growth, I would guess less than a month."

"So the crew is probably ashore and probably fairly close," Tracy said.

I couldn't tell if she was nervous or excited. I know what it made me—uneasy.

"If we sank here, knock on wood," Reid said, "and we had time for an orderly evacuation, I would haul all of our supplies to the nearest shore and make continuous trips until I had everything I could possibly need."

"Like the sails?" Tracy asked.

"If I thought we would need them for shelter or shade," he answered. "That was a loose-footed mainsail. It would come off pretty quickly. Besides, the outhaul had been cut, not unshackled, saving time."

"Did you see that when you bumped into the boom?" I asked.

"I'm trained to notice things I might have to fix later," he chuckled.

"Are we going to look for the crew?" Tracy asked.

"We have a duty to offer assistance if we can safely do so."

Reid and I began rinsing and stowing the diving equipment while Tracy went below to make lunch. She returned with quesadillas, and I didn't realize how hungry I was until the sight of melted cheese between tortillas made my mouth water. It must have been the diving.

Tracy tried hailing *The Obsession*'s crew on the radio. There was no response to her repeated attempts. We glassed the rocks for signs of survivors, but the area was deserted.

We agreed to take the dinghy and follow the shoreline behind the shoal, toward the point. We debated leaving one of us behind to guard *The Lady Anne* but finally decided that since we hadn't seen or heard anyone, it wasn't necessary.

While Reid and Tracy cleaned up after lunch, I put bottled water in the dinghy and gassed it up. Reid brought two radios with us in case we had to split up, and we set off for the shore.

We guided Tracy around the shoal and then followed the shoreline. It was composed of giant, jumbled boulders and inaccessible. We weren't sure what we were looking for, but figured we'd know it when we saw it.

The Lady Anne was still in sight when we found something. Spread across some rocks above the shoreline were three large white panels.

"Well, we know what they did with their sails," Reid said. "That's an SOS."

We slowed and spotted a landing spot. We could see where rocks and been cleared away, making an area wide enough to beach the dinghy. The was a faint path from the shore inland, like something had been dragged over the ground.

We beached and secured the dinghy. I spotted a length of line coiled upon a large rock. We eagerly inspected it. "That's a proper round turn with two half hitches," Reid said. "This was tied by a sailor. The crew made it this far."

He shouted out, "Ahoy, crew of *The Obsession*!" but there was no reply. We started toward the white panels, hoping to find a note or a sign—anything to indicate where the crew had gone.

It was a difficult trek over jagged, loose rocks but when we got to the sails, it was as Reid suspected. We found three panels cut from a sail, their mainsail judging from the sail slugs along the luff of one of the panels, each about five feet wide. Two were the same length, about twenty feet. The third was a little shorter and angled because of the leech. They were stretched over a rocky incline, secured at their corners with lines tied around nearby rocks. They would have been visible from both the water and the air.

"If you knew you wouldn't need your sail again, this is a well-made signal," Reid said.

We looked all around but didn't see any notes or arrows. The rocky ground made seeing tracks or footprints impossible, so we returned to the shore to follow the faint path we had seen from the water.

The ground was very uneven, making for slow progress. We had to step carefully, not wanting to risk a sprained ankle.

Reid would go first and then extend his hand back for me and then Tracy.

There were more of those white-striped lizards that scattered ahead of us as we approached. They had no problems speeding over the rocks. We passed some low, scrubby vegetation whose leaves contained small amounts of water. We spotted ants scurrying about the ground, the bushes, and around the little water pockets. They were big, maybe one inch long, and copper colored. A minute later we found one very large anthill. The ants paid us no attention, but we gave the anthill a wide berth in case they bit or stung.

Just past the plants, we stumbled into a large area choked with what looked like ivy. The vines were exceptionally well rooted and thick, and if you didn't step carefully, the vines would cause you to trip and fall. I found that out firsthand, hoping as I recovered my footing that I hadn't fallen into an exotic patch of poison ivy.

We slogged on, but once through the ivy, lost track of the trail, forcing us to retrace our steps. We walked the perimeter, but finally gave up trying to find where it exited.

We decided to turn back. We retraced our course back past the anthill and rested for a minute, sharing a bottle of water. Tracy switched on her radio and tried calling *The Obsession* again. There was no reply to her hail.

But I thought I heard something.

I stopped. "Did you hear that?" I asked.

"What?" Reid and Tracy asked in unison.

"Repeat your hail, Tracy."

She did. We listened intently.

Then—

Tracy put her radio away and called out excitedly, "Here puppy, puppy, puppy."

I grabbed my safety whistle and blew three long blasts.

Tracy called out again. This time, we all heard it. Barking. A dog.

And it was getting closer.

CHAPTER 56

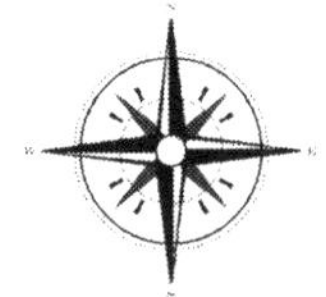

"That sounds like a small dog," I said. "Keep calling."

"Here puppy, puppy, puppy," Tracy called.

"Here boy, here boy," Reid added, louder.

There was one more bark and then a small brown, white, and black dog ran into view. It slowed down and stopped about ten feet from Tracy, its tail sticking straight up.

She knelt down, extended her hand, and spoke in a sweet voice, "Don't bite me."

The dog hesitated a moment and then ran over to her, stopping a few inches away. Its tail was still pointing up but was wagging slowly, like a pendulum. I could hear it sniffing.

"Come here, boy," Tracy said softly, kneeling down. "You're cute. Are you friendly?"

The dog ran to her, put his front paws on her knees, and tried to climb into her lap.

Tracy laughed and put her arms around him. "Good boy."

"You've got a friend," I said, slowly moving toward Tracy and the dog.

"What's your name?" she asked, petting his head. The dog snuggled against her chest and whined softly.

I bent low and offered my hand, palm up. The dog sniffed and licked my hand. He did the same to Reid's hand, but he never left Tracy's arms.

"You've really *have* got a new friend," I repeated.

"He likes me best," she said as she resumed petting him. "Are you lost?".

"What kind of dog is he?" I asked. "He looks like some kind of terrier."

"He is," Reid replied. "A skinny, dirty beagle type of terrier. And I'll bet he's thirsty."

Reid motioned for Tracy to put her hands together. He poured bottled water into her cupped hands and the dog eagerly slurped up three handfuls.

While the dog was drinking, I got a close look.

His fur was heavily matted and full of stickers. The ends of both ears had been injured by something, and when Tracy came too close with her petting, he shied away. Both eyes were clotted with puss and traces of dried blood stained the fur under his chin. The dog's breath was extra foul. His paw pads were cracked and given their condition, I was surprised he was able to walk, let alone run.

Whenever Tracy spoke, the dog looked right at her, as if it understood what she was saying.

Tracy stood, gently setting the dog on his feet. "Where's your owner?" she asked softly. "Take us to your owner."

The dog looked at her, barked, and headed back the way it had come. He continuously looked back at us, especially at Tracy, as if making sure she was following.

So off we went, following a stray dog on a rocky, inhospitable island.

The dog turned just before the ivy patch and stayed above the shoreline. We passed our dinghy and then turned again and followed the ravine we came upon yesterday. It was slow going through the rocks, and the dog frequently stopped and waited for us to catch up.

After about 100 yards of following the ravine, the dog disappeared around a sharp turn. He quickly reappeared, wagging his tail and barking, as if calling us.

When we reached him, we were overlooking a small pond with an old-style wooden dinghy floating in the middle. It was covered by a faded, blue, plastic tarp.

The dog walked slowly toward the pond, giving us time to catch up. "You don't suppose there's a body under that tarp?" I panted, trying to catch my breath.

"There's one way to find out," Tracy said, not breathing hard at all. "Reid, you go first."

We stood on the edge and surveyed the pond. The water looked stagnant and it smelled.

"How in the world did that get in there?" Tracy asked.

"The ravine we followed is dry now, but maybe that changes when it rains," Reid answered.

"Well I hope who ever put it there, rowed it in," I said. "I don't think I could carry it over those rocks."

The dinghy was wooden and of plank construction, about six feet long, painted white, and appeared to be designed for rowing, not for motoring. It was anchored about twenty to twenty-five feet out and was riding low in the water, like it was fully loaded. The pond didn't look very deep.

Tracy walked partway around the pond. The dog followed her. "It says '*Obsession Jr.*' on the transom," she hollered back.

"Ahoy, *The Obsession, Jr.*," Reid called out.

No response.

Tracy rejoined us.

"We should see what's under that tarp," Reid said. "I'll do it."

As he began to take his shirt off, the dog started barking. It had gone about fifty feet past where Tracy had turned back. It began prancing back and forth, barking furiously.

We made our way over to him and found a primitive campsite. We found a red cooler wedged in between some rocks and a blackened fry pan sitting upside down on a man-made firepit. Just past the firepit was another square of sail, stretched tight and tied to some low-growing bushes. It was barely off the ground.

"Isn't that pretty low for shade?" Tracy asked.

"I'm not sure why it's that low, but whoever tied it must have had a reason," Reid answered.

"Nice knots," Tracy said, pointing at how it was tied. "Aren't those Trucker's Hitches?"

Reid inspected one and said they were indeed Trucker's Hitches and had been tied properly. There were also two life jackets hanging over the shrubs, as if placed there to dry.

I blew my whistle again. Besides the dog barking, there was no response.

We followed Reid over to the cooler. It had a crack in one side and the red plastic lid was dented. He cautiously opened it. Laying on top was a plastic bag containing a book. He handed me the bag and kept looking.

The cooler contained several blackened cans that had probably been used for cooking or boiling water, a dozen or so empty plastic water bottles, a bent pair of reading glasses, a rusty multi-tool, some dirty utensils, and a flare gun.

There was another plastic bag containing a flashlight, a Nikon camera, two cell phones, and a portable VHF radio. None of them worked. "If I'm able to charge the camera or the phones, we might be able to see their pictures," Tracy said.

Reid and Tracy left to go check out the dinghy. I sat down and opened the plastic bag. On top of a book was a sheet of paper. In large letters was penciled, "Don't go in the water."

I immediately looked toward Reid. Tracy was holding his shirt and shorts and he was getting ready to step into the pond. "Stop!" I screamed. I could feel my heart pounding. "Don't go in the water!"

He heard me and backed away, eyebrows raised in surprise. "I found something. Come back."

They rushed back to me. I showed them the paper and the

book. It was leather bound and titled, *The Official Log of the Good Ship Obsession.*

Tracy turned the paper over. On the back was written the following:

We made a terrible mistake stowing our remaining food, water, supplies, and clothing aboard Jr. for safekeeping. Phil was bitten after setting her anchor. I now know the pond contains deadly eels. The situation has gone from bad to desperate to worse. If I can't find a way get our stuff back, I fear tomorrow. Cookie Cook.

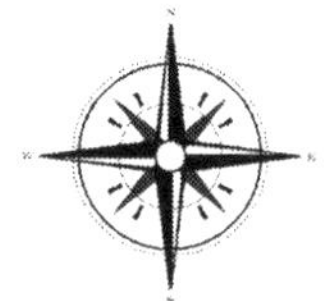

CHAPTER 57

We read the note in silence. I turned to the last log entry and read it to myself.

"They're dead, aren't they?" Tracy asked.

I nodded and closed the book.

"We'll leave everything but the electronics, the flare gun, and the logbook," Reid said. "Let's get back to *The Lady Anne*."

I took a picture of the note and put it back in the cooler, right on top where we found it.

"The dog's name is Buster," I told Tracy. "It was in the logbook."

"Is your name Buster?" she asked the dog. "Are you Buster?"

He started jumping around and barking, as if happy that we knew his name.

We started back to our dinghy in somber silence, I think each of us wondering if this was to be our fate, too.

Just as we approached the last stretch of rocks, Buster suddenly veered from leading our procession and charged after a lizard. After a short chase, he caught it.

He pranced over to Tracy, holding the struggling lizard in his mouth. He looked up at her and then dropped the lizard at her feet.

The lizard was damaged but not dead and managed to slowly crawl away. The dog alternated between looking at Tracy and the lizard. He barked a few times and appeared to be unsure what to do.

She petted him again and said, sweetly, "You're a good Buster, but I don't want your lizard. No, Buster, I don't want that nasty old lizard."

"It's probably what he's lived on since losing his owners," I said.

But Buster seemed to understand and didn't chase after any more.

Reid untied the dinghy and pushed it back until it was floating. Before any of us could board, Buster bounded through the water and jumped aboard. He leaned up with his paws and barked, as if telling us to follow.

Reid drove us back to *The Lady Anne*. I watched as the three sail signal panels faded from view. They were a solemn reminder that *The Obsession*'s crew was gone.

Buster stayed extremely close to Tracy, as if afraid of being left behind. She grinned and said, "He followed me home. Can I keep him?"

I held the logbook tightly, anxious to read it and yet afraid at the same time. Again, the question of whether we were to meet the same fate loomed in my mind.

The dinghy bumped lightly against the swim platform. Before I could step out, Buster leapt out of the dinghy, landed on the swim platform, bounded up the steps, and stood on the stern watching us, wagging his tail. He looked happy to be aboard *The Lady Anne*.

We got him a bowl of fresh water, a few slices of deli meat, and a pretzel. He eagerly took the offerings.

"Not exactly the diet approved by the kennel club," Reid said, laughing. "But the best we have."

Tracy got a solar shower ready and gave him a bath on the swim platform. Buster stood patiently while she soaped, scrubbed, and rinsed him. He was very well-behaved. When she was finished and Buster shook himself off before plopping down on the deck to dry, the three of us went directly to the cockpit table, eager to see what *The Obsession*'s log had to say.

"Before you open that," Tracy said as she dried her hands, "I have a question."

Reid pushed the log to the center of the table and said, "Go ahead. What's your question?"

"If that was one of us ashore with all of our supplies in a dinghy that was surrounded by poisonous eels, what would we do?"

She looked at me, so I answered first.

"There are lots of solutions," I said. "Build a raft, for one."

"I didn't see any logs."

"Neither did I," Reid added.

"I don't need logs, just stuff that floats. I would use the sail panels and fill them with buoyant material, like empty water bottles, life jackets, lightweight wood, et cetera. Then I would tie them like a big package and float out to the dinghy."

"Tie them with what?" she asked, seeming to enjoy playing devil's advocate.

"There were all sorts of pieces of line around. Remember the shade sail and the signal panels and the coil at the landing spot? And if that wasn't enough, I would use those cursed ivy vines we kept tripping on."

"So if you made a raft but it didn't work, what then?" she asked.

"I'm not going to just wait to die, with help only twenty feet away. This problem is not that complicated. If I would have been there, I could have gotten to their dinghy without even getting wet."

"Would you have drained the pond?" Reid asked. I wasn't sure if he was being serious or not, but I had a quick answer.

"Maybe. I would certainly walk the perimeter and if there was a natural rock dam, I would remove the rocks, drain the pond enough to reach the dinghy, and then go get my stuff."

"Okay, what if that didn't work?"

I was beginning to get annoyed by the sarcasm in her tone, but I tried hard not to show it. "If I can't walk through the water because of the eels," I said, "I wouldn't. I'd walk over the water."

"You'll be in very elite company if you can walk on water," she said condescendingly.

But Reid's expression was one of fascination. "How would you do that?"

"That place is full of rocks, right? So just start piling them on top of each other and build yourself a rock jetty all the way to the dinghy. Walk out there, get what you need, and walk back. It would take time, but if you can't reach the dinghy from shore, move the shore closer to the dinghy."

Reid smiled at my answer. Tracy didn't say anything. I could see she was thinking of a way to keep this going, but my jetty answer had pretty much stumped her.

"Great solutions," Reid said. "I probably would have concentrated on making a raft. It might not have occurred to me to build a walkway out of rocks. But that's a really good plan. I'm impressed, as usual."

"So Tracy, what would you have done?" I asked, turning the tables.

"I like to think I have some brains. After all, I do have a degree in accounting. But I have to admit, I don't think I'd have thought of anything besides making a raft. Certainly not draining the pond or bringing the shore closer."

"Do you think we should go back and try to reach the dinghy?" I asked. "Could there be something of value we could use?"

Reid was quiet for a moment. "No. I think we should leave it as we found it. Just in case…"

"Just in case someone else comes through the portal the way we did and may need the provisions more than we do." It wasn't a question.

He nodded. "Let's see what happened to *The Obsession,*" he said.

I picked up the book and began to read. "The Official Log of the Good Ship Obsession."

CHAPTER 58

Paper-clipped inside the front cover was a photo of a couple standing on a sandy beach, with a magnificent sunset behind them. Sitting between them was Buster. On the back was written, "Cookie, Phil, and Buster in St. Kitts." I passed it around.

We guessed the couple to be in their sixties. She had a slender build and short hair like mine. He had a bit of a spare tire and a heavy beard. They were both smiling and looked very happy. The photo wasn't dated, but the dog was heavier than now.

We sat around the cockpit table and slowly turned the pages, passing the log between us. Buster went under the table and lay down. We took turns scanning each entry. We were all very curious to find out what had happened to *The Obsession* since leaving St. Kitts.

We discovered that Phil and Denise Cook, or Cookie as she called herself, were from Yarmouth, Nova Scotia. Two years ago they ordered *The Obsession* from Cape Town, South Africa, and had it delivered to St. Lucia. The Cooks took possession in Castries and immediately made passage to the Netherlands Antilles. They lived aboard and explored the ABC Islands.

After their first season, they sailed east to Trinidad, leaving *The Obsession* there during hurricane season. They had her hauled out, serviced, and stored in Chaguaramas Bay while they flew back to Canada. That kept their insurance premiums reasonable because the boat was stored south of twelve degrees, forty minutes north, the "hurricane belt." That was also going to be their starting point on the next season.

Their second season began in Trinidad and they island-hopped their way north. They did much more aggressive sailing the second season, seldom spending more than one or two days in port. They even had fellow Canadian sailors join them on some of the longer, multi-day passages.

The Cooks eventually reached Puerto Rico, but instead of heading north like we did, they sailed further west, by way of Cuba. The entries between Cuba and their destination of Nassau in the Bahamas were very interesting and disturbingly similar to what happened to us.

January 03, 03:15 a.m. On set course for Ragged Island; Wind and sea conditions perfect; Cookie sleeping; Have closely observed a fascinating aircraft, possibly military, definitely high-tech hush-hush; Can't wait to see the pictures.

January 03, exact time uncertain but late afternoon. Encountered strange lights early morning; heavy mist; Cookie and I and Buster briefly irradiated by silver light; Cookie saw our fresh produce glowing silver but it tastes ok; deafening hum; violent electrical storm that crippled all electrical systems; Engine and power are out; Navigating without GPS and questionable repaired compass; Radio is out; Watches and clocks have stopped, unsure of time; Steering north best guess for Ragged Island; No injuries; No immediate threat to crew; Boat seaworthy, just without power.

"They mentioned a violent electrical storm," I said aloud. "Do you know what that means?"

"It means they went through the same electromagnetic disturbance we did and the 'fascinating aircraft' they saw was our UFO," Reid said.

"Do you think they realized they'd gone back in time?" Tracy asked.

"Let's keep reading and see," Reid said. "It's interesting that *The Obsession*'s course from Cuba to Nassau was just west of ours." He picked up the book and continued to read:

January 04, sunset. Have probably missed Ragged Island; Turning south back to Cuba to reprovision and make repairs; Have seen no other vessels; EPIRB not working; Best fishing ever but no refrigeration or ice, forcing release except what we can eat; Rationing drinking water until more located; All concerned except Buster.

January 05, late afternoon. Becalmed and still powerless, adrift; Should be south of Sargasso Sea but unsure because of heavy seaweed, numerous dolphins and whales; No signs of civilization; Still no radio or EPIRB; No way to recharge any batteries; Praying for rain from approaching front.

January 06, morning. Storm last night blew us SE best guess; Boat undamaged; Position unknown, but free of seaweed; Freshwater supply somewhat replenished by heavy rain; Bypassed solenoids and got stove working; Eating hot fish stew; Spirits improving.

January 07, evening. Made landfall in light air; Marginal anchorage sites; Island appears fairly large but rocky and inhospitable; Minimal vegetation; Fresh food running low; Still have emergency rations; Will leave when wind permits; All agree best choice is to continue S-SE to Cuba, it can't be that far.

January 08, morning. Rowed Jr. ashore; Searched immediate area but no signs of civilization; No trace of others; No signs of edible fruits or plants; No signs of drinking water except in tiny quantities from flora and scattered puddles; There is an abundance of lizards, birds, and crabs; Expect winds this evening and possibly tomorrow.

January 09, evening. Attacked by protective whale after departing; I take full responsibility for getting too close to its mate and calf; Made it partway back to shore before taking on much water near unmarked shoal; The Obsession is a fine vessel and she floated long enough to make 4 trips ashore with Jr.; Final order given to abandon ship; Fishing gear accidentally lost overboard on last trip; All alive but need help.

We looked at each other in silence, not quite believing what Reid was reading. The "abandon ship" entry was especially difficult for him, knowing now how the story was to end.

January 10, evening. Set up camp inland; Made rescue signal out of salvaged sail; Signal is well positioned for water or air spotting; Made signal fire near shore - ready to light when needed; Rowed back to The Obsession but all that remains is her mast; Can see sharks circling so any more salvage is dangerous; Unable to spot fishing tackle; Cookie said prayer for The Obsession; Buster catches lizards, crabs and birds; Cookie made hot "don't ask" soup; Will keep looking for fresh water; Can only pray and wait for rescue.

January 11, afternoon. Campsite is trouble due to ant infestation; Better site unlikely due to abundance of ants every direction; Ant bites are painful; Since large pond nearby, made decision to bring Jr. inland; Will store all supplies aboard; Will rig remaining sail so we can sleep off the ground; Still no sightings of ships or planes; Signal fire ready but unused; Tomorrow is my birthday, Cookie promises a fabulous dessert.

Reid looked up. "The handwriting changes here."

January 12. Houston, we have a problem. After loading most everything aboard Jr. to keep it clear of ants, Phil anchored Jr. in the pond. While swimming back ashore, he was bitten by an eel. The bite is now infected. I tried to swim back to Jr. for our first aid kit but he stopped me. He will not risk me getting bitten. Our fresh water is going fast. Buster is skilled at catching lizards. To conserve water I roasted one. You can't laugh at this but it did taste like chicken. I need to find more water. I need to get aboard Jr. I pray the infection goes away soon. I have nearly given up hope of rescue but I keep watch and I keep praying. I had saved our last candy bar for Phil's birthday but it's aboard Jr. and out of my reach at the moment. I sang "Happy Birthday" and he smiled.

January 13. I buried my beloved husband Phil today, the day after his 67th birthday. I don't have a shovel so I stacked rocks to make a grave. I will look for wood to make a cross tomorrow. Buster bayed while I thanked God for Phil passing quietly in his sleep. I can't remember if today is Friday the 13th or not. If it is, this is the unluckiest day of my life. I must find a way to get aboard Jr. I have only one bottle of water left and it doesn't look like rain.

Reid finished the entry. I knew there was only one more entry and it would be tough to get through it. I took the book from him and began to read.

January 14. This is the final log entry for the sailing yacht, The Obsession. I, Denise "Cookie" Cook, am all that remain of her crew. Against Phil's strict orders, I tried swimming out to Jr., our tender. I am desperate for the supplies we stupidly stored there. I was swarmed by eels less than 2 meters from shore and barely made it out of that accursed pond. I have more bites than took Phil. I know the future that awaits me. Yet I do not fear dying nor death.

Yeah though I walk through the valley of the shadow of death, I will fear no evil for thou art with me. Thy rod and thy staff, they comfort me.

I do pray that Buster can survive here. I have left him alone in this bad place. He is easily the smartest dog I've ever seen. Next to Phil, he is my best friend. I raised him from a little puppy. I think he somehow knows something is very wrong.

If anyone should find this, I am sorry to burden you, but please get it to Phil's family in Yarmouth. They will appreciate knowing what happened.

My heart is broken. I miss my dear Phil and I know I'll see him soon. I'm going for a long swim now, while I still have strength. I prefer to die at sea, a sailor's death. I don't want Buster to find me in my hammock like I found Phil yesterday morning. Phil said there were sharks about The Obsession, so that's the direction I'll go. I plan to hold onto her mast until the sharks take me.

And quiet sleep and a sweet dream when the long trick's over.
Fair winds and following seas.
Cookie Cook

CHAPTER 59

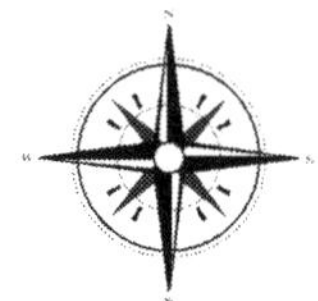

Tears burned my eyes. I closed the log and went forward, not knowing if I could keep from crying.

In a minute, Reid had joined me on the bow. He put an arm over my shoulders. "It's all right to cry," he said.

I leaned into him. "What happened to Cookie is so sad. She died because she couldn't get to their emergency rations in the dinghy. If she could have survived another six weeks, we would have found and rescued her."

He didn't say anything, he just held me.

Tracy joined us, her eyes wet from weeping. Buster followed her out, stretching out in the sun at her feet. We looked out toward the sunken *Obsession* in silence.

I went below and emerged a few minutes later with Reid's trumpet and a bottle of single malt scotch and three glasses. I asked if he would please play something appropriate.

He obliged with "Taps." It was very moving. Buster, as if understanding the context of our sadness, concluded the tribute by baying. He had an extremely mournful howl. I poured us each a double shot. We made a toast to Phil and Cookie, from Yarmouth, Nova Scotia. We made another toast to *The Obsession*, a good ship, and a third to Buster.

We moved *The Lady Anne* back to the large cove we had passed earlier as it offered more protection. We re-anchored for the night. While the engine was running, I made hot water and refilled the scuba tanks.

Tracy and I managed quick showers and then helped Reid in the galley. With Buster watching from a short distance, we made an assembly line and shelled all the crabs, setting the meat aside.

While I stirred butter and flour to make a roux, they cut up peppers, onion, and the remaining brats. He then added water, a couple of bouillon cubes, a generous pour of hot sauce, and the crab meat and let everything simmer.

The lobster was so big it barely fit on the grill. While it was cooking, we savored a bowl of fresh crab gumbo. It was delicious, even more impressive because Reid made it with limited ingredients and no recipe.

We then devoured the grilled lobster. It was messy but we laughed as Reid pulled the tail off and passed it around. Tracy slipped Buster a bite, but he proceeded to vomit about two minutes later. She agreed to feed him small portions of "calm food" until further notice. We were too full for dessert, which was a first, so we settled for another glass of scotch.

When we finished eating, Reid cleaned up the dishes, Tracy cleaned up after Buster, and I gathered and then discretely dumped all the shells over the stern, being careful not to alert any birds. I wondered if sharks would eat empty crab shells, but I didn't want to stink our trash up. I didn't see any fins, but I was positive that sharks had gathered below us. I made a conscious effort to not put my hand in the water as I discarded the shells.

As I was leaving the swim platform, Buster went down to the edge. He turned and looked up at me, then he lifted his leg and peed into the water. "Good boy," I told him.

I couldn't wait to tell the others how Buster had relieved himself. None of us had ever seen a dog trained to do that. Reid said he had sailed with a dog on board once, but it just peed and crapped wherever it wanted. He reiterated that he had only sailed with a dog one time. I was half-expecting a bad joke about unattractive sailing students, but he didn't go there.

While it had been a fine meal, worthy of a big tip for the chef, it was obvious to me that we were all depressed by *The Obsession*'s fate.

Tracy took an extra pillow and made a bed for the dog over by the hatchway. Buster quickly accepted it, lay down, and immediately closed his eyes. Then she asked, looking directly at me, "Could we survive being rammed by a whale?"

Reid began answering before I could. "Assuming the watertight doors were immediately dogged shut, we wouldn't sink right away. *The Lady Anne* is of a higher quality construction than *The Obsession*."

I added, "If we took a direct hit and ended up with a four-foot hole in our side, I'd cover it with a mattress and duct tape until we could patch it."

"You don't think we'd be screwed and all die like the Cooks?" she asked. She sounded concerned but not panicky.

"There's enough material on board for a decent repair," I answered. "Not that I want to have to find out."

"I'd run us aground on a falling tide and make sure we listed with the hole side up," Reid stated. "That would give us time to make repairs."

"So neither of you are worried about getting rammed like they did?"

Reid answered very calmly, "Any sailor would be concerned about that, but we can't let fear take over. We've already sailed through whales, hundreds of them, without incident. If it happens again, we'll just remain vigilant about not getting too close to the calves."

"Do you remember all the whales you took video of?" I asked.

"Yes." She nodded.

"Wasn't that the coolest thing ever?"

She nodded again.

"And the next whale we find will be just as cool. We'll just be vigilant, like Reid said."

"So you're really not worried?"

"Absolutely I'm worried," I said. "But it's not about getting rammed by a whale. Those odds are one in a million. I'm more worried that nobody has been by here since mid-January."

"Why do you think that?" she asked.

"Their signal marker is still there. If anybody had seen it, they would have found the camp and taken the log."

"So what do we do now?" she asked.

"I think we should leave this dreadful place and get back on course 180 degrees," Reid answered. "There's nothing here for us."

"That sounds good to me," I chimed in. "We should also leave a note on *The Obsession*'s mast, recapping what happened and warning people that the pond where the dinghy is anchored has a poisonous eel infestation."

"Should we find Phil's grave and mark it with a cross, like Cookie wanted to?" she asked.

"While that's very admirable, I'm not sure it's the best use of our time," Reid answered.

I had to agree; so did Tracy, after a moment.

We finished our scotch and decided to call it a night. The three of us slept together in our cabin, but Tracy left the door open so she could hear Buster. We needed to be together—just for the comfort of knowing there were others who had not been as lucky as we to make it this far.

CHAPTER 60

Tracy and I got up quietly the next morning and made our way topside. She watched Buster do his business on the swim platform. She was impressed.

I made coffee and brought some overripe fruit topside along with a few pretzels for Buster. We decided to let Reid sleep, so Tracy got a fishing pole and we did a little casting off the stern for fun. She caught a fish on her first cast. It was a three-foot barracuda. I unhooked it and we let it go.

We took turns casting and caught a fish on nearly every cast. It was a relief to laugh and have fun after our somber find yesterday. When Reid joined us topside, we stopped fishing and adjourned to the cockpit table.

In between bites of fruit, Tracy had a question. "Do you think it's a fluke that *The Obsession* described exactly what we went through, or do you believe that everyone else we find will report the same experience?"

"I hope I'm wrong," I answered. "But I don't think I am. I believe whoever we find will have a similar story to tell."

"You made a sundial to tell time. Can you make something to determine what year it is?" Reid asked me after a moment.

"That's going to be much harder."

"Well, you solved the problem of the unreachable dinghy yesterday. Consider the unknown year problem your next challenge," Tracy said.

I poured myself another cup of coffee and said, shaking my head, "I don't know a way to calculate the year."

They looked discouraged.

"But maybe we'll come across someone who can," I added.

"Like who?" she asked.

"Like a history museum curator who would know the approximate year by identifying the flora and fauna. Or maybe a geologist who would know the time period by the rock formations."

"And where would we find this museum curator or geologist?" Tracy asked, her tone conveying the obvious.

Where, indeed?

"What if we see a dinosaur?" Tracy asked then.

"That would be very bad because that would mean we've gone back through time millions of years instead of just hundreds or thousands."

"Who else might help us?" Reid asked.

"Well, anyone who could identify any primitive humans we find or probably someone with a deep knowledge of the constellations."

I stopped talking for a moment and then voiced one more thought. "Of course, the aliens who sent us here would know as well."

"I don't want to run into any more aliens," she said.

"And yet, that might be our best bet," I said.

"Why?"

"Because if they sent us here, they'd probably have the technology to return us to our time."

"Do you think they *would* send us back?" Reid asked.

"I think they *could* send us back," I answered. "I just don't know if they could be persuaded to do so." I could see by the expression on Tracy's face that I was making her uneasy so I added, "But I do recall people who reported alien encounters were labeled fruitcakes or nut jobs, so maybe they would feel safe in sending us back. After all, who would believe us?"

"What's going to happen if we can't find any aliens and convince them to send us back?" Tracy asked. "Are we doomed to live out our lives on *The Lady Anne*?"

I shrugged. "We'll have to keep looking for answers. I don't know what else we can do."

Tracy got up and walked forward with Buster following her. Reid and I exchanged glances, but there didn't seem to be anything else to say.

In a few minutes, Tracy called us forward and pointed

toward the shoreline. There were dozens of noisy, squawking gulls circling and diving a small area on the shore.

"Don't drop any food," Tracy warned.

Since the dinghy was still tied alongside and easily accessible, we decided to make a quick run over and see what all the commotion was about.

We tied off to a large rock a short distance from the birds. Buster was paying close attention. We carefully made our way over the rocks, but Buster charged ahead, scattering the birds a moment later.

We caught up to him and saw what had drawn the birds. They were devouring baby turtles trying to make their way to the sea over fifty feet of coarse sand that extended from the rocks to the water. We estimated there were over a thousand newly hatched turtles. We didn't see any adults.

Buster sniffed a few babies and then resumed chasing the gulls. He would charge, bark, and snap and drive one away but it would just take off and then quickly land a short distance away.

It was pretty obvious that in the daylight, a baby turtle's chance of surviving the bird army was close to zero, even with Buster unknowingly helping them.

"Let's help Buster," Tracy said. She picked up the nearest baby turtle and carried it to the water's edge, then gently released it. She then did it again and again.

"I'm not sure we should be interfering with nature's way," Reid told her.

"You don't have to help, but I'm not going to stand here

and do nothing," she replied. She didn't sound angry, just determined.

Reid and I finally joined her, and between the three of us, we transported over one hundred baby turtles to the water.

"You know Tracy," I said as I deposited a baby turtle in the water. "They're probably not going to make it past all the barracudas in this cove."

She stopped and looked at me, and for a moment, I regretted making the remark. Her expression darkened as she realized we weren't doing as much good as we thought we were.

Reid touched her arm, smiled, and said, "Come on. Let's move a dozen more and then we'll quit and get back aboard."

As we rode back, we watched the gulls swoop down again from all sides. In less than a minute, it was total bird chaos. It was as if we'd never been there.

While Tracy and Reid prepared to get underway, I decided to write a note detailing the fate of *The Obsession* and the Cooks and include a warning about the dinghy being in an eel-infested pond. I briefly mentioned who we were and our proposed heading.

I found an empty Gatorade bottle in the trash and rinsed and dried it. Its mouth was much bigger than a water bottle and allowed me to easily insert my rolled-up note. I secured the lid with a wrap of electrical tape. I remembered a bag of red cloth rags in the engine room and grabbed one, along with some duct tape, plastic cable ties, and my new, handy pocketknife.

We raised anchor and motored out, back toward *The Obsession*. Tracy put *The Lady Anne* in neutral and waited while Reid took me over in the dinghy. He held onto the mast while I taped the bottle to it. I hung the rag high on a shroud so it would wave in the breeze, a warning flag.

As Reid reversed and slowly backed away, my heart was heavy. What happened to the Cooks could easily happen to us.

CHAPTER 61

We had decent wind so we cleared the area, raised sail, shutdown the engine, and resumed course. I made a sad log entry about the Cooks, *The Obsession,* and the birds feeding on all of the newly hatched baby turtles. Buster jumped on a cushion in the cockpit and rested, only opening his eyes when one of us would pass. He was obviously very comfortable sailing.

When the radar showed us twelve miles offshore, I showed Tracy which valves to open and close and we macerated the wastewater tank, discharging its contents overboard. She made a quick stop in her cabin to put on her skimpy red bikini top.

As I suspected, it didn't cover anything.

"Don't tell me you want to get laid," I whispered.

She looked in the mirror and smiled. "My period should

start tomorrow and you're having yours now, right?" she whispered back, eyeing her reflection. "Do you think he'll like the top? It's pretty revealing."

I looked away but didn't answer right away. Finally I said, "Don't say anything, but I'm late."

"Uh-oh."

"Yeah, a big uh-oh. I better not be pregnant."

"We've been taking our pills together," she said, leaning in close. "You only slept with Reid once. You were careful, weren't you?"

"I've been very careful. I haven't missed a pill and he wore a condom."

"Well, give it a couple of days. Maybe all the electrical excitement messed things up."

I looked at her for a moment and said, "I brought one extra package of pills with me, how about you?"

"Me too."

"So what are we going to do when we run out of pills and he runs out of condoms?"

She put on a T-shirt and replied, "There's always oral, but I've got a more important question. What happens when we run out of tampons?"

With that, she went up. I followed, trying not to think about her last question.

As we joined Reid at the helm, he said, "I've been thinking."

Tracy and I sat down, not sure what to expect.

"Since Pat believes we've gone back in time, until we can find a marina to disprove her theory, we should sail more and motor less."

That made sense and we both nodded our approval.

"We should also take inventory and start using perishables first." He looked at Tracy. "And we should eat more fish. Tracy, why don't you try your luck now?"

Tracy perked up at that, so I took the helm while she picked the next lure. She selected a green-and-white plastic streamer rigged with stranded wire instead of heavy fishing line. Buster followed her aft while I tacked to avoid a patch of seaweed, and Reid helped her position the lure to drag through our wake.

I heard the line go out and Buster bark before Tracy could shout, "Fish on."

I knew the drill so I heaved to, really concentrating on stopping us on my first attempt. I succeeded. Reid told me to get the fighting belt and the camera, that Tracy had hooked a nice fish. Then he went down to the swim platform, gaff in hand, ready to assist.

It took a while, but Tracy finally tired the fish enough to bring it close. It was a huge dorado. Reid gaffed it on the first try and managed to drag it up on the swim platform by himself. The dorado was easily eight feet long, and Reid estimated it weighed close to two hundred pounds. The head was much bigger than the one we had lost to a shark.

"It followed me home, can I keep it?" Tracy asked, grinning.

"When I said for you to catch a nice fish, I probably should have clarified one that would fit in the fish box." Reid sounded serious, but his grin betrayed him.

Reid tried to fillet the dorado but it was too wide for his knife. I got him our biggest knife from the galley and assisted as he gutted and then hacked the once beautiful dorado into manageably sized chunks, then into serving-size fillets and steaks which I rinsed off and packaged in freezer bags. We toted the fish below but had too much for the freezer, so we stored about twenty pounds in the fish box, with ice.

Tracy took the helm and resumed course while Reid and I discarded the waste off the stern and washed away all the blood. We had made quite a mess, but we got everything cleaned up. Before I could mention we'd probably draw sharks, Reid pointed astern and said, "Shark."

There were twenty dorsal fins following behind us, drawn by the blood. Tracy called Buster to the helm for safety. We joined him. Falling off of the swim platform here would have been savagely fatal.

"How much fish is in the freezer?" Tracy asked, still all smiles.

"About seventy-five pounds and another twenty in the fish box," I answered.

"We'll have grilled dorado for dinner," Reid said.

"Well, you two smell like fish, so go shower. Clean up and don't fall in."

Reid and I showered on the stern side by side. Showering in the nude with him so close by felt strangely erotic but there was no fooling around. I was concerned that my period was late, and while Tracy's remark that it might have been the electrical field that disrupted our cycles sounded plausible, I was not willing to take any chances. If it could make me late, it very well might render my birth control pills ineffective too.

Something that didn't appear to have crossed Tracy's mind.

I left Reid to go below and put on fresh clothes. When I came back to rinse off the fishing gear, Reid was in the galley.

Tracy pulled me aside. "Did you and Reid do it?"

I shook my head.

"You weren't turned on showering with him?"

"Not really. Dorado guts have never been my favorite aphrodisiac."

She stared at me for a moment. "I swear, Pat, I don't know what's wrong with you."

I started to tell her my theory that we should be extra careful until we knew if our cycles would regulate when Reid came topside balancing a bag of popcorn, a pitcher, and three glasses on a tray.

"I would like to propose a toast," he said cheerfully, pouring us each a glass. "To wives and sweethearts." He paused and winked. "May they never meet."

We all laughed. Tracy tossed some popcorn for Buster to catch. I looked astern. The sharks were gone.

"And here's to Tracy catching our dinner," I added.

We all clinked. It was amazing how refreshing ice water could taste. I poured a little for Buster. He loudly slurped it up. Then he lay down near Tracy's feet, opening his eyes when he heard us ruffle the popcorn bag. I noticed Tracy kept dropping popcorn conveniently right in front of him.

CHAPTER 62

Tracy called out that our last landfall was now off of the radar. What happened to the Cooks saddened us all over again.

"I wonder how long Buster would have lasted if we'd hadn't found him," she said.

His ears perked up when he heard his name and she scratched his head.

We decided to sail on for three more hours. If we didn't have any radar contacts or sightings by then, we'd start taking naps so we could sail through the night. If the person on night watch found something, they'd heave to and wait for daylight. Tracy offered to take the first nap with Reid. I didn't say anything.

We were a little hungry for something besides popcorn, so Reid went below and later returned with chicken salad wrapped in lettuce leaves and celery sticks stuffed with peanut butter.

Buster enjoyed one stick of jerky, a pretzel, and a few peanut butter/granola balls. We had good wind, and with Reid at the helm calling out fine-trim adjustments, we were heeled over, making better than ten knots. The ocean stretched before us, reaching seamlessly to where it blended with the sky. Sunlight reflected off the water, blinding in its brilliance and sparkling like diamonds on the surface.

Tracy pointed. "Are those gigantic flying fish?"

I grabbed the binoculars. "Those aren't flying fish. They're manta rays, big ones."

We watched in amazement as a ray would launch out of the water, flap its massive wings, propel itself several feet, and then re-enter the water with a whack and a splash.

Soon we were sailing through the rays and could watch their antics close-up. Most of the rays had twenty-foot wingspans but a few were considerably larger. Their white underbellies and the tips of their wings really stood out against their dark bodies. One of the larger ones jumped right by us. It had swirls of white near its head.

Tracy was shooting video and asked, "Is it my imagination or is the water changing color?"

It wasn't the camera; the water was changing from blue-gray to blue-green. We had been so busy watching the rays, we'd neglected to notice.

Reid read the depth meter. It had suddenly shallowed to sixty feet. He changed course, keeping deep water beneath us.

"Do you suppose the rays are feeding over a reef?" I asked.

"Or something from the reef might be feeding on them, chasing them to the surface," he replied.

I slowly glassed the area but didn't see any sharks or whales. We sailed on past the jumping rays, Reid staying just alongside the shallower water. A band of light green stretched on before us, seemingly forever.

"Do you suppose we're following a reef or underwater canyon?" I asked.

"Could be anything," Reid answered. "But whatever it is, it seems to be running due south, like us."

A little while later, the radar displayed another tight grouping of blips twenty-three miles away. We couldn't see anything, but we held our course, watching as the distance decreased.

Tracy was sitting next to Reid at the helm when I saw a shadow in the distance. I glassed it and pointed. "Land ho."

The radar put it at twelve miles, and we were steadily approaching. The hued water seemed to go straight toward the land.

At four miles out, we could clearly see a black streak winding down through the rocks, right to the sea—the remains of a volcano's lava flow.

We turned and paralleled the shoreline four hundred yards out. The jumbled black rocks that had once been molten lava were clearly visible. We passed a cave along the shoreline that was easily large enough to hold a powerboat. Our consensus was that it was a lava tube.

The depth had shallowed to ninety feet, so we reduced sail and slowed down. Reid handed off the helm to Tracy. Bird activity around us was increasing. There were hundreds of birds in flight and more in the water. Several large flocks passed high overhead.

Flying fish, loosely clustered and following along the shoreline, traveled along with us. I spotted a shark with two dorsal fins. It was at least fifteen feet long. Based on the coloring and the fins being nearly equal size, Reid thought it might be a bull shark. He said they could go from salt water to fresh water and were very dangerous. It followed us for a while and then submerged.

Tracy executed short tacks, steering out and then back in, trying to keep us close but in no less than seventy-five feet of water. Sea birds were ever present, wheeling and cavorting about, diving and soaring with ease. Their cries and calls could be heard over the crashing of the surf against the rocky shore.

As we continued, seals began surfacing near the boat. They were slapping the water and grunting at us. We couldn't tell exactly how big they were because we just saw their heads, but there were several dozen of them, all around.

Finally one swam right alongside us. It was about ten feet long, had a brown body with light yellow patches on its belly, had a pointed snout, and oversize flippers. I got it on video. It had a "cute" face.

"Reminds me of a joke," Reid said.

I groaned.

"No, this is good. A seal broke its flipper. A shark came

over to eat it. 'You can't eat me,' the seal said. 'Why not?' the shark asked. 'Because everybody knows, you shouldn't eat if the seal is broken.'"

In spite of myself, I laughed.

"That's funny," Tracy said.

And as usual, Reid laughed at his own joke, repeated the punchline, and then laughed some more.

We soon cleared the seals and continued following the deeper water.

Tracy shielded her eyes. "Is that smoke up ahead?"

Reid took the binoculars and worked his way forward for an unobstructed view.

"Sure looks like it."

I sniffed the air. "I don't smell sulphur, so I doubt it's volcanic activity." My heart started racing. "It could be either a settlement or a signal fire."

CHAPTER 63

We continued on toward the smoke, the atmosphere onboard a combination of excitement and apprehension.

A cove appeared ahead. Its mouth was wide, but it narrowed and appeared to curve at the far end. The smoke was coming from around the curve. There were some large white rocks scattered throughout the cove. We decided to heave to and make a plan.

"What do you think?" I asked.

"Well, we definitely found something," Reid said. Then echoing my words of a moment before, he added, "A settlement or a signal fire."

"So what do we do now?" Tracy asked, still looking through the binoculars at the smoke.

"I'm going to take the dinghy and investigate," Reid answered.

"I'll go with you," I said.

Reid shook his head. "No, you two will stay here and guard the boat. I'll take a radio and let you know what I find."

Tracy lowered the binoculars. "Why can't we all motor over there together?"

Reid was quiet for a moment, as if choosing his words carefully. Finally, he said, "We don't know who made that signal. They could be friend or foe. If they're a friend, I'll call you and you can bring her in." He paused and lowered his voice. "But if they're not friendly, you'll need room to maneuver."

"Maneuver? What does that mean?" Tracy asked, frowning.

I answered before Reid could. "It means we turn around and get out of here."

"I'm not leaving Reid here," Tracy said.

"Nobody is leaving anybody," I said. "We're just discussing a worst-case scenario." I turned to Reid. "Look, I don't mind you investigating what is likely a signal fire, but as captain, my first responsibility is to my vessel. My second responsibility is to the crew, which is you two. And my third responsibility is to offer assistance, if it can be done without putting the vessel or the crew in jeopardy."

Reid nodded. "So you *were* listening in class. Good. And for you to fulfill your responsibilities, you need to make the best use of your crew. Me. I'll take the dinghy in and let you know if it's safe for you to follow."

"As captain, I should take the dinghy and investigate," I said, standing up.

Reid stood up as well. "I want you two to remain onboard. Don't take that as a sexist remark. Just please stay here, guard the boat, and wait for me."

His tone wasn't rude, sexist or condescending. I saw the wisdom in what he was saying. We had no idea what or who might be behind that signal fire. If it turned out to be an unfriendly bunch, two of us would have a better chance of rescuing him than just one. I nodded agreement and we got ready for him to go ashore.

I topped off the dinghy's gas tank while Tracy got him a working radio—and the shotgun.

Reid pushed the shotgun back at her. "Keep it on board. Just in case," he said.

She looked like she was going to argue but Reid held up his hand. "You need to stay topside, stay alert, stand by the radio, and be patient," he said. "And shoot anybody who tries to board."

I looked hard at him. He was deadly serious. "How will we know if you run into trouble?"

After a quick discussion, we agreed to have a code word. If he used it, we were to assume the worse and leave. If we used it, he would return as quickly as possible.

Tracy suggested the code word "honey."

"Why honey?" he asked.

"Because it's innocuous. People use it all the time."

Reid nodded. "Honey, it is. If you hear the word, continue south and don't return without help."

Tracy and I looked at each other. "Help? And where exactly are we going to find help?" she said.

"Doesn't matter. You two have become competent sailors and I am very proud of both of you. You'll figure out what needs to be done."

I held up a hand. "Nobody is going anywhere. You're going to find a couple of people who got stranded the same way we did. If you get a good vibe, rescue them. If not, leave them and get back here pronto."

Reid got a bottle of water and boarded the dinghy. I pushed it off and threw him his line. He slowly motored away and then increased speed and headed off toward the end of the cove. We watched him until he curved out of sight.

"Now what?" Tracy asked.

"Try and be patient I guess," I said. "And keep our fingers crossed."

CHAPTER 64

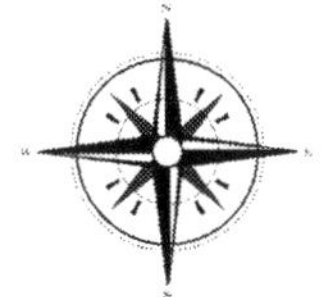

Tracy and I returned to the cockpit. The shotgun was laying on the table and I made sure the safety was on and pointed away from us. Reid called us on the radio and told us to move *The Lady Anne* further out from shore.

We did as instructed, re-heaving to about one thousand yards offshore. A short time later he radioed again.

"Hey, you two," he said. "If you do come in here, don't forget to raise the keel."

"Got it," Tracy replied.

I was glassing the waters toward the shore. Seeing the gun on the table made me a little nervous. Could I shoot someone trying to board? Could I sleep at night if I did? I was debating the answers to those questions when Reid radioed again.

"Found them. A woman with two kids. They're waving and excited to see me."

"Do you see a boat or a plane?" Tracy asked.

"Neither."

"I think you should drive around a little before getting out of the dinghy," I said.

"Good idea," Reid said.

"Are they by the smoke?" Tracy asked.

"Yes, by the fire."

I took the radio. "Ask them how they got there?"

There was a brief pause and then, "In a fishing boat, and it's anchored further down the shore."

"Ask them about the captain."

"The woman said he didn't make it."

Tracy and I exchanged glances and then Reid radioed again. "I'm going to go look for their boat, stand by."

A few minutes later, Reid radioed that he had found their boat anchored bow and stern, close to shore, further down the shoreline, just past a large jumble of rocks. It was a big white fishing boat with a flybridge and a tower.

"The name on the transom is *Day Dream*, Turks and Caicos."

"How big?" Tracy asked.

He reported it to be about a forty footer. One outrigger was partially lowered, drying some T-shirts and shorts.

"Does it look seaworthy?" I asked.

"She's floating and appears undamaged, but the blue Turks and Caicos flag is flying upside down and there is an orange flag with a black ball and square."

From our sailing classes, Tracy and I knew these were distress signals.

"Are they properly anchored?" I asked. "Or does it look like a woman and two kids did it?"

"It's properly anchored, but remember that you and Tracy can properly anchor a much larger sailboat."

He was right, but somehow my instincts were telling me something was off about the situation. If Reid was concerned, his voice didn't convey it.

"So now what?" Tracy radioed.

"I'm going in to talk to them," he replied.

"Please be careful," I said.

Tracy grabbed the radio from me. "And stay in constant contact."

"Roger. Stand by," he radioed.

"Standing by," Tracy acknowledged.

"Now what?" Tracy asked.

"I guess we stand by."

We sat at the cockpit table, the gun within easy reach.

After about fifteen minutes, Tracy pointed and said, "Has the smoke signal changed?"

It had changed. What had been a single lazy spiral was now two lazy spirals. The wind was blowing but wouldn't have split the smoke column like that. I wasn't sure what had happened. We continued to watch until Buster ran aft, barking.

Tracy and I both jumped up.

A half-naked man was climbing onto the swim platform.

"Oh, fuck," Tracy screamed. "Get the gun."

I grabbed the gun and headed aft, commanding the man to stop and put his hands up.

He was a large man, built like a defensive football player, wearing only a pair of white briefs. I guessed him to be in his forties. He was very tan, but his face was hollow and in spite of his size, his ribs were visible.

"Who the fuck are you?" Tracy asked while I kept the gun pointed at him. Buster was on the stern, growling and baring his teeth.

He didn't seem fazed by the gun, but he did put his hands up. "You can't shoot me," he replied.

"Why not?" I asked.

He grinned. "Radio the shore and ask Captain Rick why you can't shoot me."

Tracy looked at me, her face red, her breath coming in shallow gasps.

"Go. Radio ashore. See if Reid answers," I told her.

Tracy went over to the radio. I moved in between her and the man. His hands were still up but his expression had changed. He watched Tracy, his eyes narrowed. My palms were sweaty, but I held the shotgun steady. The safety was off and my finger was on the trigger.

"Reid, honey, are you there?" Tracy asked.

"This is Captain Rick. Put Carl on now."

The voice that came back was not Reid's.

Tracy took a deep breath, glanced over at Carl, looked at

me, and then answered, "Carl can't come to the radio right now, but I'm supposed to ask you why we can't shoot him."

"Listen carefully, you on the sailboat," Captain Rick said. "If I hear a gunshot, or even think I hear one, I will cut this man's head off and you can listen to him scream as he dies."

CHAPTER 65

Tracy glanced back at me. I could see how upset she was, but her voice remained calm. "His name is Reid," she said. "And I need to talk with him now."

"Reid, huh?" There was a pause and he said, "Say hello, Reid, nothing else."

"Hello, honey," Reid said.

"Honey. Are you okay?" Tracy asked, her hands gripping the radio so tightly, I saw her knuckles turn white.

"Okay, bitch." The reply came right back. "He's alive. At least for now. Do as Carl tells you and do it quickly or he won't be."

I waited for another broadcast, but the radio was silent. Reid had called us honey, meaning he was in trouble, and despite the fact that Tracy had used the code word too, I was pretty certain Reid couldn't help us. Tracy and I were on our own.

Carl didn't move but said, "There are five of us shipwrecked and we need an immediate ride to the nearest port."

"That's going to be a problem," I replied.

"This boat is plenty big enough," he remarked, looking at me. "What kind of problem are you going to cause?"

"I'm not your problem," I said. "Since the electrical storm, there has been no radio contacts, no cell phone service, no signs of civilization, and we found a shipwreck from January and they hadn't seen anything or anyone either. But the sailors who wrote the log entries are dead."

"That's their dog," Tracy said, pointing at Buster. "That's all that's left."

"Assuming I believe you, which I'm not saying I do," Carl said, "exchange one half of your fuel, food, and water for your man ashore. You can take your boat and get out of here. We won't take anything else."

"Do you expect us to believe that?" Tracy asked.

"Believe what you want, but you've got no choice. If Rick hears a gunshot, he will do what he said, cut your man's head off."

"Maybe we should just kill you without using the gun," Tracy threatened.

"I'm weak from not eating much and tired from swimming out here, but I'm still strong enough to take two scrawny bitches and your poor excuse of a watch dog."

I wished that Buster was an attack-trained Doberman, but

he wasn't. My mind was racing, trying to come up with a solution to a grave situation.

Carl lowered his hands and started forward. "You can't fire that or your man is fucked. Captain Rick isn't bluffing."

Buster charged him, snarling and snapping, but Carl was quicker than he looked and easily tossed Buster off the end of the swim platform, into the water.

"Buster," Tracy yelled.

But I was watching Carl. He had started up the steps and was watching me. He repeated, "You can't fire that or they will hear."

"Do something," Tracy hollered.

The gun was no longer an asset, it was a liability. If it went off, intentionally or in a struggle, Reid would likely be butchered. I backed away, through the cockpit, toward the hatch.

For an instant I debated luring Carl below, closing the hatch and then firing. I dismissed that for two reasons. One, they might still hear the gun. Two, I couldn't risk blowing a hole in the hull.

"Pat," Tracy panted. "Do something."

I stopped, turned the gun on its side, held the release, and ejected all of the shells onto the deck. I quickly tossed the now-unloaded gun below. It landed with an ominous thud.

"You're fucking stupid," Carl hollered. "Now you're completely unarmed."

"Do you know what you're doing?" Tracy asked, backing away slightly.

"Go get Buster," I told her.

Then I looked at Carl and hissed, "Now they won't hear when we stop you."

"You definitely have balls," Carl said. "I was just going to take one half of your food, fuel, and water, but now I will take the two of you back to *The Day Dream* so Rick can fuck you and stop staring at my wife."

I almost smiled. I was counting on him being macho and overconfident.

Tracy helped Buster out of the water and as I predicted, Carl turned to look at her. That put him between us. He could no longer watch both of us at the same time.

When he was watching Tracy, I signaled her to lift her T-shirt. I knew she was wearing her skimpy bikini top underneath and I counted on him staring.

She saw my signal, turned to face him, and lifted her shirt. Her bikini top had shifted and wasn't covering anything. He got a really good look at her breasts.

That gave me a few seconds to get my rigging knife out of my pocket. I quietly locked open the marlin spike, quickly showed it to Tracy, and then hid it behind my hand and slowly moved toward him.

He briefly looked toward me, then looked back at Tracy, and moved toward her. I needed her to keep his attention, so I made eye contact and signaled her again. I signaled her by pumping the air.

She pulled her shirt over her head, cradled one breast in each hand, and said, "How much time do we have? Reid is

Pat's man, not mine. And she won't share. I haven't been fucked for months. Your wife will never know."

He stopped dead and stared, obviously not expecting that.

I moved close behind him and with all of my might, thrust the pointy marlin spike into the side of his neck.

But he was taller than I calculated, and the spike just bounced off his collarbone. It grazed his neck but didn't go in. He whirled around and grabbed me by my throat. I could feel his fingers tightening. I could barely breathe. I panicked and dropped the knife, grabbing his wrists with both hands.

Buster tried to bite his leg, but he kept kicking him away.

His face was a few inches from mine and I heard him say, "Now you and your friend are going to wish you were dead."

CHAPTER 66

"Pat. Pat! Can you hear me?"

Tracy's voice echoed in my head from far away. I tried to open my eyes, tried to swim toward it, but my limbs were heavy.

"Pat!"

My face stung. I jumped. Was she hitting me?

Another crack and explosion of pain.

My eyes flew open. "Goddamn it, Tracy, stop hitting me."

The next instant, I could hardly breathe she was hugging me so tightly.

"Sorry, sorry. I had to get you to wake up."

I pulled myself into a sitting position. "What the fuck happened?"

She pointed toward the deck. Carl was spread-eagled, blood pooling from a gash in his neck.

I felt my eyes go wide. "Did you do that?"

She nodded slowly. "I gaffed him. He was choking you. I had to do something."

This time it was me hugging Tracy until she gasped and pulled away.

The radioed crackled. "Carl, are you there?"

Tracy and I exchanged glances. In the distance, we heard the guttural sound of the dinghy's engine being fired up.

"What do we do now?" Tracy asked. "They're coming."

I had an idea. "Help me drag Carl over to the steps and prop him up so he'll be visible on the stern. Put Buster in the forward cabin and tell him to be quiet, no barking."

Tracy and I positioned Carl's body so it looked like he was watching us on deck. When Tracy returned from taking Buster, she had the shotgun and shells and something else.

"Let's put these on."

My nose wrinkled as I slipped into the bloody shirt. "Great idea. Thank you, Mr. Dorado, your sacrifice was not in vain."

She put on Reid's shirt. I reloaded the shotgun. "You lay here," I said. "Now let's hope Reid figures out what we're doing."

In a moment, as the sound of the dinghy drew nearer, I laid beside her, the shotgun clenched in sweaty hands beneath me.

The radio squawked again. "Damn it, Carl, what's going on?"

When there was still no answer, Rick repeated his call. The

dinghy was so close now, we could hear the aggravation in his voice not only through the radio.

The Lady Anne was hove to and slowly oscillating back and forth. It was very quiet; only the dinghy's motor could be heard in the distance.

It grew closer, slowed down, and came to a stop.

"Oh my God," a woman's voice screamed. "They've killed my husband."

The scream made my heart pound. I know I jumped. I imagined Tracy had, too, but hoped the sight of Carl's bloody body had drawn their attention away from us.

"I have to go to him," the woman shrieked.

"Just wait," Rick commanded. "Something's not right."

The dinghy circled *The Lady Anne* two times before taking up position close astern.

"Wait here," Rick said.

He boarded *The Lady Anne*.

I held my breath. I could hear soft footfalls as someone boarded from the swim platform.

In a moment, a voice. "Carl is dead, but from the looks of it, he took the two women with him. Let me get tied off and then you can come aboard. And bring him with you."

"They ripped his throat out," the woman sobbed a few minutes later.

"Judging from the blood-soaked corpses, he gave better than he got," Rick said. "Is this mess your crew?"

"That's them," Reid said softly.

"I'll keep you alive for now. Pay your last respects and then the bodies are going over the side. I would have preferred a decent burial for Carl, but he won't care."

"No," the woman said. "We take him back with us. His children need a chance to say goodbye."

Reid must have separated himself from the two, because suddenly, he was standing beside me. He mumbled how sorry he was and that this was all his fault. Then, suddenly, he leaned close and said in my ear, "I'm clear. Shoot."

I rolled over, raised up, and pointed the gun. "Captain Rick, don't flinch, don't blink, don't move."

Tracy jumped up next. She looked like a bloody apparition rising from the dead. She was covered in blood, but she was holding our two largest knives. She snarled at the woman who was standing over Carl's body on the steps to the swim platform, "Don't fucking move, bitch."

Rick stood still, his mouth open in surprise. We took a gamble—played possum—and it had worked. I could only imagine what we looked like, fish blood and guts covering us from neck to knees. A bloody mess that hid the fact we were alive and had weapons concealed beneath our "bodies."

Reid walked over to Tracy, extending his hands so she could cut him loose. "You have no idea how glad I am that you're both alive," he said, grinning.

"No happier than we are," she said as she sawed through the fishline. She took a hard look at him. "Is that blood? Are you bleeding?"

"I'm okay," Reid replied. He twisted his hands apart and

began rubbing the feeling back in his wrists. "Captain Rick over there bushwhacked me with a rock."

I kept the gun leveled on Rick and the woman. "It took you long enough to figure out what we were doing," I said, raising an eyebrow.

"The blood kind of threw me," he replied, shaking some feeling back into his wrists. "But then I noticed Tracy was wearing the shirt I wore when I cleaned the big dorado." He glanced at me. "And Pat had on the shirt she wore, too, when she helped me clean the fish. Buster was nowhere to be found and unless Carl had chucked him overboard, he'd never leave Tracy's side. Combine all that with the fact that I didn't see the shotgun laying around, the puzzle pieces snapped into place."

"Good job, Sherlock," Tracy said. She jerked a thumb toward Rick and his companion. "What are we going to do with them?"

"Tie them up," I answered. "Nice and tight."

Tracy went below and got some line. Buster came up with her. Reid tied their hands tightly behind their backs. Buster stayed in front of Tracy, growling the entire time.

When Reid was finished, we seated them on the steps, near Carl's body. There were sharks circling astern. Carl's blood trail, oozing into the water, had drawn at least two dozen sharks. Given the size of their dorsal fins, a few of them were pretty big.

Reid made introductions. "Captain Rick, meet Captain Pat and First-Officer Tracy. Pat and Tracy, meet Captain Rick. And this is Bonnie, mother of two and now a widow. Her late husband is the one bleeding all over the deck. His name was Carl."

Our prisoners didn't say anything, but Rick looked very pissed off. Bonnie hung her head and was quiet. For the first time, I looked, really looked at her. She was maybe forty, tall, thin. Her face was gaunt, but I imagined she must have been beautiful when they started on their ill-fated fishing charter. She bore a striking resemblance to a young Elizabeth Taylor— the same deep blue eyes and raven hair.

No wonder Carl suspected Rick of lusting after her.

I lowered the gun and switched the safety back on. My hands hurt from holding it so tight. My knees were weak. I figured the adrenaline rush was ebbing. I sat at the helm.

"You murdered my husband."

Bonnie's eyes were hard as she looked at me.

No," Tracy said, coming around to stand between us. "I killed your husband in self-defense. He boarded us, threatened us that Captain Rick would kill Reid if we resisted, told us he was taking one half of our fuel, food, and water, and then told us he was going to kidnap us for Captain Rick's pleasure to stop him from staring at you."

She turned and pulled the neck of my shirt open. "See those bruises, Bonnie? That's what your husband was doing when I killed him. Choking my friend unconscious."

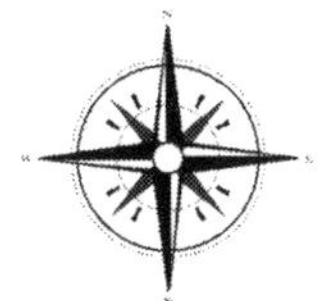

CHAPTER 67

Bonnie began to sob. "He was only trying to help us," she said. "We're running out of provisions and we have children."

"Then he should have asked for help," I snapped. "And not threatened to steal from us."

"And that gave you the right to kill him?"

Rage suddenly flared inside me. I stood and released the safety on the shotgun. "He gave us the right to kill him," I barked. "The same way I'd have a right to kill you two right now. Piracy is still a capital charge in a lot of countries and by boarding my boat illegally, you've committed piracy. I'm right about that aren't I, Reid?"

Reid had come up to stand beside me. "She's right."

But he reached over and gently took the gun from my hand. "But we're not cold-blooded killers." He took my arm and steered me back to Tracy. She put her arm around my shoulders, and we sat together on the deck.

"Reid," she said. "We still don't know what happened to you over on the island. Fill us in."

I could tell Tracy was trying to take my mind off my anger. What she didn't know was that part of my fury was directed not only at Carl, but at Pincus and what he had tried to do to me. When Carl had his hands on me, the only thing I kept flashing back to was being bent over the salon table. If Carl had had his way, I'd be back on the island with Rick and Bonnie, and Tracy and I would once again be at the mercy of a madman.

I didn't realize I was shaking until Tracy's arm tightened around my shoulder. "It's okay," she said. "We're back in control. No one can hurt us again."

I looked into her eyes and realized she understood more than I thought. I pulled myself together. "Yeah," I said, turning to Reid. "What happened after you spied Bonnie and her kids on the shore?"

Reid rechecked Rick's and Bonnie's knots before starting. "You heard my reports about spotting Bonnie and her kids."

Bonnie interrupted. "The kids have names, Max and Joey. Max is ten and Joey is twelve."

He nodded. "Okay…spotted Bonnie and Max and Joey." He waved a hand. "I found the boat, *The Day Dream*, and when it seemed secure, motored back to the fire. The three of them were still standing on the shoreline. Bonnie wanted me to call the Coast Guard or the Navy or radio for a helicopter. I told her I hadn't been able to make contact with anyone."

Reid placed the shotgun down on the deck beside us. "She wanted to know who I had been talking to earlier on my radio. I told her that my portable radio only reached my vessel. I also told her we had been unable to contact the Coast Guard and my phone didn't work, which was true."

He began pacing. "She didn't believe me. She insisted we take them to the nearest phone or marina. I asked how many of them were there. She told me there were only three of them; the others were dead."

Bonnie didn't respond but she fidgeted uncomfortably. I wondered if she was uncomfortable being tied up or having to hear how she had lied to Reid. Regardless, Reid continued.

"There was something in her voice that made me suspicious. Maybe it was the fact that she was so calm. Maybe it was because the clothes drying on the outrigger looked like men's clothes, not a woman's or a kid's."

He looked down at Bonnie. "I was thinking about what to do when she took off running. She sprinted about fifty feet, screaming hysterically, and then tripped and fell facefirst onto the rocks. She sat up and looked back toward me. Her face was bloody. The kids caught up to her and started crying."

Bonnie spoke up for the first time. "Rick made me do it. He had spotted your vessel approaching the island. He said it was critical that we either get a ride or get fuel, food, and water. Then when Reid motored past us in his dinghy, we saw he was alone."

Bonnie turned to face Rick. "You sent Carl back to their vessel, instructing him to hide in the rocks and wait for a signal. The signal would mean the dinghy and its driver had been captured. Carl was to swim out to the vessel and persuade its crew to either take all of us with them to the next port or leave us some supplies. Carl was to radio when he was aboard and Rick would explain what would happen if there were any gunshots."

"The double smoke signal was the signal for Carl to board us," Tracy asked. "Wasn't it?"

"Yes," Bonnie responded.

I turned again to Reid. "What happened next?"

CHAPTER 68

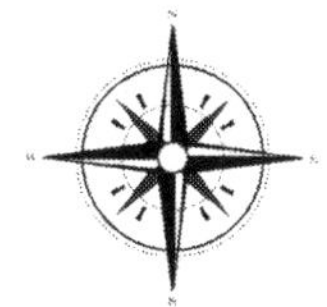

Reid continued. "I hurried ashore, tied off the dinghy, and ran over to Bonnie. Her nose was bleeding and she was crying. I tried to help her, but then suddenly everything went black."

"Let me guess," I said. "*Captain* Rick had been hiding, snuck up behind Reid, and hit him in the head with a rock."

Bonnie blanched and nodded. "The way Reid collapsed, I thought he was dead."

I went over and inspected Reid's head. There was a trail of dried blood running down his neck and shirt and a giant bump. His scalp was scraped and raw. His hair was matted with blood. He said he had a headache but no longer felt dizzy. I felt anger bubbling up again. I whirled on Bonnie and Captain Rick. "If you had killed him, I swear to God you'd both be dead by now."

Reid put a gentle hand on my arm, pulling me away. "I'm all right. When I came to, my hands were tied. The kids were tending a second fire." He nodded at Tracy. "The signal for Carl to board *The Lady Anne*. I debated getting up, but I was groggy and with my hands tied, I knew that Rick had every advantage.

"About that time Tracy radioed and Rick explained what would happen to me if he heard any gunshots. The way he glared at me, I knew he was serious about killing me. When the radio call was over, he smacked me and demanded to know how many persons were aboard. I didn't tell him. It didn't seem to matter. He was very confident that Carl would complete his mission and they would either leave with our boat or get fuel for their boat."

"What was going through your head while all this was happening?" I asked him. "Were you scared?"

Reid smiled. "Not for myself. I was scared for you and Tracy. The way I figured it, I had one chance and that was to convince them we had a better chance to get through this together than apart. So I asked them if they took photos or video of the same things we had—those strange lights—right before they went through hell's electrical storm. I suggested we should compare notes. That brought Bonnie and Rick right over."

"Then what happened?" Tracy asked.

"Rick wanted to know what I knew. I told him I knew they had lost power, had no radio or cell phone service, no GPS, no working compass, and had no idea where they were, despite the fact that he probably thought he knew these waters like the back of his hand."

"That's when I told Rick not to kill him," Bonnie said. "I knew he had information about what had happened."

Reid continued, "I asked Rick where he would go if he took our boat. He said he'd go back to Provo. I explained that he wouldn't find Provo because Provo wasn't there. I told him we hadn't spotted one landfall that was on the charts. There was no GPS and there was no satellite service.

"I told how we found another shipwreck but that the crew was all dead, poisoned from eel bites. I explained that their log described the same electrical phenomenon we all encountered, but back on January 3rd. I confirmed their log stated they hadn't seen any boats or planes either. Rick was skeptical but Bonnie seemed to believe me, saying they had been in trouble since Christmas week.

"I asked them why they hadn't figured out that the lights they had encountered were a UFO. I told them that when they filmed it, it silenced them by sending them back in time."

Reid shook his head. "Of course, Rick called me full of shit, but I told him that deep down, he knew things hadn't been right since the electrical storm. Things he couldn't explain—the utter failure of all communication, the fantastic schools of fish, the hundreds of whales, the thousands of dolphins, the sky black with birds, the recent volcanic activity, and the complete lack of other people, ships, or planes.

"I could tell Bonnie was beginning to come around. Rick, while he insisted he did not believe in aliens, could come up with no alternate explanation. When he hadn't heard from Carl, he decided to dinghy back to *The Lady Anne* and see what was wrong. I convinced him to take me with him and Bonnie joined us."

"How did you sell that idea?" Tracy asked. "It sounded like he was ready to kill you."

"I asked him how he was with sails. He had a sarcastic response about God inventing motors so fisherman wouldn't have to depend on the wind. So I asked how non-sailors would handle a sixty-eight-foot sailing yacht under sail alone through a narrow channel."

I realized Reid hadn't mentioned that we restored engine power and when he gave me a sly wink, I knew he was keeping that quiet. We sailed into their view, so how could they know anything else?

Reid continued, "I asked if they knew how to deploy and retrieve an anchor under sail alone. I asked that when they left, how they would handle twenty-foot swells when there was too much wind for the sails but they needed steerage. Bonnie knew they needed me and told Rick that she was coming along. She told him that she could watch me while he and Carl handled our crew."

Reid sat down and rubbed a weary hand over his face "So, they left the kids by the fire and the three of us came back in the dinghy. You know the rest of what happened."

CHAPTER 69

"So what are you going to do now?" Rick asked.

For no longer being in control, he still looked and sounded arrogant. I wanted to slap that arrogance right off his face. "I do believe the penalty for piracy is death," I said calmly, hefting the shotgun.

"If you kill us, my kids will be alone," Bonnie said. "Please. You have to promise to take Max and Joey with you."

"We're not bringing any kids with us," Tracy snapped. "What do we look like, a day-care center?"

"You should have thought about the future when you sided with Rick," Reid said. "He's a cowardly bushwhacking son of a bitch and you aided him when you lied and then deliberately injured yourself, luring me ashore."

"I was desperate," Bonnie pleaded.

"Under nautical law," Rick interrupted, "you have a responsibility to offer assistance to shipwrecked survivors."

Reid walked over to him. "You left off the last part of that rule: if such assistance can be rendered without endangering your vessel or personnel. If I remember correctly, you threatened to cut my head off and broadcast my screams over the air."

Rick didn't respond, but he didn't look away either. I got the feeling he wasn't intimidated or scared.

"I vote we push Carl over the side and shove this bastard in after him," Tracy said coldly. "After the sharks have finished, we can take Bonnie back to shore with a few supplies. She can take care of her kids."

"I don't think we can survive without him," Bonnie said, her voice trembling.

Rick hissed at Reid, "If you kill me, the three of them will die of dehydration in a couple of days. If you leave them water, starvation will follow within a week. I hope you got a good look at Max and Joey back there because their death will be on you."

"But," I said, "if we let you go, what's to stop you from waiting for the next vessel and attacking them the way you did us—without warning, hesitation, or mercy?"

"You killed Carl and can claim self-defense," Rick stated. "But if you kill me, you are committing murder. Cold-blooded murder."

"He may be right," Reid said. "Tied up like this, he is no longer a threat. While the penalty for piracy used to be hanging, that isn't the case anymore. I believe the only action against Somali pirates was arrest and seizure of their vessels."

Bonnie started to cry again. "Think of my kids. My God, they're only ten and twelve years old. We were on winter vacation. Deep-sea fishing was supposed to be a surprise for the boys. How could we have imagined something like this…"

Tracy had been sitting on the deck, Buster at her side. Now she looked up. "If our situations were reversed, what would you do?"

It got quiet. Rick looked over at Bonnie, but didn't say anything. Bonnie had stopped sobbing. She drew a deep breath. "If you can't let us both go," she said quietly. "Will you at least leave my kids provisions to last a month or so? Enough to last until another boat comes by?"

"There's no guarantee another boat will come by," Tracy said, her voice hard. "And we don't have a lot extra we can spare. We are provisioned for three, not five."

Rick snorted. "Then it looks like you'll have to kill me, kill Bonnie, and then go kill Max and Joey." He glared at Tracy. "And I'll bet even a cold bitch like you doesn't have the balls to commit quadruple homicide. Pushing us over the side is easy, killing two young boys in cold blood isn't."

But Tracy didn't bite. Instead she met his eyes. "I had balls enough to kill your partner when he went after my friend. And you're making it so easy to want you dead. You shouldn't push your luck. If it was up to me, you'd be shark bait already."

For once, Rick had the good sense to keep quiet.

I considered that a victory—score one for Tracy.

Still, we were no closer to a decision than we were before.

Reid shrugged. "Options?"

I thought for a moment and then replied, "One, we can leave them here. Two, we can take them with us. Three, we can bury Carl at sea and have Rick accidentally fall in after him."

At the last suggestion, Rick glared at me, but Tracy clapped. "I vote for three," she said.

But we needed to discuss between us what to do—out of the earshot of our captives. We checked that they were securely tied and went forward bringing the gun, making sure to keep them in our line of sight.

One by one, Tracy, Reid, and I discussed the pros and cons of each option. If we left them here, we could send help back for them when we reached civilization. However, if I was right about my time travel theory and there was any civilization to find, who knew if anyone would be in a position to offer aid.

Besides, we all agreed that leaving them here would put the next boat that found them at risk.

Our discussion continued with taking them with us. If Rick got loose, he would surely make trouble. Since Bonnie had proven both a liar and an accomplice, coupled with the fact that Tracy and I had killed her husband, regardless of the circumstances, it was pretty clear that she couldn't be trusted either. Even if we locked Rick and Bonnie in a cabin, her kids might try to free them. Tracy again reminded us that our supplies were limited.

Rick called out to us. "I have an idea," he said.

We rejoined them aft, not having come to any conclusion.

"What is it?" I said.

"Tie us up in my boat, tow it, feed us just enough to keep us alive, and then turn us in at the next port."

Tracy laughed. "Next port? If Pat's time travel theory is correct, there won't be a next port."

I shook my head. "Besides, Reid said your boat was a forty footer. *The Lady Anne* was not designed for towing anything as big as that. We would sail at a snail's pace."

Since Rick had no idea we could motor-sail, I didn't add that using our precious fuel to pull a fishing boat for even a few days was foolish. Unless we were lucky enough to find replacement fuel, what we carried was all there was. I was suddenly glad we had topped off the tanks in Provo.

"You three honestly believe we went through some kind of time portal?"

The sneer in his tone said it all.

"Pat's very smart," Tracy said. "You should listen to her."

He lunged forward, strained against the rope. "Fuck this," he said. "Whatever you're going to do, do it. Just do it. Fuck you. Fuck all three of you."

CHAPTER 70

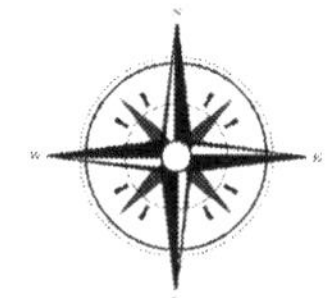

It took a lot of time and effort, but we were finally ready to get underway. We still had a decision to make, but first things first.

Reid told Bonnie not to look. We had Tracy get underway and then Reid pushed Carl's body over the stern. Bonnie screamed when she heard the splash. Sharks swarmed his body and in minutes, all that was left was a stain on the water.

Reid placed a hand on Bonnie's shoulder. "I'm sorry for your loss. I understand desperate people do desperate things, but your husband could have killed Pat. What happened to him was the result of bad choices."

She hung her head, quiet sobs her only reply.

Rick sighed. "So, what now?"

For once, his tone was free of sarcasm and belligerence.

"We're not sure yet," I answered. "Right now, we're going

to clean this deck and get out of these clothes. I'll bring you water in a few minutes."

Reid washed the blood off the deck and I told Tracy to sail a short distance further before heaving to again. When I checked over the side, none of the sharks had followed us.

After Tracy and I cleaned up and changed clothes, with Reid standing guard, it was time to have another crew meeting. We needed to decide what was to be done with Rick and Bonnie. We discussed returning them to their camp, the concern being that if they got *The Day Dream* up and running, they could easily chase after us. And they'd catch us—the fishing boat was faster than *The Lady Anne*. The thought nagged at me that I was already looking over my shoulder for Pincus; I couldn't bear the thought that Captain Rick might be after us as well. It boiled down to the fact that there were two things we could do about that—one, scuttle the ship, or two, make sure the fuel tanks were empty and take the keys.

"It goes against every fiber of my being to sink a boat," Reid said. "But I used to teach the diesel engine maintenance class. In five minutes, I could permanently disable the engine. Even if they did manage to obtain fuel, they could never get it running."

"To me, the bigger problem," Tracy said, "is how to alert the next poor sucker who happens upon them that Rick is a dangerous son of a bitch."

I shook my head. "Nothing we can do about that."

Reid thought for a minute. "Wait a minute," he said, snapping his fingers. "Don't we have some paint on board?"

It took me a moment to remember. "We do! In the workroom."

"Then we'll paint a message on the side of *The Day Dream* . . ."

Tracy gave a little squeal. "Danger, pirate ahead," she said.

"Or 'Watch your back-Captain Rick is not to be trusted,'" I suggested.

"And we'll sign it, crew of *The Lady Anne*," Reid said.

Sounded like the most reasonable plan we could come up with. None of us had the heart for more killing. Secretly, I wished we could take Bonnie and her kids with us, but realistically, I knew it was impossible.

We decided it would be prudent to drop them a reasonable distance away from their camp to have time to paint the warning on *The Day Dream* before they got back. We didn't know where the kids would be, but hoped when they saw us approach with their mom, they'd follow the dinghy to where we released her.

We dismissed the possibility of them starving or dying of thirst. They'd managed to live this long, so they must have found a fresh water source and Rick was the captain of a fishing boat, after all, so he'd have plenty of equipment. Fishing in these waters was good.

Still, I insisted we put together a carc package. I rescued two dozen empty water bottles from our trash, rinsed them, and refilled them with fresh water. Reid seasoned some of Tracy's dorado, double-wrapped four portions in foil, and put them in a small box containing a bag of ice cubes. Tracy added two candy bars, labeled Max and Joey.

We donated a bag of potato chips, eight juice boxes, one onion, one lime, one green bean pepper, and four cans of vegetables. Tracy added a bottle of rum from our casino night. I packed everything into a trash bag and tied it shut. I also got the bolt cutters and our largest hammer, at Reid's request.

I piloted *The Lady Anne* across the channel to the far shore. As the crow flies, we were only a ten-minute dinghy ride from their camp, but having to walk along the shore, we guessed we had at least two hours before they'd get back. I knew they could save time by swimming directly across, but I figured the large number of feeding sharks across the channel would be a deterrent.

After I heaved to, I managed the gun while Reid seated Rick and Bonnie in the front of the dinghy, hands still tied. Tracy would stay on board *The Lady Anne* with the shotgun. I placed the goodie bag in the back of the dinghy.

"There's some fresh fish in here," I told Bonnie. "Better cook it tonight."

I motored along the shore, about fifty feet out. Reid had Rick stand up. He cut his hands loose and them immediately shoved Rick over the side. Reid did the same with Bonnie. We waited until they made it to shore, then I sped the dinghy across the channel to where Max and Joey were standing on the rocks. I got Reid in close enough to leave the goodie bag on the rocks.

The boys reached it first. While they carried it back to

their camp, Reid and I motored around to *The Day Dream*. The paint we found was really a red metal primer, but it did the trick.

"Beware: Captain Rick is dangerous. Proceed with Caution."

We signed it with our names and leaned back to inspect our work.

"What do you think Rick will say when he sees this?" I asked.

Reid picked up the hammer and bolt cutters and smiled grimly. "I hope I never get the chance to ask him," he said. "Now give me a few minutes to get aboard and disable the engine and then let's get the hell out of here."

CHAPTER 71

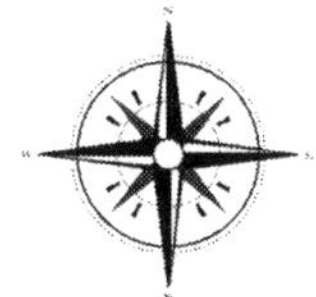

We were back on board *The Lady Anne* and under sail when Tracy asked, "What if the next people we find are as desperate as Rick and Bonnie?"

"We'll just have to be careful," Reid said.

"But she's got a good point," I said. "Who knows how many people have been trapped here. As long as we continue to sail in this area, it stands to reason anyone we encounter will be just as desperate to leave as they were—as we are." I paused. "And their desperation is most likely to be directly proportional to how adept they were at finding food and water."

Tracy was quiet for a moment. "Do you think we should have taken Bonnie and her kids with us?"

I shook my head. "No. We're not provisioned for three more. All we can do is keep searching for a way to get back to our own time, and maybe then we can figure out a way to send help back to them."

"I feel sorry for the kids," she said, frowning. "As far as Rick is concerned, I hope he never gets out."

Buster had been lying at her feet. He rose and stretched and made his way back to the swim platform. We watched as he did his business, then trotted back to us.

"Good dog," Tracy said, scratching his head.

Reid had been listening to our conversation. "The problem is," he said, "Rick couldn't accept the likelihood that they were transported back in time. Even when I described the events that brought us here and Bonnie was astounded that it was exactly what they experienced, Rick couldn't accept it. For him, it will always be finding the closest marina."

"Do you think we should change course?" Tracy asked.

I shook my head. "I think we should stay on course and hopefully come upon another contact. If I'm right about this whole time portal thing, we'll see how well they have fared since they came through."

"So if the next people we find confirm they got here the same way we did, then what?" she asked.

"Then we have to decide to stay here or go somewhere else."

"Somewhere else?" Tracy's voice rose in frustration. "Where the hell else could we go?"

"We could go anywhere," Reid answered. "We've got a fine ship, a water maker, and provisions for weeks if we eat smart and continue to catch fish."

"And be trapped in whatever time period this is." Tracy leaned over and scratched Buster's head. Finally, she said quietly, "But what if we don't want to accept this time?"

There. That was the question I'd been waiting for. "Then we should stay within the Bermuda Triangle," I said. "And focus our efforts on finding the aliens that sent us here."

Both Reid and Tracy looked at me in surprise.

"It was alien technology that brought us here, it will have to be alien technology that sends us back."

Abruptly, Tracy stood up. She walked forward toward the hatch and then just as abruptly stopped, turned around, and said, "How the fuck are we supposed to find the aliens?"

As she disappeared below deck, Reid said, "Tell me you have an idea."

"Ever hear Shania Twain's song, 'Dance with the One That Brought You.'"

"Meaning what exactly?"

"Meaning, since we found aliens by videoing them at night, we sail at night and keep the video camera handy."

"So now you want us to sail at night, in waters full of whales, without GPS or accurate charts, and take video of any strange lights that happen to go by?"

"Yes," I replied. "That's exactly what I want."

"So supposing we do see them, what then?"

"Then we figure out a way to communicate. They have no reason to send us further back in time; there's no one here we could show the video to. We try to negotiate with them to return us to our time. We can even destroy the camera as a gesture of our sincerity."

"Well," he said, after a moment. "We've got nothing to lose."

Tracy returned topside with a bag of trail mix, three Gatorades, and a piece of jerky for Buster.

She passed around the drinks. "So, what did you two decide?" she asked.

"We're going to do some night sailing and look for aliens," Reid replied.

If we expected another outburst, Tracy surprised us. She handed the trail mix around, saying nothing until, "If we are going to be sailing all night, I'm going to need a nap."

CHAPTER 72

"We'll keep going on 180 degrees magnetic for a while and see if we find land. If we don't, we can start making adjustments for shifts," I answered.

Rick's island fell off the radar about an hour after we finished snacking. It was smooth sailing under a clear sky and for the first time in days, I felt myself begin to relax. Later that afternoon, we came upon another radar contact and altered course toward it. I had mixed feelings. The knot in my stomach caused by our run-in with Carl, Rick, and Bonnie had just begun to loosen.

Reid must have sensed my concern, because he ducked below and returned with the trail mix and a big bowl.

"Come on you two," he said. "Help me pick out the raisins. I have an idea for dinner."

"Trying to distract us?" I said.

He grinned.

"Tracy, you help Reid. I'll take the helm."

So while I steered, they sorted out the raisins. Reid took everything below and rejoined us a few minutes later.

"Are you making raisin bread?" Tracy said, giggling.

"Nope, something much better," he said with a wink.

As we got closer to the radar contact, it became apparent the blips were multiple islands. Keeping an eye on the depth, I headed for the closest one. I closed to a safe distance and paralleled the shoreline. It was rocky, desolate, and inhospitable.

I made a few tacks and sailed in between two of the islands. There weren't any coves or inviting anchorages here either, but we passed a protected spot behind some big boulders.

I sailed a little while longer but found nothing better, so we returned to the big boulders. I had to motor in because between the boulders and the rocky island, there wasn't enough wind. I made one pass to check the depth and then gave Tracy the helm and helped Reid with the anchor.

"You know what's nice about this big, flat, barren island?" he asked me as we prepared to anchor.

"There's no one hiding ashore to swim out here later?"

"Exactly." He smiled.

Soon we were anchored. Tracy stayed topside to make sure the anchor was set and Reid headed for the galley. Since the engine was running, I began recharging batteries.

"If you get me your radio, I'll top it off," I told him, holding up the empty charging base.

"I think it's in the dinghy," he replied. "At least, I hope so."

I hollered up for Tracy to check the dinghy for Reid's radio. A few minutes later she hollered back it wasn't there. I went topside to help her look. We couldn't find it.

"Any luck?" he asked, poking his head through the hatch.

Tracy shook her head and asked, "Where did you last see it?"

He grimaced. "Rick had it."

"Did he bring it with him on the dinghy?" I asked.

"I don't remember. Bonnie was holding a knife on me and I was trying not to get stabbed."

"I have a feeling they've got our radio," I said. "But it's not worth going back for. The only thing they could do with it is contact us while we're in transmission distance and we're probably out of that by now."

Satisfied the anchor was holding, Tracy joined Reid below. After the batteries were charged, I shut down the engine and rejoined everybody below. "What smells so good?" I asked.

Tracy handed me a glass of red wine and grinned. "Reid made sauce with this so now we've got to finish the bottle."

I took a sip and smacked my lips. "Good."

As Reid served us dinner, he apologized for butchering one of his best recipes, Tournedos with Raisin Cabernet Sauce. "I had to use hamburger. I usually use filet mignon."

"Well, this is really good," Tracy said, taking another bite.

"It's better with fresh raisins, and I was missing several ingredients, but I'm glad you like it."

"He soaked the raisins in wine until they plumped up," Tracy added. "I'll have to remember that."

"Filet mignon or not, right ingredients or not, this is fantastic." I smiled and raised my glass. "Here's to the chef."

Reid peered into his glass and said, "Knowing Charles, this is probably a five-hundred-dollar bottle of wine."

"So?" Tracy asked.

"If the vintner knew I used that bottle for cooking, he'd go nuts."

I shook my head. "No he wouldn't. He'd take one bite and offer you a case if you'd cook this for the guests at his vineyard."

Reid smiled and said, "Speaking of wine, when I was looking for a Cabernet for tonight's dinner, I spotted the perfect wine for tomorrow night's fish dinner."

"Which one?" she asked.

Reid winked at me and then replied to Tracy, "The dorado in the cooler topside."

"No, silly, which wine?"

"I found a bottle of Pouilly Fuisse," he said, looking extremely pleased.

"What kind is that," I asked.

"It's French for fussy pussy," he said very seriously.

"I don't speak French, but I'm pretty sure that's not how it translates."

"That's how it always translates on late-night comedy," he said.

"I'll translate for you," Tracy announced as she finished her glass. "It means Reid's not fussy about whose pussy he gets later tonight."

I shook my head. Tracy was back in form.

We had finished and I was taking the plates to the galley when Reid opened another bottle of wine, refilled our glasses, and asked, "Do you know what's good and bad about that recipe?"

I looked down at the empty plates I was carrying. "No leftovers. Not even a scrap for Buster."

CHAPTER 73

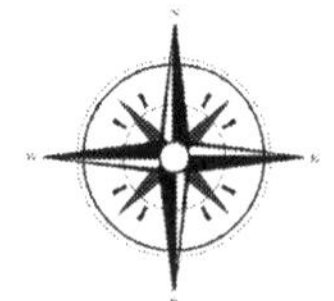

Buster's barking woke me. He needed to go topside. Tracy and Reid had spent the night in his cabin. The barking didn't appear to wake them, so I got up and let him out. He went straight to the swim platform.

I walked once around the deck. Everything was fine and Buster soon joined me. We returned below and I slipped him a pretzel while I started making breakfast. I tried to be quiet, but my puttering in the galley brought a sleepy-eyed Tracy. She stumbled into the galley and went straight for the coffee. Five minutes later, Reid joined us, and we gathered around the table.

"So, what's the plan for today?" Tracy asked, spearing a slice of bacon.

Reid answered, "Explore any radar contacts we come

across today and if we don't find any survivors, begin night sailing tonight."

Tracy turned to me. "Do you really think we'll spot a UFO out here?"

"I think it's our best bet," I answered her.

"What do we do if we find someone else?"

She didn't mention Rick and Bonnie by name, but it was clear by the hesitation in her voice that they were on her mind.

Reid answered her question. "We'll be careful, very careful."

"We don't have much to barter with except fresh water," I said. "That's one thing we have plenty of."

"We have fish," Tracy said.

I nodded. "True. We could trade them fish and water for information. Maybe confirm if they got here the same way we did and if our speculation about *how* we got here makes sense to anyone else."

"You mean aliens," Tracy said. "Asking if anyone else thinks they've been stranded by aliens."

I shrugged. "I think most people that have survived here will be more willing to accept what happened to them than Rick was. If they've observed the same things we have and they're logical in their thinking, they'd have to consider it."

We finished breakfast and got underway. The sea was calm and glassy, only a faint breeze now and then to ripple the surface, so we motor-sailed.

We debated stowing the dinghy and not towing it, but

decided to wait a while in case we needed to go ashore. We passed several small islands, but there were no signs of boats or people. No signal fires or messages on the rocks, no radio contact of any kind. We had the area to ourselves.

We found wind in an open area. Before Tracy shut down the engine, I ran the water maker and topped off our fresh water supply.

In a while, Reid spotted some dark shapes on the water and we cautiously changed course to investigate. We soon found ourselves sailing through hundreds of sailfish that were lying directly on the surface. They had their beautiful blue sails raised and appeared to be sunning themselves. They were gorgeous fish, about twelve feet long. Since we were over-stocked with fish, we left them in peace, settling for making a video record of the encounter.

High noon found us navigating around the last island in the group. There were still no signs of people, so we heaved to for a quick lunch.

While we were eating, I told Reid and Tracy something I'd been thinking about. "If we heave to again and send the dinghy to shore, whoever is left aboard needs to move the boat every fifteen minutes or so."

Tracy nodded. "Yes. If someone tries to swim out to us again, let's not make it too easy. Carl barely made it out to us, but he did make it. If we'd have moved a couple of times, he might have been forced to turn back."

"I think that's a brilliant idea," Reid said. "We may not ever come across someone as devious as Rick again, but we have too much to lose to take chances. *The Lady Anne* makes a tempting target for anyone stranded without a boat. May as well not make ourselves an easy target too."

We finished eating and were soon back on course.

One hour later we got another radar contact, twenty-three miles distant. We adjusted course and trimmed the sails. *The Lady Anne* heeled nicely and our speed increased. Tracy had the helm, smiling like crazy as she steered.

There were clouds scattered here and there, providing interesting patterns to decipher. Fortunately, the clouds didn't appear threatening. We had perfect conditions for sailing. I kept looking for dolphins near our bow but never saw any.

We spotted a few whales but maintained our heading. Tracy kept us in a nice, straight line, trying to sail as efficiently as possible. Reid was the first to grin, point, and holler, "Land ho."

Tracy grinned back and asked, "Who are you calling a ho?"

At seven miles away, land was clearly visible. There were two distinct mountain peaks, separated by a low area. Sporadic patches of green streaked down toward the valley, primarily on the left side. The other side appeared rockier.

Buster was enjoying himself, sitting next to Tracy at the helm.

Reid suggested we head for the leeward side of the island. "But don't sail too close to the shoreline. The prevailing wind is blowing onshore. We don't want our boat to get blown into the rocks."

"How close is too close?"

"Stay out at least one mile. That would give us time to get the engine started or room to deploy the anchor if we need to."

"I should have known that," Tracy said. "I believe that was a question on one of the sailing tests."

Reid smiled. "Yes, it was. And what else do you need to be on the lookout for?"

"The current or a tide," I chimed in, "can also trap you against the shore. But the wind is most dangerous because it can shift without notice."

Tracy adjusted her course and I trimmed the sails. She closed to one and one-half miles offshore and angled to parallel the shore. We had just left the deep, cobalt-blue water and the water was now a dark green. She kept an eye on the depth, calling it out occasionally. There were large flocks of birds flying about, dive-bombing the water and squabbling with each other.

A sleek gray and white bird with a black head and beak and a long split tail landed on the starboard lifeline and looked at us. Buster leapt off the seat and charged, but the bird flew away before he could get there.

Tracy stayed at a safe distance just outside of the light-green shallows and paralleled the shoreline. It was rough, rocky, and desolate with scattered patches of sparse vegetation. Reid tried another hail, but there was no answer.

We got around a point and we now had the wind offshore blowing us away from the rocks. Tracy tacked and angled along the shore. There was a long band of flat water where the island was blocking the wind. It looked like a highway. We paralleled the band devoid of wind and waves. We weren't exactly sure what we were looking for, but we were confident we'd know it when we saw it.

About two hours later, Reid was glassing the shore when he suddenly exclaimed, "Oh, shit."

"What's wrong?" Tracy asked.

He turned to face us. "I guess boats aren't the only ones here." He pointed above the rocks, toward the wreckage of an airplane.

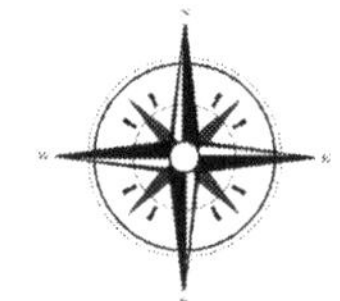

CHAPTER 74

We heaved to for a better look. It was definitely an airplane. It looked to be a single-engine plane, upside down. The closest wing had been ripped off and was laying on the rocks a short distance away. There was a big hole by the tail section and the cockpit, smashed.

"You think it got here the same way we did?" Tracy asked.

I shrugged. "I have to suppose so. From this angle, I don't see any area flat enough for a landing," I said.

"I hope I'm wrong, but it doesn't look like a wreck anyone would have walked away from," Reid said softly.

"Do you suppose we should get a closer look?" Tracy asked.

"We absolutely need to go see, but I think we should wait until morning."

"Why do you want to wait?" I asked.

"We can't anchor here. It's too exposed if the wind shifts during the night."

"We passed a nice cove back there," Tracy said, pointing.

"I figure it will take an hour to get there and get anchored. That plane isn't going anywhere and we haven't seen anyone around, so I vote we go anchor and return tomorrow."

We did as he suggested. The cove contained some birds, but other than that it was desolate. Reid grilled some of our fish while Tracy made a salad. I kept watch to be certain the anchor was holding since we had anchored in deeper water than usual.

When we were settled for the night, Reid poured us each a glass of Pouilly Fuisse. He had used the rest for cooking the fish, wrapped in foil. The wine tasted like Chardonnay and was very good. It complemented his fish creation perfectly.

"This is just fish and wine and butter and garlic?" Tracy asked, taking another piece.

"There's a few spices, but using foil packets lets the wine semi-steam the fish."

"Well, as usual, Reid, this is another perfect meal." I beamed.

"Here's to Charles," Tracy toasted.

"To Charles," I said and clinked glasses.

Tracy looked at her glass. "Do you suppose he calls it fussy pussy?" Tracy said, laughing.

I smiled and shook my head no. "I wouldn't think so, but then I wouldn't have expected him to wager *The Lady Anne* for sex either."

Tracy was eyeing Reid, and I got the hint. "Go ahead," I said. "I'll clean up."

Tracy took Reid's hand. "Sure you won't join us?"

I shook my head. When they left, I set about clearing the dishes and tidying the galley. Then I went topside, calling Buster to follow. We walked around the deck and then adjourned to the cockpit. I scratched him a few times and then just gazed out over the anchorage.

After a while, Tracy joined me and Buster topside. She was naked, but carrying fresh clothes, shampoo, soap, and a towel. She grinned and told me she had fucked his lights out and he was recovering.

"Has your period started?" I asked while she got a bottle of water. I wasn't sure if I really wanted to hear the answer, but I needed to know.

"Not yet," she replied.

"Aren't you worried that neither of our periods have started?"

"I'm not going to worry about what I can't control."

"Good point," I said.

She finished her water, took a second bottle, and headed for the solar shower. I went below and made coffee.

In ten minutes, she joined me at the cockpit table, towel-drying her hair. She winked at me and said, "It's been about thirty minutes. He's probably recharged by now." She looked at me and grinned. "Unless you want a turn."

"Don't you ever get enough?" I asked.

Tracy looked at me. "Enough? You mean, am I a nymphomaniac?" She laughed. "Not at all."

"So it's Reid? Are you in love with him?"

She laughed again. "If Reid wasn't here and another man was, I'd behave exactly the same."

"You admit it. You're promiscuous."

"Not at all. In fact, I'm monogamous by my own definition. One lover per set of sheets."

That caught me off guard and I hesitated, wanting to choose my next words carefully.

But Tracy didn't wait for my reply. "You think I'm a whore?"

She didn't look insulted or angry. Just curious.

"I was thinking more along the lines that you have a relaxed moral compass."

"You don't really know me, Pat. Our friendship back in the real world was casual. You surprised the shit out of me when you made that bet with Charles. Before that, the idea of sharing a lover with you would never have occurred to me. I can see it still doesn't go down easy with you."

Her response wasn't emotional but very matter-of-fact.

"I can't help who I am any more than you can help who you are," I replied. "I have no idea what possessed me to take that bet. Maybe the same thing that makes you a different person when you're on vacation. A chance to live another life. But once that bet was settled and we were on our way, the old Pat came back."

"Think what happened with Pincus has something to do with that?"

I winced. "You were unconscious through most of that. You didn't see what he almost did to me."

"*Almost* did to you."

I stared. "That makes a difference? The fact that he didn't actually rape me?"

Tracy shook her head. "No. I'm sorry I said that. I don't know what happened to you. Just like you don't know what's happening to me."

"Then tell me."

"It's a long story." She sighed, leaning back in her chair.

"I haven't heard Reid moving about," I said sarcastically. "So we've got time before you jump his bones again."

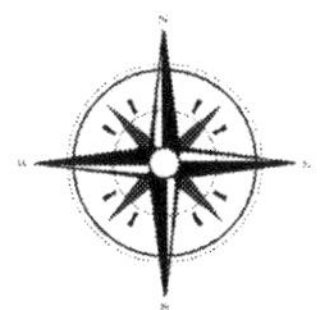

CHAPTER 75

Tracy moved closer to me and lowered her voice. "I don't want Reid to know this," she said. "Promise me.

I had no idea what she was about to tell me, but her expression was so serious, I agreed.

"I'm thirty-four years old. The women in my family don't make it past fifty."

"What?"

"My mother, my grandmother, my aunts. Dead. Cancer." She took my hand and continued, "The past twenty-six women in our bloodline were all buried before their fiftieth birthdays. We can have children, but we do so knowing what the future holds if the children are girls."

I could think of nothing to say to that, so I squeezed her hand to continue.

"When I got divorced, I knew I would never marry again.

I don't have the energy to fall in love, and my biological clock for childbirth is nearly done ticking. I told myself it was time to live. It was time to eat, drink, and fool around. Life is not a dress rehearsal; this is all we get. So don't judge me if I want another pitcher of hurricanes, a second piece of cheesecake, or another fuck."

"Why don't you want Reid to know?"

"Oh, yeah. That's the first thing I want him to know. That I'm going to die in sixteen years, maybe less, of rare, stealthy, aggressive ovarian cancer, but it's okay to fuck me now because I'm not contagious." She waved a hand. "I'm not looking for sympathy fucks. And I'm not telling you this so you'll feel sorry for me. I want you to understand that the way I'm living my life right now is because I don't know how long I have. And there's another reason. My ex knew. He promised 'til death do us part. But he lied. He married me, he insured me, and then he left me. What I have with Reid is uncomplicated. I want it to stay that way."

We lapsed into silence, watching Buster chase a bird that kept taunting him by landing on the lifelines.

After a moment, Tracy asked, "Do you think I can go inspect the plane wreckage this time?"

"Are you trying to change the subject?"

She shook her head. "I don't know what more I can say. You either understand or you don't. But, and I mean this, it doesn't change how much I value our friendship. You are important to me, Pat. I hope you know that."

I sighed. "You're important to me too. I don't know how

I'd react if I was in your situation. Maybe the same way. In any case, as long as we're stuck here on this boat, you and Reid can fuck like bunnies if you want. He sure seems to enjoy it, so who am I to object?"

"I am serious about one thing though. If you want a turn with him, just say the word. I can share."

I started to make a sarcastic remark about what Reid would think of our passing him around like a party favor, but thought better of it. Instead, I said, "I have no objection to you going to the crash site. You are likely to find bodies. Will you be okay with that?"

"So now who's changing the subject?"

I waved a hand. "Are you afraid of staying alone on the boat?"

"I'd rather take my chances ashore than have to fight off another boarder," she admitted. "Face it, Pat, we were lucky."

"I think that if we don't stay hove to for very long at a time, a swimmer from the shore probably couldn't do what Carl did."

"And that behooves us to keep a better watch. Still, if it's okay with you, I'd like to go ashore, either with you or with Reid."

"That's fine," I answered. I stood up, stretched, and yawned. "I'm turning in," I said. "You can get back to Reid. He's probably wondering where you went."

Tracy grinned and snapped the air with her towel. "I love you, Pat," she said.

"I love you, too, Tracy. Good night."

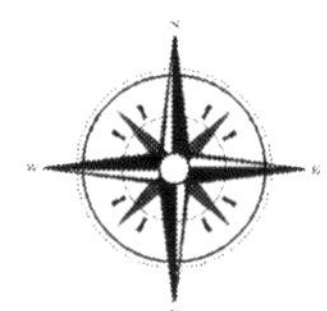

When I got to the galley the next morning, Tracy was already laying out breakfast. She handed me a cup of coffee. "Still okay with you if I go inspect the wreckage this morning?"

"It's fine with me," I said. There was movement from Reid's cabin and Reid appeared to join us.

"What's fine?" he asked, sitting down next to me.

"I want to go and look at the plane," Tracy told him.

"The way that plane looks, there's a good chance you'll find victims, not survivors. Are you okay with that?"

"Just what I told her," I said. "But she wants to go."

"Do you want to go alone?"

"No. I'd really like to go with Pat and leave you aboard this time." She looked intently at him, like she was expecting him to argue.

"Okay," he said. He turned to me. "Is there any more coffee?"

When we were ready, we motored back to the plane. Reid said he would circle while we went and checked out the wreckage. He wanted us to take the gun, but we refused. We did take a radio and also took Buster with us.

"Hurry back," he said as he kissed Tracy.

She grabbed his shoulders and kissed him back. "Guard the boat," she replied.

Then he kissed me on the cheek and told me to be careful. He smelled like toothpaste. "I will."

Tracy drove and I guided her to a space between some rocks. I tied the dinghy to a big rock and then rechecked my knot. Buster got wet jumping to shore but shook himself off and looked eager to go exploring.

"We're headed up to the plane, stand by," I radioed.

"Standing by."

"If there are bodies up there, they won't be able to tell us anything," Tracy said as she stepped carefully over the rocks.

"They might, if they wrote anything down before crashing."

"Are you still convinced about us really going back in time?"

"I hope I'm wrong and we'll find a marina around the next bend, but the longer we're here without finding civilization, the more credence I'm giving my theory."

A minute later, my feet slipped on a rock and I landed

hard. "Fuck," I yelled, examining a good-size scrape on my knee.

Tracy came back and gave me a hand up. "Are you okay?"

I looked at the scrape and sighed. "Just what I need, another bruise."

"Put some of that aloe cream on it when we get back," she told me. "It's done wonders for your face. The bruises are nearly gone. That cream really works. Are you using it on your neck too?"

My hands went to my throat. "I have been. It's still sore where he was choking me."

I shook away the memory of Carl and pointed. "Almost there."

A moment later we arrived at the wreckage. I radioed, "We're here, stand by."

Reid acknowledged.

"This thing is really smashed," Tracy said.

The damage up close was much worse than it appeared from the water. One wing had been sheared off and the other wing was torn in several places, almost as if it had been made of foil. The tail section was also dented, and there was a large hole where it had tried to rip away from the cabin section. The side door was closed and severely dented. I doubted it would open. All of the plane's windows had shattered, leaving a perimeter of broken glass.

Peering in through the missing cockpit windshield, Tracy said, "There's no one here and I don't see any blood, but it's hard to tell because of all the debris."

I looked inside through the hole near the tail, being careful not to cut myself on the jagged edges. Buster tried to join me, but I pulled him back. I didn't want him to get cut on any of the sharp, exposed metal or the broken glass.

It was dark inside and hard to see, but what from I could make out, there were no bodies inside and there was no smell.

"Do you have a flashlight?" I asked Tracy.

"No. Stupid to have forgotten to bring one. And no phone either since I figured why bother. There's no service. Never thought about the light. Why, do you see something?"

"Nothing," I replied.

"So now what?"

I joined Tracy in the front of the plane. "Are there any notebooks or logs? Pilots are required to file flight plans so there should be something in the cockpit."

"No, but we can look around some more."

The radio startled me when Reid asked if we were okay.

"We're okay. Give us a few more minutes and we'll come back. It doesn't look like there's much here," I responded, then added, "No bodies that we can see either."

He acknowledged again.

"Look at that, Pat," Tracy tapped me on the shoulder and pointed.

I had been so preoccupied with the obvious damage that I had walked right past it, but now it was clearly visible: a large arrow on the attached wing. I took a close look at it. It was black and about a foot long and maybe four inches wide. The pointy end was symmetrical and neat, obviously man-made.

I touched it.

"Is it paint?" Tracy asked.

"No, it's grease or oil or something," I replied, wiping my finger on my shorts. "But it definitely means there was someone who survived the crash."

"So now what?" she asked me again.

"Let's see if there's another arrow on the other wing, then we'll call Reid."

We made our way around to the other wing and inspected it. It had been cleanly separated, leaving more exposed tubes and wires. There were stains on the rocks where fluids had leaked out, but there was no matching arrow.

I radioed Reid and told him what we had found. Since no signs of survivors were immediately visible to us and we had no idea how far away whoever painted the arrow might be, or if they were still alive, we decided it was prudent to return to *The Lady Anne* and reevaluate.

We drove the dinghy back and rejoined Reid aboard. "Well," I said, sipping a bottle of water, "we know someone survived the crash, at least long enough to paint that arrow."

"But why would they move so far from shore where rescuers wouldn't be able to see them?" Tracy asked.

I shook my head. "Maybe they found a fresh-water supply and thought it best to camp close." I looked at Reid. "I think we should cruise the shoreline."

Reid held up a finger. "We'd have to motor-sail," he said. "Or sail quite a distance offshore. The island is blocking the wind."

I knew what he was saying. "If we motor out to the wind and raise sail, we might be too far out to see survivors," I said. "So how long do you think we should motor-sail? I know we want to preserve our fuel."

"No more than thirty minutes, and if we haven't found anybody, we head for the wind."

Tracy took the helm, and Reid and I stood near the lifelines, binoculars handy. Buster stood between us, looking toward the rocky shore as well.

Twenty minutes later, Tracy shouted and pointed high. "Is that a flare?"

I looked where she was pointing just in time to see a bright spot of light fall from the sky and disappear, leaving a smoke trail.

"That's a flare," Reid confirmed. "Change course."

About one minute later, we saw another ball of fire race skyward, arc, and then drop before burning out.

"Zigzag," Reid instructed. "Let them know we see them."

Tracy brought the bow over so hard that Reid had to hold me so I didn't fall over. When she brought the bow back, I nearly fell again. Thankfully, Reid had been holding on and was stable enough for us both. Buster slid into our legs which kept him upright. As soon as he regained his balance, he gave us a look and headed below.

"Hey," I hollered at Tracy. "You're sitting down, we're not."

"Sorry, hang on." Then she repeated the maneuver, but we were ready this time. Finally she straightened out, heading in the direction of the flare.

We quickly closed the distance and ahead on the shore saw two people, one of them waving a bright orange panel. Tracy throttled back and as the engine slowed and quieted, we could hear them screaming.

"Ahoy," Reid shouted. "Is there anywhere close and deep enough to anchor?"

"Not for a boat that size," the man answered.

"Now what?" Tracy asked.

"How about if we find somewhere to put ashore and see what we're dealing with," Reid said.

I looked through the binoculars. The man looked to be in his late sixties, skinny, with bad hair, a wild beard, and overly tanned skin. He was wearing tattered cargo pants with a rope for a belt, a badly torn shirt, and was barefoot. He was also carrying what I initially thought was an orange panel but was really a Home Depot plastic bucket.

The woman was barefoot, wearing cut-off shorts and a man's once-white T-shirt. I put her in her sixties. She was so tanned that her skin looked like leather. She also looked malnourished and had a short, ragged, do-it-yourself haircut.

"They look harmless," I said. "But so did Bonnie. We don't know if they're alone."

"Stand by," Reid called out to them.

Tracy steered a big, lazy circle while we discussed our options. The couple ashore quit waving and sat down on the rocks, watching us.

"What's the plan?" Tracy asked.

"We need to find out what they know," he replied. "And if they're alone."

"Do you want me to circle out here while you two take the dinghy?"

"That's probably best since it looks like the wind for heaving to is a couple of miles offshore."

"Should I just shut the motor off and drift?" Tracy asked.

"Don't do that," Reid replied, suddenly looking serious. "Remember what we talked about. If conditions change and she doesn't start right away, you'd be in trouble against the rocks. Just motor real slow and protect *The Lady Anne* at all costs."

Tracy nodded and then warned, "Take a radio and remember the code word, just in case."

CHAPTER 77

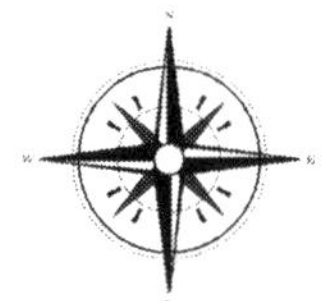

Tracy steered out to give us plenty of space. Reid drove the dinghy to within about twenty feet of the rocks and slowed down. The water was clear and beginning to shallow.

As Reid looked for a spot to land, the woman called out to us. "Do you have water?"

I nodded and held up two bottles. Then I radioed Tracy we were going ashore.

"Keep in touch," she said. "And be careful."

I climbed out on a big rock. The man and woman rushed out to help us, and when the dinghy was secure, the woman grabbed me in a hug.

"My name is Gertrude Kohler," she said. "Gert. You can't imagine how happy we are to see you."

Reid stepped between us. "I'm Reid Adams, third mate of *The Lady Anne,* and this is Captain Pat Taylor."

I handed her a water bottle. "Are you two alone?"

Gertrude nodded and gestured to the man who had come up behind her. "This is Morrie Morris. Mo for short. He and I are alone on this godforsaken island."

I gave the man the second bottle. "Did you survive that plane crash we saw earlier?" I asked them.

"I landed my Beechcraft perfectly and walked away without a scratch," Mo said. "What you see now is compliments of a hurricane." He told us how he had tied the plane down, but the storm was too powerful, and had ripped it loose and smashed it where we found it. "But we didn't end up here together." He looked at Gertrude.

"I was the only survivor of *The Splashy*, a tour boat that hit a reef and sank," she said.

"What happened?" Reid asked her.

"I booked a spot on a whale-watching boat out of Cockburn Town in the Turks and Caicos. We were caught in some crazy electrical storm. It must have rendered us all unconscious because the next thing I knew, we had come to and our boat was drifting, powerless. Surf drove the boat onto a reef. The crew and all the passengers abandoned ship. I had to jump without a life jacket but managed to hold onto a floating cushion to keep from drowning. The next morning, some dolphins found me and two of them gave me a tow all the way here."

Reid and I exchanged looks.

Gert caught it and said, "Really. I'm not making that up.

Dolphins found me and two of them gave me a tow all the way here."

I smiled. "No. I believe that. Dolphins are very smart."

"I'm also lucky Mo took a walk along the shoreline that morning or else the birds would have finished me and I wouldn't be here right now."

Mo took a long pull from his bottle then said, "She's luckier still the dolphins found her first and not the sharks."

"Did you find anyone else from the boat?" Reid asked.

"No, we kept looking but found nothing else—no bodies, no debris, nothing."

Gert put an arm around Mo's shoulders. "He stayed with me while I regained my strength. I owe him my life."

"So about the electromagnetic disturbance you mentioned earlier," I said. "Did you happen to be filming or photographing anything unusual before it began?"

"If by unusual you mean UFOs then yes, I was trying to follow a UFO with my plane," Mo said. "And yes, I did manage to take its picture, several times actually."

Gert nodded. "Everyone on *The Splashy* saw what we figured was a UFO. We all took video and pictures. Suddenly we were enveloped in fog."

"And then you lost power and went through an electrical portal of some kind?" I asked.

Mo looked straight at me and answered, "And then we were shifted backwards through time, just like you were."

Reid smiled at me and said, "Time travel was her theory as well."

"Well, it's theory no longer," Mo said. "Welcome to Earth's past. By my calculations, the aliens have sent us 25,700 years backwards through time."

Reid and I looked at each other.

"You sound pretty confident about that number," I said.

"In my former life I was a space scientist for NASA. I might be off a few hundred years, but I'd wager I'm pretty darn close."

It got quiet again while Reid and I digested what he said.

"I was fairly certain we had gone back in time, but I had no idea we went back that far," I said. "How long have you been here?"

"Six months, one hurricane, and two bad storms," he answered. "How about you? Are we the first people you've come across?"

We quickly told them about first finding *The Obsession* and later about finding Captain Rick. I omitted the part about Carl.

Gert listened but finally nudged Mo and said, "Tell them about the aliens."

"What about them?" Reid asked.

"Do you have a working compass?" Mo asked back.

"Not with me but, yes, we have one."

"You need to bring it to our camp and take bearings off the markers I've made to track the alien's course."

"Markers?" I asked. "What are you talking about?"

"We watch the aliens fly overhead nearly every week," Gert said.

Mo waved a hand. "It's really a five-day cycle."

Gert glared at him momentarily and then started over. "We watch the aliens fly overhead every *five* days. Mo uses rocks to track their direction."

"The problem is," Mo said, "while I can guess at their course by the stars, I can't provide a navigational bearing without a compass."

"Why five days, do you think?" I asked.

"I believe the aliens require five days to get to Earth. If you examined a chronological record of reported alien sightings, I predict there would be a regular pattern."

"Are you saying that aliens come to our planet every five days and no government or military or investigative reporter has said anything about it?"

Mo gave me a look of frustration mingled with irritation, and I knew why immediately. "The cycle is five days now," I said, correcting myself. "There must be a different cycle in our time, because you're right, if they were that common, they'd be reported."

Mo paused, then said, "I'm certain the cycle is five days. That being said, it's difficult to spot them during daylight hours or when the night skies are cloudy or rainy. In addition to that, the other variable is not keeping a twenty-four-by-seven watch. After all, there's only two of us and we do need to sleep." Mo looked a little tired and sat down.

"Where do you think the aliens are headed?" Reid asked as he sat next to him.

"Mo thinks they have a base here and I concur," Gert answered.

"How far away is it?" Reid asked.

"Certainly within range of your sailboat," Mo said, looking toward *The Lady Anne.*

"What do you propose?" I asked.

"Take us with you," Gert said.

Mo waved Gert's comment off with a hand. "First things first. What if you go back to your ship, get your compass, and then accompany me to our camp? I've got to get my notes and take readings off my markers."

"Then what?" Reid asked.

Mo looked like he was beginning to get impatient, but he calmly answered, "Then we go find the aliens and ask them to return us to our time."

"Hey, are you guys all right?" Tracy's voice blared from the radio, making us all jump.

I rolled my eyes at how we reacted. We had been so intent with Mo's story, I almost forgot Tracy would be waiting to hear from us. "Sorry, Tracy," I replied. "Yes. We're okay."

"When are you coming back?"

Reid took the radio and replied, "Stand by a minute."

Then he excused himself and motioned for me to follow. We walked a short distance away. Mo and Gert sat down on a rock and looked out over the water, away from us, giving us some privacy.

"What do you think?" Reid asked in a hushed voice.

"I think that if we intend to find the aliens, he's our best bet."

"Do you believe he's serious about knowing where they go when they pass by?"

"He certainly seems confident, and neither of them have any problem believing we were all sent back in time by aliens," I replied.

"How do you think Tracy will react if we want to bring two passengers aboard?"

"One way to find out."

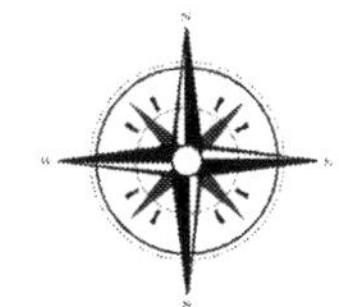

CHAPTER 78

We radioed Tracy our situation. There wasn't much to discuss. They obviously needed help and we were the only ones in a position to provide it. Plus, they had the knowledge we'd been looking for.

She agreed completely. "I'll be ready to receive Gert."

Reid and I ferried Gert back to *The Lady Anne* and left her with Tracy. Then we returned to Mo with our compass. At Gert's urging, we brought him another water and a granola bar.

On the way back to Mo, Reid slowed the boat down. "Pat," he said. "I have a feeling you aren't completely happy with the way Tracy and I..."

He paused as if unsure to how to continue, so I did it for him. "The way you and Tracy can't keep your hands off each other?"

Color flooded his face. "So, it does bother you?"

"I need to ask you a question," I asked, leaning close. "As a red-blooded, heterosexual, sexually active male, I fully understand Tracy's appeal. She's always ready to fuck." This time I paused. I knew why Tracy did what she did. Did I have the right to even ask Reid how he felt about it?

I could feel Reid watching me. After what seemed like an eternity, he sighed. "I don't want you to repeat what I'm going to say," he said. "Promise?"

I nodded.

"There's something driving Tracy. She uses sex like a weapon. She's a living, breathing, beautiful play toy. But all she craves is an orgasm. She has minimal interest in foreplay or in her partner's experience. She's like a dessert buffet available twenty-four/seven. After a week of four or five trips each and every day, you get buffeted out."

I almost felt guilty asking, but I couldn't help myself. "Are you getting Tracyed out?"

"Twenty years ago I never would have said this." He grinned again. "But going at it with Tracy three, four, five times a day is going to give me a fucking heart attack, and I mean that literally. She's a handful, right on the line between your greatest fantasy and your worst nightmare. I'm not complaining, really, but I do have a favor to ask you."

I was sure he was going to say something about asking if I was bisexual and if so, would I finally agree to a three-way so he could get a break. I had already formulated my answer when he asked, "Would you share my cabin every other night and pretend to be my lover?"

That I was not expecting.

"I need Tracy to give me a break, which she will if she thinks you are taking your turn. You can have the bed, I'll take the deck, and nothing has to happen."

I looked away. Should I be honest? Tracy certainly wasn't being honest with Reid. He had no idea what was behind her take-no-prisoners-in-bed attitude. And she did say I was free to "take a turn with Reid" if I wanted.

"What if I don't want to pretend?" I said. "What if I want something to happen?" I silently gulped as I said that, my heart beating a tattoo against my chest. "Do you want to make love to me?"

Reid raised an eyebrow. "Did you really think I would say no? We've only been together once, but you were a passionate, wonderful lover." He waved a hand. "Not that Tracy doesn't have her moments, but she's a hardcore sex machine, part porn star, part contortionist, part nympho, and totally insatiable."

I took that as a yes. *The Lady Anne* was too far away for Tracy to see us, so I kissed Reid—a long, lingering kiss that left us both breathless. "Your secret is safe with me," I said.

Reid resumed speed and we made our way back to Mo, who was seated on a rock, waiting patiently.

As Reid was securing the dinghy, Mo handed me the Home Depot bucket which I set out of the way. I noticed it contained an orange flare pistol and four flares. He ate half the granola bar and then we followed him uphill toward their camp.

"Aren't your feet sore?" I asked, wondering how he could manage so well barefoot over the rough rocks.

"They used to be, but the salt water ruined my shoes so I had no choice. It was amazing how fast they toughened up," he answered, giving me a grin.

"How have you two managed to survive here?" Reid asked.

"I've got a manual emergency desalinator back at camp that can produce about a quart of potable water an hour."

"Is that what the Home Depot bucket is for?" I asked.

"Yes. Every time we come down to the shoreline, we take a bucketful of salt water back with us."

"Do you also bring your flare gun with you?"

"Of course."

"What have you been eating?" Reid asked.

"Gert eats lobsters when she can catch a shallow one, and we both eat birds, lizards, conch, occasional eggs, a few berries, and tiny fruits."

"Does anything else grow here?"

"I tried to grow some seeds, but nothing happened."

"What kind of seeds?"

"I had a little food with me and saved the apple, pepper, tomato, cucumber, and lemon seeds, but like I said, none of them would germinate, not even in water. Not even my onions would sprout. I'll tell you my theory about that later."

He stopped to catch his breath in a wide, mostly flat area. "Is this where you landed?" I asked.

He nodded.

I didn't see any camp ahead but hoped we were getting close, for his sake. I used the break to radio Tracy. She answered but cut the call short, saying she was busy. Since she didn't use our code word, I didn't worry.

While we were resting, he explained how he had gotten here. He was flying his plane to Cat Island to spend the weekend with some friends when he spotted the aliens and gave chase, just to see what would happen. He stated he was very fortunate to have emerged from the time portal in daylight and close enough to this spot for a dead stick landing.

"But this isn't Cat Island," I said. "It's too small."

Mo nodded and resumed walking. He appeared to be headed for the ridge ahead.

"Why are you so sure we've gone that far back in time?" I asked as I made my way over the rocks.

"Based on my calculations, I estimate we are in roughly the same geographical place, but approximately 25,700 years in the past."

"If we're in roughly the same place, why can't we locate these islands on our charts?" Reid asked.

"Your charts are off due primarily to the present ice age changing the oceans depth, and to a lesser extent, tectonic deformation. Your magnetic compass is off as well, due to magnetic declination and geomagnetic storms."

"How did you figure 25,700 years?" I asked. "That's rather an exact number. Why not twenty-five or twenty-six thousand?"

"It was actually a rather simple calculation," he answered. "My number is based on having an accurate timepiece, a sextant, a nautical almanac, and observing the positions of the constellations. If there is any error, it's due to my arithmetic and not having a calculator."

"How did you come by an accurate timepiece?" Reid asked. "All of our watches and clocks stopped working. The only reason we know the time now is because Pat made a sundial."

Mo stopped and proudly displayed his wristwatch. "This is a World War II vintage Bulova A-11 that needs winding every day but still works perfectly. Because it has no battery or electrical requirements, it wasn't affected by the portal's electromagnetic interference like other instruments were."

Just before the crest of the hill, we came upon a large swath of low, sparse foliage. He smiled and said we were getting close and then turned and proceeded down through the vegetation.

There were lots of lizards up here and several dozen nested birds as well. I commented it was interesting that we could walk right next to the birds without spooking them. Mo stated they had no fear of humans, which worked to his advantage when needing food.

I still didn't see any camp, but the flatter ground allowed Mo to walk easier and his pace increased. Reid pointed behind us toward *The Lady Anne*. She was quite a ways offshore and appeared to be hove to, but without binoculars we weren't certain. I debated using the radio but decided not to bother.

As I followed Mo, I asked, "When we were going through the electromagnetic time portal, what do you think the clockwise bright light signified?"

Mo slowed down slightly and answered, "It was a complete cycle around the ecliptic, or what is known as a Platonic Year."

"In English please," Reid asked.

Mo smiled. "It's when the planets and the constellations go once around the sun and end up where they started. Clockwise would indicate going backwards in time, while counter-clockwise would indicate the opposite."

"I'm not familiar with what you just described, but isn't Polaris still the pole star?"

"Yes, Reid, it is because we went back one Platonic year. If we'd have gone back half a Platonic year, roughly thirteen thousand years, the constellations would be rotating around Vega, not Polaris."

"So if the stars are back where they started, how exactly did you calculate the time?" I asked. "Isn't the night sky about the same as it was when we left?"

"The constellations are in the same place, but a number of other stars have moved. The distance they moved supports my calculations."

"Finding Polaris is easy using the Big Dipper," Reid said. "But how do you find Vega?"

"Either find the constellation Lyra or find the Summer Triangle. I'd be happy to show you some evening. Oh, and by the way, we're here. Camp is straight ahead."

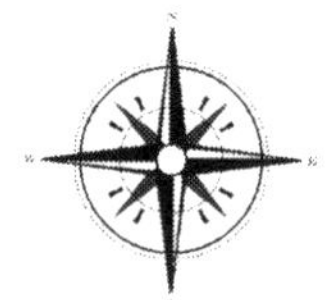

CHAPTER 79

There wasn't much to Mo's camp. There was a large silver tarp rigged against some aluminum struts, courtesy of the wrecked plane I surmised, making a crude lean-to. There were two seats from the plane near some blackened rocks outlining a firepit. And there was a small pile of something covered by a smaller blue tarp.

Regardless of first impressions, Mo graciously welcomed us to his camp. "Let me show you the markers I spoke of earlier."

We followed him a short distance to a smooth patch of ground, outlined by conch shells, forming a square about three feet across. He knelt down in the middle of the square, placing his knee next to a piece of metal that had been pounded into the ground, probably an alignment point of some kind.

About twenty feet away was a rock marker. Another twenty feet past that was another. "If you stand here, the aliens go straight overhead in a line with both markers," he said, obviously very excited to be showing someone his work.

"May I go take a look at those?" I asked.

"Certainly, but please don't touch."

Reid and I made our way to the closet one. Mo had stacked several large, flat rocks in the general shape of a pyramid. There were two conch shells sitting on the top, with their natural sides facing each other and their pink centers facing out. There was a white arrow drawn between them, pointing to the next marker. The entire marker was waist high.

"What are the shells for?" Reid asked.

"Those were recycled after dinner. I kneel low and sight between them, like I'm aiming a gun."

"Is that why there's a stick atop the other marker, like a rifle's front sight?"

"Exactly right, Reid. Gert lined it up for me and now it's spot-on."

"Why the painted white arrow?" I asked.

"That's so I can realign my sights when the wind blows the shells over," he answered, then he added, "By the way, Pat, that's not paint."

I laughed. "Let me guess. It's bird shit."

He nodded. "Guano," he corrected, and laughed with me.

I walked over to the other marker. It was of similar construction, but it wasn't a wooden stick that was protruding out the top. It was another aluminum piece from the plane. There was a small white circle around the post, probably to line everything back up if it got disturbed.

Reid and I followed Mo back to his camp. Under the blue tarp were two army-style duffel bags, a large, bright-green backpack, two plastic totes, a tool box, a small suitcase, and some torn, black, plastic trash bags. There were also a number of green sticks that had been sharpened and then blackened on the pointy end.

I held one up and gave him a questioning look.

"Those are our roasting sticks."

He moved the upper tote and opened the lower one. He removed a plastic bag and inside there was a spiral notebook and a stubby, hand-sharpened pencil.

"My notes," he proclaimed proudly. "We'll need these."

"What goes back to the boat?" I asked.

"Everything except for the seats, if that's okay?"

"That's fine," Reid answered.

"You don't know how long I've waited for this day," Mo said, fighting to hold back tears.

"While you and Reid take some compass bearings off your markers, what would you like me to do?"

"Start schlepping what you can carry; it all has to go."

CHAPTER 80

Reid and I made two trips in the time Mo made one, but eventually we got everything but the airplane seats from his camp to the dinghy. The hill was steeper than it looked, and by the time we were finished, we were both breathing pretty hard. Reid and I took a full dinghy out to *The Lady Anne*.

I felt a little bad leaving Mo to wait in the hot sun, but Reid explained to me he didn't want to leave Tracy outnumbered. Besides, Mo was happy to wait for us and finish the granola bar.

The ride provided an opportunity for a brief rest and a chance to talk in private. "Are you one hundred percent all right with bringing them aboard?" Reid asked.

I balanced the equation. If we didn't bring them with us, they would surely suffer the same fate as the *Obsession*'s crew. If we did bring them, we would consume *The Lady Anne*'s supplies at a faster rate.

Eventually, I nodded. "Mo is a treasure chest of information about the time period, and he definitely knows more than we do about the aliens. Has the thought that Mo and Gert might turn on us like Captain Rick and Bonnie flashed through my mind? Absolutely. The possibility is there, but I think it highly unlikely. Nothing in my brief conversation with Gert or my longer interactions with Mo raised any red flags—none at all. I think they're good people in a bad way. So I'm totally fine with our decision." I paused. "Are you?"

Reid smiled. "Me too. They're a cute old couple. I don't see any risk at all. Let's get everything unloaded and return for Mo and the rest of his stuff."

We quickly unloaded the dinghy and headed back. Mo was right where we left him. We reloaded the dinghy and then all of us motored back to *The Lady Anne*. Mo waived goodbye to the island and thanked us again.

Tracy and Buster were waiting on the swim platform. I didn't see Gert, but Tracy was smiling and waving. Buster trotted over to sniff our new shipmate, took one whiff, and retreated behind Tracy.

Mo climbed aboard *The Lady Anne* and introduced himself.

"Where's Gert?" he asked Tracy.

"She's below. She had a chance to clean up and is changing clothes." Tracy smiled. "You won't recognize her."

"You're very kind, allowing us aboard like this."

"You may revise that opinion after I ask you to take a shower as soon as the dinghy is unloaded," Tracy replied. She leaned away and held her nose.

Mo winced. "That bad, huh?"

"Well, you probably don't smell it, and I don't know if you noticed, but even Buster is keeping his distance," Tracy said, chuckling.

"Should I go below to shower?"

"Please no, it would be best if you showered on the stern, like Gert did. I'll show you where."

"No problem," Mo said. "Thank you for being honest."

Gert came topside just then, smiling like she had won the lottery. If it hadn't been for her super dark tan and bare feet, I might not have recognized her. She was wearing an elegant blue silk dress. Her hair, freshly shampooed, framed her face. The dress was a little big, but other than that, she could have been a passenger on a cruise ship heading for dinner at the captain's table.

Mo stopped dead. "Who is this beautiful woman?"

Gert's face reddened, but she did a little pirouette, fanning the skirt so it billowed around her. "Do you like it?"

"You are positively radiant."

"Can you do that for me?" Mo asked. He laughed. "I don't mean the dress, of course."

We laughed with him and Tracy said, "The dress belonged to the late wife of the former owner of *The Lady Anne*. And I believe she would be happy to see her clothes put to such good use." She winked. "And yes, there are some men's things too.

Reid, why don't you show Mo where to shower? Then he can go below and pick what he wants."

Before he left, Tracy added, "As for sleeping arrangements, do you want separate cabins, or will you share?"

"Whatever is available is fine with us," replied Mo, looking very appreciative. "We've been sleeping on the ground."

Tracy smiled and cleared her throat. "I guess I'm asking one bed or two? We have two available cabins, but they both have stacked single berths. Each cabin does have its own bathroom or head if you want to speak nautical."

Reid interjected, "However if you want to share a bed, my cabin has a queen-sized bed and I'm used to sleeping in quarter berths with canvas lee cloths, so I'm happy to take the port-side forward cabin."

Gert and Mo both shrugged. "Which would be easier for you to accommodate us?" she said.

"It's about the same," Tracy said. "Either we move supplies out of the crew's quarters, or we move stuff out of one of the other forward cabins."

Reid suggested Mo shower and then we'd go below and show them their options. Reid, Gert, and I unloaded the dinghy while Tracy rigged another solar shower and retrieved a plastic disposable razor that Pincus had left below.

As Mo showered, at Reid's insistence, we went through their gear scattered about the deck, looking for bugs. Reid apologized to Gert for disrespecting their privacy, but she fully understood.

It soon became apparent that none of their clothing was salvageable, being either torn beyond repair or moldy. Gert didn't argue but went below and cheerfully returned a few minutes later with some fresh clothes for Mo. She took them to him while we continued looking through what we brought from the island.

One thing for sure, Mo had an impressive selection of survival gear.

Besides the Home Depot bucket and the flare gun, there was a first aid kit, two wrinkled silver space blankets, the portable desalinator he had mentioned earlier, a blackened aluminum pot with a lid, a well-used plastic water bottle with some purification tablets, a partial roll of duct tape, a large survival knife, a hatchet, and a small plastic box of fish hooks and small weights but no fishing line, rod, or reel.

Gert returned while we were sorting the fishing gear. I held up the hooks and weights.

"Mo lost all his fishing gear to a big fish," Gert said, shaking her head. "It just pulled his rod and reel right out of his hands. Another reason why we were so happy to see you. We had lost our chief source of fresh food—the fish he caught."

Tracy held up a wooden stock. "Is this a rifle?"

"Yes, it is. Mo showed me how to assemble and shoot it. All the parts fit in the stock."

"Do you have any ammo left?" Reid asked, examining the gun.

"Yes, we've used it very little since it's easier to just walk up to a bird and grab it by the neck than try and shoot it. Besides, the noise scares all the birds away."

We started laughing and Tracy told Gert about our adventure with the swarming gulls.

"What's this?" I asked, holding up a small piece of metal attached to a key chain.

"That's a block of magnesium that Mo uses to start fires," Gert replied. "You strike it with the knife and direct the sparks to your tinder. It's pretty ingenious."

Tracy found a piece of chain. "What's this?"

"Be careful with that," Gert warned. "It's really sharp. That's chainsaw chain and it cuts through wood faster and easier than the hatchet does."

Reid held up two survival whistles and smiled at me.

"Those are really loud," Gert said.

"Yeah," I said. "I have one just like it and Buster will start barking if you blow it."

"I don't see a life raft," Reid stated. "Wouldn't there have been one on the plane?".

"We had one, but it ripped loose in the hurricane that destroyed the plane and we never found it."

"Other than the water purification tablets I saw earlier, I don't see any food," I said.

"Mo had enough food and water to last two people for seven days in the event of an off-airport emergency landing."

Reid looked surprised. "That's it?"

"It was nearly gone when he found me, but he shared what

he had left and then we ate what he caught, killed, and cooked."

I picked up a strange-looking flashlight. The body was clear plastic and there was a coil of copper wire where the batteries should have been. As if reading my mind, Gert held out her hand, smiled, and said, "Just shake it for a bit and you'll get four to five minutes of light." I handed it to her, and after a brief shake, there was indeed light. Not overly bright but certainly bright enough to work with.

"Have you used this?" Tracy had a booklet entitled "Survival Guide" in her hands.

"I've read that several times. The best part is it wants you to keep an enthusiastic, positive attitude, which we've tried to do," Gert answered. "But we knew we were losing weight and slowly spiraling downhill, so you have no idea how glad we were to spot you."

Her voice trembled and tears filled her eyes. I patted her arm. "You may have saved us too," I said. "If we use Mo's calculations and track and find the aliens, we may just have a chance to get out of here and back to our own time."

Gert swiped at her eyes with the back of her hand. "It's nice to have hope again. I'd almost given it up."

We started a bag of discards to stay topside. We also sprayed and wiped their gear with Lysol. Satisfied there were no hitchhiking critters around, we took a break while waiting for Mo to get dressed.

Mo joined us wearing Charles's clothes, pleated trousers, and a silk shirt. He was still barefoot, and the clothes were way too big, but at least they were fresh and clean. He had also shaved off his beard, completing the transformation from desperate castaway to classy gentleman.

The four of us clapped when he approached, and color flooded his face. He had bundled his old clothes. "What should I do with these?"

"Right here," I said, pointing to the discard heap. "We'll set this stuff on fire after dinner."

Tracy rubbed her hands together. "And wait until you've tasted Reid's cooking. He's a marvel in the kitchen."

Reid waved the compliment away. "Let's go below and get you settled."

After checking the various quarters, Mo and Gert decided to share the crew's cabin. It was filled with supplies and we started right in transferring everything to the larger front cabin. We fashioned an assembly line and quickly emptied the crew's quarters, leaving only the bags of clothing for Mo and Gert to go through.

"Won't all this stuff be in your way now?" Gert asked.

"This forward cabin is mostly storage anyway," I replied. "Tracy and I share the owner's cabin and Reid has the larger forward cabin."

Tracy grinned. "It's probably better you've decided on crew quarters. I sleep most nights in Reid's cabin and we're not always quiet, if you know what I mean."

Gert smiled. "So, you're a couple?" she asked.

Remembering my earlier conversation with Reid, I answered, "Actually, Tracy and I both sleep with Reid. We take turns." I smiled up at Reid. "I think tonight it's my turn, right?"

Tracy winked and gave me a thumbs-up. "You go, girl," she said.

Gert frowned. "You're both sleeping with Reid?"

"Kind of robbing the cradle there, aren't you, Reid?" Mo asked.

He might have been attempting humor, but his voice betrayed his distaste.

Tracy and I looked at each other. It had suddenly gotten very awkward and very quiet.

Tracy broke the silence. "Look, if the fact that we're both fucking Reid is going to be a problem, let's go. I'll drive you back to the island myself."

Not exactly the way I would have put it, but considering how we literally saved the lives of these two, their judgmental attitude was puzzling.

"The three of us have become extremely close," Reid said. "Just like you, we're trying to survive, together but alone, lost in the past and depending on sixty-eight feet of boat for survival."

He gathered his thoughts for a second and added, "I am making love with two women who happen to be considerably younger. If you can't get beyond that, then you need to say something."

Tracy stepped beside Reid. "You two have been together for six months. You mean there's never been any—" She paused, fluttering her hands. "Any fooling around between you? I know you're older than we are, but you're not dead."

Gert crossed her arms over her chest, but Mo allowed a smile to play at the corners of his mouth."

He looked at Tracy and chuckled. "I'm from a different generation. A generation not so free with expressing what's in one's heart. I admire your ability to state what's on your mind."

Tracy shook her head. "You mean you have feelings for Gert you never expressed? Not even when the two of you were alone on a goddamned island in the middle of fucking nowhere? What if we'd never come along? You'd have taken the secret with you to the grave, denying yourselves the only pleasure left to you because of what? Some old-fashioned delusion of honor?"

"Yes," Gert said. "We are both old and old-fashioned."

"I'm a victim of a lifetime of conditioning," Mo replied a moment later, his expression and tone returning to normal. "I've fallen in love with a woman I never would have dated had circumstances been different."

"Because she isn't Jewish?" I said, looking at her necklace.

He nodded. "I didn't plan to fall in love with her, but I did, and I can't imagine life without her."

Gert quickly added, "We *are* both old and old-fashioned. Still, that's no excuse for our rudeness. Or our hypocrisy." She took Mo's hand. "Mo didn't tell the truth. We have made love. And I hope to do so again."

Tracy grinned. "Then you're on the right boat!"

CHAPTER 81

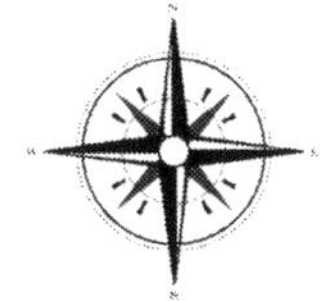

After Mo and Gert were moved into the crew's quarters, Reid suggested it was probably best to return to our previous anchorage. We "un-heaved to" and got underway. Reid took the helm, allowing Tracy and me to go below and change into nicer clothes, so Mo and Gert wouldn't feel so awkward. We sailed until the land blocked our wind and then motored in the rest of the way and anchored.

I took advantage of engine power to wash the towels they had used and one load of our laundry. While I had power, I also ran the water maker.

Tracy helped Reid make dinner while I joined Mo and Gert topside, watching to make sure the anchor was set. A little while later, Reid came up carrying a large platter of fish fillets, seasoned and arranged on bamboo skewers. As he started the grill, Mo stood up and said, "I don't want to seem at all ungrateful, but I'm not sure my stomach can handle that."

"Mine either," added Gert. "It looks delicious, but after five months of severe dieting and serious weight loss, I better stick with something simple."

"It's not a problem," Reid answered, smiling. "We have soup on the stove, just for you two."

"Is it chicken soup by chance?" Mo asked, sitting back down.

Reid laughed. "Jewish penicillin."

Mo clapped his hand. "Perfect."

Tracy joined us topside and handed our guests glasses of what looked like a milkshake or perhaps a smoothie. One was pink, the other was creamy white.

"Ensure." She grinned. "Strawberry and vanilla, compliments of the previous owner's personal supply."

Reid checked the fish and Tracy went below to check the soup. A few minutes later, dinner was served. Grilled fish from the sea and chicken noodle soup, green beans, and peaches from a can.

Mo asked permission to say a prayer, so we all held hands. He said a short prayer in Hebrew, which he followed by translating that he was thanking the Lord, King of the universe for all things. He teared up before finishing the translation. So did Gert. It was very sweet.

They had finished their Ensure, so Mo raised his water

bottle and made a toast. "To righteous gentiles." He said it very proudly.

We all took a drink.

"Do you know what the term *righteous gentiles* refers to?" he asked then.

Tracy, Reid, and I glanced at each other and then shook our heads.

"*Righteous gentiles* were those non-Jews who risked their lives to save Jews during the Holocaust. It's the highest honor a Jew can bestow on a non-Jew."

We were quiet for a moment before Reid said, "We may not deserve that honor. We didn't risk our lives to save you."

"Maybe, but you still may be risking your lives. There are five of us now, and we are going to consume sixty-seven percent more supplies than three."

"We'll do fine," I replied. "We've got a water maker and have been catching lots of fish."

"We've also got a big bag of rice that we haven't opened yet," Tracy added. "So if you like fish and rice, we've got you covered."

"With canned chicken and a pinch of spices, I can make gallons of chicken with rice soup." Reid smiled, not wanting to be outdone.

"You know what I'm really going to like here?" Gert asked, her eyes twinkling.

She raised her own water bottle. "Toilet paper," she said.

"To toilet paper," I echoed, and we all drank to that.

They each managed to eat half a bowl of soup and a few peach slices before they said they were stuffed. Of course Tracy, Reid, and I made short work of the grilled fish. It was really good. Buster ate several small bites but seemed to prefer a pretzel spread with peanut butter, with a piece of jerky stuck on top. I felt bad feeding the dog when Mo and Gert were so thin it was scary. But I noticed even Gert gave Buster a head scratch when he passed close to her.

I cleared the table and carried the dishes below. Tracy joined me in the galley and whispered, "Can you believe Gert's attitude earlier? I was ready to punch her lights out."

"Let it go, she's old and cranky."

"You know that when you held my hand when I was shaking mad, they both thought we were lesbians."

"Yeah, I caught that. But wasn't it nice of Reid to defend us and say all those sweet things?"

"He's right." Tracy nodded. "The three of us have grown extremely close. He really cares for us. Both of us."

"I thought she was going to have a heart attack when you said we were both fucking him and either like it or get off the boat."

"She just pissed me off. How dare she say one word about our lifestyle when they'd probably be dead in another month if we hadn't stopped to explore that plane wreck."

"Like I said earlier, they're old and cranky, like old people get."

"Well, she better watch her mouth," Tracy softly threatened. I didn't respond.

We got everything cleaned and put away and then made

our way topside. The others were at the stern rail, watching the sun disappearing below the horizon. Above the brilliant white spot of sun, the immediate sky basked in hues of orange, fading to yellow. We joined them aft. I noticed Tracy, still smarting from Gert's original reaction to us, stayed away from Gert.

There were fingers of whiten reaching toward us over the water. As the fingers touched the water, they produced shimmers of light that almost looked like stepping-stones, marking a path to the horizon. Higher above, most of the clouds had dark tops and lighter bottoms. The upper sky was slowly turning a grayer shade of blue. As the sun dipped below the horizon, it left a purple aura, a marker for the night ahead.

"We've seen a lot of beautiful sunsets," Mo said as he returned to the cockpit table. "But tonight's seems especially magnificent."

"I think it's the company," added Gert, smiling.

"I want to thank you all again for sharing your provisions with us," Mo stated, looking directly at each of us.

Then Mo asked how I came to be the captain of such a luxurious boat, and I gave them an abridged version of the poker game, omitting the more salacious details of the bet and how Pincus, enraged by losing his job, came after us.

"Have you encountered anyone else after passing through the portal?" Gert asked.

I started with finding *The Obsession* and how sad we were that we hadn't arrived in time to save the crew. I bent down and lifted Buster onto my lap. "But we did rescue Buster," I said, getting a sloppy kiss in return.

Tracy took over then, telling them about the crew of *The Day Dream*. She was honest about killing Carl, though it was obviously in self-defense and neither Gert nor Mo condemned us for it. In fact, they expressed anger that Captain Rick had tried to commit modern-day piracy.

"We left them with what we could spare," she said. "And we painted a warning on the side of their fishing boat in case anyone else happens upon them. We've noted their position in our logs and if—"

I shot her a look.

"And *when,*" she amended hastily, "we get back to our time, we will try to send a rescue boat back."

"That brings you up-to-date with us," Reid said then. "Now we want to hear about your journey."

"I admit I'm curious," I said to Gert. "What put you on a whale-watching boat in hurricane season?"

She sighed. "It's always cheaper to travel in the off-season."

"Don't you worry about why the rates are so much less?" Tracy asked.

"I'm a retired teacher and have to wait tables twenty hours a week just to make ends meet. Money is always a problem. At the same time, I love to travel. I have to take the deals when they come up."

"I thought teachers had pensions," I said.

"I do have a pension, but it doesn't go as far as I originally calculated. Hence, I still work part-time. But I do indulge myself with one discounted vacation every two years or so. Off-season bookings, cheap flights, and inside cabins are my new best friends."

Mo stared at her. "I had no idea you had financial problems. You never mentioned it."

Gert shook her head, her face reddening. "Why would I? I was shipwrecked on a deserted island 25,700 years in the past, facing the very real prospect of starvation. The last thing I'm going to do is tell you I need help with my credit card."

Gert was obviously embarrassed by the turn the conversation had taken. Reid shot me a sideways glance and cleared his throat. "So before you photographed the alien that sent you here, did you see any whales?" he asked her.

"We only saw one and didn't get very close." Then she closed her eyes. "I'm sorry. I think I'm more tired than I thought." She stood. "Will you all excuse me? I need to get some rest."

"Of course," Reid said. "It's been a long day."

Mo stood, too, and reached for Gert's hand. "Let me take you below."

She squeezed his hand but then dropped it. "No. You stay. Tell them what you've found. The sooner you all put your heads together, the sooner we have a chance of getting back home."

"Are you sure?" Mo's face reflected concern.

She touched his cheek. "Yes. I'll be fine." She straightened her shoulders and looked around. "Good night, all. And thank you again. For everything."

She turned and started below. Mo watched for a moment, then followed, pausing only to excuse himself. "I'll be back," he said. "I want to make sure she's all right."

I smiled to myself. Gert might be a gentile, but there was no doubt in my mind that Mo loved her.

CHAPTER 82

While Mo was below, Reid used the time to complete the day's log entry. I hung the damp laundry that I had forgotten about and Tracy made herself a drink.

After about ten minutes, Mo rejoined us.

"Is she all right?" I asked.

"It was a pretty eventful day," he replied. "I think the emotion and excitement of being saved caught up with her."

"Saved?" I repeated. "Not sure of that yet, but I'm glad we found you. I have a few questions if you don't think you're too tired. But if you'd like to go to bed, I understand, and we can start tomorrow."

Mo shook his head. "The sooner the better."

I agreed and turned to Reid. "Let's start with the compass bearings you got off the markers."

"I took five readings," he answered. "And Mo took five. We agreed the aliens were following course 025 degrees."

Tracy joined us too. "Won't that heading take us into open ocean?"

Reid nodded.

I looked at Mo. "Any idea how far away the aliens might be when they land?"

"That calculation isn't as exact," he answered.

"Best guess?" I asked, turning my palms up.

He didn't respond right away. Instead he took a sip of water and then looked toward the sunset again. Finally he spoke. "I took liberties calculating their angle of descent without proper equipment, but I feel somewhat confident their base is between six hundred and one thousand miles distant. And thanks to your compass, we now know their heading."

"You think the aliens have a base out in the middle of the ocean?" Tracy asked.

Her tone didn't exactly drip with sarcasm, but it didn't ring with endorsement either.

"Gert and I have observed, and my notes will confirm, that aliens fly overhead about every five days." He smiled at me and continued. "I say about because we aren't watching every single minute of every single day and even if we were, sometimes the clouds, or rain, or daylight makes them hard to see. While the times vary, the number of days between sightings has remained fairly constant."

"How much does the time vary?" I asked.

"You're welcome to review my notes, but you'll see most of the sightings have occurred within a twelve-hour window, and the majority of those have occurred in the early evening."

"Why would aliens come to Earth every five days?" Tracy asked. "And why wouldn't that get reported?"

I repeated the conversation we had on shore about just that subject. "Five days is the cycle now, but in the future…"

"It might be different." Tracy sighed. "What could they be doing here if you're right about us being 25,700 years in the past?"

"In my former life at NASA," Mo said, "I was involved with the Hubble Space Telescope, which as you may know is a bus-sized telescope orbiting the earth. Its job is to take pictures of the planets, stars, and galaxies, and it can see billions of light-years away. That's all it does, take pictures and send the data back to Earth."

Mo continued. "So to answer your question, Tracy, I believe the aliens are doing what the Hubble does; they are observing the planet we call Earth. But instead of merely taking pictures and relaying the data, they are making first-hand observations."

"What would they be observing way back here in time?" she asked.

"I like to think of it as a science project."

"What do you mean, science project?"

"What if your assignment was to observe something, say a plant, and then keep observing it through time and report on the changes you saw? Over time, the plant would grow, it would flower, and then it would die, but hopefully not before propagating itself."

Tracy nodded and told him she liked his analogy.

"Observing your plant could be done on your patio over the period of say one season, right?"

She nodded again.

"At a preset time each day, you would look at your plant and write down what it was doing. You might measure its growth or count its leaves or even take its picture."

"I follow you," she said.

"But what if your job was to observe not a plant but the life on a planet over a long period of time, say hundreds or thousands or millions or even billions of years. How would you accomplish that?"

"I couldn't," Tracy replied. "No human could."

"Not given *our* lifespan and technology," I interrupted. "But given advanced alien technology, they might be able to move between the centuries, or even the eons, as easily as I could go forward to the bow."

It got very quiet. Mo smiled and then sat back. After a moment, he asked quietly, "Did you ever hear of Atlantis?"

Tracy nodded. "Of course. But it's a myth."

"The theory of Atlantis has countless critics, but one theme resonates, and that is that if Atlantis truly did exist, it was likely inhabited by an advanced civilization. It's also a given that the alien technology we have encountered is far in advance of our own." Mo paused here, took a breath, and continued. "My observations suggest they are arriving and landing somewhere, but since I don't see them leaving, it's probably safe to conclude they are staying."

"Or they might be leaving from another location or in another manner we aren't familiar with," I interjected.

"Perhaps, but let's focus on what is certain or at least highly probable. An alien craft is landing x-hundred miles from here in that direction"—he pointed—"at regular intervals. So to answer your question, Tracy, I believe the aliens are observing the life on our planet, like you would watch a plant's growth through the cycle I described earlier."

"And you think they're based on Atlantis?" Tracy asked.

Before he could reply, I interrupted with another question. "Or do you believe the entire civilization inhabiting Atlantis is alien? If you see aliens arriving but don't see them leaving, there might be quite a few there by now."

"At this time in Earth's history," Mo replied, "there are primitive humans spread across the planet, but if I remember correctly, they are primarily inhabiting the continents and probably aren't capable of long ocean crossings."

"So if we find Atlantis, we might be the only humans there."

"Well, if we are looking for aliens, they'd be easy to spot if we're the only humans," Reid said.

"There's a simple way to find out," Mo stated confidently. "What's the range of *The Lady Anne*?"

"Assuming the wind holds, with three watches," Reid replied, "she can easily have two-hundred-mile days."

"So that's roughly five days out and five more back?"

Reid nodded.

So did I.

Reid turned to me. "You're the captain," he said. "What do you think?"

I took my time formulating an answer. "I believe that Mo believes what he's saying. I also think he has sound reasoning behind his theories." I turned to Tracy. "What about you?"

She turned to face Mo. "If we head out on course 025 degrees and sail for a thousand miles but don't find anything, are we going to turn around and come back?"

"We'd have to evaluate our options at that point."

"If we stayed on that course and didn't find anything but didn't turn around, where would we end up?"

"Probably Iceland or Greenland if we sailed that far," Mo replied. "But that's a guess since I don't have a 25,700-year-old chart with me."

"Well, I don't want to go to either of those places," Tracy said with a grin. "So if we don't find Atlantis, can we change course for Europe? I'd like to go see the Mediterranean or possibly Norway and the fjords."

"It's about four thousand miles across the Atlantic so it would be closer to turn around, but if you wanted to keep going, it'd be okay by me."

"Are you two serious?" Reid asked.

"Well, you know what they say about Caribbean islands," I joked. "If you've seen one, you've seen them all. So why not? Let's give Mo's theory a try and if we come up short, we can head east and add a transatlantic crossing to our sailing resumes."

Mo agreed. Tracy smiled. Reid shook his head but didn't say no.

I looked from one of them to another, wondering if they had the same question I did. What would it be like to be completely alone crossing an ocean?

CHAPTER 83

There was a little more discussion about venturing a thousand miles into the Atlantic, but Reid, Tracy, and I knew *The Lady Anne* was up to the task. Reid had two final concerns: not knowing the weather forecast and not having any chance of rescue if anything went wrong.

Mo told us there hadn't been any storms in weeks and the winds had been very reliable. He was confident hurricane season was over.

Then he added that surviving ashore was just as problematic as surviving at sea, as evidenced by his condition after only six months. After answering a few more questions, he excused himself below and bid us all goodnight.

"It was interesting to watch him defend going to search for Atlantis," I whispered.

"He definitely believes it exists," Reid said, also whispering. "But like I said, we'll be one hundred percent on our own."

"He sounds like he can take us to the aliens," Tracy added. "So if you two still want to do that, he's our best chance."

"If we want to get back to our time, we don't have a lot of choices," I said quietly as I stood.

"We can discuss it in the morning," Reid whispered and then went below.

Tracy yawned and stretched and asked me to see if Buster needed to go aft. "I'm beat," she said.

I quietly called Buster to the swim platform and then waited while he did his business. The stars were close and bright. They really were magnificent. I wondered which star the aliens came from.

I made my way quietly below, turning off lights as I went. Tracy was in our cabin, getting ready for bed. "So you're taking a turn with Reid tonight?" she asked, smiling. "Good for you."

I didn't say anything. I wondered if I would make love to him or just maintain the illusion so he could get some rest.

The decision was made for me. Reid was already asleep when I slipped into bed. Was I relieved or aggravated that he didn't wait up for me? It didn't matter.

I was also the first one awake the next morning. Reid hadn't even changed position that I could see. I watched his chest rise and fall beneath the sheet, debating whether to wake him with a kiss.

The fact that I had to ask the question made me realize I

wasn't as ready to commit to a physical relationship as I thought. I sighed and dropped silently out of bed.

Buster was waiting by the hatch, so after letting him topside, I tiptoed into our cabin and got dressed. Tracy was still fast asleep too, so I closed the door behind me and went to the galley to make breakfast.

I wanted to make something Mo would really appreciate. He was very smart, and I liked having him aboard. I remembered the resort breakfast with Charles the morning I first saw *The Lady Anne* and decided to make bagels.

I carefully sliced the last three bagels into fourths so it looked like more than it was. I found the remaining lox and then thinly sliced an onion and tomato as well.

The house batteries were drained more than normal, which I attributed to having non-sailors aboard. Rather than use the inverter, draining them even further, or starting the engine or generator which would be noisy, I "toasted" the bagels in a frypan and made coffee on the stove. I set out the cream cheese, poured juice, and set the table for five.

Reid appeared just as I put the finishing touches on our breakfast platter. He came up behind me and put his arms around my waist. "Why didn't you wake me last night? Or this morning?"

I turned to face him. "You obviously needed your rest. I didn't have the heart to disturb you." I smiled up at him. "Besides, giving you a break from sex duty was the whole idea, wasn't it?"

He started to say something, but the sound of Mo and Gert talking announced their arrival in the galley.

Reid stepped away and motioned to the table. "Right on time. Breakfast is ready."

Mo and Gert were wearing what looked like golf attire, shorts that hit just below the knee and colorful short-sleeved shirts. The only thing missing were shoes—they were barefoot.

Mo said, "It's really nice they left these clothes aboard. It's just a pity none of their shoes fit."

"It's also a pity that we have the clothes because one of them died and the other lost his yacht in a poker game," Gert chided.

Mo's face reddened. "You're right, of course. My apologies to the Williamses."

I gestured to the table. "Sit down. Tracy is still asleep, so we'll go ahead and eat before the bagels get cold."

Mo looked at the spread. "Lox and bagels? Am I dreaming?"

I put two slices aside for Tracy. "Enjoy them. This is the last of our lox and bagels. From now on breakfast will consist of cereal and fruit."

Mo beamed. "I appreciate you sharing them with us." He turned to Gert, grinning. "This is a perfect Jewish breakfast."

We had finished eating when Tracy joined us. She apologized for sleeping so late and voraciously devoured what I had set aside. She gave Buster one half of the last bagel slice, spread with peanut butter.

Before we left the table, Mo said he had something important to say. The way he emphasized "important" concerned me.

"I forgot to include an essential piece of information in last night's discussion," he began.

"Uh-oh," Tracy said, leaning away.

"I woke up early this morning and went through my notes, looking for the last time the aliens had passed by."

"What's wrong?"

"Nothing is wrong, but I sighted an alien the evening before we saw and signaled you, so that was two days ago, right?"

"Correct," Reid confirmed.

"Assuming the aliens stick to the five-day cycle, there should be another pass by here in four days. Are you with me?"

"Are you asking me if we can be one thousand miles from here in four days?" Reid asked.

Mo shook his head. "It might not be that far, so I believe our timing will be good. What concerns me is that I saw an alien ship two days ago, but according to your log, that was five days after you came through the time portal."

"Was your previous sighting five days before that?" I asked.

"Yes, it was."

"So are the sightings here corresponding to the sightings in the future?" I asked.

"Apparently so."

"So was I right last night?" Tracy said. "Aliens really are coming and going every five days, but nobody is reporting it?"

"That seems entirely possible," Mo answered.

I thought for a moment. "See if this makes any sense," I said finally. "Suppose the aliens got videoed by Joe Blow on x-day, in his time. They swiftly propel him back in time, 25,700 years. On that same day, the same aliens fly over Mo's island and he sees them and records it."

"Mo's island, I like that," Mo said, smiling and looking at Gert. "But maybe it should be Gert's island?"

Tracy laughed, "Or Mo-Gert's island, like yogurt with an *m*."

I waited for their laughter to subside and then finished. "So when they send Joe Blow through, perhaps they come with him, since the time portal would be in place and big enough to accommodate two vessels, Joe's and theirs."

"So when I see aliens, they may not be alone. Another vessel, another ship or plane, might come through with them," Mo said. "But why wouldn't I see that too?"

I shook my head. "I can explain why we didn't notice the alien craft when we came through. We had all passed out. But why you wouldn't spot it from the ground, I have no idea. And maybe it doesn't happen every time." I let my imagination wander. "Maybe it takes so much energy, even for them, to create their time portal that they are just being efficient by using it if they need to when it's open."

"I'll have to think about that for a while," Mo said. "But if you're right, someone else might have come through two days ago."

"Where would they be now?" Tracy asked.

"They could be anywhere. It would depend on where they were when they documented the aliens."

"So what's the bottom line?" Reid asked. "Should we search awhile to see if we find another vessel or follow our intended course?"

"We have no idea where to look for anyone else," Tracy said. "I vote we follow our original plan."

I nodded. "I agree. Finding the aliens should be the best way to get back to our own time. After that, we can try to figure out how to bring whoever is still trapped here home."

Mo and Gert were nodding in assent. "It still seems to be our best option," Mo answered, sounding confident.

"Okay, then," Reid said. "North, northeast on course 025 degrees magnetic, toward the Atlantic Ocean it is. Let's get underway."

CHAPTER 84

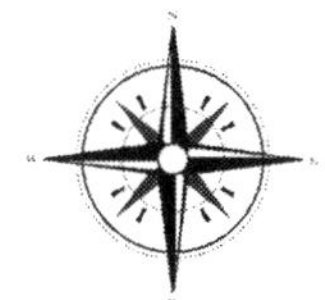

Reid sent Tracy, Mo, and Gert topside while I saw to clearing away our breakfast things. Then he called me to join him, wearing his PFD and carrying Tracy's and mine.

"We've been neglecting to wear them the last few days," he said. "But given that we will be headed way offshore, it's time to get back in the habit."

We went topside and he opened a locker, giving Mo and Gert each a life jacket. He instructed them to wear them at all times topside and to stay in the cockpit unless they were clipped in. They both agreed.

He asked Mo and Gert if they had any sailing experience.

"Not sailboats," Mo answered. "But I have flown a glider, does that count?"

"The last boat I was on sunk," Gert answered and then chuckled. "But it wasn't a sailboat."

"Do you two mind if we go over some basics before we get underway?" Reid asked, using his teaching voice.

"Should I be taking notes?" Mo asked.

"Wouldn't hurt," I replied, thinking of our first few days on board. "Just a minute."

I ducked below and got him a sheet of paper and a pencil. He was quite happy having a new pencil, like a kid getting a surprise birthday present.

Reid began, counting off rules on his fingers as he went. "Don't fall overboard. Don't get hit by the boom. Don't get your hand caught in a winch. The decks get slick so don't fall. And last and most important: get Pat or Tracy or me if you see anything that doesn't look right."

Mo had him repeat a few of those so he could write them down correctly. Gert read over his shoulder and told him his *i* looked like an *e,* but she was pretty sure that Reid has said winch, not wench. Then she started laughing.

Tracy did too. "Yeah. Don't get your hand caught in a wench."

"You know, I've never had any of my students make that mistake before," Reid said, laughing along with everyone else. "But it's not so funny if it happens. Getting caught in a winch, I mean."

Tracy giggled and then had Mo add to his list, "Nothing goes in the toilet that you didn't eat or drink first."

"And please don't waste water or power," I said. "When you leave your cabin, turn off the light. Brush your teeth with a half glass of water, not thirty seconds of running water."

"Is that why you use the solar showers?" Mo asked. "To conserve water?"

"Charles had them aboard. They are very efficient," I answered.

"I even try not to stack dishes," Reid said. "Why wash both sides? Oh." He paused. "And remember to stay hydrated."

"We'll try to be more efficient," Mo stated as he finished writing.

Gert nodded. "I'll try, too, but you might have to remind me a few times. I have to get used to having lights to turn on and off."

Reid told Tracy to start the engine and brought Mo and Gert forward to help he and I stow the dinghy since we didn't think we'd be using it. After it was secured, we raised the anchor. Gert went back to the cockpit to join Tracy, who took us out toward the wind. Tracy let Gert take the helm, seated right next to her, coaching. I used that opportunity to lower the keel.

"I never knew you could see wind," Gert said as she looked at the wind line ahead of us. It was very obvious where the calm water ended and the windblown water began. "It's fascinating."

Mo accompanied Reid and me below and we showed him the electronics and gave him a brief overview of *The Lady Anne's* systems. He asked good questions and was very impressed.

Reid rummaged around in the salon and finally found

what he was looking for—the two spare pairs of sunglasses I had bought at Costco. He handed them to Mo, advising him not to drop them overboard since they weren't corded. I made a mental note to take care of that tonight. I had some paracord that would work.

We made our way topside, just in time to watch Tracy unfurl the mainsail while Gert steered into the wind. Before long, the engine was shut down and we were under full sail. Tracy used the compass and steered 025 degrees. Mo and Gert were thrilled to be moving so quickly under wind power alone.

With no chart on which to plot our course, Reid drew a long line on a sheet of paper and marked one end with the time and speed and wrote "Atlantis - 025 degrees," at the other end.

"This is our course." He showed everyone. "We'll do our best to stay close to this line and figure the distance traveled by knowing the elapsed time and our speed."

Mo looked at the sketch and asked, "How did you calculate the time?"

I showed Mo my sundial, borrowed the compass, and got it properly oriented. Sundial time was within eighteen minutes of his watch. He was impressed. I smiled.

Tracy let Gert steer but stayed close by. Gert was really enjoying herself and called Mo over. "You've got to try this," she bubbled. Mo handed her sunglasses and took the helm.

"This is similar to flying," he announced, grinning widely.

"It's very similar to flying," Reid told him. "Both use physics, except our wings are vertical instead of horizontal and we call one a sail and the other a keel. Where wings have lift, sails have pull."

I trimmed the mainsail for the course we were on and *The Lady Anne* heeled over slightly, and then heeled further as I adjusted the traveler, genoa, and mizzen sail. That made them both grin even more. Mo was fascinated that minor adjustments to sail trim had such a profound effect on performance.

"I'd like to learn how to do this someday." He smiled as he held the wheel.

"Well, you've got a thousand miles in which to learn," I quipped. "And Reid is the finest instructor there is."

CHAPTER 85

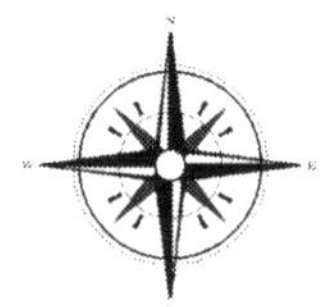

Reid busied himself making a new watch schedule. It was the same as before, two hours on, four hours off during the day and three hours on, six hours off at night.

Mo, peering over Reid's shoulder, questioned why he and Gert weren't included, especially since Reid's schedule showed one double shift. Reid was frank in explaining that he didn't feel they were ready. After all, neither had sailing experience.

"If you're serious about learning, though," he said, "I'll pencil you and Gert for the ten o'clock to twelve o'clock a.m. morning shift. One of us—Tracy, Pat, or me—will always be awake by then if you run into trouble."

Since it was close to eleven, Mo asked if he and Gert could take over until twelve. Reid reluctantly agreed to let them have the helm by themselves until noon, after which time the schedule would begin in earnest and Reid would take over. Mo and Gert eagerly accepted.

Tracy, Reid, and I went forward. I could tell Tracy wasn't comfortable leaving Mo and Gert by themselves at the helm. In fact, as soon as we were out of earshot, she turned to Reid.

"I don't think that was a good idea."

Reid held up a hand. "Listen, they've got to have a chance to learn if they're going to be any help to us. We're on course, trimmed, and shouldn't have to tack or retrim unless the wind changes. Besides, the three of us are right here."

Tracy shrugged. "I suppose it's all right." She looked to the horizon. "I want to fish but we're moving too fast." She held up a hand to shield her eyes. "I guess I'll keep a lookout for dolphins or whales instead."

I left her and Reid and made my way below. I rinsed out and refilled water bottles with desalinated water. It was very tricky moving about below, and I found myself having to hold on with one hand because we were heeled so far over.

I took some water to the helm for Gert and Mo. I also handed Gert a jar of my aloe cream and told her it would help her dried skin.

"Dolphins," Tracy shouted, drawing our attention. "Dead ahead."

"What should we do?" Mo asked, his hands tightening on the wheel.

"Hold your course," I answered.

"Won't we hit them?" Gert asked.

"Nope, they know exactly what they're doing. They're playing a game with us."

Reid had joined Tracy forward on the windward side, away from the genoa, and they were laughing and pointing.

"Can we go look?" asked Gert, now sounding excited.

I took over the helm and let them go forward, one at a time, warning them to hold on and be extra careful.

When Gert came back, she was flushed with excitement. "There are so many of them," she said. "And they swim right along beside us."

Mo motioned her back. "Go, enjoy the show. I'll be all right here with Pat."

We watched Gert make her way to join Tracy and Reid. "Now that it's just you and me, I have a question for you" I said, sitting beside him. "I'm curious. Why didn't you take off after you landed that first time? Couldn't you get the plane started? Was the battery dead? All our batteries were drained from the trip through the portal, but we managed to get them charged again."

"I might have been able to do that too. I even started clearing rocks to make a smoother runway."

"So what happened?"

Mo shrugged. "When I calculated how far back in time I had traveled, it was clear there was nowhere better to go. I didn't have enough fuel to dead reckon back to the US, even if that had been possible. I eventually decided I was better off staying put. And as it turns out, I was right. First, Gert came along. Then the three of you with *The Lady Anne*."

I nodded. "It's clear you've given a lot of thought to the way this world works, so I have another question. Why do you think your seeds wouldn't grow?"

Mo drew in a breath. "You might not like my answer to that question," he replied. "Do you really want to know?"

"Yes. From your expression, I gather what you're about to tell me is not something I'm going to be pleased to hear. But like you, the scientific curiosity in me is strong."

Mo paused as if gathering his thoughts. "Okay," he said after a moment. "My theory is that as long as we die in this time period, nothing inorganic we leave behind will be around in 20,000 years when recorded history starts. No notes, no pictures, no shipwreck, nothing. Everything will have decayed, decomposed, or rotted away. There will be absolutely nothing to show that any of us, including *The Lady Anne* and my plane, were ever here."

"But you said nothing *inorganic* would survive. What about something organic?"

"Ah," Mo said. "You've almost answered your own question. Anything organic, like plants for instance, might survive, reproduce, and change nature, perhaps even change history."

I snapped my fingers. "Is that why we found all the dead bugs on board after we went through the portal?"

"I didn't know you had, but it makes perfect sense. The aliens don't want twenty-first-century bugs scurrying around in this time period, nor do they want them to perhaps mutate and disrupt the natural order of evolution."

"But I'm organic and I'm obviously not dead."

Mo peered at me. "Connect the dots. I said the aliens don't want plants surviving and *reproducing*."

I suddenly felt weak in the knees as the import of what he was saying struck home.

Mo looked at me and said, "I see by your reaction that you just figured it out."

"Is that why neither Tracy nor I have had a period?"

"I would imagine so. And if you did a sperm count, Reid would be found to be shooting blanks. As would I, and even Buster."

"So to keep us from reproducing in this time period, you think we were sterilized on the way back through time."

"You, me, Gert, Tracy, Reid, Buster, and all the fruits and vegetables you were carrying. We could try your seeds, but they're not going to germinate either, I'm positive."

Mo looked up as Gert approached. "Hi, there Gert, how were the dolphins?"

I stood and gave Gert my seat. My mind reeled at the implications of Mo's theory. I heard Gert talking and laughing, but all I could think of was that I had to get away to think. I waved her into the chair.

"Talk to you later," I managed to say before rushing below.

CHAPTER 86

I covered my head with a pillow and started crying. I don't even know why Mo's theory affected me the way it did. Having children was not something I had given much thought to. But if Mo was right, the aliens took that option away along with everything else. Anger and frustration made for bitter tears.

Tracy found me in our cabin. "What's wrong?" she asked. "What the hell happened?"

I wiped away the latest round of tears. "Close the door," I said.

Tracy pulled the door closed behind her. "Did Gert say something to upset you? I swear—"

I shook my head.

"Then what is it? Tell me."

I stared at her, not knowing where to begin.

She handed me a tissue and very softly said, "You need to tell me what's wrong."

I closed my eyes to compose myself, but before I could form the words, Tracy headed for the door

"I'm going to go get Reid," she said, panic washing the color from her face. She rushed out before I could stop her.

I got another tissue, mopped at my eyes, and blew my nose. I wasn't sure I wanted to see Reid. Not until I had my emotions in check. But I had no choice. Reid bolted in, Tracy on his heels. She sat on the edge of the bed and took my hand. "What is it?"

I drew in a deep breath. "Mo has a theory," I began. "It explains why seeds don't germinate. Why all the bugs on board the ship died when we went through the portal. Why Tracy and I haven't had a period. We've been sterilized."

Reid frowned. "Sterilized? Why would he think that?"

I repeated his theory about disturbing the evolutionary process.

"We don't know he's right," Reid said, holding my hand. "We haven't had unprotected sex."

"It makes sense though. What else could account for our not having periods? For seeds not germinating?" I lowered my head. "And the way you and Tracy go at it, are you *sure* you've always used a condom?"

Tracy didn't say anything, she just looked away. Reid too. I knew then I was right.

"They had no right to do that." Tracy stood, hands in fists

at her side. "I may not have seen children in my future, but what if Pat had?"

Reid held our hands for a few seconds and then said he had to go but would be right back. In a moment, the boat stopped heeling and then tacked before slowing down to oscillate back and forth.

"We just heaved to," Tracy said.

A few minutes later Reid was back, asking if he could come in and saying that Gert was with him.

"It's open," I replied.

"Mo should have let me tell you," she said. "He's very smart, but he's not very tactful. And it's just a theory. Maybe the process will be reversed when we get back to our own time."

"She's right," Reid said. "Maybe when we go back through the portal, everything will be the same as before."

"But we can't know that," I argued. I threw up my hands. "What difference does it make anyway? We may never get back. We may be stuck in this time warp until we die. We may —" My breath caught.

Reid stood. "Would you please excuse us, Gert?" he said. "I'm sorry I dragged you down here."

"I'll be at the top of the hatch if you need me." She smiled sadly at us and closed the door softly behind her.

Reid, Tracy, and I remained in the cabin. I lay back on the bed, Tracy beside me, while Reid sat in the chair opposite us. I couldn't think of anything else to say. It was too much to take in. But being together was comforting in itself.

In a while, we made our way topside. Reid got us back on course, then handed off the helm to Mo.

Gert asked if we were okay and told us she had yelled at Mo for being so insensitive.

"He answered my question," I said. "And he was truthful. If he's right, we may as well be prepared to accept the fact that we've been changed, and that change may be permanent. It's not his fault."

It was getting close to noon and Reid took the helm, thanking Mo and Gert for taking a turn.

Tracy went below to make lunch and Mo sat next to me in the cockpit. He apologized for being so blunt earlier.

"As I told Gert, you were honest," I replied. "I'm not going to shoot the messenger for answering a question I asked."

He moved back to the helm and sat by Reid. Gert looked like she wanted to say something to me, but thankfully she didn't. I really wasn't in the mood to discuss my feelings.

Buster preceded Tracy topside, wagging his tail. She had two plates of sliced fruit, two cereal bowls with spoons, and some pretzels. She handed one bowl to Gert and took the other to Mo.

"What is this?" I heard him ask.

Tracy grinned and said, "It's mo-gert."

"What's in it?"

"Ensure and granola. Enjoy."

She took Reid a plate of the fruit and a couple of the pretzels, then sat down near me to share the second plate. She gave

Buster one of the pretzels, which he dispatched with his usual enthusiasm.

Reid stood up and announced, "There's a contact at the edge of the radar. It's probably one of the islands we passed when we were sailing south. We'll just steer around it and then get back on course. Any objections?"

"You're not going to stop and go ashore?" Tracy asked.

"I didn't plan to. I'd like to stay on schedule. Why?"

"I wanted to burn some of our trash and bury the rest ashore. I was going to say something this morning but forgot."

"Unless we stop for another reason, that will have to wait."

"We can double bag it and store it in the dinghy for now," I said.

"Good idea," Tracy agreed. "Thank you."

Reid finished his shift without incident. The wind was holding, and he had been coaching Mo on the fine points of sail trim. *The Lady Anne* was heeled over and really hauling ass.

"The more we heel, the faster we go," Mo told Tracy as she took over the helm.

Tracy smiled indulgently. "Yes, but heeled over like this is hard on anyone below, especially if they're trying to sleep or cook," she replied. "As you might find out in a very short while."

"Well, I'm going below but I'm used to it," Reid said. "So just hold your course."

Tracy steered around the island, staying in deep water but holding her speed. Mo used the binoculars but reported he didn't see anything.

I noticed Gert was getting pale and offered her some water. She took a few sips then put her head down on the table. "Are you feeling okay?" I asked.

"I don't feel good," she replied. "I don't think that mo-gert stuff agreed with me."

"Hang in there," I said and then I went below to tell Reid Gert was a getting sick.

I found him in the workroom. The door was closed. Strange enough, but stranger still when he didn't let me in but asked what I needed through a partially open door. I told him. He said to give Gert some ginger ale and that he'd be up in a few minutes. He wouldn't tell me what he was doing, and I couldn't see around him. Puzzled, I left.

Gert was kneeling at the lifeline, puking over the side. Mo was at her side, keeping her steady. I felt bad for her, but there wasn't anything to do but wait until she was finished. Since Tracy was at the helm, Mo and I helped her back to the table.

She washed her face, rinsed out her mouth, and sipped a little ginger ale. Mo used a solar shower to rinse off her life jacket.

"Sorry," she said, looking very weak and very tired.

About then Reid came topside. He told her to sit where she had the wind in her face and sip the ginger ale. She moved toward the windward side and sat down. Mo sat next to her, holding her hand. Reid returned below without saying much. His behavior was suspicious.

The rest of Tracy's watch went without incident. We sailed around an island and got back on course. Gert told us she was feeling better, her stomach settled. We saw more dolphins and lots of birds, but no whales.

I went below to take care of our waste just as Reid was coming topside. He was carrying a handful of juice boxes. He looked very pleased.

"Will you be long?" he asked me.

"I don't think so. I'm going to macerate our waste. Why?"

He grinned. "Just come up as soon as you're done."

I pumped out the waste and quickly returned topside, very curious to see what Reid was up to.

"I have an announcement to make," he said. "So please gather at the helm if you would."

He quietly handed everyone a juice box. Then he took two small plastic medicine bottles out of his pocket.

Curiouser and curiouser.

He got down on one knee and handed one bottle to me and one to Tracy.

"In front of these witnesses," he said. "I am pledging my undying love to Tracy and to Pat."

I looked at Tracy and she looked at me.

"I think he wants you to open the bottles," Mo finally whispered.

I opened mine. Inside was some string, or actually, it was paracord. "What's this?"

"You'll see," Reid replied.

He looked very pleased with himself.

I pulled out the paracord. It was a necklace with a gold pendant.

"I have one too," Tracy exclaimed, holding hers high.

"Imagine that, so do I," Reid said.

I examined the pendant. It was a piece of one of our gold coins with a hole drilled in one end.

"If you put them together, you'll see they all fit," Reid said.

He held his piece out. Mine fit on one side. Tracy's fit on the other. They indeed formed a Canadian Maple Leaf gold coin.

"Did you make this?" Tracy asked, smiling.

He nodded and shifted his weight to his other knee. "Do you accept?"

"Wait," I said. "Is this a proposal? You're proposing to both of us?"

"I am."

It grew very quiet.

Reid was obviously waiting for one of us to say something. I wasn't sure what to say. The fact that Tracy didn't say anything made me guess she wasn't sure what to say either. Mo and Gert, meantime, were watching all three of us, waiting for someone to say something.

It was very awkward for what seemed like an eternity.

Finally, Reid said, "I can't stay knelt down much longer. Please say something."

Tracy spoke first. "Reid Adams, are you seriously proposing to two women with a homemade charm and a juice box?"

He nodded. "I am."

"Why a juice box?" I asked.

"You know my policy on alcohol while making way. This was the best thing I could come up with."

"Well, I do love you, and I'm very charmed," Tracy said, fingering her necklace. "Pun intended, so yes, I accept."

They both looked at me.

I grinned. "I'm very impressed with your resourcefulness and the symbolism behind cutting the coin into thirds. I don't know how we're going to make this work but, yes, Reid Adams, I, too, accept."

"Mazel tov," said Mo loudly, raising his juice box high. "Congratulations."

Gert started clapping and then Mo joined her. She gave Tracy and me each a big hug and said she was so happy for us. Tracy wiped away a tear. So did I.

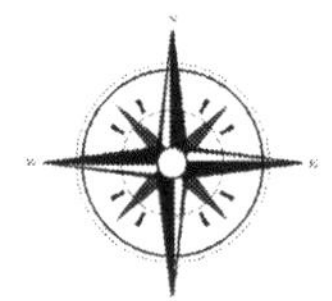

CHAPTER 87

Reid placed our necklaces around our necks, first mine, then Tracy's, kissing us as he finished. Then he went below and came back with his trumpet.

Mo looked at him with surprise. "You play?"

Reid nodded and warmed up with a scale. I stayed at the helm with Tracy. Mo and Gert were at the table, and Reid took a position in the middle.

The first song he played sounded familiar, but only Mo and Gert knew it was "Kiss to Build a Dream On." The next one we all knew, "Take My Breath Away" from the *Top Gun* movie. The last one, "My First, My Last, My Everything" got him a standing ovation.

I found myself rubbing my coin necklace and smiling. He had made me very happy.

"That had to be the craziest fucking proposal in the history of crazy fucking proposals," Tracy whispered to me. "But he's very sweet."

Reid put his trumpet down and made his way back to the helm.

"I hope you like your necklaces." He smiled.

"We love them," Tracy said. "I can't believe you made them. Have you been planning this long?"

"Actually it came to me because of what Mo said."

"And what was that," I asked.

"He said he'd be lost without Gert, and I feel the same way —that I'd be lost without you two."

Tracy smiled and took his hand.

"You know," Reid said, pointing to Mo and Gert sitting together at the table, their heads close together. "Those two probably had a week or two left if we hadn't have found them."

"Meaning what?" I asked him.

"Meaning, regardless of how this alien thing goes, our time here is limited. There is nobody else I would rather spend the rest of my life with than you two." He paused. "My whole life I've looked for love and I finally found it, here on a sixty-eight-foot sailboat."

Tracy threw her arms around him, letting go of the wheel. "I've never heard anything so beautiful in my whole life."

The Lady Anne began to veer. I grabbed the wheel and regained control, thinking ironically that this was probably how life with the three of us would go—Tracy giving in to impulse and me coming to the rescue. Next, she'd be dragging Reid below.

But Tracy surprised me by letting Reid go off to visit with Mo and Gert and taking the wheel back.

"You thought I'd want to consummate our new relationship right now, didn't you?" she asked me, grinning.

"It did cross my mind," I said.

"Well, this is a reformed Tracy. I won't shirk my duties and I won't monopolize Reid. In fact, if you want to…"

I shook my head. "No. I can wait."

She tossed her head. "Well, don't wait too long. Unless you're ready for the three of us to share a bed."

I may never be ready for that, I thought, realizing this new "reformed" Tracy was not much different than the old "unreformed" Tracy. Suddenly, the glow of optimism cast by Reid's romantic gesture dimmed. I sighed and went below.

The rest of Tracy's shift went without incident. I took over promptly at four o'clock, as per the schedule. We passed another island, but it wasn't in our path so no course adjustments were necessary. The wind had shifted a bit, but I adjusted the sails and tried to keep our speed up.

We didn't see any whales but saw lots of birds, dolphins, and the biggest sea turtle Reid had ever seen. It was massive, probably over ten feet long, and Reid guessed it weighed a ton or more. Tracy tried to get some video, but it was gone before she could get the camera ready.

I was the only one topside just before six o'clock p.m. The others had gone below to prepare dinner. I eased the sheets and reduced our heeling to make it easier for them while below.

There was another large contact on the radar, but it was twenty miles away and not in our path. A small, brown bird had landed on the stern rail and was watching me. "Don't get used to that spot," I told him. "The mighty Buster will be up here soon and chase you away. He hates birds."

The radio squawked and startled me so much I jerked and twisted my neck. We had left it on out of habit but had completely forgotten about it.

I rubbed my neck, cursing them for calling me on a portable. "Not funny, guys," I mumbled.

Just then the radio blared again. "Calling the sailboat. Can you hear me?"

CHAPTER 88

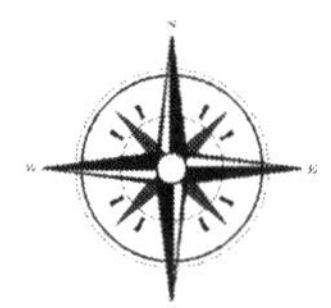

I reached for the handset just as Reid charged through the hatch.

"Was that the radio?"

As if in answer, the radio blared again. "Can anybody hear me?"

"I hear you," I fairly shouted. "Who is this?"

"Bonnie," she replied, her voice shaking.

I glanced up at Reid. "Bonnie? Of Rick and Bonnie?"

"Yes."

"Where are you?" I asked. "I can hardly hear you."

By now, Reid, Tracy, Mo, and Gert were at the helm, listening. Reid held the wheel so I could focus on the radio.

"I'm hiding below. I have the radio you left behind."

Bonnie sounded more than nervous. She sounded scared.

I replied, "Is Rick there? Why are you hiding?"

"He's driving. I turned off the circuit breaker that powers his radio. He can't hear me."

Reid motioned to attract my attention. "Ask her what he's driving."

"Driving what? *The Day Dream*?"

"No, not *The Day Dream*. *The Aquaholic*." Bonnie's voice was beginning to sound frantic.

"What's *The Aquaholic*, and where are you?" I asked.

"*The Aquaholic* is a charter catamaran that Rick took over. He's completely lost it. He's killed three men, beaten one woman into a coma, and has been assaulting the other two wives. We're prisoners. You have to help us."

Reid took the handset away from me and said, "Bonnie, this is Reid. Where are you?"

"Hiding in the head."

"No, where is your boat? Where is *The Aquaholic*?"

"Coming right at you."

I looked at the radar. Except for the land I had seen earlier, it was clear. I adjusted the sensitivity like Reid had done before. A very faint blip appeared periodically, about three miles out.

Without being told, Mo grabbed the binoculars and rushed forward, Tracy right behind him, followed by Buster.

"There's a boat ahead, maybe two or three miles," Tracy hollered, pointing dead ahead.

Reid asked, "Bonnie, does Rick have any guns?"

There was no reply. Reid repeated his question.

"Are you still there?" she answered.

"We're still here. Does Rick have any guns?"

"This radio is running out. The battery light is flashing. Rick has a gun, just like yours."

"Does he have ammo?"

"I don't have time for twenty questions," Bonnie hissed. "Shut up and listen. If there is shooting, my kids might get hurt. I need to know if I stop Rick, will you take all of us with you?"

Reid stopped transmitting and looked at me.

"He's killed three men?" I asked, not wanting to believe what I had heard.

"That's what she said," Reid answered.

"Are you still there?" Bonnie radioed, pleading.

"I'm still here," Reid answered.

I took the handset back. "Bonnie, this is Pat. Don't confront him. He'll kill you. Can you and your kids jump overboard and we'll pick you up?"

"That won't work. I can't leave the others here. I need to know, will you take us with you?"

"Stand by," I answered.

"We need to help those women," Gert said anxiously.

"We have a duty to offer assistance," I said. "But only if it can be rendered without putting our vessel or ourselves at risk."

Reid nodded. "If Rick is indeed armed, we will be at risk of getting shot. That's a pretty big risk."

Tracy and Mo returned to the helm. "What's going on?" Tracy asked.

I quickly filled them in. "We're debating if we should offer assistance or not," I answered. "Rick has a shotgun and has already killed three. I don't want to be target practice."

"My little rifle has more range than a shotgun," Mo interjected. "I'm a pretty good shot, even from a heaving, moving vessel."

"We can't just sail by while Rick violates those women," Gert added.

"Are you going to help me or not?" Bonnie's voice cracked over the radio.

"Just a second," I answered. "Reid, what would you suggest?"

Reid looked at the radar screen, looked forward, and then answered, "If Bonnie is telling the truth, Mo's rifle gives us a slight advantage in firepower. I'm confident *The Lady Anne* can outsail a charter catamaran under the command of a fishing boat captain who has limited sailing experience. If Pat, Tracy, and Gert handle the boat, Mo and I will be free to shoot if we have to."

"That sounds like we have the advantage," Tracy said.

"Of course there's always the possibility Bonnie is lying, trying to lure us into a trap," Reid said softly. "She's done it before."

"And if we do this thing," I added, "we'll have many more mouths to feed."

"But we'll also have another boat to accompany us into the Atlantic," Reid said.

"Are you guys still there?" Bonnie radioed. Her voice was low, but her tone conveyed desperation.

"Thumbs-up or thumbs-down?" I asked, putting my thumb up.

Reid raised his thumb and said, "The enemy of my enemy is my friend."

I sure hoped he was right. As I made eye contact, one by one, everyone signaled thumbs-up.

I nodded and spoke into the radio. "Okay, we'll take you with us," I replied. "What are you going to do?"

There was no response.

"Bonnie, can you still hear me?"

"Stop transmitting," Reid commanded. "Maybe she can't answer. We don't want Rick to hear."

Reid started below, saying he was going to get the gun.

Gert followed behind. "I'll get Mo's too."

"What should I do?" I asked, a wave of fear washing over me.

"Hold your course," Reid answered. "If Rick didn't hear us, he doesn't know that we'll be ready for him."

CHAPTER 89

Reid checked the shotgun and put extra shells in his pockets. Mo had finished assembling his rifle. He placed the extra magazine in his pocket.

Reid insisted Tracy, Gert, and Buster go below. Tracy argued that Buster could be put below but the rest of us should stay topside to steer and make any necessary emergency maneuvers. Gert said she wasn't a very good sailor, but she could work the second winch.

Reid reluctantly agreed they could stay.

"So, what's the plan?" I asked Reid. I tried not to sound scared, but I'm sure he could see me shaking.

"Mo and I will stay low, out of sight. Pass them port to port. When the shooting starts, duck."

The cat was in sight now, coming right at us. It was a very wide vessel, its twin hulls intimidating. Its mast looked taller than ours.

The salon windows were heavily tinted, making it impossible to see inside. I couldn't tell who was at the helm. I altered course slightly, intending to pass broadside within about forty feet.

"I don't like this," I said. "We're going to be close enough to shoot, but so is he."

"Hold your course," Reid instructed. "Fall off if he swerves toward us. Be alert and be quick. You can do this."

Tracy switched places with me, insisting she take the helm as she had more experience driving. I took up position at the winch so I could quickly trim the sails for any course changes. Gert went to the other winch, watching me for instructions.

With less than 200 feet to go, Reid disengaged the safety. My heart started pounding so hard I was sure everybody could hear. My hands were sweating so badly I had to wipe them on my shirt.

Just then, the cat swerved. Only it didn't swerve toward us; it veered the other way.

"Fall off," Reid yelled as he jumped up and raced for the stern, shotgun at the ready. Mo lost his balance a little but regained his footing and followed Reid.

Our sterns passed fairly close and Reid and Mo were ready to fire, but I didn't see anybody onboard the cat.

The cat held its course away, towing a small dinghy behind it. Its sails weren't adjusted for its new course and began to luff. The cat began to slow.

"Jibe," Reid hollered. "Circle behind them."

"Jibe ho," Tracy yelled.

Gert and I worked the winches. *The Lady Anne* responded and crashed through the waves, really jolting us.

The cat had slowed. Its huge mainsail was luffing, beginning to flap; so was its smaller jib. Their boom was dangerously swinging from side to side. The paint job was unlike anything I had ever seen. The hulls had black striping, like a psychedelic zebra.

A figure appeared at its stern, waving. It looked like Bonnie.

I released the genoa to luff too, slowing us down. We passed astern of the cat.

"I need help!" Bonnie shouted.

"Where's Rick?" Reid yelled, gun pointed.

"I got him," she yelled back. "He's dead."

Reid surprised me when he answered, "Nice try, but I've heard that before."

Then he told Tracy to keep going and circle around again but not get too close.

"He's really dead," Bonnie shouted, waving frantically. "Don't leave me here. You said you'd take us with you."

Tracy circled around, keeping our distance. Gert and I continued to work the winches.

"I was born at night, but it wasn't last night," Reid exclaimed. "You pulled that shit on me once and I'm not falling for it again."

"What do you want to do?" I asked.

Bonnie was still waving as we passed by again. "Look at his

blood on my hand," she shouted, holding her right hand up. It appeared to be bloody.

"Nice try with the fish blood but I've seen that before too," Reid shouted, glancing at Tracy and me.

He had a good point.

"Alright, I'll fucking prove it," she yelled, and then headed back inside the salon, out of sight.

"Keep moving," Reid ordered. "Circle around again, not so close this time. Mo, you stay alert. Your gun has the most range and accuracy."

We sailed by, but Bonnie wasn't visible. Neither was anyone else.

"One more pass," Reid commanded Tracy. "Same speed, same distance."

My heart was still pounding. Gert and I were doing our job with the sheets and Tracy was handling the helm as Reid instructed. I was secretly glad Reid had taken over, because I feared my engineer training might have forced me to overanalyze the situation.

The Lady Anne swung around, and Tracy began another pass. Bonnie appeared again. Her face and shirt were covered in blood. She raised both hands up. They were bloody as well. The closest object to me looked like a hatchet or perhaps a kitchen cleaver. I couldn't quite see what was in her other hand.

"Oh my God," Tracy said, turning away and covering her mouth.

Gert turned too, bent down, and held her stomach.

Finally I saw it.

Bonnie was holding a severed head.

"Fuck you, Captain Rick," she screamed. Then she tossed the head toward us. It hit the water with a splash, still oozing blood.

"I'd say Captain Rick is dead." Reid turned and looked at me.

"I'd say he's dead fucking dead."

"Eat shit and bark at the moon," Tracy shouted.

"*Gay kaken ofn yahm*," Mo added. Then he translated the Yiddish to English: "Go shit in the ocean."

CHAPTER 90

It took some doing, but Reid threw Bonnie a line and we eventually got both boats tied together, or "rafted" as it is called in nautical terms. As neither Tracy nor I had ever actually "rafted" before, Reid quickly explained to stagger the masts and use lots of fenders so the vessels wouldn't rub together.

While Tracy and Gert held the guns, Reid, Mo, and I climbed over to the cat. Reid quickly furled the cat's sails, hollering back for Tracy to do the same. Both vessels were quickly de-powered and began to bob up and down, drifting.

Bonnie was covered in blood and appeared to be in shock. She was still holding the cleaver but surrendered it to Mo without arguing. There was a headless corpse in the main salon and needless to say, it looked like the set of a horror film. The helm was sprayed with blood and the steps down to the salon were bloody as well.

There was a shotgun, just like ours, laying a few feet from the body. Reid ejected one shell and then passed the gun over to Tracy. I guessed that Bonnie must have stabbed Rick while he was at the helm and when he followed her to the salon, she finished him off. She was hysterical, but managed to say that everyone else was below. I could see blood had pooled in what looked like gashes but were probably cleaver cut marks in the fiberglass sole.

Reid checked Rick's person and pockets for keys or anything important and then he and Mo disposed of the body over the stern. Nobody said any prayers. We didn't linger to watch the sharks feed. I feared the feeding sharks might damage the *Aquaholic*'s dinghy, so I moved it further forward.

Bonnie stripped out of her clothes and tried wiping off as much blood as she could, leaving everything she touched stained crimson. Gert came over with a mop and bucket and started cleaning up the mess, mumbling that she wasn't sure where to begin.

Tracy tossed over one of the resort T-shirts she had used as a rag so that Bonnie could cover herself. Then we went below, starting on the starboard hull.

Each hull contained two cabins and two heads. Both cabin doors had been tied so they wouldn't open. Fortunately, I had my rigging knife with me and rather than untie knots, I quickly cut the lines.

Bonnie's kids were in the aft cabin. They were scared but

looked all right. They were glad to see their mother. Knowing it was still bloody topside, Bonnie told them to wait in their cabin but left the door open. She then accompanied us, continuously glancing around as if still very afraid.

The forward cabin contained Angie, the late skipper's wife. She was tied to the bed and was naked and unconscious, but she was breathing and had a pulse. Her face was badly bruised and there was a large bump on the side of her head. We untied her and covered her with a blanket. She never moved or opened her eyes.

We crossed over to the other hull. The forward cabin was where Bonnie had been held captive. She put on some clean shorts and shoes. The aft cabin was also tied shut and it contained two women, Ashley and Donna, both naked, tied to the bed, and gagged. The different colored bruises suggested repeated beatings, but both women were conscious, watching us wild-eyed. The cabin reeked of urine, vomit, and crap. I opened the overhead hatch.

They began thrashing about and struggled violently when Reid started untying them, so he let me cut them loose. They were scared and started screaming, but finally calmed down when Mo made them understand that Rick was gone and wouldn't ever touch them again. Bonnie got them blankets, which they grabbed to cover themselves. They looked afraid of her as well, which was slightly puzzling.

Bonnie tearfully told us the three husbands had been murdered by Rick, who had gone berserk. She didn't elaborate and we didn't press her for details.

Bonnie rushed back to her kids and Mo started helping Gert clean up the blood. He began by cleaning the bottoms of our shoes and then wiping up our bloody footprints.

Reid and I went topside to talk to Tracy. We explained what we had found. She was mortified and then thankful because that could have been us.

"What's the plan, Reid?" I asked.

"These women all need a hospital, especially Angie. But since we don't have one, *The Lady Anne* will have to suffice."

"What's after that? Are we still going to Atlantis?" Tracy asked.

"Part of me says go find a place to anchor and let the injured recover," Reid said. "And part of me says we need to go and find the aliens now more than ever and get them to send us back where there are medical facilities."

"Will everyone fit aboard *The Lady Anne*?" I asked.

"Probably, but if this cat is seaworthy, and it looks like it is, we'd be foolish to leave it," he answered.

"What's with the crazy paint job?" I asked.

"Don't know. I've never seen anything like it, but it looks high-maintenance."

"There's no land for eighteen miles in the wrong direction and the sun is going down, so what do you want to do?" Tracy asked.

"We should probably split into two crews and sail both boats," he replied. "And we should probably get going."

"You might not want to put Bonnie with us," I mentioned. "After all, Tracy and I did kill her husband."

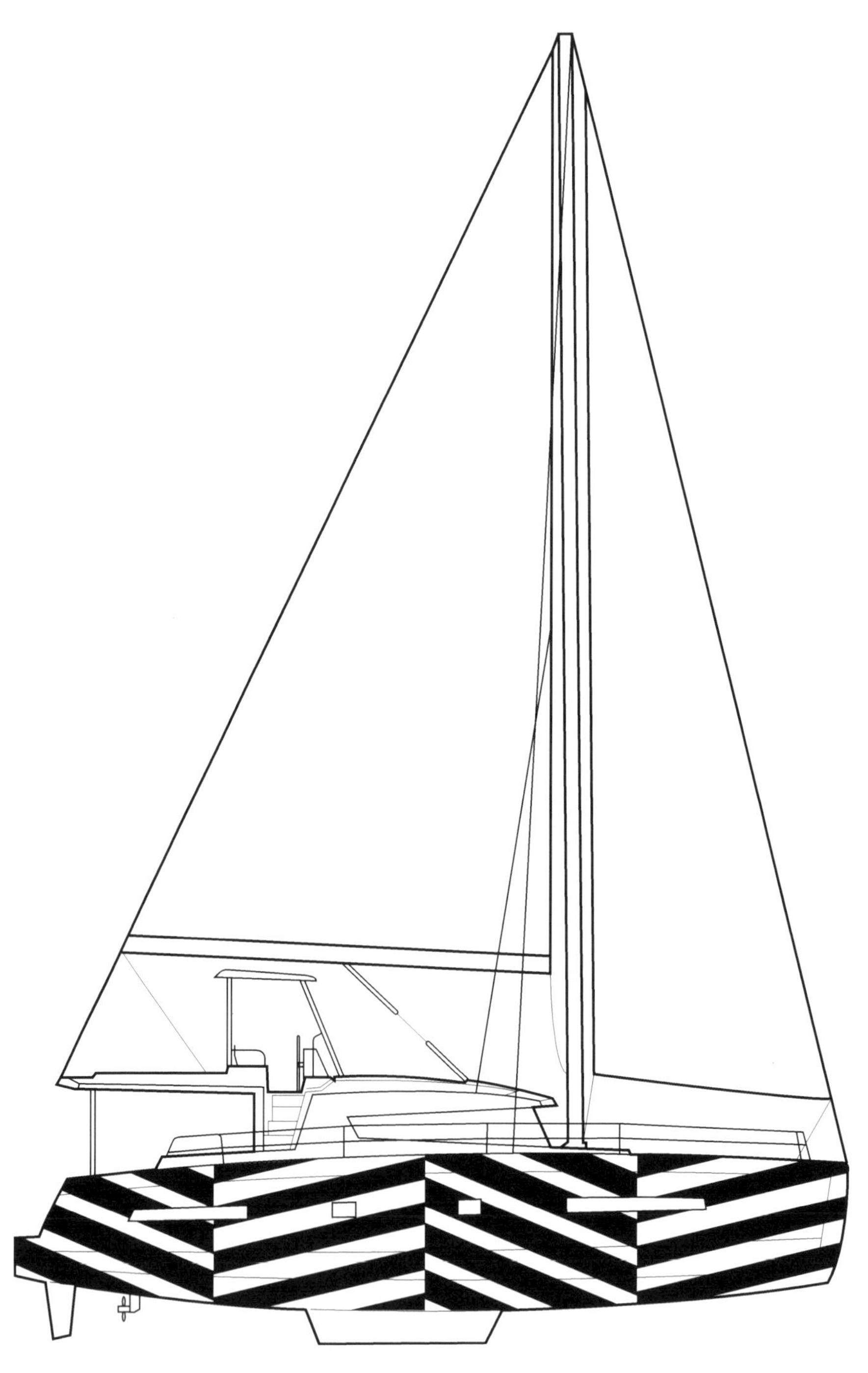

THE AQUAHOLIC
VESSEL OVERVIEW
NOT TO SCALE

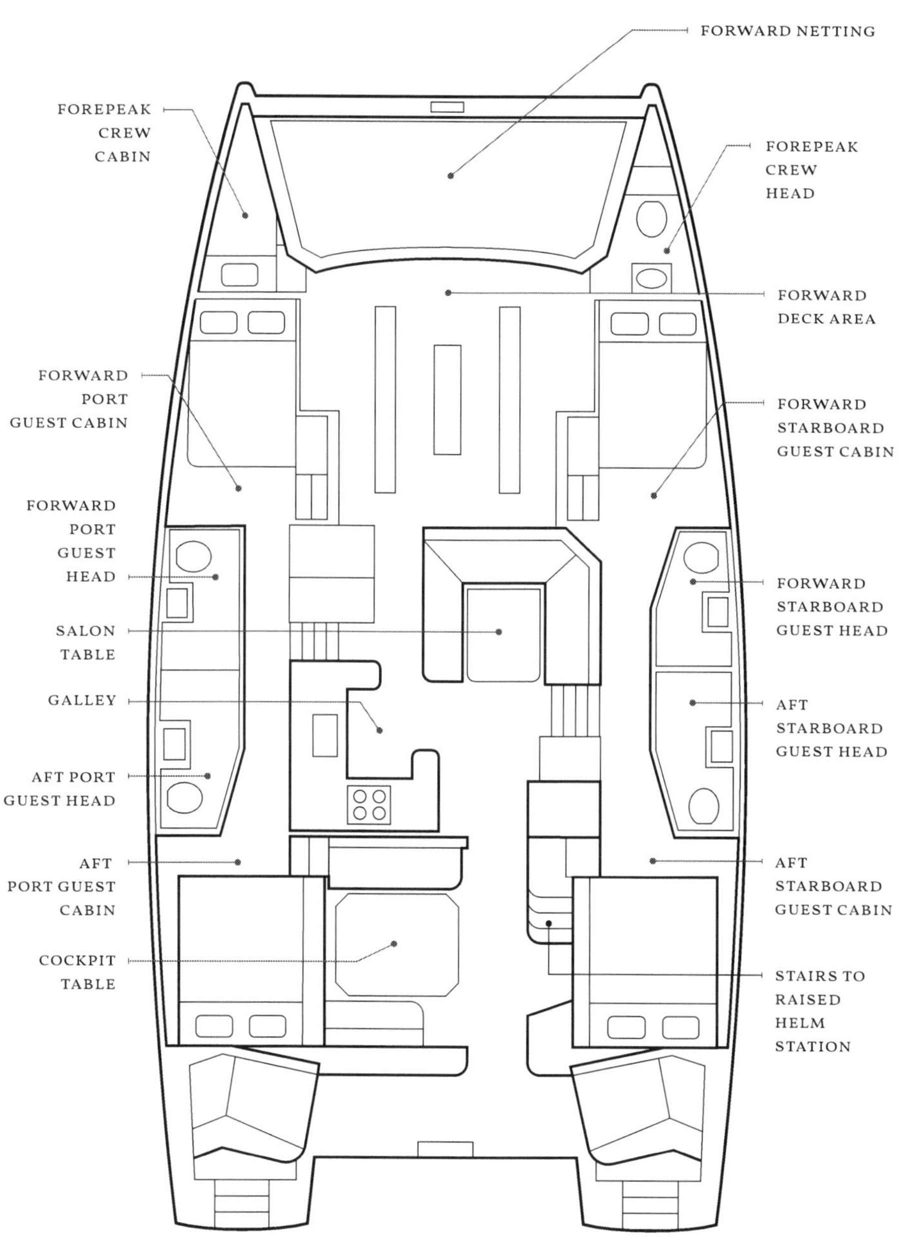

FORWARD NETTING
FOREPEAK CREW CABIN
FOREPEAK CREW HEAD
FORWARD DECK AREA
FORWARD PORT GUEST CABIN
FORWARD STARBOARD GUEST CABIN
FORWARD PORT GUEST HEAD
FORWARD STARBOARD GUEST HEAD
SALON TABLE
GALLEY
AFT STARBOARD GUEST HEAD
AFT PORT GUEST HEAD
AFT PORT GUEST CABIN
AFT STARBOARD GUEST CABIN
COCKPIT TABLE
STAIRS TO RAISED HELM STATION
THE AQUAHOLIC
CABIN LAYOUT
NOT TO SCALE

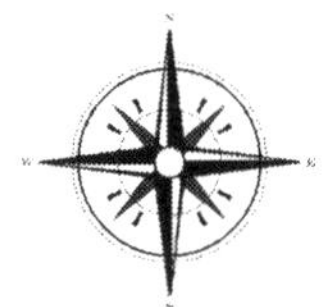

Reid took the cat with Mo, Bonnie, her kids, and Angie, the unconscious skipper's wife. We all agreed it was best to not move her, at least not until she regained consciousness.

That left *The Lady Anne* with me, Tracy, Gert, Ashley, Donna, and Buster. Reid initially wanted one man aboard each vessel, but we told him that wasn't necessary. He apologized for being sexist. I knew he hadn't meant anything by it; that was just his generation.

The cat had power, water, fuel, and a ton of food. Mo switched the radio circuit back on, establishing communications. I exchanged the handheld radio Bonnie had been using for one that was fully charged, so they'd have a spare.

Reid checked the two forepeak cabins that were only accessible via a deck hatch. One contained a quarter berth. The other contained a small head. He reported both were empty. I was surprised there wasn't access from below. It seemed like an awkward design. I silently chuckled; the designer had to be a man.

We got the vessels untied and *The Lady Anne* and *The Aquaholic* both got underway. Almost immediately Reid radioed there was no working compass aboard, so he'd have to follow *The Lady Anne*. Both vessels switched on their running lights and Tracy, Gert, and I watched as *The Aquaholic* maneuvered about one hundred yards astern and then followed our wake.

Ashley and Donna were very traumatized. I put Ashley in her early thirties and Donna maybe a little younger. Ashley was brunette and built like Tracy but not as cute, although that probably wasn't fair because of the bruises.

Donna had shoulder-length, dyed magenta hair and was a skinny little size two who could probably eat three desserts and lose weight. I forced myself to not hate her. Neither of them said much, but they did manage to eat some soup. We pointed to *The Aquaholic*, telling them that was where Angie, Bonnie, Max, and Joey were.

They did not want to talk about Bonnie or anyone else. They didn't want to go below either, and were satisfied with resting at the cockpit table. They were very smelly and reluctantly allowed me to hose them off with the solar shower.

I noticed both women had sores on their backs, rears, and calves. I gave them some Band-Aids and antiseptic lotion. I surmised they were bed sores, no doubt caused by being tied up.

We had neglected to bring any of their clothing over, so Gert and I went below and got them some clean clothes. They stayed in the cockpit, huddled under blankets, nervously watching *The Aquaholic* trailing us.

I got some rest and Tracy promised to wake me at midnight or when she got tired. It took me a long time to fall asleep. The cabin seemed really empty. I also had recurring images of being tied up, beaten, and raped, but it wasn't Captain Rick who was raping me, it was Pincus.

I relieved Tracy just before midnight, having been dozing fitfully. I sailed through the night, anxiously watching *The Aquaholic* pace us.

I found the red and green illumination from their running lights strangely comforting. I knew they could only see our white stern light and guessed they found that equally comforting. Save for our lights, it was eerily dark, and the ocean felt more vast than usual.

Gert napped topside, waking up to talk to me every so often. Reid radioed me every hour until Mo took over about two thirty a.m. He continued the hourly radio checks. Mo didn't sail as efficiently as Reid, but he stayed close enough, always in sight but weaving in and out of our wake.

Sunrise found both boats close together. By my calculations, we were way behind schedule, but the wind was holding so we kept going. Since both boats needed to recharge their batteries, we furled the sails and got tied together again, engines running.

Reid said he would make breakfast for everybody, but Ashley and Donna refused to go aboard *The Aquaholic* with Bonnie there.

"What do you supposed happened?" Tracy whispered.

"I don't know," I whispered back. "But something is definitely wrong. The tension is palpable."

Reid sent over breakfast burritos, and Ashley, Donna, and I ate topside at the cockpit table. Gert, Tracy, and Buster ate aboard the cat with the others.

Reid looked tired and I missed him. He said he talked to Angie after his shift was over, hoping she would hear him and wake up. She hadn't responded, but he wasn't going to give up on her.

Forty-five minutes after rafting together, we untied and resumed course, *The Aquaholic* following *The Lady Anne*. I remembered to have Bonnie send over some of Ashley's and Donna's clean clothes.

Tracy took the helm and I convinced Ashley to take another shower. She refused to shower on the swim platform but agreed to shower below, but only if I would stay with her the whole time.

Showering made Ashley so frightened, she started crying. I hoped it was claustrophobia, but deep down I knew it wasn't. She quickly finished, dried off, changed into her clothes, and rushed topside. Donna refused to shower, and I didn't push it.

Gert and I sat down on the bed in my cabin and we were both so tired, we immediately fell asleep.

Both boats rafted together again for dinner. Bonnie had heated frozen lasagna. She sent a large portion over, along with some garlic bread. It was really nice of her and thankfully, she didn't mention Carl. Gert passed on the lasagna and had a can of soup instead.

During dinner, Ashley became less frightened and more talkative, and she told us about going through an electrical disturbance and becoming lost. Her story was very similar to ours, even the part about videoing a UFO before the mayhem started, everything and everyone glowing a gray-silver color, and having to clean crud off of the solar panels. They too had used a portable generator to get their main batteries charged.

I learned from her that *The Aquaholic* was a crewed charter boat out of Eleuthera that had been booked by three couples for a ten-day charter. One couple failed to show up and forfeited their deposit. In hindsight, they were the lucky ones.

Angie was the crew and cook and her late husband was the skipper. The boat had been provisioned for eight persons for ten days. That explained why they had so much food aboard.

She told us how they made radio contact with Captain Rick, who came aboard and seemed friendly enough, but then killed the men one at a time by slicing their throats with a fillet knife. She gave a surprisingly gruesome description.

She told us how Angie tried to fight back, but he hit her in the head with a fire extinguisher, knocking her out.

She didn't speak about being tied up and none of us asked.

Donna listened to Ashley's entire story but didn't say much except that she would now like to take a shower. I felt that was progress.

I got to spend a few minutes with Reid before he went back to *The Aquaholic*. We missed each other. It was sad to split up again, but we were still behind schedule.

Gert, Tracy, and I split the night shift. Ashley stayed topside until ten o'clock p.m. then she went to sleep. Donna did take a shower, but mostly stayed below. She seemed to enjoy petting Buster, and he liked the attention.

The next morning, I talked to Reid on the radio. The good news was that while Angie hadn't woken up, the bump on her head was getting smaller and she had rolled over. He described multiple sores on her back, and he treated them with antiseptic ointment. The bad news was that we both had the same problem: Bonnie and Ashley had noticed the sailing conditions were getting harsher and demanded to know where we were going.

CHAPTER 92

The sailing conditions had changed. It was noticeably cooler, the wind had increased, the swells were bigger, there weren't many birds, and we were seeing large pods of whales, which Gert appreciated but which made Ashley and Donna nervous.

Reid decided we should raft together for a group breakfast to let Mo and I talk to everybody about our intended passage and answer the questions they were sure to have.

While we were motoring to get into position to tie together, I ran the water maker and recharged our batteries. Since Donna refused to go aboard *The Aquaholic*, Ashley helped Gert set *The Lady Anne*'s cockpit table. Bonnie and her kids came aboard with fruit and toasted English muffin, Canadian bacon, and egg sandwiches.

Mo was next to cross over, and he pulled me aside and

asked if I would please run the briefing. I didn't especially want to be in charge but I nodded, remembering his lack of sensitivity about certain topics.

Reid went to check on Angie one last time. I got everyone situated around *The Lady Anne*'s cockpit table and introduced myself as, "Pat Taylor, engineer, general contractor, co-owner, and captain of *The Lady Anne*." I nodded at Tracy.

"Tracy Palmer, accountant, first mate, and the other co-owner of *The Lady Anne*."

Tracy had just finished her introduction when Reid hollered across, "Bonnie, I need you. Angie's awake."

"Let's wait for them to join us," I announced. "So in the meantime, please eat and let's continue introductions."

"Gert Kohler, retired schoolteacher."

"Ladies and youngsters, I am Morrie Mordechai Morris, but please call me Mo. I used to be a space scientist, working for NASA on the Hubble Space Telescope. My plane crashed on the Isle of Mo-gert." He winked at Tracy. "And now Gert and I are grateful passengers aboard the sailing yacht, *The Lady Anne*."

"My name is Max. I'm twelve years old."

"My name is Joey and I'm almost eleven. Max is my brother. I like the dog. Can I have him?" he asked, looking right at me.

I shook my head no.

"Ashley Morgan, my husband was murdered, he sold insurance, I helped run the office."

"Donna, my name is Donna Kincaid."

Right after Donna introduced herself, Angie appeared at *The Aquaholic's* stern. Reid and Bonnie were supporting her, and she was upright but looked shaky. I guessed her to be in her thirties. She was nearly my height but probably fifty pounds heavier.

She saw us and managed to raise her hand. Ashley stood up and applauded loudly. "Welcome back, Angie."

Angie managed a feeble smile. Donna watched but didn't say anything.

Reid and Bonnie stayed with Angie aboard the cat while I continued the meeting.

Tracy introduced Reid. "Over there is our resident sailing expert, musician extraordinaire, and world-class chef. He has been called Mr. Talented, but you can call him Reid Adams."

Reid waved at Tracy's silly introduction. She waved back.

"And that is Bonnie," I said and pointed. Bonnie quickly introduced herself, barely speaking loudly enough to be heard. "Bonnie. Bonnie Buckman. Houston. Houston, Texas."

"And next to you is Angie," I said, and then raised my voice so she could hear. "Angie, can you tell us about yourself?"

She looked confused and didn't reply, so Bonnie told us simply that Angie was *The Aquaholic's* crew and cook.

Bonnie didn't say anything else about Angie or her condition. With the possible exception of the kids, everybody knew what had happened to her.

That completed the introductions.

"Where are we going?" Ashley asked rather loudly.

"I'm going to answer that by reading you some log entries," I answered.

I then had Tracy read *The Lady Anne*'s log portion about the portal. Ashley was surprised to hear about all the dead bugs because *The Aquaholic* had experienced that as well. Mo read his notes about his encounter. Gert said that she hadn't written anything down but quickly told her story. Bonnie pretty much echoed the same thing about *The Day Dream*'s experience. Her kids collaborated her story.

Reid read *The Aquaholic*'s entries, which made Angie start crying because her late husband had written it. Then I managed to read *The Obsession*'s entries without bursting into tears. Most everyone had moist eyes after hearing Cookie's last entry.

"The point of reading all of these log entries is that all of us have experienced basically the same thing," I said, closing *The Obsession*'s log.

"Now before I answer your question, Ashley," I continued, "I'm going to have Mo, our resident NASA scientist, tell you what or who he thinks is responsible for the electromagnetic disturbance we all encountered."

Mo calmly announced that he strongly believed aliens had initiated the phenomenon we had all experienced.

"And this is going to sound crazy," I said. "But Mo, would you please explain to everyone what year you believe it is and how you arrived at that conclusion?" I took a sip of juice. I was really nervous how this news would be met.

Mo told everyone that we had been transported 25,700

years into the past and then offered numerous examples to support his claims about the aliens and the year. As expected, there were strange looks and total disbelief from Ashley and Donna.

I said that Mo's theory about the year was the only plausible explanation as to why no GPS units would work, there was no radio contact, no cell phone service, no Internet, no satellite phone connection, and no spotting of airplanes, ships, or inhabited islands.

"But where are we going?" Ashley asked again, sounding quite distraught.

Mo and I both explained that if they accepted that aliens were responsible for our predicament, and if they accepted that we had really gone back in time, then there were only two possible scenarios. Either stay here in the past, or try to get the aliens to return us to our time, return us to the future.

"So you're telling me we're out here in the middle of the Atlantic looking for aliens and the lost continent of Atlantis?" Donna asked, her tone betraying her disbelief.

"We're not exactly in the middle of the Atlantic," Gert answered her. "But if you were paying attention, you heard Mo say that since tomorrow is the fifth day from the last sighting, which I witnessed by the way, he predicts that aliens should be somewhere near here sometime tomorrow, probably tomorrow evening."

There weren't any immediate questions, mostly just blank stares from Ashley, Donna, and Bonnie. Max and Joey did say that finding aliens would be awesome, but Bonnie gave them a long-distance "ahem" and they stopped talking.

Before adjourning the meeting, I stated that life jackets were to be worn anytime anyone was topside. I also reminded everyone to please conserve battery power and to not waste electricity, food, or water. Tracy added the part about not putting foreign matter in the toilets. Reid mentioned safety at sea, emphasizing the need to avoid any injuries. Angie gave him a strange look, to which he replied, "Sorry."

There was a little more discussion about UFOs and some more general questions, and then the meeting ended and everyone left the cockpit. I pulled Mo aside and quietly thanked him for not mentioning his sterilization theory. He smiled and said he had learned his lesson from Gert's chastising.

I didn't notice Bonnie come aboard, but when she cornered me at the stern, I got really nervous, knowing a confrontation about killing her husband was coming.

Instead she apologized for holding me responsible for Carl's death. After what she had gone through and had watched the other women endure, she realized that Tracy and I were only protecting our vessel and ourselves.

Then she said something else I hadn't expected. She thanked me for not making her share the boat with Ashley and Donna. "They don't like me because they think I was Rick's girlfriend."

"Girlfriend? Why would they think that?"

"Because I was sharing his cabin and his bed." She wiped

away a tear. "The day after Carl died, that monster delivered an ultimatum—spread my legs or listen to my kids cry when they got hungry. I had to cooperate because not protecting my children was never an option."

"Your kids didn't know what was happening, did they?" I was beginning to get really angry again. Not at her, but at Rick.

"I don't think so. The man was diabolically clever. He would walk Max and Joey thirty minutes down the shoreline to a 'good fishing spot' and set them up fishing. Instead of returning to camp, he would go to his boat where I had to be naked and ready for him. He was really pissed at you guys for disabling his engine by the way. He was mechanically savvy enough to have recharged the batteries using a portable generator, but repairing the engine was impossible without proper tools and parts."

She looked down. "They usually went fishing twice a day, but sometimes the kids would be gone for the whole afternoon. That was worse for me. I cried myself to sleep every night and wanted to kill the motherfucker and take my chances. But I was afraid what would happen to my kids if I failed."

Her voice trembled as she continued. "Then he captured *The Aquaholic* and made me help him. I had to watch over his captives, giving them food and water and potty breaks. Having my children's lives as power over me, he forced me to clean up the women before and after he raped them. He was a sexual demon. After he killed her husband, Angie tried to fight back. He hit her so hard I'm surprised she's alive."

"Why couldn't the three of you team up and overpower him?" I asked.

"I kept thinking about what Reid had said about going back in time," Bonnie answered. "If that was true, and if we did manage a mutiny, Angie, the only one of us that could sail and really work the boat, was in a coma. And if she did wake up, what would happen to us after we ate all the food? I had visions of my kids slowly starving to death, either aboard a floating prison or ashore on another worthless island."

I thought about her situation and probably would have killed Rick in his sleep anyway and taken my chances. But that was me. And I didn't have kids to consider.

Then she said, her voice trembling, "In between rapes and naps, he focused his energy on finding *The Lady Anne* and plotting what he would do to Reid and you and Tracy, especially Reid for fucking over *The Day Dream*'s engine. He had found *The Aquaholic*'s gun and now thought he could win a fight."

"He *wanted* to find *The Lady Anne*?" I asked.

"He guessed you would sail south, so that's the general direction he headed. Then you made it easy by sailing back toward us."

I shook my head at my stupidity. Mo's course of 025 degrees would put us on a nearly reciprocal heading to 180 degrees, bringing us back near *The Day Dream*. It never dawned on me.

"Rick really lost it after Carl was killed," Bonnie continued. "He wanted vengeance. Then when *The Aquaholic* came along, he saw his chance. He managed to cover the warning you had painted on his boat. He calculated exactly how to trick *The Aquaholic* into thinking he could help them. He was so obsessed, he nearly torched *The Aquaholic* after he captured it, initially only wanting their food, diesel fuel, and engine parts. I talked him out of setting fire to it, telling him he was foolish if he picked a diesel-only boat that might or might not run over one that could sail and motor."

"You called him foolish?"

"He punched me for saying that, but he would have punched me anyway for something else."

"I'm so sorry you had to go through that," I said. "We should have killed him when we had the chance."

She wiped away another tear and then looked around, making sure we were still alone before saying, "You gave him a chance. You were compassionate. Don't blame yourself. Rick was a fiend. A horrible monster. I'm glad I killed the fucking bastard."

She left me then and went over to her kids.

"I am too," I said.

CHAPTER 93

Tracy came over and whispered that she thought the meeting had gone well. I confided I was a little disappointed that Donna wouldn't participate.

"Give her time," Tracy told me. "I know how we felt after what almost happened with Pincus. I can't even imagine what they're going through."

"What a nightmare," was all I could say.

Before splitting up and resuming course, there were two crew changes. Max and Joey wanted to sail aboard *The Lady Anne* and be with Buster. They didn't say it directly, but sort of implied that they wanted a break from mommy. And I wanted to be with Reid, at least until the next time we stopped.

Mo double-checked my rudimentary calculations on Reid's Atlantis diagram and confirmed we had stayed more or less on course and had sailed approximately 525 miles. He asked if we could push it hard today and be in position when the aliens showed up tomorrow night.

"Have you thought about how we should signal them if they do fly overhead?" I asked.

"Flares, lights, cameras, radios, screaming, waving flags, sailing in circles, anyway we can," he replied.

Mo and I climbed over to *The Aquaholic*. The first thing I noticed was the strong smell of chlorine, but at least I didn't see any blood so that was good. Mo and Gert had really cleaned. It didn't even look like the same boat, although there were still gashes near the entrance to the covered rear deck. Reid sent me forward to untie the bow line.

Reid went to the stern and hollered, "Tracy, today's lesson is racing. Be across the line in five minutes."

"What line?" she asked, looking at the knot he was untying.

"The starting line." Reid laughed as he untied the stern line and pushed us apart.

While coiling his line, he explained to Mo and Bonnie that obviously there was no starting line, no committee boat, no timekeeper, no officials, no race course, and no spectators, but there were two sailboats headed in the same direction, so by definition, it was a race.

Bonnie smiled. "Sounds like fun. And God knows we could use some of that."

Mo agreed. "It's the same when flying. Game on!"

Tracy and Gert got *The Lady Anne* ahead early because Mo and Bonnie took time to help Angie take a seat, leaving me to crew for Reid aboard an unfamiliar vessel, a catamaran no less. We had to tack to get into position and being so wide, the cat tacked really slow. Once Reid finally got *The Aquaholic* on course and properly trimmed, we quickly gained on *The Lady Anne*. We waved as we passed. They didn't wave back.

Reid sailed several boatlengths ahead and then slowed down considerably. "Why are we slowing?" I asked, my competitive juices flowing.

"I'm trying to keep it fair since, with the possible exception of Angie, I'm the only one here with any offshore racing experience," he replied, smiling. "Plus they aren't going to catch Angie's boat."

"Angie doesn't happen to be the hooker from the Hilton, does she?" I asked grinning. "Should I be worried? Do you need to borrow some money?"

"No," he replied. "That Angie was"—he paused and grinned back—"hourly."

Being so close and seeing him smile made some other juices start flowing. "How about letting Mo and Bonnie take the helm?" I whispered in his ear. "I need to show you something below."

Mo gave me a crooked smile, as if he heard what I'd said. "Take all the time you need," he said with a wink.

Bonnie grinned. "Use my cabin. Clean sheets."

Angie remained seated, her expression emotionless, her eyes looking straight out at sea. Remembering the medic's comments about Tracy, I purposely bent down and looked at Angie's pupils. They were equal size.

I felt bad for her. But not bad enough to keep from leading Reid below. I think the fact that Tracy was on *The Lady Anne* and not breathing down our necks helped too. I very seldom had Reid to myself.

We were naked in Bonnie's cabin in twenty seconds. I didn't need much foreplay. Neither did Reid. Our first coupling ended much too soon. But it wasn't long before Reid was ready again and this time, our passion mounted more slowly, each of us driving the other forward with lips and hands until we could hold back no longer. We didn't even try to be quiet.

Later, *The Lady Anne* was still astern as Reid and I rejoined the others.

Mo and Bonnie grinned at us.

"So, what's the status?" Reid asked, trying very hard to sound casual.

"I might ask you the same thing," Mo said. "I think your T-shirt is on backwards."

Reid's face reddened. I couldn't help but laugh as he drew it over his head, turned it right side out, and then pulled it back on faster than I would have thought possible.

Mo laughed. "We're still ahead."

Reid went forward and observed the wind conditions for a few moments. "I'm going to reduce sail," he said after a moment. "The wind has increased, and I don't want us to become overpowered."

When he came back, he asked me, "What's the first thing you notice about *The Aquaholic*?"

I shrugged. "You mean besides the paint job?"

Mo waved a hand. "I can explain that," he said. "I'm something of a history buff. It's called razzle-dazzle paint and was used during the war to confuse U-boats by presenting various hull patterns. How Angie and her husband came to use it I can't imagine, but I like it."

Bonnie confirmed that one of Angie's mom's great-great-aunts was an artist during the war and painted model ships so the navy could evaluate each design's effectiveness. *The Aquaholic* sported one of that woman's original designs. And the ship that received that paint scheme survived the war without being torpedoed.

I found myself wincing. "It makes me kind of nauseous," I said, turning back to Reid. "Anyway, what was I supposed to notice about *The Aquaholic*?"

"Cats don't heel," he said. "Notice how flat we are?"

I hadn't before, but now that he mentioned it, *The Lady Anne* was heeled way over while we were ninety-eight percent flat with only a tiny bit of heeling. As a consequence, the ride aboard *The Lady Anne* wasn't nearly as smooth as aboard *The Aquaholic*.

"Don't you have anything to say about this fine catamaran?" he asked me then, smiling.

"Think Angie would like to play some poker?"

It was meant as a joke, but when I glanced at Angie, still locked in her own thoughts, I felt ashamed I'd said it.

"They'll never catch us, will they?" Mo asked Reid.

I was glad for the change of subject.

"In light air on a course that required a lot of tacking, they'd have the advantage. But out here, in these conditions, on this point of sail, no way."

"Does Tracy know she can't catch us?" I asked.

"No, and don't tell her. Let her think she's doing well."

The Lady Anne stayed in our wake until early afternoon. We ran into some heavy rain and both vessels slowed down. Luckily there wasn't any close lightning, just rain.

Both vessels had water makers so there was no need to catch rainwater. The rain obscured the sun, rendering the solar panels on both boats ineffective, but our batteries were well charged and I assumed *The Lady Anne*'s were as well.

We slowed and let *The Lady Anne* catch us. Tracy sailed alongside, close enough to yell back and forth but not close enough to hit us. Max and Joey weren't feeling well and wanted to come back to *The Aquaholic*. Joey said our boat was too *crooked*.

Tracy asked if I'd switch places with her, and Gert wanted to be with Mo for a while. I asked Ashley and Donna if they'd help me sail *The Lady Anne* and they both agreed.

Rather than tie up together and raft in the pouring rain, we used *The Aquaholic*'s dinghy to swap personnel. I really struggled motoring an empty dinghy across to *The Lady Anne* by myself. Between me, the motor, and the gas can, a lot of the weight was in the stern. If I applied too much power, the bow raised up, threatening to catch wind and flip me. If I didn't apply enough power, the wind blew me off course.

I got scared, thinking I wouldn't make it to *The Lady Anne*, and then even more scared realizing I might not be able to get back to *The Aquaholic* either. Fortunately, Tracy noticed my predicament, steered closer, and Gert threw me a line.

After making crew changes, I watched as Tracy drove back. Going the other way was easier because the dinghy was loaded with her, Max, Joey, and Gert. With the weight more evenly distributed, the dinghy plowed through the waves and made it back to *The Aquaholic* without incident. Using *The Aquaholic*'s small dinghy made me really appreciate the fine dinghy *The Lady Anne* had.

I took the helm of *The Lady Anne* and resigned myself to the fact that I couldn't catch the cat, even though *The Lady Anne* was now much lighter and *The Aquaholic* was equally heavier. Buster stood near the lifeline and barked at Tracy a few times. He finally realized she wasn't coming back and returned to the cockpit, getting out of the rain. He put his head down between his paws.

Donna reached over and scratched his ears. "Don't worry," she told him. "She'll be back."

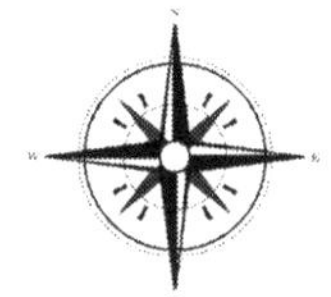

CHAPTER 94

We sailed through the rain and then continued under partly cloudy skies until five o'clock p.m. The radar showed patches of heavy weather all around us, but I managed to avoid most of the squalls.

The Aquaholic stayed ahead the whole time. When I would adjust my course through the storm, *The Aquaholic* would adjust a few minutes later. It felt like we were somehow being followed by the boat in front of us. I couldn't remember if *The Aquaholic* had radar or not, but I guessed she didn't.

Ashley was very helpful and seemed interested in learning the basics of sailing, but Donna kept saying that she wanted to go home. She would burst into tears without warning, but she stayed topside and operated the winch as instructed.

Reid radioed to slow down, that it was time to change crews again, back to our original assignments. He drove

Tracy and Gert across, powering the dinghy right up onto the swim platform. Ashley helped them all aboard. Donna just stayed by her winch, staring at *The Aquaholic*. She started crying again but Ashley went over to her and tried to be soothing.

I was really glad to see Reid and welcomed him aboard with a long, deep, wet, passionate kiss. I kissed him so hard we accidentally bumped our teeth together. I was beginning to understand how Tracy felt around him. I wondered if it was possible for the three of us to continue as lovers. I also found myself wondering if Tracy had made love with him while she was on *The Aquaholic*. I recognized a pang of jealousy and tried to squelch it.

I felt Reid watching me. "Are you all right?"

I kissed him again. "I am now."

He held me a moment. "It would be really easy to stay, but I've got to get back," he said at last.

Reluctantly, I backed away.

He went to the dinghy and retrieved a grocery bag. Buster sniffed it intently, his tail pointing straight up.

"It's dinner," Reid said. "Don't let it get cold."

I took it. "Anything you need from *The Lady Anne*?"

"Now that you mention it, there is something you can get me. I need a condom."

Tracy had come up beside us. She and I exchanged glances. "Oh?" I asked, eyebrow raised. "Why would you need a condom?"

"You certainly don't need it with us anymore," Tracy said.

Reid laughed at the implication. "It's not for me, it's for Mo."

"I don't think he needs it either," I replied. "Unless Bonnie and Angie don't know everything about coming through the portal."

"He's going to use it to make a barometer," Reid said.

"Seriously?" Tracy asked.

"Seriously," Reid answered. "I'll get what I need."

We watched him disappear below.

"Could you make a barometer out of a condom?" Tracy asked.

"Barometers record the change in air pressure so maybe. I've never really thought about it."

Before shoving off, Reid kissed us again, first Tracy and then me. I was sorry he had to leave, but I understood.

Reid had to fight the waves with the nearly empty dinghy as he motored back, the same way I had. It made me realize that I hadn't been doing anything wrong earlier. He was sitting further forward than I had been, but it was still slow going. I was relieved when he finally made it across.

Once we were back on course, Gert took the helm, telling us to eat. She had already finished, and the rest were waiting for us below. Tracy went first.

Reid radioed then, saying he was going to get some rest and reminding us to switch on our running lights. He maneuvered *The Aquaholic* to fall in behind *The Lady Anne*, letting us take the lead.

I left Gert at the helm and joined Tracy, Ashley, and

Donna at the table. Reid had delivered a nice dinner. We had hot chicken soup that looked and tasted homemade, roast beef sandwiches loaded with fresh lettuce on really good sourdough bread, grapes, and brownies for dessert. He had even prepared and labeled a meat sandwich treat for Buster.

Donna ate a little soup and then excused herself. As soon as her magenta hair disappeared into her cabin, Ashley asked, "So it looks like you are both fooling around with Reid? Isn't he a little old?"

Tracy held up a hand. "Don't start," she said. "Yes, there is an age difference but he's the best lover I've ever had."

I elbowed her lightly. "Excuse me, the best lover *we've* ever had, and actually, he proposed to both of us two days ago."

We showed her our necklaces.

"Do you really expect your love triangle to last?" she asked, examining both sides of my pendant.

There was something about her attitude that I didn't care for. Maybe because I felt guilty for having the same thoughts.

Tracy sliced her sandwich in half, then glanced at me, probably hoping I would reply.

"Do you remember the end of *The Obsession*'s log entries, when Cookie buried her husband and then swam out to the mast and waited for the sharks?"

Ashley lowered her eyes and said, "That was really sad."

"In her final words, Cookie wrote that her husband and her dog were her best friends. That's because the three of them had a special bond. Once she lost them, she had nothing else to live for," I said.

Neither Ashley nor Tracy said anything, they just waited for me to continue, so I did. "Whether or not you believe Mo's theories about aliens and time travel, you know survival here is very difficult. Mo and Gert might not have survived another week if we hadn't found them. But they have a special bond and although they knew they were literally wasting away, they were together and they were happy. I imagine their final log entry would have been another tearjerker, like Cookie's was." I sighed. "What Reid, Tracy, and I have is unconventional and you may be right, it might not last, but the three of us have that same special bond. For now, it's enough."

"It's like gravity," Tracy added. "You can't touch it, hear it, or taste it, but everybody knows when it's working."

At that, Ashley smiled.

CHAPTER 95

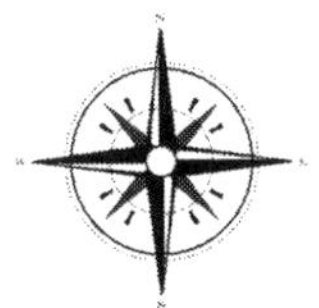

We made it through another night passage without incident and without needing a formal watch schedule. Gert and Tracy sailed till they got tired, which was after eleven o'clock p.m. I woke Ashley and she stayed at the helm with me until Tracy and Gert relieved us around three thirty a.m.

During that time, the subject of Rick came up. She confirmed she had been repeatedly violated. She told me she would never forget the image of Rick slashing her husband's throat. It was seared into her brain. So was the image of Rick sweating on top of her and laughing while he raped her.

She was initially very hostile toward any mention of Bonnie. She blamed her for being cozy with a rapist. She didn't know about Rick's leverage with the kids and how

Bonnie was made to do unspeakable things to protect her children.

She knew Rick had been killed and she obviously saw all the blood, but she didn't know the specifics. I told her what had happened, including how Bonnie had severed Rick's head to prove to us that he was dead.

She listened very intently. There was a long period of silence. "Maybe I've misjudged Bonnie," she said.

I sensed that was enough for now and asked her if she'd talk to Donna. She said she would.

Then Ashley called Bonnie on the radio. She told her she now knew the whole story. She thanked Bonnie for getting even with Rick and then apologized for the way she had been treating her. Bonnie accepted her apology.

With Tracy and Gert at the helm, Ashley and I went below for some much needed sleep. We were rummaging around in the galley for a quick snack when we heard screaming. Buster was with us and started barking. We rushed forward to Reid's cabin.

Donna was yelling, "Get away, get away."

I switched on the light. Donna's hair had caught in her life jacket. Each time she moved her head, her hair caught and pulled.

Ashley and I rushed to her. We untangled her hair and when she was awake, told her she'd been having a bad dream.

"You're okay," I told her. "Everything's okay."

Donna clung to me a moment.

Ashley climbed into bed beside her and motioned to me that I could leave. "I'll take care of her now."

I nodded and left them alone.

The next morning, I made my way topside to see how Tracy and Gert had fared on the early morning watch.

I hadn't slept well. Donna's nightmare had awakened memories of Pincus and what he had tried to do to me. I was lucky. The Coast Guard prevented him from raping me. No one had come to Donna's or Ashley's aid. I wondered how long it would be before either of them had a night's rest without seeing Rick's face.

Tracy yawned when she saw me. "Quiet as a mouse, but I'm glad to see you. I'm beat."

She and Gert wasted no time but headed below, and I took up position at the helm.

The skies were dark and cloudy and perhaps a bit more threatening than yesterday. I predicted there might be more rain. We got the boats into position and rafted for breakfast. Reid had tied a monkey's fist knot at the end of his messenger line and nearly hit me with it when he threw it across.

"Hey! What's in here?" I hollered as I hefted the knot. "A rock?"

"Actually it's a big lead sinker from *The Day Dream*'s tackle," Reid replied. "Captain Dead Fucking Dead transferred all of his fishing gear aboard, so tell Tracy that when she wants to fish, I've got lots of stuff, even some pink lures."

I tied a sheet bend knot between his light line and a

heavier line and after he drug that across, we pulled both vessels together.

It was good to see him. He told me Mo had showed him how to find Vega and had also given him a first-class sextant lesson. He looked a little tired but said he'd get some sleep later.

I filled him in on what had transpired with Donna the previous night. Ashley finally talked her into going aboard *The Aquaholic*, as long as she didn't have to go below.

We all met aboard the cat. Its table was larger than *The Lady Anne's* and easily accommodated all eleven of us.

Angie served breakfast. She was feeling better and had made pancakes with sliced, overripe bananas, but Reid vetoed serving maple syrup. She poured everyone cranberry juice or coffee or both. She was wearing her apron and looked pretty happy to be back in the galley.

"Who made the soup yesterday?" I asked.

Mo raised his hand.

"That was the best chicken soup I've ever had," I told him.

Everyone echoed that feeling, even clapping for him. Reid and Angie both said they had learned a lot watching Mo cook.

"What kind of a Jew would I be if I couldn't make Jewish penicillin?"

"What's your secret?" Tracy asked. "Why was your soup so good?"

He finally admitted he had been very wasteful and used two sets of vegetables. One set when the chicken was cooking and then he replaced them with a second set later. He explained that's why the celery and carrots were so crisp and not soggy or cooked into mush. Reid smiled and added that given the circumstances, he had saved Mo's "used vegetables" and would use them in something else later.

"Do you really think we're going to see aliens today?" Bonnie asked.

Mo's answer hadn't changed. He was still confident they'd pass by, he just didn't know when. He was concerned that cloudy skies would reduce visibility. He mentioned the barometric pressure was falling.

"I didn't know there was a barometer on board," I said.

"There wasn't, I made one," he replied, looking quite pleased with himself.

He showed us his invention. He had slipped the "special balloon," as he called it, over the top of an empty can and secured it in place with a rubber band. There was a thin piece of wood taped to the top. He had taped the can to a shelf and there was a pencil mark with the day and time on a piece of paper, taped to the bulkhead directly behind it.

"The stick is pointing lower than it was yesterday," he said, pointing at the mark, "indicating the pressure is falling and we could be in for some bad weather."

"Nice job," I told him. "I'm very impressed."

"Thanks for sparing the condom, I mean special balloon." He grinned, then looked up. "But I still hope the weather clears."

Since the kids were lingering nearby, Tracy whispered, "I

can't believe I'm with people who can make sundials and barometers out of cereal boxes and condoms."

"Rube Goldberg would be proud," I said.

"Rube Goldberg was Jewish," Mo said.

"Who the hell is Rube Goldberg?"

Tracy had obviously never heard of him or the contraptions bearing his name.

Mo and I exchanged glances and then he explained that Rube Goldberg was a cartoonist that drew complex machinery performing simple tasks.

"Engineering students compete nationally to design and build a machine to do something we take for granted," I added. "Like hammering a nail or blowing up a balloon and then popping it."

Tracy shook her head and walked away.

Mo and I "high-fived" each other and grinned.

After breakfast, we got back to our boats and prepared to get underway. As usual, I used engine power to run the water maker and charge the batteries. I debated running the washing machine for one community load, but Donna offered to hand-wash everything, saying she wanted to help. Ashley winked at me and said she'd keep her company.

Mo took some time and gathered all of the flares, then split them evenly between each boat. He made sure each boat had whistles, working flashlights, charged radios, and signal flags. He was very methodical.

I asked Tracy, half-jokingly, "What are we going to say to an alien if we find one?"

She thought for a second and then answered, "Well, we probably shouldn't ask them if they're from Uranus."

It took a minute for that to register, but she started laughing, which made it click. I laughed too. It really was pretty funny.

Gert left us for *The Aquaholic*. Besides wanting to be with Mo, she said she didn't feel any queasiness aboard the cat. I didn't question her. I was confident Tracy and I could sail *The Lady Anne* with Ashley's and Donna's occasional assistance. We untied and resumed course.

The wind increased and the swells got larger. Tracy and I reduced sail area by reefing the mainsail and the genoa. As conditions continued to deteriorate, we furled the genoa ninety-five percent and furled the other sails all the way in. We sat at the helm together, guiding *The Lady Anne* through the roller-coaster swells. Our course had become secondary to keeping *The Lady Anne* bow first through the waves and swells and not getting blown sideways.

The Aquaholic was further behind us but still in sight. She appeared to have dropped her mainsail and was sailing under partial jib alone. I radioed Reid to ask if the cat was okay. He said his passengers were getting nervous, but he, himself, was sure the *Aquaholic* was in no danger. He had us switch on all of our lights so he could keep us in sight easier.

Even with the surface clutter, the radar indicated numerous squalls ahead. They were in a line—not circular, indicating a hurricane—so that was comforting until Tracy pointed to the anemometer. It was reading winds of between forty-five and fifty knots. That's gale strength.

The wind soon roared as loud as any freight train, and the blowing foam from the waves stung our faces like angry hornets. The deck was covered in spray. Tracy and I both donned our offshore rain gear. It was doing its job of keeping us dry, except for our exposed hands and faces. I made a mental note to find gloves next time I was below.

Lightning flashed all around and the thunder was louder than shotgun blasts. Great clouds of blowing foam turned the sea white. The waves were massive. I guessed their height to be around thirty feet. Visibility was lousy and with the rain blowing sideways, I felt like I was driving *The Lady Anne* through a car wash.

Ashley and Donna huddled together in the cockpit, wearing their life jackets and safely tethered to the jackline. They had gone below but couldn't stay because it was too rough. They were completely soaked. They were watching me, eyes wide.

I cautiously made my way to them, utilizing *The Lady Anne's* strategically placed handholds. The seas were treacherous and falling overboard now would be fatal. I crouched next to Ashley and Donna. They were shivering. I wasn't sure if they were cold or scared or both.

"We're okay," I said. "*The Lady Anne* is an ocean crossing yacht and has been through many transatlantic passages. She's handling the conditions just as she's supposed to. There's zero chance of capsizing."

"I think they said the same thing about the *Titanic*," Ashley said.

I smiled. "No icebergs on this trip."

They smiled back, though not very convincingly. "I'm

going below for just a minute," I told them. "I need to make sure all the hatches are closed. Stay right here and you'll be just fine."

Donna looked as if she was going to object, but Ashley took her hand and nodded at me to go ahead.

I unclipped from the jackline and ducked below. All the hatches were closed. The bilge was dry but just for safety, I closed the watertight doors too.

I looked longingly into our cabin. I was bone-tired and wanted a nap, even a quick one, but even if it hadn't been too rough to sleep, I couldn't leave Tracy alone that long. I did find some work gloves, not waterproof, but better than nothing. I also put Buster in Reid's cabin. He barked at first but finally stopped.

The Aquaholic had switched on all of her lights and was following us. We knew she was there but we would regularly lose sight of her, only to see her reappear over the next massive swell.

It was unnerving when the big cat went completely out of sight; even her anchor light atop the mast would disappear. Neither Tracy nor I liked the feeling of being totally alone. Neither of us had been this far offshore before, nor had we ever sailed in conditions like this. I radioed Reid and checked in.

"I'm fine," he said. "But even Angie is getting nervous."

"So are Ashley and Donna. Do I need to get the sea anchor ready?"

"No. I questioned Angie and they never bought one, never

anticipating needing a drogue for Bahamian charters." He didn't sound concerned. "If you deploy your drogue, we'll have a hard time staying with you."

"How about the storm jib?" I asked, remembering there was one below. "Should we rig that?"

"Not now. It's too dangerous to go forward in these conditions. Good job reefing when you did, by the way. A minimal headsail is all you need. You're doing fine. This blow will be good for your confidence. I'll see that it counts toward the Offshore Passage Making class experience."

I heard the smile in his voice but sighed. "It's scary when you drop out of sight."

"We're not dropping out of sight," he said. "I thought you were."

Hearing him joke made us all feel better.

CHAPTER 97

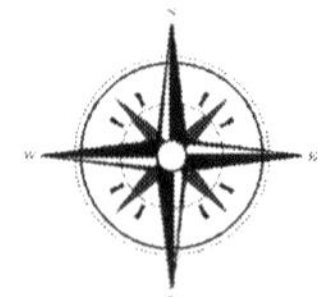

Just after two o'clock p.m., the sun broke through the bleakness and the wind abated considerably. We were through the worst of it and the radar showed mostly clear ahead. The swells were still huge, but the ride smoothed out and everyone's spirits improved.

I celebrated by passing out ginger ale and granola bars.

"Mazel tov," I radioed. "We just weathered our first gale. Thank you all for your help."

There followed a few minutes of pleasant chitchat over the radio. Both crews were very thankful to be through the storm.

Tracy reduced the reefing, exposing slightly more sail. I took a compass reading. We were off course, but not bad, all things considered. I checked below. Other than some items that had landed on the deck, the bilge was dry and everything looked good.

Tracy came below, looking exhausted. "Ashley and Donna say they can handle it, so we have a two-hour break."

"Can you believe we got through a real gale all by ourselves?" I asked on the way aft to our cabin.

Tracy shook her head. "I tried not to show it, but I was really scared every time the swells were higher than we were. That was frightening."

I agreed, though frightening or not, I think we were both asleep the moment our heads struck the pillow.

Donna woke us exactly two hours later, surprised that we had been able to sleep with the way the boat was rocking.

"How are you?" I asked her. "Any problems?"

"Nope. Doing okay." She turned to go back topside. "Take your time. Come up when you're ready."

Within a few minutes, we rejoined them topside. We left Buster below again, just in case we ran into more weather. It was far safer for him to be safely tucked in a cabin than loose on a slippery, rolling deck.

We found Ashley steering, and although she had a death grip on the wheel, she was doing fine so we let her keep driving.

At five o'clock p.m. Reid radioed it was still too rough to raft or launch the dinghy, so we'd be on our own for dinner. He also told us that Mo wanted more separation so the *Aqua-holic* would be dropping back even further but not to be concerned.

"Why does Mo want more separation?" Ashley asked.

"He doesn't want us shooting each other with flares when

we're signaling the alien," Reid responded, chuckling. "He also wants two people on lookout duty when possible, one watching forward, the other aft. Radio right away if anybody sees anything. And leave all of your lights on."

"Got it, thank you. *The Lady Anne* over and out." Ashley glanced at me and smiled.

I gave her a thumbs-up at being able to steer and work the radio. It was obvious once she accepted *The Lady Anne*'s seaworthiness, her confidence had grown. During the storm, she had handled an extremely stressful situation quite well.

I told her one of Reid's lame jokes. "The sailing student asked if boats like this sink very often. The instructor answered, 'No, usually they only sink once.'"

She shook her head and rolled her eyes.

It was approaching dinnertime, but no one was very hungry. Tracy stayed with Ashley at the helm and I worked my way forward while Donna went aft. It was still overcast, but less than before, and as it got darker, we began to see faint stars. Conditions continued to improve and slowly, more stars became visible, a few at a time.

At eight o'clock p.m., I went below. I was tired of watching for alien lights and I needed to pee. I also wanted to get everybody some snacks, cold water, and do a little stretching. My neck was sore from looking skyward. I didn't think I'd be missed for five minutes.

I hadn't been below thirty seconds when I heard Ashley and Tracy begin to yell.

"Pat, get up here," Tracy said. "We see one."

CHAPTER 98

"Hang on," I hollered back. I debated rushing topside immediately but the urge to pee was pretty strong, so I took care of that in record time and then went up.

I could hear Angie's voice over the radio saying Gert spotted it first. I clipped to the jackline and headed aft. Donna was at the stern, pointing. Ashley was next to her. Tracy was driving.

Tracy smiled as I passed by. "Mo was right—five days, in the evening. I can't believe it." Her eyes were wide with excitement.

I took a spot at the stern rail, on the other side of Donna. I spotted it immediately, a pale-yellow light. It moved horizontally and then dropped straight down. It was low in the sky and probably less than a mile away, but it was difficult to judge the distance exactly.

It dropped again. I tried to guesstimate its trajectory and speculated it would pass over us, this side of *The Aquaholic.* Suddenly I heard a distant whistle and saw a flare race skyward. *The Aquaholic* had fired a flare and was signaling. Nearly simultaneously the radio blared, "What are you girls waiting for? Light it up." It was Reid and he sounded serious.

I began giving orders. "Tracy, steer as erratically as you can without tacking or dumping us. Maybe they'll notice our drunken course and stop to investigate. Ashley, bring me the flare gun, a flashlight, and the whistle. Donna, go below to the electrical panel and turn off the breaker for the anchor light; count two, three, four, then turn it back on and count two, three, four again. Repeat and keep repeating, slowly flashing the light. Let's go now, we may not get another crack at this."

The Lady Anne was suddenly a blur of activity. Tracy was swerving one way and then back. Donna had gone below and was rhythmically flashing the anchor light. Ashley handed me the flare gun and four flares. She then held out the whistle and the flashlight, but paused when *The Aquaholic* fired again.

Bonnie's voice came loud and clear over the radio. "Calling the aliens, can you hear me? Calling the aliens."

"Wave the light, blow the whistle, and don't fall overboard," I told Ashley, trying not to chuckle at Bonnie's radio calls in the background.

I loaded a flare and pointed the orange flare pistol in what I hoped was a safe direction. I didn't want to hit the sail, or hit *The Aquaholic,* or have the flare blow back onto us and start a fire. I aimed towards the yellow light overhead and fired.

A ball of fire shot skyward like a Fourth of July celebration. It arced and then dropped. The yellow light was passing overhead and moving fast. It was low, but that was relative because it was still much higher than the range of the flare gun.

"This isn't working," I yelled as I reloaded. It was difficult to be heard over Ashley's whistle. "I don't think they see us."

My heart sank at the realization we had sailed so far and were now so close, but there was no reaction from the alien ship. In a few minutes we would be way behind it.

I motioned for Ashley to stop blowing the whistle. That had been a stupid idea to begin with, and my ears were ringing. I told her to follow me.

I went to the helm and directed, "Ashley, take over. Stop veering and just hold her steady." Then I said to Tracy, "Go get the camera. That got a response once, maybe it will again. And tell Donna she's doing a good job with the light and to keep it up." I headed forward with the flare gun. I could still hear Bonnie trying to hail the aliens.

I drug my tether through the cockpit and over the dinghy and took up position at the bow. I had three flares with me. I fired forward at an angle, aware the falling flare would be hot enough to burn anything it touched. The yellow light continued, not responding.

Tracy made her way forward and took position next to me, aiming the video camera directly at the aliens. I reloaded and fired again. The alien light didn't change course. There was no visible reaction.

I reloaded, aimed, and said, "Come on, honey, see us." Then I fired my last flare.

The yellow light kept going and continued to drop and was soon out of sight, having gone over the horizon. Tracy videoed another full minute, but it didn't reappear. Dejected, we made our way back to the others. As we passed the hatch, I hollered for Donna to leave the light on and come back up.

We regrouped at the helm. Bonnie was still hailing but there was no enthusiasm in her voice. *The Aquaholic* had stopped firing. Compared to the hectic action a moment ago, all was very still. I was very disappointed the alien ship had gone right on by.

"We're not going to stay out here another five days are we?" Ashley asked, her voice echoing the despair we all felt.

"I can't believe they didn't see any of those flares," Tracy added.

"This fucking sucks!" Donna exclaimed as she left the helm and sat down at the cockpit table. "It feels like we just missed the last exit. I need a drink."

"Me too," Ashley said. She went below and came back with a bottle of rum, a couple of cans of ginger ale, and some glasses.

She started to pour but Tracy took the bottle from her hand. "Let me do that," she said and poured us all drinks that were three-quarters rum.

CHAPTER 99

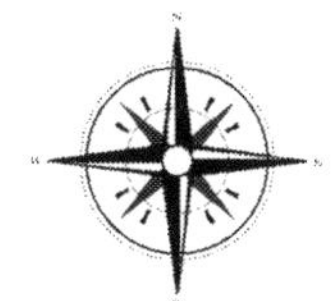

Tracy and I took our drinks to the helm. She looked at me with such discouragement, I thought she was going to cry. "Is Donna right?" she asked. "Did we just miss the last exit?"

"I don't know," I replied. "Either they didn't see us, or they saw us and didn't care. If we had it to do all over again, I'm not sure what we could have done differently."

Bonnie finally quit transmitting, so I got on the radio and asked to speak to Reid.

"What's the plan?" I asked, trying not to sound as glum as I felt.

"The kids thought that seeing the alien light fly by was the coolest thing ever." He paused. "The rest of us probably feel about the same as you do over there."

"Tell Mo I'm impressed with his alien course prediction.

He was right on," I replied.

"We probably need everybody on for a conference call," Reid said. He sounded like he had something on his mind.

Ashley and Donna heard him and came back to the helm, drinks in hand.

"We're ready whenever you are," I radioed.

Mo spoke first, thanking everyone for following him on what turned out to be a wild-goose chase. Angie was next; she said she wanted to go home. Ashley and Donna seconded that idea.

Bonnie and her kids agreed with them. As I expected, Gert was adamant to stay with Mo, whatever he decided to do or wherever he decided to go.

"Where's home exactly?" I asked, not trying to sound flippant but at the same time, I was peeved at everyone stating the obvious.

Reid came back on then. "Angie and Bonnie want to take *The Aquaholic* due west, back to North America. They want Ashley and Donna to join them. The rest of us can go back to *The Lady Anne*. They'll share their food with us for rescuing them, but they want to get started as soon as the storm clears."

"Mo, do you have any ideas?" I asked.

"I can't believe the aliens didn't see us, so I have to conclude they aren't going to bother with us. Short of shooting at them with my rifle, we signaled them with everything at our disposal. I had not expected them to just ignore us."

He paused a moment and then continued, "Gert and I would like to stay with you three aboard *The Lady Anne* if that's all right. We'll abide by whatever you choose to do—either sail away or continue looking for Atlantis. We'll stay out of the way and we don't eat much."

I chuckled at his attempt at humor.

"Stand by," I answered. "I'm calling an executive meeting with my partner Tracy. We'll call you right back."

Tracy and I went below. Buster was really glad to see us. Tracy gave him a pretzel and then poured two glasses of single malt scotch. "Here's to nothing," Tracy toasted, chugging her drink. I took a small sip. I didn't want to mix scotch and rum and get sick.

"This is a major decision with significant consequences," I said. "As I see it, we've got three options. One: Weather permitting, we could resume course for Atlantis. If we haven't located it in five days, we can try to signal the aliens again if they fly over. If we did locate an alien base or civilization, we could try to communicate with them.

"Two: We could give up hope of making contact and head east to Europe. *The Aquaholic* has offered us some of their provisions and after sailing through a gale, I'm one hundred percent confident in *The Lady Anne*'s abilities to get us there safely.

"Three: We could turn back with *The Aquaholic* and head for North America. We'll have company and there obviously is safety in numbers."

I concluded, "Regardless of which option we choose, bringing Mo and Gert with us won't be a problem. They are good company and have become competent crew."

Tracy poured herself another triple shot of scotch and downed that as well. We discussed the pros and cons. Either direction we picked wouldn't offer any civilization because any 25,000-year-ago humans we encountered would be very primitive.

Either continent was likely to offer more native plants and wildlife than Mo's island, so finding food and fresh water would no doubt be easier. Obviously, North America was closer.

We agreed that if we didn't stay in the area, there was probably no chance of finding the aliens again. Mo had been right about the day and time and even the course they would be on. The radar was too cluttered to give clear readings. It didn't read the alien light and it didn't read any nearby land masses, but there could have been an entire continent just out of range.

His theory about Atlantis was still plausible and the alien light had continued on the same heading and was decreasing its altitude, so we figured it was probably landing somewhere. Why not Atlantis?

"I'll stay with you and Reid." Tracy smiled, rubbing her gold coin pendant. "So I'll leave the decision entirely to you. You're the best." She was slightly slurring her words and I knew three stiff drinks on an empty stomach was catching up to her.

I was rethinking my analysis when I felt and heard stomping on the deck and Donna hollering, "Get your asses up here. Here comes another exit."

CHAPTER 100

We rushed topside, accidentally letting Buster follow us. Ashley was steering but Donna was at the stern, motioning for us to hurry. I noticed that *The Aquaholic* had caught up and was nearly even with us.

"Watch between the swells, over there." Donna pointed. "There's a light beneath the water. Reid is sure it's the aliens. So is Mo."

"I see it," Tracy yelled. "It's just like before. This is so cool."

Sure enough, a bright, emerald-colored light was closing on us, heading right between us and *The Aquaholic*.

"Should I get you the flare gun?" Donna asked, so excited she was practically dancing in place.

"No," I replied. "I think they know we're here."

The light was clearly visible, but something else was happening too. Something remarkable. The wind had suddenly stopped and the seas had suddenly flattened. I could see swells a few hundred yards away, but we were entirely becalmed with no wind, no swells, and no waves, not even any ripples. It was like being in the middle of a puddle.

I rushed back to the radio and transmitted, "Reid, if you see any indication we are getting sent through time, you need to immediately disconnect the batteries. Do the starting battery first, then the house battery and finally, portable radios, GPS units, flashlights, et cetera. Did you get that?"

Thankfully, he acknowledged. Ashley wanted to see what was happening, so I took the helm. A minute later I joined everyone aft. The was no need for a helmsman. *The Lady Anne* wasn't moving; she wasn't even drifting. It was eerie to have come to a complete stop, but we had.

The light broke the surface, right between *The Lady Anne* and *The Aquaholic*. The water radiated shades of jade and emerald in all directions. The light surrounded us and was intensely bright for a moment and then faded. As it dimmed, an object surfaced a short distance away.

It was about twenty feet across and resembled a sphere made up of angles, like a giant soccer ball. It glowed pale-yellow. It looked more fluid than solid, seeming to change consistency with each pulse of light. It was suspended a few feet above the surface.

In what looked liked a video test pattern, bands of different colors appeared, moving across the side of the sphere that was facing us. There were bands of reds, blues, greens, and yellows. There were also colors that I had never seen before, some murky, other metallic, some very opaque and some quite intense.

The colors appeared, got brighter, then dimmer before vanishing, only to reappear somewhere else. It resembled a random color generator, testing each pixel on the screen. The pattern was primarily circular, moving around the sphere horizontally. There was a burst of bright white followed by a flash of no color at all. Then the color process repeated, only now it was progressing vertically, mostly up and down.

"This is really freaky." Tracy leaned in close and stammered. I could smell the alcohol on her breath.

"You better sit down," I replied.

"Are you guys seeing these colors?" Reid radioed.

I went over to the radio and confirmed we were and then asked, "What stopped us?"

"I've never experienced anything like this in all my time on the water." There was a pause, then, "Wait, what's happening?"

The light pattern had stopped and we began hearing sounds. They seemed to be emanating from the sphere. They weren't words or musical notes but were more like a test of frequencies. The pitch would go from low to high. It would change from shrill to deep, from crisp to fuzzy, and from barely audible to rock concert loud. It didn't sound instrumental, but more electronic.

Then all was quiet. A faint purplish light illuminated the

sphere. I sensed a pressure change, a slight increase. It was subtle and not enough to make me want to clear my ears, but I definitely felt something.

I put down the radio mike and headed aft towards the others. The purple light slowly shaded back to pale yellow.

Suddenly…

"I have many things to say to them." Mo's booming voice shattered the stillness.

Startled, we flinched as one, spooked by the volume of Mo's cry.

"What the fuck?" Tracy exclaimed. "That was really loud."

Even though *The Aquaholic* was probably fifty yards away, Mo's voice was as near and as clear as if he had been standing next to us, shouting in our ears. Buster started barking, which got amplified and was so loud, too, it was nearly painful.

"No barking," Tracy scolded Buster. Like the others, her voice was thundering.

Yet she wasn't yelling.

The sphere suddenly darkened and was then reilluminated with a blueish-white glow. A shape began to appear on the side facing us, flickering for a second and then stabilizing. It had a green tint. There was a slightly oversized head and what appeared to be arms and legs and it looked vaguely human, but small featured and childlike.

Just like every image I've ever seen of an alien in movies and comic books.

"Is that a little green man?" Tracy whispered to me, looking quite amused and obviously feeling the booze.

"*We have assumed a non-frightening form and are using comprehensible language, Tracy Palmer. What is your next question?*"

I stared in disbelief. The voice had come from the image on the sphere.

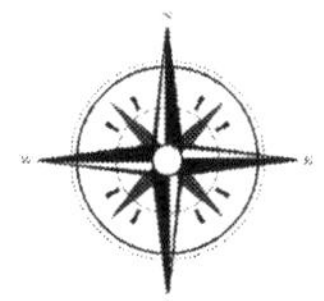

Tracy didn't say anything but slowly looked out toward the sphere. Her eyes were narrowed, as though she was trying to focus. "That looks like a little green man, but I've been drinking." She sat her glass down. "So it might not be. Does anyone else see this?"

I heard Ashley whisper to Donna, "She's drunk."

"Ask them…" Mo started to say over the radio. His voice was no longer amplified.

Puzzled, I returned to the helm and radioed back, "Ask them what?"

There was no reply. I didn't know if we were transmitting or not but apparently our radio was no longer receiving.

Ashley rushed toward me, a panicked look on her face. "It's Tracy. Something's wrong."

I looked back at Tracy. She was still standing where I left

her, but her body had taken on a luminescence that cast a bright glow around her. She was looking down at her hands, and turning them over and back, as if trying to understand what she was seeing. She giggled and held her hands up. "Look, Pat. This is so cool."

I approached her but I wasn't sure she could see me. When I tried to touch her, I felt a strange, moist resistance, like trying to press my hand through wet sand.

I waved my hands in front of her face. "Can you see or hear me?"

There was no response. Her gaze had shifted to the alien image on the sphere.

We have established an audible connection with Tracy Palmer, a voice from the sphere spoke. *And will communicate only with she who asked the first question. The others of her species can listen but not interfere.*

The monotone voice originated from the sphere, but was all around us, like a surround sound audio system. It sounded more computer generated than human with no accent, inflection, or feeling. Thankfully it was now normal volume, not earsplitting.

Tracy stared. "Who are you?" she asked. "Who's talking to me?"

The scotch was still affecting her. She was swaying slightly, her words running together. However, the force field, or whatever it was surrounding her, seemed to be keeping her upright. It didn't move when she steadied herself against it.

I never should have let her drink—hell, none of us should have been drinking. Reid would have been furious if he knew.

The voice came again. *We are observers from outside your galaxy.*

As it spoke, the sphere's image appeared to move its mouth, but the voice was out of sync with the movement.

I glanced at Donna and Ashley. I had a pretty good idea what they were thinking. They probably found it as ironic as I that we had succeeded in finding and communicating with an alien, but the one doing the communicating was inebriated.

Tracy giggled again. "So if you guys are aliens from another galaxy, why are you here?"

We study the evolution of planetary life over the span of time.

"Is this what you really look like?" She was laughing now. "Like something out of a B movie?"

That question made me wince. I could only imagine what the others aboard *The Aquaholic* were thinking. Here was the chance we'd been waiting for to win over the aliens enough to send us back home and Tracy was asking why they looked like a cartoon.

But there was nothing any of us could do but listen and wait.

You are right to laugh. Our normal form would be too chal-lenging for you to communicate with. This form was chosen to be humorous and acceptable.

Donna, Ashley, and I exchanged looks, and I shrugged. Who would expect the aliens to have a sense of humor?

"How come I can understand you?" Tracy asked then. "When did you learn to speak English?"

"Really?" Ashley said. "She's communicating with an alien and all she can ask is how they know English?"

If you prefer another language or communication medium, specify.

"I'm cool with English," Tracy stammered. "Why did you send us back in time? Was it because I took your picture?" Her tone was suddenly coy, like she was flirting with a hunk in a club.

Ashley noticed it too. "Oh my God, is she flirting?"

"That's Tracy," I said, sighing.

Evidence documenting our existence is suppressed whenever possible. Relocation through time is our preferred response.

"Why didn't you just vaporize us or something?"

"Oh shit, don't ask them that," Donna said.

We have no offensive weapons.

"So, what have you guys learned about us?"

Your species generally acts without considering consequences.

"Consequences? What kind of consequences? Consequences for what?"

One example you will understand, Tracy Palmer, concerns the earth's oceans. Overfishing and apex predator reduction, coupled with extreme pollution, will eventually threaten your own species' survival. But if you prefer, we could discuss the consequences of diminishing freshwater supplies, increasing population, or defor-estation.

"No, no. I don't want to talk about that stuff," Tracy

retorted. "One thing I don't miss here is the evening news. Why don't you help us fix things? You're obviously advanced enough to have traveled here from another galaxy, you must have the ability to show us the way to improve things. Don't you?"

Her tone was accusatory, brash, like she was reprimanding them.

I winced again. How would they react to being bawled out?

Our mission is to study, not to interfere.

"I can't take much more of this," Ashley said, exasperated. "Why did they have to pick her to communicate with? Why couldn't they have picked Mo or Reid?"

Tracy couldn't hear any of our conversation. She asked, "Do you guys live in Atlantis?"

One of our transit points for Earth has been called by many names: Devil's Triangle, Bermuda Triangle, Atlantis.

I hoped she wasn't going to ask to go to Atlantis with them. "You're not picking someone up Tracy," I whispered. "Get back on track. Focus."

We heard her snicker and then giggle, and I feared the worst, but her next question was, "Will you send us back to our time?"

"Good job, Tracy," Ashley whispered.

"Finally," Donna echoed.

Why is there desire to return, Tracy Palmer?

CHAPTER 102

Tracy didn't immediately answer. I prayed she was thinking of a good response. I whispered to Ashley and Donna that I was hopeful since the aliens asked why instead of saying no, we had a chance.

"What is the right answer?" Ashley quietly asked me.

"I'm not sure, but I'm afraid if she simply says she doesn't like it here or she misses her old life, those are probably the wrong answers."

"She better not blow this," whispered Donna. "I wish they were talking to someone else. The stakes are huge."

My thoughts raced to the poker game and the stakes of *that* wager, which seemed huge at the time.

Why is there desire to return, Tracy Palmer?

It was the same question, but I was relieved to hear the

tone hadn't changed. There was no frustration or anxiousness, only curiosity.

"Please say something, Tracy," I whispered, wondering what was taking her so long. "Make it good. This is Final Jeopardy for the championship."

None of us could do anything but wait. It seemed to take forever, but finally Tracy responded.

"I have two reasons," Tracy said. "The first is that there are those among us who have sustained serious medical injuries. Angie, Donna, and Ashley have been beaten and assaulted and require medical attention. Mo and Gert are dehydrated and malnourished and have lost so much weight they may die. Bonnie and her kids lost a husband and father and need professional counseling for what they've been through. If you return us to our time, we could get them the medical and professional attention they need."

I smiled; that was a decent answer. Ashley, Donna, and I held hands and waited for the alien's response.

What is the second reason, Tracy Palmer?

"Why don't you just call me Tracy? You don't have to be so formal. I feel like I'm in trouble."

What is your second reason, Tracy?

All three of us sighed in unison. Donna whispered, "Come on, Tracy, please have another good reason."

"My second reason is you aren't consistent. You say you only study and observe, but you do interfere if we happen to take your picture. You send us back to a time where survival is all but impossible. I get that we humans are tough on our planet and on each other and we are shortsighted and we don't always consider consequences, I know I don't, but right or wrong, isn't that our choice?"

She was starting to roll, and I just smiled and listened.

"There must be something about us that you admire. If nothing else, what about our curiosity? It was curiosity that caused the caveman to strike rocks together and discover fire. It was curiosity that sent sailors across the unknown oceans. It was curiosity that made Mo work on a telescope to study and observe other galaxies. And it was curiosity that caused me, and probably everyone else that's here, to take a picture when we saw a strange light fly by.

"You are here studying Earth because you are curious, yet you have punished us for being curious about you. You say you don't interfere, but you have. You have put us in a time where we don't belong and can't survive because you are trying to keep *you* being here a secret. If you want to make things right, interfere again and return us to our own time."

I smiled. *Good job, Tracy*, I thought.

The aliens weren't long in responding. *If we return the others, will you, Tracy, in exchange, remain behind, knowing you cannot survive?*

"They're not making this easy, are they?" Donna asked.

"I'm glad they didn't ask me that," Ashley said.

"I prefer to be with Reid and Pat," Tracy said, sounding sober for the first time. "The three of us love each other very much. But if you want me to stay here, if that's the price to pay, I will. Send the others back. They need help more than I do."

That was the most magnanimous thing I had ever heard. Was she really offering to stay here alone? My eyes filled with tears.

You have demonstrated pity, compassion, and kindness. You surprise us, Tracy.

"So, what's your answer? Will you demonstrate pity, compassion, and kindness as well?"

She sounded anxious, excited, and cautious, all at the same time. I knew she was taking a big gamble. There was a chance she could get stuck here, alone. I found myself holding my breath, waiting for the alien response.

Finally, it came. *All records must be destroyed.*

"What records?"

A soft white beam of light emanated from the sphere, lighting up both vessels. I guessed it was several-million candlepower because I could almost "feel" the light, but it wasn't blinding. Everything lit up.

A minute or two later the beam was extinguished and the voice spoke: *Any and all documentation of our existence must be* destroyed.

"Like my camera?" Tracy asked.

All records must be destroyed.

"How would you like me to destroy my camera?"

Place all records into the heat.

"What heat?" Donna asked, looking around.

I heard a splash directly astern and saw a hole appear in

the water. It was perhaps two feet across and radiating an intense, searing heat that I could feel from where I was standing. There were no flames and there was no steam rising, but there was serious heat.

I got the video camera and returned to the stern. I looked at it for a second, knowing it contained irreplaceable video, but I threw it into the hole. It disappeared with a little puff of smoke.

All records must be destroyed.

"What records do you want, exactly?"

Physical records and other digital records exist. Both vessels must comply. We will display.

The image on the sphere changed to a series of pictures. I recognized my cell phone and Tracy's. There was also a picture of *The Lady Anne's* logbook and *The Obsession's* as well. There were pictures of other cell phones, *The Aquaholic's* logbook, other cameras, Mo's notes, notebooks, papers, and several other items. The pictures were large and easily identifiable. They were in color and the quality was impressive.

"Where did they get those pictures?" Ashley asked.

"Probably from scanning us earlier with the bright light," I replied and then headed below.

Both vessels must comply, the voice repeated.

It was interesting that when I tossed my cell phone into the hole, its picture was removed from the gallery. I saw the picture of another cell phone go away, indicating *The Aquaholic* was doing as directed. I reasoned there was another "heat hole" behind them as well.

I got rid of Tracy's phone, *The Obsession*'s logbook and then, painfully, our logbook. Those pictures were immediately removed. One by one, our evidence of seeing aliens and being here was incinerated.

Donna and Ashley returned with their cell phones. "My life is in this phone," Ashley said, gripping it tightly.

"My life *was* in this phone," moaned Donna as she threw it into the hole. Finally, Ashley followed suit, tossing in her phone too.

We waited as items were destroyed and pictures were removed. I was surprised by the number of seashells that had to be destroyed. Even a bird's big feather that might have been collected by one of the kids appeared on the display. The pictures of all the fish we had kept and Mo's roasting sticks were eventually removed. The last picture was of Reid's Atlantis course paper. I crumbled it into a ball and threw it into the hole.

There were no more pictures on the sphere and the alien's image returned but was silent. I knew we were all wondering what was next.

Finally the voice said, *Public discussion of this encounter will cause authoritative intervention.*

"We understand," Tracy said. "We're all aware there will be consequences if we talk about you."

That assurance is often broken.

Tracy looked surprised. "Then you have returned others to their time?"

Infrequently. Agreements are broken and we are forced to take steps to discredit the ones we were trying to help. Please don't make us sorry we are helping your friends here today.

I glanced back to where the heat hole had been. I wondered if one of the *steps* was to make the "discredited" disappear like had been done to our records. I shivered at the thought. Then something else the alien had said registered: "Don't make us sorry for helping your friends."

"Oh no," I shouted. "They aren't going to return Tracy."

"What?" Donna asked.

"Didn't you hear what they said about not making them sorry for helping her friends?"

"Oh, shit," Donna exclaimed. "Wait, Tracy, stop this, they're keeping you here."

But Tracy couldn't hear her.

Prepare, the voice said suddenly.

Tracy held up her hand. "Wait, I have one more question. When you return us to our time, can you reverse us being sterilized?"

Ashley and Donna looked at each other. Judging from their expressions, they didn't know about that part. I looked down and away and waited for the answer.

Action not reversible.

"You guys don't want to interfere, but sterilizing us isn't interference?"

That is done to make your stay here easier. Procreating in this time would upset the natural order.

Tracy shook her head. "Listen, I have a hint for you. If you don't want to be seen by Earthlings, fly with your lights off.

Or come through with the noon sun behind you, or in a thunderstorm where lighting would obscure the lights. Do something that wouldn't draw attention."

That made me chuckle, but she had an interesting point. Why didn't the aliens eliminate or at least camouflage their telltale light? Had it not been for their strange light and flight pattern, we would never have taken notice.

But it wasn't a question, and the image on the screen began to flicker.

There will be no more questions, Tracy. Prepare to remain here alone, on the vessel of your choice. You have sixty of your minutes. Connection paused.

CHAPTER 103

"No, no, no!" I shouted at the image. "Don't leave Tracy here alone." But there was no response. The image was static, not moving.

Tracy was silent. I couldn't imagine what she was thinking.

Ashley threw up her hands. "Wait. I have more questions. Tracy, ask them if they can return us to a time before my husband was killed?"

"Please, can you do that?" Donna begged. "Please, we miss our husbands."

I understood why they asked, but I was disappointed. They were going to be returned in time and they wanted to know about their husbands, not seeming to care that Tracy would be stuck in the past, where she could not survive.

The alien image was nonresponsive. The force field that had been surrounding Tracy was suddenly gone. She stumbled and nearly fell over, but I caught her. She looked dazed, with a deer-in-the-headlights look.

Donna and I led Tracy back to the helm. I didn't know what to say to her, how to express how brave she had been to sacrifice herself for the rest of us.

"*The Aquaholic* is coming," Ashley pointed.

I looked. It was indeed headed our way, probably under power judging from the way her sails were trimmed.

I took Tracy's hand. "Do you know what you've agreed to? That you're staying here alone?"

She nodded. "It's the right thing to do. The others need help. I'll be okay."

Her words rang true, but I knew she was scared. How could she not be?

The Aquaholic was alongside, about twenty feet away. "Prepare to raft," Reid hollered.

Tracy rose up to help deploy fenders, but I told her to stay put and rest.

We got rafted together and soon Reid, Mo, and Gert came aboard *The Lady Anne* and headed straight for Tracy.

"I'm staying here with you," Reid said. It wasn't a question.

"So are we," Mo added, squeezing Gert's hand.

Ashley and Donna were at the lifeline, talking to Angie and Bonnie. Max and Joey were a few feet away. I couldn't hear what they were saying, but Tracy was listening.

"There is no way I'm leaving without you," Reid repeated.

Tracy sighed, turning to Reid. "No, my dear Reid, you are going with the others. You and Pat are taking everyone back to our time onboard *The Aquaholic*. I'm going to stay here, onboard *The Lady Anne*, with Buster. Don't worry about us; we'll be fine."

I made up my mind too.

I walked over to where I could clearly see the alien image. It hadn't changed. "There has been a change of plans," I said. "Tracy will not be staying here alone. Reid and I are staying with her."

I waited and when there was no response, I repeated my statement. Reid joined me, taking my hand. "We're staying with her. We're not going back. Return the rest."

The image flickered and then responded.

Tracy agreed to stay alone so the rest of you can be returned to your time. There will be no changes. You are wasting time.

The image froze again.

"What are we going to do?" I asked Reid. The thought of leaving Tracy 25,700 years in the past, alone aboard a sixty-eight-foot yacht, was impossible to accept.

"They're not being very flexible," Reid said softly. We made our way back to Tracy.

She watched us approach. "I heard what they said. I love you both for trying, but they aren't changing their minds and neither am I. Get your stuff and get everyone onboard *The Aquaholic*."

Mo and Gert joined Reid and me at the helm.

"Gert and I took a vote," Mo announced. "Regardless of what they say, we are going to stay. They can send Bonnie and her kids back along with Ashley, Donna, and Angie."

"Listen, you guys," Tracy said. "It is very sweet that the four of you would stay here with me, but you all know that is the wrong decision."

She wiped away a tear and continued. "I insist that you all leave. That was the goal when we set out to find the aliens, right? Get returned to our time? Well, we accomplished that. But there is a price. There are consequences. I'm happy to take one for the team."

"The price is too high," I said.

"I have my reasons for agreeing to stay. Once you're on the other side, Pat, you can explain it."

I knew exactly what she was referring to. The women in her bloodline died of a nasty cancer before reaching the age of fifty. She had sworn me to secrecy with that information and I hadn't told anyone.

My mind raced. She'd have many years to survive before the cancer took her. At the most, there were four to six months of supplies on board. That meant she'd have to live off the land or the sea for over a decade. Based on Mo and Gert's condition, her survival that long seemed doubtful. I didn't want my friend, my best friend, to be sacrificed. I shook my head. "No. It's not right."

Tracy rose and took my hand. "Please don't make this any harder than it is. It's a business decision. Keep your heart and emotions out of it. Save the others. Return them to where they belong."

Tears coursed down her cheeks and in a moment, I was blithering too. I grabbed her in a hug. "I love you, Tracy."

"I love you too, Pat." She pushed me gently away. "Now take everything you need, leave whatever food and clothing you can spare, and get aboard *The Aquaholic*. Don't miss the boat."

I tried to smile at her last remark but couldn't. Tracy went from person to person giving hugs.

Reid cleared his throat. "I need a moment to say goodbye. I want the rest of you to start unloading *The Aquaholic*. Pat, will you be in charge of that? We might be at sea three or four days before making landfall, so keep what food we'll need but leave Tracy as much as you can. And Angie, Donna, and Ashley, don't forget your passports and IDs."

With that, he took Tracy's hand and led her aft, down the steps to the swim platform.

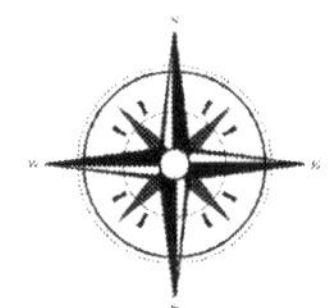

I took some of my clothes, a portable GPS unit, identification, and a few personal items and made my way over to *The Aquaholic*. Angie and Bonnie were setting aside food. Max and Joey were bringing up fishing gear, probably from what Captain Rick had transferred from *The Day Dream*.

Ashley and Donna made their way aboard. They were holding hands and whispering. I figured they were telling each other *The Aquaholic* was now safe.

Gert came over next, carrying one small duffel bag. She said that Mo wanted to give Tracy a lesson in using his survival gear. Her eyes were red from crying.

Reid finally came aboard toting one of his duffel bags. It didn't look very heavy. He looked like he had just buried his best friend. Maybe he had. I told myself he had been coaching her on the logistics of solo sailing and extended living aboard, but I knew he had also professed his love for her and apologized for having to leave.

I looked over at the alien's image on the sphere. It was still there, still frozen. "I really don't want to leave Tracy here alone," I said to it. "Your price for returning us is too high."

The aliens did not respond. I hadn't really expected they would.

I was afraid we might be running out of time. I gave the order to send the food and whatever supplies had been gathered across. We fashioned an assembly line and we began passing items to *The Lady Anne*. I was happy to see there was a lot of food, more clothing than I would have expected, and a lot of *The Day Dream's* fishing gear.

I returned to *The Lady Anne* and waited at the bottom of the hatch while supplies were passed down. Mo and Tracy were gathered at the cockpit table. His survival gear was spread about. He was explaining to Tracy how to put his rifle together.

I started crying again. My beautiful Clarriage was going to become Tracy's life sentence. Until she decided to transition to land, it was going to be her floating prison. The realization of that made me tremble so hard, my hands slipped and I dropped a heavy tackle box. It landed with a thud.

Mo saw my condition and called topside for someone to relieve me. I wanted to stay but I listened to him and returned to *The Aquaholic,* switching places with Bonnie in the assembly line.

Finally we were done. Everyone crossed over to *The Aqua-*

holic, everyone except for Tracy. It got quiet. Reid and Mo untied the boats. Tracy began untying *The Lady Anne*'s fenders. Buster was watching intently. I silently hoped the aliens would let her keep the dog. He would be her only company. I then knew exactly how Cookie Cook felt after burying her husband

Tracy looked like she had been crying and was forcing a smile. I knew it was temporary. I was still trembling and had no more tears to shed. Numbness had replaced sorrow.

The sphere flashed a bright light several times. We all looked at it. The alien image faded and then the sphere began to sink into the water. There was no further communication. The connection went from paused to terminated.

"Get some distance, you guys," Tracy shouted. "We all know what needs to be done." She drew a hand over her face. "Thank you for everything you sent over. I'm sure I'll use it all. After you leave, I'll put everything away." She paused, a wry smile touching the corners of her mouth. "Or I may not. After all, I'll have lots of time to get organized, won't I?"

"Remember to practice assembling the rifle a few more times," Mo shouted, his voice loud but shaky.

Bonnie stood at the rail. "Thank you for letting us return," she said. "My kids and I will never forget you."

"You're a very strong woman," Ashley stammered next. "You are going to be okay." She put her arm over Donna's shoulders who echoed what her friend said, tears streaming down her cheeks.

Max and Joey waved. So did Gert. Angie waved, too, adding to be sure to use the perishable items first.

It was my turn. There were a million things I wanted to say. Somehow the words didn't come. I wanted my last words to be perfect, to be something Tracy would remember. My head ached with the effort. I was losing my best friend and I could think of nothing to say except, "Take care of yourself, Tracy Palmer."

Reid came up beside me. "Take care of *The Lady Anne*," he added. "And she will take care of you."

"When you get into trouble, ask yourself what Reid or I would do," I managed to add, voice shaking. "Take your time, evaluate your options."

Mo spoke again. "If you go ashore, don't eat anything the birds aren't eating."

Tracy nodded.

Reid leaned over to whisper, "Everyone should go inside the salon now."

I nodded. It was time to disconnect the batteries and prepare for the jump. I opened the GPS unit that was in my pocket and removed its battery. I looked over at Tracy once more and raised my hand in farewell before ushering the rest below.

I heard Reid shout, "Fair winds and following seas, my love."

I didn't hear what Tracy said in reply.

CHAPTER 105

Having disconnected batteries and assorted electronics, we congregated in the galley. I knew what was coming, we all did. Fog appeared ahead of us on the calm sea and *The Aquaholic* was drawn right into it.

"Go and find a spot to lie down," I said. "That way you won't fall down when you pass out."

Bonnie, Max, and Joey went to the starboard hull, Angie, Ashley, and Donna followed them.

Mo and Gert went below on the port side. I followed them. Reid wanted to stay at the helm, but I reminded him the static electricity component of time travel was dangerous. He agreed and went below, looking back toward *The Lady Anne* one last time.

Mo and Gert had taken the forward cabin, the one that Bonnie had been forced to share with Rick, her tormentor.

Reid and I were left with the aft cabin. It still smelled from Ashley and Donna's captivity, but I knew the smell of ozone would soon mask the stench of bad hygiene.

We lay down on the bed and I had a vision of Ashley and Donna, naked and bound. Thankfully that vision evaporated when Reid squeezed my hand.

"She is going to be okay," he told me.

"She is going to be all alone," I replied.

I put my head on his chest and closed my eyes. He felt safe.

I forced myself to relax and think about how I would survive alone 25,700 years in the past. How I would prepare.

First, I would take inventory, noting what food I would have to consume first and what could keep. Then I would decide where to go. I had a fully functional, fully equipped Clarriage, large enough to cross an ocean and live aboard for an extended period. No. I dismissed the thought of crossing an ocean. The European continent did not have anything to offer that North America didn't. Going to Africa or South America also seemed pointless.

No, I told myself, my best choice would be to sail to North America or back to the Caribbean.

Mo and Gert had not been flourishing on the island of Mo-gert. While Rick, Bonnie, Max, and Joey appeared to be faring all right where *The Day Dream* was wrecked, I couldn't help but think of the fate that claimed Cookie of *The Obsession* on her inhospitable island with its deadly pond of eels.

So the Caribbean was probably not the best choice. Better to sail west to North America and then follow the coastline.

There was enough fuel for the dinghy to allow for several dozen trips ashore. I could manage my supplies, catch a few fish, and look for a suitable landing. One that would provide a source of fresh water, food, and shelter.

Living aboard alone, I easily had enough supplies for several weeks. That should be more than enough time to find a new home.

"I would rename North America Tracyland," I muttered, the last thought I had before everything went dark.

CHAPTER 106

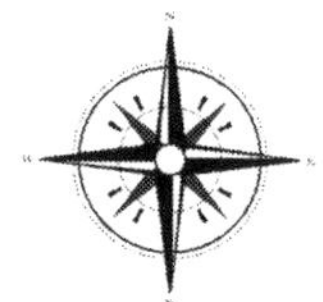

I imagined a knocking sound. It competed for my attention with a triple-migraine headache. I opened my eyes. It was daylight. Reid was lying next to me, still out.

The knocking grew louder. I shook the cobwebs from my head and focused on the sound. I was in a strange cabin, but I could see the door. As I rose up, the door opened.

It was Gert. "Are you and Reid all right?"

I rubbed my temples. "Except for a bitch of a headache. Reid is still out."

Gert took a step into the cabin. "Mo told me that everyone in the other hull was up and at it. He sent me to wake you two."

I gingerly shook Reid. He moved a little and then opened his eyes. "Is it over?"

"We're through the portal," Gert assured us. "Mo and

Angie are reconnecting the batteries. Donna and Ashley are topside. Max and Joey are still in their cabin with their mom, but they're awake."

"Is there any sign of *The Lady Anne*?" I asked hopefully.

"No. We're the only ones here."

"I'll be up in a few minutes," I replied. "Reid, get up when you're ready."

Gert closed the door.

I sunk back on the bed, my mind racing. Tracy was no longer with me. She was stuck in the past. I would never see her again, nor ever know her fate. Would she enjoy her adventure or be miserable? Would she manage to find others that would accept her? Or would she run afoul of others and get into trouble?

And what about us? Where were we? "We don't have a working compass to navigate by," I uttered. "We left it for Tracy."

Reid was sitting up now. He caressed my arm. "Don't worry about it. We have GPS, a satellite phone, and a VHF radio that should all be workable."

His remark about having GPS made me remember the unit in my pocket. I pulled it out, replaced its battery, and switched it on. A moment later it was acquiring satellites. I heard the *Aquaholic*'s engines start. The rumble was strangely comforting.

Reid and I joined the others topside. My GPS had located coordinates for our position, but Mo had already plotted them on a chart, thanks to *The Aquaholic's* GPS, which was also working.

"Seven hundred miles from Nassau but only two hundred from Bermuda," he announced.

We took a quick vote and it was unanimous that we set sail for Bermuda.

Angie passed around a bottle of Tylenol and I took three. So did everyone else. Bonnie even gave Max and Joey one each.

Reid retrieved his trumpet and played "Somewhere Over the Rainbow," dedicating it to Tracy. Even with my headache, it sounded good and was very appropriate. I started crying again.

Donna and Ashley gave me a hug, telling me they were so sorry. I turned away. The thought of Tracy trying to sail *The Lady Anne* through a gale all by herself made me cringe.

But I knew the deed was done and she was gone. I made a mental note to get ahold of Charles as soon as possible. He needed to know Tracy's fate, and the fate of *The Lady Anne*. I remembered the alien's warning not to talk about what had happened, but Charles needed to know.

I walked forward, wanting to be alone. While I was staring out to sea, I saw what appeared to be fog building from nowhere.

"What's that?" I shouted, pointing.

CHAPTER 107

"The aliens wouldn't be coming back to get us again, would they?" Ashley asked, her voice trembling. "Could they have changed their minds about letting us go?"

The fog was very dense. Fog materializing this far at sea, with a slight breeze and clear skies, had happened before. I understood Ashley's concern. This had to be the work of the aliens.

Angie was at the helm. "Slow down," Reid said. "Keep your distance."

Angie slowed and shifted into neutral.

"Maybe we should get out of here," I said.

As soon as the words were out of my mouth, the fog abated, leaving a vessel in its place.

My breath caught. "Oh my God," I shouted. "It's *The Lady Anne*."

I turned to Angie. "Take us over there," I said. "Ashley and Bonnie, deploy our fenders. Reid, Mo, and I will raft us together and see if Tracy is aboard."

If Tracy is aboard. She had to be. Why would the aliens return the yacht without her?

It seemed to take forever, but finally we were rafted alongside *The Lady Anne*. Despite Reid's insistence that he go first, I jumped aboard.

The hatch was closed. I got it open before Reid and Mo caught up with me. "Tracy," I said cautiously. "Are you there?"

There was no reply. She wasn't in the main salon either. It was cluttered with stuff but no Tracy. I went aft. Except for the fishing gear we had transferred from *The Aquaholic*, the crew's quarters were empty. I checked the owner's cabin.

I found nothing except a big bunch of clothing spread out on the bed. It looked like she had been sorting through what everyone had left behind for her.

Reid's voice broke the silence. "They're in here," he called. "Come forward, my old cabin."

I went forward so fast, I nearly tripped over some boxes that hadn't been put away.

There she was in Reid's cabin, lying on his bed, Buster next to her.

Reid gently touched her face. "Tracy, it's me Reid. Can you hear me?"

I wanted to get closer, but Mo held me back. "Let Reid make sure she's okay."

Why would he say that? I pulled away. She had to be okay.

Unless the aliens returned her because she was sick or hurt.

No, I told myself, she's merely out from transiting the time portal. The way we all were.

Reid felt her neck with two fingers. "Strong pulse," he announced.

My heart raced. Why wasn't she waking up?

Suddenly Bonnie and Angie were in the cabin with us.

Angie looked at Reid. "What's going on?"

If he answered her, I wasn't paying attention. I was watching Buster. Except for his chest rising and falling, he was motionless. But he was alive. So was Tracy if she had a pulse. I told myself to be patient while they recovered from the effects of the time portal.

We stood around the bed, waiting. When Tracy's hand moved, I jumped. When she reached up to rub at her temples, I squealed with relief. Finally she opened her eyes and saw us standing over her.

"Am I dreaming?" she asked, groggily. "Are you really here? What's going on?"

"You're back with us," I said, laughing. "You're not dreaming."

Reid climbed onto the bed with her. "How do you feel?"

I settled myself on her right side. "Headache?"

Before she could respond, Gert said, "Give her some room. She's just disoriented."

She was right. Reid and I pulled back. A little. I was so happy to have her with us I didn't want to let go of her hand. So I waited, holding her hand with one hand and lightly petting Buster with the other. Finally, Buster opened his eyes, looked up at me, and then closed his eyes again. I wondered if dogs got headaches and if they did, was it safe to give a dog Tylenol?

"I'm okay," Tracy announced after a time. "Help me up."

Mo and Reid settled her at the salon table. Angie got her a bottle of water. Bonnie shouted across to the others aboard *The Aquaholic* that Tracy and Buster were fine. I heard cheering from *The Aquaholic*.

After she drank some water, I had to ask what I was sure everyone wanted to know. "How in the hell did you get the aliens to return you?"

Tracy shrugged. "It was weird. After you guys disappeared in the fog, I started putting things away. I didn't have a plan but I wanted to clean up the boat a little so I wouldn't trip on anything. And to keep myself distracted."

I smiled. So did Reid.

"Buster went topside and suddenly started barking. I followed him, half afraid of what I would find. My heart almost stopped when I saw the alien sphere had returned."

"What did they say?" I asked, leaning in close.

Tracy took her time to answer, seeming to enjoy having everyone's undivided attention. She grinned as she said, "I had passed the test."

Reid and I looked at each other. "What test?" we said in unison.

"I asked them that very question," she replied, taking another drink of water.

She was really enjoying torturing us. Angie handed her some Tylenol and we had to wait some more while she took two, downed them with a swig of water, and wiped her lips. Just then Buster joined us in the salon, sniffed at Tracy, and settled himself down at her feet.

If she starts playing with Buster, I thought, *I'm going to scream.*

Tracy glanced at me, and the look on my face must have betrayed my thoughts. "Okay," she finally said. "I passed the test of selflessness. They were impressed that I would give up a chance to go home so that my friends could."

"It's called *mitzvah*," Mo said. "Performing a good deed with no expectation of recognition or reward. I'm thankful your generous act of courage was appreciated by the aliens as well as by us."

Mitzvah seemed very noble. In fact, what Tracy had done for the rest of us was likely the most noble or selfless thing I had ever witnessed.

"So are we back where we belong?" Tracy asked. "Did they keep their word?"

"They did and we are," Reid answered. "Two hundred miles out of Bermuda. The GPS units are working and everyone is glad to be here, thanks to you."

"What's the plan?" she asked.

I paused before answering. There were definitely going to be some hoops to jump through before we could show up in Bermuda and announce to the world that we were back. Not only back, but with another boat and eight extra people!

Bonnie and her family had no passports. Gert was the sole survivor of a lost tourist boat, and Mo survived a plane crash. Charles no doubt had people searching for us. Would he be able to pull some strings if we explained what we'd been through? If there was one thing I was sure of, we'd need his help and his connections.

I released a breath. "First, we're going to reprovision the *Aquaholic*, decide on crews, and set sail for Bermuda. I'll call Charles on the way and see if he can't meet us offshore." I waved a hand. "We're returning with not only a second boat but extra people—people who have no papers. I'm sure he'll be able to help with that and maybe bring a doctor to check everyone out."

Tracy shook her head. "I figured we weren't going to sail in and have nobody notice."

"Speaking of sailing in," Reid said. "Did you remember to disconnect the batteries before you entered the time portal?"

She shook her head.

"Did you remember to tighten the shipping screw on my compass?"

Again she had forgotten to do that.

"Well, it doesn't matter." He grinned, hugging her. "We're all glad you're back."

"I'm especially glad you're back," I told her. "You may never want to sail another boat in your life, but if you do, I can't think of a better partner."

"Not want to sail again? Are you kidding?" Tracy laughed. "I wasn't alone very long, but I'd already made up my mind to try to contact those aliens again. I wasn't ready to give up on the future you and I talked about when you won *The Lady Anne*. Only the next time when we sail around the world, there'll be no video cameras."

I nodded and put my arms around her. "And no phone videos. We'll lock up the phones and only take them out in an emergency."

"And only if we're nowhere near The Bermuda Triangle." she said, hugging me back.

"Only if."

The End

(For now)
Books two and three on the horizon.

Nautical Glossary

Abeam	The area at a right angle to the vessel.
Aboard	To go on or into a vessel.
Adjustable keel	The ballasted structure on the bottom of the vessel's hull that can be raised or lowered to suit conditions.
Adrift	Moving on the water but not under power or control.
Aft	At or toward the stern.
Aground	Stuck on the ground in shallow water.
Ahoy	1. A nautical greeting. 2. A shout used to attract attention.
Alarm tone	A loud tone that sounds when the diesel engine is first started, indicating low oil pressure. Once the oil begins pumping and lubricating the engine, the tone stops.
Amidships	Area in the middle of the vessel, either front-to-back or side-to-side.
Anchor	A device, usually deployed from the bow, used to secure the vessel to the bottom to keep the vessel from moving away. Anchors come in different shapes and sizes to optimize holding in different bottom compositions (mud, sand, rock, etc.)

Anchor alarm function	A device using GPS to monitor the vessel's position and sound an alarm if the vessel moves outside of a preset boundary.
Anchor light	One or more white lights shown at night when a vessel is at anchor. Sailboats often have this light atop the mast.
Anchor station	Topside area where the anchor is kept.
Anchor storage compartment	A compartment where the anchor and associated tackle are kept. On a dinghy, this is often in the bow. On some vessels, there are provisions for a freshwater rinse of the anchor and its chain/line.
Anchor windlass	See windlass.
Anchoring	A process of deploying or retrieving the anchor.
Anemometer	An instrument for measuring wind speed.
Astern	The area behind the back of the boat.
Autopilot	A device of various designs to automatically keep the vessel on a preset course.
Backstay	A support, often made of cable or rod, that leads downward and aft from the upper part of the mast. It is used to support the mast and to control sail trim.

Baja Ha-Ha race	An annual fall sailboat rally that begins in San Diego, California and ends in Cabo San Lucas, Baja, Mexico. It is not officially a race, but there is a lot of "informal" competition.
Bareboat Chartering class	Instruction to take the Bareboat Chartering test, an advanced-intermediate level of certification to be able to charter (rent) sailboats, between 30 - 50 feet in length, for sailing in moderate wind and sea conditions, within sight of land, during daylight hours. The prerequisite is usually the Coastal Cruising certification or equivalent. There is normally textbook, classroom, and on-the-water instruction, including an overnight sail.
Basic Keelboat class	Instruction to take the Basic Keelboat test, a beginning level of certification that demonstrates ability to prepare the sailboat to sail, get away from the dock, raise sail, perform basic sailing maneuvers such as tacking and jibing, and get the boat safely back to the dock. There is usually no prerequisite as this is a beginning level course. There is normally textbook, classroom and on-the-water instruction, including learning several knots.
Battery selector switch	A mechanical switch to select which battery (house or starter) to use (charge or discharge). It usually can be switched to either battery, both, or neither.

Beam reach	A point of sail where the wind is coming over the side of the vessel at a roughly 90-degree angle. The sails will normally be adjusted further out when sailing on this point of sail.
Becalmed	A condition that exists for a sailboat when there is no wind whatsoever.
Belay that	A command to cancel the previous order.
Below	The area beneath the deck. Also - belowdeck.
Bermuda Triangle	An area loosely bordered by points in Florida, Puerto Rico, and Bermuda where dozens of ships and planes have disappeared, some under mysterious or unexplained circumstances.
Berth	1. A sleeping space aboard a vessel. 2. A vessel's allotted space at a dock.
Bilge	1. The lowest, deepest part of a vessel where the bottom curves up to meet the sides. 2. The water (often dirty and smelly) that collects in the bilge.
Bimini top	A temporary cover that can be deployed for shade or protection from the elements over the open cockpit of a boat. They are often made of a treated material to resist fading and are usually collapsible.
Bitter end	1. The inboard end of the anchor line, hopefully secured to the vessel. 2. The end of a line that is not attached to anything.
Board/boarded	To get on, or allow others to get on, a boat.

Boarding ladder	Temporary steps allowing people access to a vessel from the water. Boarding ladders are usually near the stern and often fold for storage.
Boat	A small vessel propelled by oar, paddle, sail, pole, or an engine. Rule of thumb: A boat will fit on the deck of a ship, but a ship will not fit on the deck of a boat.
Boat hook	A long pole, sometime telescoping, with a hook on one end used for grabbing or pushing something.
Boom	1. A long spar of various materials protruding out from the mast, holding the foot (bottom edge) of the sail. The boom can be released (eased) to swing from side to side. 2. The last sound you hear when you are unexpectedly hit in the head by the boom. This can be very dangerous, even fatal.
Bow	The front of the vessel, also called the pointy end.
Bow pulpit	A railing, usually metal, at the bow of the vessel. It sometimes extends forward past the deck. On larger vessels, it may hold the anchor.
Bow wake	A wave that forms at the bow of a vessel as it moves through the water.
Bowsprit	A spar or pole protruding forward from the bow to which sails or rigging can be attached.

Brass Bell	The ship's bell, made of brass or bronze, used to signal the time or produce required sound signals. They are normally engraved with the vessel's name and can be quite ornate.
Bulb keel	A specific type of keel, ballast filled and usually teardrop shaped.
Bulkhead	A support or dividing wall between compartments to strengthen the vessel.
Buoy	An anchored float, normally used as an aid to navigation or to display warnings or mark dangerous areas.
Cabin	An enclosed area on a vessel that may or may not be tall enough to stand up in.
Canadian-flagged boat	A boat displaying the Canadian flag.
Capsizing	To turn over or upside down in the water.
Captain	The person in charge of the vessel and responsible for its safe operation and the safety of the crew and passengers.
Catalina 470	A 47-foot-long American sailboat, first built in 1998. They were built by Catalina Yachts but are no longer in production.
Catamaran	A vessel with twin hulls, running parallel to each other.

Channel	1. A navigable length of water, often marked with aids to navigation, connecting two other, often larger bodies of water. 2. A specific band of frequencies used in radio or television.
Chart	A nautical map, paper, or electronic used for navigation. It usually shows the water depth, land features, markers (buoys), traffic lanes, distances between islands, the method to convert magnetic to true north, etc. Charts are marked in degrees latitude and longitude. The depth can be shown in feet, meters, or fathoms (6 feet in a fathom).
Charter boat	A vessel for rent or hire, normally located in island or coastal destinations.
Circumnavigation	The process of sailing (or traveling) all the way around something, often the world.
Clarriage Sixty-Eight	A fictional luxury sailing yacht designed to cross oceans and then live aboard for extended periods in complete comfort.
Clipped in	Attached to the boat by various methods so as not to fall overboard.
CO2 cartridge	Some PFDs are inflated using a compressed gas (carbon dioxide) cylinder that contains enough gas for one inflation.

Coastal Cruising class	Instruction to take the Coastal Cruising test, an intermediate level of certification that adds to the Basic Keelboat instruction. Advanced topics include reefing, anchoring, heaving to, docking under power, and additional proficiency with knots. The prerequisite is usually the Basic Keelboat certification or equivalent. There is normally textbook, classroom, and on-the-water instruction.
Cockpit	The location of the controls on a vessel, normally outside the deckhouse and often recessed slightly into the deck. There may be a separate helm station on some designs.
Cockpit curtains	Side and aft curtains, often with a see-through panel, used to enclose and protect the occupants from the elements. Usually used in conjunction with some type of roof structure or Bimini top. The curtains are often made from a rain-resistant material.
Cockpit table	A table, usually in the cockpit of a boat. They can be of several designs, including pedestal, drop-leaf, fold-down, adjustable height, etc. and can be made of various materials (various species of wood, plastics, fiberglass, acrylics, metal, composites, etc.) with varying degrees of resistance to the harsh marine environment.
Compass	An instrument to determine directions that contains an easily rotating magnetized pointer (needle) which shows the direction of magnetic north and bearings from it.

Compass needle	The magnetized pointer in a compass.
Compass rose	1. A circular reference tool on a nautical chart displaying true north, magnetic north and indicating adjustments for compass variation. 2. A decorative figure displaying north, south, east and west and perhaps points in between.
Compass variation	The angle or difference between magnetic north (on a compass point) and true north (on the meridian towards geographic north). Variation changes in amount and direction, based on location and year.
Crew	The person or persons who assist in the operation of the vessel.
Crew's quarters	A spartan but efficient living space to offer the crew some privacy. Somewhat self-contained and may or may not have minimal galley facilities.
Crewed charter boat	A boat for charter (rent) that comes fully equipped (food, drinks, dishes, linens, towels, fuel, captain, cook, crew, etc.) so all the guests have to do is bring personal items and relax.
Cruising/cruisers	1. Those that sail from place to place, living aboard for extended periods, for pleasure. 2. Vessels designed specifically for cruisers. 3. Those persons who fix their boats in exotic locations.

Cruising guide	A publication, either hard copy or electronic, dedicated to a specific area, giving various levels of information and details about the area. May include information such as marina locations, yacht clubs, approach/departure routes, monitored radio frequencies, facilities, lodging, shopping, marine repair, sightseeing, dining, fishing, custom's information, etc. May also include chart excerpts for specific locations.
Current position	Accurately obtaining the vessel's location by electronic or other means. Caveat - If the vessel is moving, the position you obtained and noted may be several minutes old.
Cutlass	A short, broad sword sharpened on the cutting edge. They could be straight or curved and were a common weapon during the age of sail.
Deck	A floor-like surface, permanently covering one or more level(s) of a hull or compartment and serving to strengthen the hull.
Depth finder	A device, usually electrical or electronic, to measure the depth of the water.
Diesel engine	The most common engine in sailboats over 25 feet long. Compared to gasoline fuel-powered engines, diesel fuel-powered engines offer higher torque, higher available horsepower, lower maintenance costs, no carbon monoxide production and less sensitivity to moisture. But diesel engines are heavier, noisier, and more expensive, initially.

Diesel generator	An additional way to provide electricity other than using a diesel engine. Diesel fuel is safer to store than gasoline because diesel fuel doesn't vaporize as easily and is less combustible.
Dinghy	A small open boat, often carried on or towed behind a larger vessel. A dinghy can be used as a tender (transport), for recreation or even as a lifeboat. Dinghies can be rowed, sailed or motor driven. Their hull can be inflatable or rigid or a combination.
Distress signal	1. Any of various internationally recognized indicators (either visual or audible) signifying a vessel is in danger. 2. A request for assistance.
Divider	An instrument used by navigators to measure and transfer distances on a nautical chart using the latitude scale.
Dock cart	A wheeled, wagon-type carrier used for moving supplies to or from the vessel when docked. Some dock carts fold for compact storage aboard.
Dock line	A specialty line used to secure the vessel to the dock. Dock lines often have a factory spliced loop at one end, are water and fade resistant, and provide some stretch. They vary in size, load rating, and length, depending on application.
Dock(s)	Man-made walkways in the water for which to access boats. Many docks are floating to allow for tides or fluctuating water levels.

Dogged	To close something (watertight door, port-hole) and latch it closed.
Dorado	The Caribbean name for the dolphinfish, a species of fish with its dorsal fin running the length of its body. Also called mahi-mahi in Hawaiian waters.
Draw	The depth of water necessary to operate the vessel without grounding (running aground).
Drifting	At the mercy of the wind or current, having no means of directing the motion of the vessel.
Drogue	An external device attached to the vessel's stern used to slow the vessel down in a storm and designed to keep the hull perpendicular to the waves.
Duffel bag	A type of bag, traditionally cylindrical in shape and closed by a drawstring or zipper. The bag got its name from Duffel, a town in Belgium where the cloth was first made. Duffel bags are preferred by sailors because unlike a suitcase, they can be collapsed when emptied, thus saving precious space.
Ease	To slacken, let out, decrease tension, or pay out slightly.
Electronic chart overlay	Using GPS and an electronic chart, an electronic method to synchronize the vessel's autopilot to keep the vessel on a predetermined course.

Engine compartment	A usually limited space to access the vessel's engine. On sailboats, the engine compartment is often located behind the ladder leading belowdecks. The steps are removed to access the front of the engine and then additional panels can be removed to access the remainder of the engine.
Engine room	A specific room or larger compartment dedicated to housing the vessel's engine. There is usually comfortable and well-lit access to all sides of the engine for inspection or maintenance purposes. The engine room is normally well insulated to reduce the diesel engine's noise.
Engine throttle back	To manually slow the engine down, usually by pulling backwards on the throttle handle or lever.
EPIRB	An Emergency Position Indicating Radio Beacon (EPIRB for short) is a distress beacon used by mariners worldwide to alert (using satellite technology) search and rescue forces that they are in distress.
Eye of the wind	Exactly where the wind is coming from.
Fair winds and following seas	1. A nautical blessing for a safe journey. 2. A favorable wind blowing in a desirable direction of travel for the mariner.
Fall off	To turn the sailboat away from the direction of the wind.
Falling tide	A movement of a tidal current away from a shore or down a tidal river or estuary.

Fender	A bumper placed outside the hull, used to prevent damage to the vessel. Fenders are often deployed when docking or rafting two vessels together. Fenders can protect both the vessel(s) and the dock.
Ferry	A specially designed boat or ship to carry passengers, vehicles, and/or limited cargo across a normally small body of water at regular intervals.
Fighting belt	A fishing accessory designed for use when fishing standing up. The belt straps around the fisherman's waist and has a receptacle that mates to the end of the fishing rod. The belt spreads the load across the fisherman's thighs and provides a mechanical advantage when fighting large gamefish.
Fillet knife	A specialty knife designed for filleting fish. It typically has a very sharp, flexible blade to allow the blade to easily cut underneath the fish's skin, just above the backbone.
Fish box	A container, built-in or freestanding, in which to keep the fish you have caught fresher, longer. A fish box should offer good insulation, a smooth interior finish, and adequate drainage to keep ice and the day's catch colder and speed the clean-up process at the end of the day.

Floorboards	The floor of the vessel, also called the sole. It is often made of long pieces of a species of wood that is resistant to water damage, such as teak. Some floorboards are removable to access the space(s) beneath them, such as the bilge.
Flybridge	The flybridge is a small, often open area situated high on the vessel (usually larger fishing boats), offering duplicate controls, where the vessel can be steered. The flybridge usually offers greater visibility due to unobstructed views of the fore, aft, and sides of the vessel.
Flying the spinnaker	Having deployed the spinnaker sail. See spinnaker.
Following sea	Waves coming from behind the vessel.
Foredeck	1. The deck at the forward part of a vessel. 2. The forward part of a vessel's main deck.
Forward	At or toward the bow.
Full sail	When all of a sailboat's sails are set, raised, unfurled, or deployed.
Furl	To roll a sail over itself by using the roller furling mechanism. Opposite of Hauled out, def. # 1.
Gaff	A handheld hook, often attached to a rigid handle of various lengths, used for holding or lifting heavy fish. The hook can be barbed or not and is often fairly sharp and pointy.

Gale	A strong sustained wind. A gale at sea is accompanied by large waves and regular whitecaps. There may be blowing foam or churning seas. It is stronger than a breeze but weaker than a tropical storm.
Galley	The kitchen area aboard a boat or ship.
Gangplank	A portable walkway or bridge used for boarding or leaving a ship.
Gated pier	A locking gate, often made of metal, across the entrance to a pier or dock.
Genoa	A sail set near the bow that does extend aft of the main mast. A genoa is larger than a jib.
Gimbaled rod butt	A fitting mounted into or onto the butt of a saltwater fishing rod that fits inside a mating fixture that is attached to a fighting belt or a fighting chair.
Ginger ale	A carbonated soft drink, flavored with ginger. Ginger is thought by many boaters to help reduce vomiting, a typical result of being seasick.
Glassing	To scan one's surroundings with binoculars.
Gnomon pointer	The part of a sundial that casts a shadow.

GPS	A satellite navigation system (Global Positioning System) used to determine the ground position of an object. The GPS receiver uses multiple signals from orbiting satellites to calculate a fairly accurate position using a process called triangulation.
Grab rail	A safety device, often in the shape of a railing or bar, used to provide the sailor with a strong and convenient handhold while moving about the vessel.
Gulf stream	A warm ocean current flowing north from the Gulf of Mexico, along the east coast of the United States to an area off the southeast coast of Newfoundland where it becomes the western terminus of the North Atlantic current and flows toward Europe.
Hail	An attempt to establish contact by various methods, including a radio call to see if anyone is listening.
Halyard	A line that raises a sail (or flag) up and/or down.
Hand bearing compass	A handheld magnetic compass, capable of one hand use.
Handed off the helm	1. Literally, to not let go of the wheel or tiller, until your replacement has a hold of it. 2. To relinquish control of the helm to a replacement.

Harbor	A place on the coast where vessels may find shelter. Harbors are usually protected from rough water by land, piers, jetties, sea walls, or other artificial structures.
Hatch	1. An opening in the deck leading to a lower level through which cargo, personnel, and even air can be passed. 2. A covering for such an opening.
Hatchway	A passage or opening leading to or from a compartment. See hatch.
Hauled out	1. To deploy a sail that has roller furling by pulling it out by the clew (one of the corners on a triangular sail). 2. To physically remove the vessel completely from the water, usually for service but sometimes in advance of approaching storms.
Head	1. The bathroom on a vessel. 2. The top corner of a triangular sail.
Heading	A direction or course to steer.
Headsail	Any sail set forward of the most forward mast.
Heave to	A technique for (nearly) stopping a sailboat by positioning the sails to contract each other. The vessel will oscillate slowly from one direction to another and then back again.
Heavy weather	Strong winds and large waves. May or may not be accompanied by rain, thunder, and/or lighting.

Heel/heeling	The angle the boat sails at. The more the boat is heeled, the steeper the angle.
Helm	1. The tiller or the wheel that controls the angle of the rudder. 2. The area of a sailboat from which the boat is steered.
Helmsman	The person who steers/drives the vessel.
Horseshoe	A throwable cushion used for lifesaving. It is usually mounted on the stern rail at the rear of the vessel. Larger vessels may have them placed at strategic locations.
House battery	The battery that provides power to run the vessel's lights and electrical equipment but not used to start the engine.
Hove to	Past tense of heave to. A sailboat that has heaved to.
Hull	The main body of a vessel including the bottom and the sides.
J/44	A 44-foot-long American sailboat, designed as both a racer and a cruiser, first built in 1989. They were built by J Boats but are no longer in production.
Jackline	A temporary line, webbing strap or wire, strung tightly from the bow to the stern to which a safety harness can be attached, allowing a crew member to safely move about the deck when there is a risk of falling or being swept overboard.

Jeanneau 45	A 45-foot-long French production sailboat, designed with lots of space for cruising in comfort, first built in 2007. They were built by Jeanneau Yachts but are no longer in production.
Jib	A sail set near the bow that does not extend aft of the main mast. A jib is smaller than a genoa.
Jibe	A maneuver to bring the stern of the boat through the eye of the wind.
Jibe ho	A command issued (normally by the helmsman) while jibing, just prior to the boom swinging across to the other side.
Keel	An extension of the hull that goes deep(er) into the water and provides stability from heel and sideways resistance to the wind.
Ketch	A type of sailboat having two masts, the second of which (the mizzen mast) is generally shorter than the main mast.
Knot	1. A measurement of speed at sea equal to one nautical mile per hour. 2. Used to fasten (tie) a line to itself or another object.
Knot meter	An instrument, normally electric or electronic, that measures the vessel's speed through the water.
Ladder	The stairs or steps between decks, so named due to their steepness and narrowness.

Land ho	An expression shouted by the vessel's watch to inform the crew that land has been spotted. After long passages at sea, Land ho was very comforting to hear.
Latitude	The angular distance, measured in degrees, minutes, and seconds, running north or south of the equator.
Lazarette	A small compartment or locker used for storage.
Lee cloth	A sheet of canvas, or other fabric, attached to the open side of a berth. It can provide an illusion of privacy but is primarily used to keep a sleeping person from falling out of bed when the vessel heels during sailing or rough weather.
Lee shore	A nearby shore that is downwind from your present position. They are particularly dangerous to mariners because with the wind blowing toward them, it is very difficult to get away from it against the oncoming waves.
Leech	The back edge of a triangular shaped sail.
Leeward	1. On or toward the side sheltered from the wind. 2. The side sheltered or away from the wind. (The side opposite windward.) (Pronounced loo ward, like steward with an L.)

Life jacket	A flotation device, designed to keep the wearer afloat in the water. They are available in different styles and are designed for various purposes and sea conditions.
Life raft	A smaller boat, used in emergencies, often inflatable. Some life rafts provide a cover that can be used as shade. Some life rafts are designed to be difficult to sink in rough seas.
Lifeline(s)	A wire or cable that runs along the outside of the deck, designed to help restrain passengers (or crew) from falling overboard.
Lifeline gate	A section of the lifeline that can be unhooked to allow easy access on or off the boat without having to step over the lifeline.
Light stick	A self-contained, short-term source of light. It consists of two plastic tubes containing chemicals that, when mixed together, begin glowing. They are available in different colors and intensities, although usually the brighter the glow, the shorter the time they last. (Also called a glow stick.)
Line	Rope or other forms of cordage that have come onboard a vessel. Lines with specific uses may be called by other names.
List or listing	When the vessel heels (tips) with no outside forces being applied.

Log	1. A book in which all matters concerning the vessel are notated. Similar to a journal. 2. To make a notation of an event worth recording.
Long tack	A sailing vessel being on the same tack (point of sail) for a long period of time.
Longitude	The angular distance, measured in degrees, minutes, and seconds, running east or west of the prime meridian running through Greenwich, England.
Loose-footed mainsail	A method of attaching the mainsail to the boom, using only the two lower corners of the sail as attachment points.
Luff	1. The leading edge of a triangular shaped sail. 2. A sail fluttering or flapping in the wind.
Macerate	The act of using a machine to grind solids (including sewage and food waste) in wastewater into small pieces so they can be discharged directly into the sea (normally when a minimum of 12 nautical miles offshore).
Magnetic north	A compass bearing relating to the magnetic poles rather than the true north and south poles.
Main mast	The primary, usually the tallest, mast aboard a sailboat.
Main salon	The primary indoor guest area on a vessel.

Mainsail	The primary source of power for a sailboat. The main sail is attached to the main mast and the boom.
Mainsheet	The line that controls the mainsail, bringing it in or letting it out, from side to side.
Making way	A vessel moving through the water.
Man-overboard drill	Various techniques used to retrieve a person who has fallen overboard. The method used will depend on the type of vessel, the prevailing sea conditions, and whether the victim is conscious or not.
Marina	A normally sheltered or protected area where yachts and small vessels can dock, refuel, and get repairs and supplies.
Marlin spike	A pointy tool used in marine rope work. It may be a separate tool or one item on a specialty pocketknife.
Mast	A tall upright spar of various materials and designs, erected vertically, generally along the centerline of the vessel. On a sailboat, the mast(s) carry the sail(s).
Mayday	The international distress signal that a vessel uses to declare they have a life-threatening emergency.
Messenger line	A light line, used to haul a heavier line, between vessels or to the shore.
Mizzen mast	The mizzen mast is aft of (behind) the main mast.

Mizzen sail	A sail affixed to the mizzen mast and mizzen boom. The mizzen sail is usually smaller than the main sail.
Mizzen sheet	The line that controls the mizzen sail, bringing it in or letting it out, from side to side.
Monkey-fist knot	1. A knot in the category of heaving knots, tied to the end of a line serving as a weight, making it easier to throw. 2. An ornamental knot. (It is so named because it resembles a bunched fist or paw.)
Monohull	A vessel with a single hull.
Motion sickness pills	A medication in pill form, used to relieve the symptoms of travel or motion sickness.
Motor-sailing	The act of a sailboat using engine power while keeping the mainsail up (for stability).
Multi-tool	A versatile hand tool that combines several individual functions (screwdriver, knife, pliers, etc.) into a single unit.
Nautical mile	A unit used for measuring distances at sea. Historically it was equal to 1 minute of 1 degree of latitude. Now it is equal to 1,852 meters, 6,076 feet or approximately 1.151 statute (regular) miles. It is abbreviated "nm."

Nautical white	A clothing style borrowing from naval officer's designs. Uniform will be white in color, not blue. Shirts have epaulet straps. Epaulets (an ornamental shoulder piece) may be plain or striped, with or without an insignia. Pants are often a solid color and may be pleated. Belt may have nautical themed designs, possibly signal flags, and the buckle may have an insignia. Hats are captain's style, with or without gold striping, insignias, and/or scrambled eggs (leaf shaped embellishments) on the visor.
Navigation station	A dedicated area of a vessel that house the navigation tools and equipment. On a sailboat, it is usually below deck, often near the radio and the electrical circuit breaker/switches.
Newport-Ensenada race	An international sailing yacht race, first run in 1948. It begins in Newport Beach, California and ends 125 nautical miles later in Ensenada, Baja, Mexico. It is an annual event with numerous classes of competitors. It is often abbreviated N2E.
Night watch	A lookout during the night or a person(s) keeping such a lookout.

Noon sun shot	A navigational method to give a close approximation of your current latitude. It requires a sextant, an accurate timepiece, and a current copy of a Nautical Almanac. The calculation is fairly straightforward if the sighting is at LAN (local area noon). A close approximation of longitude can be determined in this manner as well.
Ocean crossing	1. The passage of passengers (and/or cargo) across an ocean. 2. An ocean crossing vessel is designed to handle rough seas and long passages.
Offshore Passage Making class	Instruction to take the Offshore Passage Making test, an advanced level of certification. It is a weeklong (or longer) live-aboard class, consisting of nearly nonstop sailing for a minimum of 600 miles, 250 of which are at least 50 miles from shore. The prerequisites are usually the Bareboat Chartering certification and the successful completion of a Coastal Navigation course and possibly a Celestial Navigation course, or equivalent. This is a capstone class for those wanting serious sailing instruction in real-world conditions. Instructors for this class will be highly qualified.
Offshore	1. At sea, often out of sight of land. 2. A wind that is blowing away from the land.

Offshore rain gear	Foul weather gear designed for consecutive days or weeks of use in extreme conditions. It must be durable, waterproof, highly breathable, and made of heavy-duty, high-quality fabrics, components, and construction.
Outboard motor	A small internal combustion engine with a propeller integrally attached for mounting at the stern of a small boat.
Outhaul	A sail control line that allows adjustments to tension the sail.
Outrigger	A pair of long poles, fitted on both sides of a fishing boat, designed to hold fishing lines apart from each other and away from the boat. They are often used for trolling multiple fishing lines.
Overhead hatch	A hatch leading to the space above. They can be used for ventilation, light, or if they are large enough, as an emergency exit for personnel.
Overtaking	To come up (on another vessel) from behind.
Owner's suite	Normally the most luxurious accommodation/cabin aboard in terms of size, comfort, location, and features.
Pan-pan	The international urgency signal that a vessel uses to declare they have an urgent situation, but for the time being, the situation is not life-threatening or posing an immediate threat to the vessel itself.

Paper chart	A nautical chart printed on paper. They are often laminated or a heavy-duty, smudge-resistant paper. See chart.
Paracord	A lightweight nylon rope originally used in the suspension lines of parachutes but now used as a general-purpose utility cord.
Parallel rules	A drafting instrument used by navigators to draw parallel lines on charts. It consists of two straight edges joined by two arms which allow the edges to move closer or further away from each other while always remaining parallel.
Passageway	A hallway or corridor between areas of a ship.
Pelican cooler	A brand of deluxe coolers, heavily insulated and rated for extreme temperatures. They are made of sturdy plastic, have freezer-grade gaskets, and are leakproof.
PFD	Abbreviation for a Personal Flotation Device, see lifejacket.
Pier	A man-made structure that protrudes from the shore.
Piracy	The practice of attacking and robbing, stealing from, or committing illegal violence against vessels at sea.
Pirate	One who engages in piracy.

Pirate flag	A flag, sometimes displaying a white skull and white crossbones on a black background, flown to indicate a pirate ship. The first recorded use of a flag displaying such symbols dates to the seventeenth century. Other pirate flags featured a skeleton and could be black or red. The pirate flag was usually only flown when the pirates wanted to announce their presence, i.e. just before a raid or battle.
Pitching	An up-and-down movement of the bow and stern of a vessel at sea.
Plot a course	Basically drawing a line between two points on a chart, calculating the distance between them, and determining the compass heading.
Polarized sunglasses	While ordinary sunglasses can reduce the total amount of light reaching your eyes, they don't eliminate much glare. Polarized lenses filter out most of the glare and block nearly all the damaging UVA and UVB (ultraviolet) rays.
Port	1. The left side of the vessel when aboard and facing forward. 2. Where vessels come in to dock.
Portholes	A round, window-like opening with a hinged, watertight glass cover in the side of a vessel for admitting air and light.

Position	Also called a fix, is the determination of the vessel's location, arrived at by various methods, usually expressed as precise coordinates in degrees, minutes, and seconds of latitude and longitude.
Powerboat	1. A boat propelled by an engine. 2. A fast boat used in racing.
Primary helm station	When there are steering wheels on both sides of the boat, the side where the engine controls are also located.
Prop	Short for propeller - a rounded blade that rotates in a circle and moves the vessel forward (or backward) through the water.
Propane locker	A vapor-tight compartment enclosing Liquid Propane Gas (LPG) tanks and some of their associated connections, separated from the interior of the vessel, or outside of the vessel in a location where leaking gas will not drain to the interior of the vessel.
Quarter berth	A sleeping space (bed) aboard a vessel, often a single bunk, and sometimes placed where there is minimal space.
Radar	Equipment to, or a means of, sending out radio waves to detect objects in the distance that may be obscured by weather, darkness or are simply out of sight or difficult to see.
Radar blip	A generic term for a radar echo or radar response from an object displayed on the radar screen or other type of display.

Radar reflector	A device designed to reflect radar waves in order to make the vessel more highly visible on radar screens. The radar reflector should be sized for the vessel it will be used on and mounted as high as is practical. Radar reflectors are often lightweight and modular for ease in storage. When assembled, they usually contain at least three intersecting planes and are often, but not always, circular.
Raft	1. Buoyant materials fastened together to make a floating platform. 2. To tie two (or more) boats together, side by side, while in the water, away from a dock to assist in easily moving between them. 3. Two or more boats tied side by side are said to be rafted. 4. Abbreviation for life raft.
Raise sail	The act of hoisting, unfurling or deploying the sail(s).
Reaching	A point of sail where the wind is coming from a direction approximately between 2-5:00 or 7-10:00.

Red and green lights	A type of navigation light used at night by vessels at sea. They are called sidelights or combination lights. One of them will be visible to another vessel approaching, or being approached from the side. Both of them will be visible on a vessel that is approaching/overtaking your vessel from behind. The red light indicates the port side of a vessel while the green light indicates the starboard side of the vessel. However, when either color is used in conjunction with one or more white lights, it may mean something else entirely.
Reef	1. To decrease sail area (make the sail smaller). 2. A ridge of jagged rock, coral, or sand just above or below the surface of the water/sea.
Reefing	The act of making the sail smaller.
Regatta	A rowing, powerboat, or sailing race or a series of such races.
Repel boarders	Any action used to keep people from coming aboard a vessel uninvited or unwelcomed.
Replacement canvas	Another name for spare sails, even if the sails aren't made of canvas but another material instead.
RIB	Abbreviation for a Rigid Inflatable Boat. A lightweight but high performance, high-capacity boat constructed of a solid and an inflatable hull. (See dinghy.)

Rigging	1. Standing rigging are the cables, shrouds, and stays that support the mast(s). 2. Running rigging are the sheets, halyards, and lines that control the sail(s) or parts of the sail(s).
Rigging knife	A specially designed knife used to cut heavy lines. It may have a serrated edge for sawing through the line. It may have an extra-heavy blade, suitable for pounding with a mallet to drive the blade through the line. The folding models often come equipped with a marlinspike for convenience. (See marlinspike.)
Rigging station	A dedicated area in a vessel containing rigging equipment, specialized tools, and supplies, often including an assortment of lines and fittings and perhaps even extra sails.
Round turn with two half hitches knot	A two-part knot, commonly used to secure a vessel to a dock post. The first part (the round turn) passes the line around the object, encircling it, while the second part (the two half hitches) secures the end of the line to itself.
Rudder	An underwater appendage that controls the direction of the vessel when moving through the water.
Run aground	The act of getting the vessel stuck (on the bottom) in shallow water. See aground.
Running lights	Navigation light(s) is/are a source of illumination on a vessel that give information on the vessel's type, position, heading, and status.

Sail slugs	A fitting on the sail that allows it to attach to the mast by fitting into a slot.
Sailboat	A vessel that uses wind power to propel it forward through the water.
Sailing certifications	A certification, issued by various sailing organizations, stating the individual has completed progressively advancing levels of training. Proof of certification, including presenting a sailing resume, is often a requirement to charter a sailboat, especially the larger ones. There are also various levels of certifications for sailing instructors.
Sailing gloves	Gloves designed to protect the hands from abrasion and blisters that often occur when handling lines. They are available in different styles, fabrics, and colors, depending on the expected usage.
Sailing shoes	Comfortable, casual shoes usually made of canvas, suede, or leather, with non-marking rubber soles designed for use on slippery surfaces. (Also known as boat or deck shoes.)
Salon table	The primary dining table in the salon of a vessel. Some salon table can convert into a berth for sleeping.

Sargasso Sea	A region of the North Atlantic Ocean bounded entirely by ocean currents. It is the only sea without a land boundary. Unlike most of the Atlantic Ocean, the Sargasso Sea has characteristic brown Sargassum seaweed and calm blue water.
Satellite phone	A telephone that transmits and receives voice (and possibly short messages) from orbiting satellites, providing coverage around the world.
SCUBA certification	A certification, issued by various dive organizations, stating the individual has completed required levels of training, normally consisting of coursework, pool work, and open water experience. Proof of certification, including presenting a logbook with recent dives, is a requirement to have dive tanks refilled (with air). There are also various levels of certifications for diving instructors.
Sculling	To move the boat forward by rapidly swinging the rudder back and forth.
Scuttle/scuttling	To deliberately sink a vessel, often by making holes in the side or bottom of it.
Sea anchor	See drogue.
Sextant	A precision astronomical instrument used to determine latitude and longitude by measuring the angular distances, especially the altitude, of the sun, moon, and stars.

Sheet bend knot	A type of knot used to tie together two lines of unequal diameter.
Sheet-in	To tighten, bring in, or increase tension on the sail for sailing closer (higher) to the wind.
Sheet(s)	A control line(s) for a sail. Sheets control the sails side to side.
Ship	A large vessel. Rule of thumb: A boat will fit on the deck of a ship, but a ship will not fit on the deck of a boat.
Shipshape	A desirable condition aboard a vessel where everything is clean, neat, tidy, organized, and in good order or condition.
Shipwreck	1. An accident in which a vessel is destroyed, lost, or sunk, especially by hitting a reef or running aground. 2. The skeletal structure of such an unfortunate vessel.
Shipwrecked	Those persons affected by a shipwreck.
Shoal	A shallow area of rock or coral.
Shore power	The provision of shoreside electrical power to a vessel at berth while its main and auxiliary engines (or generators) are shut down.
Shroud	A wire or cable supporting the mast from side-to-side.
Signal flag halyard	A line specifically used to display a signal flag.

Signal flags	1. Various flags used internationally by vessels at sea to spell out short messages. When used in certain combinations, they may have special meanings. 2. Signal flags were used in military operations to communicate while maintaining radio silence.
Single-hand	To pilot or sail the vessel alone or without help.
Skiff	Any type of shallow, flat-bottomed, open boats with a sharp bow and square stern. See dinghy or tender.
Skipper	See captain. Skipper is a less formal title.
Slip	1. The area of water that is between docks, piers, or wharves where vessels can be moored. (A space to park/secure your vessel that has shore access. See berth def. #2) 2. To fall or lose one's balance.
Slip fee	A fee paid to keep your vessel in its slip/berth/allotted space at a dock.
Solar shower	A device originally designed for campers, it consists of a container that absorbs the sun's direct heat to raise the temperature of the inside water. It will have a hose and shower head, with a valve to regulate the flow and normally a hole or hook from which to hang it.
Sole	The cabin or deck floor covering, often made of teak or other marine environment tolerable materials.

Spar	A long, cylindrical object made of wood, metal, or composite material, such as the mast or the boom.
Spinnaker	A large, usually colorful, three-cornered sail, typically bulging when full, set near the bow, used when running (sailing downwind).
Spinnaker pole	A spar used to help support and control the spinnaker. It can also be used with other headsails when sailing downwind without the spinnaker.
Spreader	A horizontal support for the shrouds that sticks out from the mast.
Stacked berths	A bed on a vessel, stacked one above the other, like bunk beds.
Stanchion	A vertical metal support along the outside of the deck, supporting the lifelines.
Standing rigging	Cables that support the mast, usually braided wire. These have specific names depending on location. The cable in the front of the mast is the forestay, the cable on the side(s) of the mast is a shroud, and the cable at the back of the mast is the backstay.
Starboard	The right side of the vessel when aboard and facing forward.
Starter/starting battery	The battery that provides power to start the engine.

Steerage	Having enough speed through the water to be able to steer/control the vessel's direction.
Stern	The aftermost part of the vessel.
Stern rail	A railing, often metal, at or near the stern of a vessel, designed to help restrain passengers (or crew) from falling overboard. It is usually more substantial than a lifeline. May also be called the "stern pulpit."
Stow	To put something away on a boat.
Surface clutter	Unwanted echoes (blips) in the radar system causing sometimes serious performance issues. Such echoes can be returned from ground, sea, rain, atmospheric turbulence, etc. Sometimes the "clutter" can be eliminated by adjusting the radar's sensitivity controls.
Swells	Big waves that travel over long distances in the open ocean.
Swim platform	A structure on the stern of a boat designed to make getting into or out of the water easier.
Tack/tacking	A maneuver to bring the bow (front) of the boat through the eye of the wind.
Tall ship	Although not strictly defined, it refers to any large, traditionally rigged sailing vessel. Tall ships usually have more than one mast and often have square sails.

Teak	The wood from a teak tree. It is strong, durable ,and resistant to insects and warping and frequently used in ship building.
Tender	A small boat used to ferry crew to and from a larger vessel. See dinghy.
Tether	A short lead for a safety harness.
Thru-hull plug	A fitting, often made of wood, that can be used to temporarily plug a leaking thru-hull fitting. (A thru-hull fitting is an intentional hole through the hull, fitted with a metal or plastic device, through which fluids can flow in either direction.)
Topside	On or toward the upper deck of a vessel.
Tower	An elevated structure on some deep-sea fishing boats, used as an aid in spotting certain species of fish.
Traveler	A track which allows for side-to-side adjustments of the mainsail (or mizzen sail).
Trim	1. To adjust the sails to be more or less efficient. 2. To pull in or let out a sheet.
Trucker's hitches knot	A type of knot used like a block and tackle to increase the amount of tension in a line.
True north	North according to the earth's axis, not magnetic north (according to a compass).
UFO	Any unidentified flying object, often associated with sightings of alien ships.

Underway	Moving through the water.
Unfurled (the sails)	See Hauled out, def. # 1.
United States Coast Guard	A branch of the United States Armed Forces, responsible for the enforcement of maritime law and for the protection of life and property at sea.
Vented locker	A storage compartment utilizing vents to offer increased or maximum ventilation and airflow.
Vessel	Any boat, ship, yacht, or watercraft.
VHF radio	A common type of radio used in marine applications. VHF (very high frequency) refers to the marine frequency range of 156 to 174 MHz, inclusive. Channel 16 (156.8 MHz) is the international calling and distress channel.
Wake	The waves caused by the motion of the vessel through the water. The wake from a large vessel, like a cruise ship, can be dangerous to small craft getting caught in it.
Wastewater	Wastewater is the product contained by the vessel's sewage system. Numerous laws and rules govern where and when wastewater can be discharged overboard. It is normally referred to as "greywater" when without fecal contamination, such as that from sinks, baths, showers, or dishwashers. It is normally referred to as "blackwater" when having fecal contamination (from toilets).

Watermaker	A device used to obtain potable water from seawater by the process of reverse osmosis. Also called a "desalinator."
Waterline	1. A line that marks the level of the surface of water on something, usually the vessel's hull. 2. A line marked on the outside of a vessel that corresponds to the water's surface when the vessel is afloat.
Watertight door	A special type of door, found on vessels, designed to prevent to the ingress of water from one compartment to another during flooding or accidents.
Weather fax	A facsimile machine designed to receive and print high-quality, high-definition weather charts and satellite images.
Weigh anchor	To retrieve the anchor when ready to get underway.
Wheel	Used to steer the sailboat by controlling the rudder. Some wheels fold to save space when not in use.
White light	A type of navigation light used at night by vessels at sea.
Winch	A mechanical, drum-shaped device using gears and a handle (or electric operation) to increase the tension in a line.
Windlass	A machine (usually powered by electricity) used to feed or retract the anchor chain (or line). Essentially a winch for the anchor.

Windward	1. Facing the wind or the side facing the wind. 2. The side or direction from which the wind is blowing. (The side opposite leeward.)
Workroom	A room (or compartment) containing specialized tools, parts, supplies, and/or equipment for making repairs or building needed things.
Yacht	Any sail or power vessel used for pleasure, cruising, or racing. Conventionally, any watercraft over forty feet in length will likely qualify as a yacht but the minimum length to be considered a yacht is debatable. And the category of "mega" or "super" yacht can also be very subjective.
Yacht club	A club organized for the enjoyment of sailing (and boating).

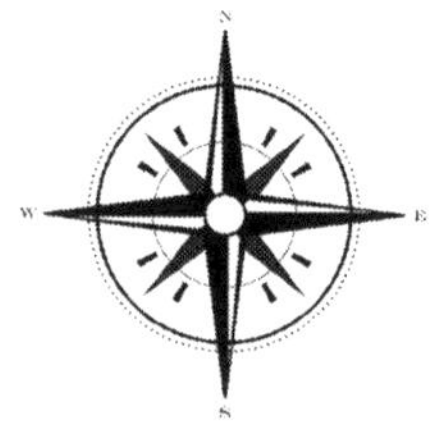

ABOUT THE AUTHORS

Jim Schoendaller

Jim Schoendaller is a Certified Sailing Instructor, ironically teaching in the landlocked state of Colorado. He is a retired public-sector employee who is enjoying writing novels instead of contracts. He is an avid traveler, having visited 5 continents so far, and is an accomplished Ballroom dancer.

Jeanne C. Stein

Jeanne C. Stein is the national bestselling author of the Urban Fantasy series, The Anna Strong Vampire Chronicles and most recently, The Fallen Siren Series written as S. J. Harper. There are nine books in the Anna Strong series and two books and two novellas in a series written with Samantha Sommersby under the S. J. Harper pseudonym. She also has more that a dozen short story credits, including the novella, Blood Debt, from the New York Times bestselling anthology, Hexed and The NYT bestselling anthology, Dead But Not Forgotten edited by Charlaine Harris. Her short stories have been published in collections here in the US and the UK. Her latest, an Anna Strong novel titled Paradox, was released in November 2019.

Made in the USA
Columbia, SC
12 February 2020